APERTURE

A P E R T U R E

Gene Farrington

Water street press

Published by Water Street Press

Healdsburg, California

Water Street Press paperback edition published 2017

Copyright by Gene Farrington, 2017 ✦ All Rights Reserved

Cover: Sally Eckhoff

Interior: Typeflow

Produced in the USA

Library of Congress
Control Number: 2017955763

ISBNS:

978-1-62134-390-5 (PRINT)

978-1-62134-392-9 (EPUB) ✦ ISBN: 978-1-62134-391-2 (MOBI)

This is for Mary.

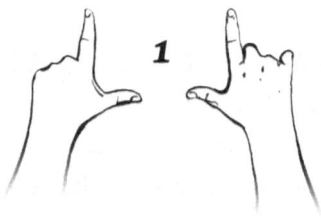

Open Aperture

CLICK. SNAP. I was conceived at age ten. Mummy and Daddy were gone. I was hammered upon the Humber. Spoke English English, so dropped the aitches and was "'ammered upon the 'umber." Did not quite understand the nature of 'ammering at the time, but it somehow sounded right. Born? I was born in the blitz. A footnote to the underground. I had to re-conceive that later. London bombed, yes. The Blitz to come. My math was screwed, but that's a ten-year-old, and while I thought I knew everything I admittedly was mistaken.

I picture the world through my own lens. Or I will. I didn't quite see things on that day crossing the suspension bridge as I would in days that followed.

"The Thames looks quite murky this forenoon," I told her as we rattled across the suspension span in a 1934 Dodge Sedan. I sat alone in the back. I preferred that. The curtains were tied neatly back at the windows. If she wasn't a woman she could have been my chauffeur. Women could drive ambulances in the Great War. I don't think they were allowed to be chauffeurs. I could pretend she was a man. She was tall enough. Six two. Six three. I don't know how many stone she weighed because I didn't understand conversion. I only knew pounds. We could stick her long hair under a cap. But she had so much of it, great wallows of flame red, she called it, curls.

"What are you mumbling about, Garnie?"

"My name is Nigel. And I said, my dear, the Thames looks quite bleak, so dark and wintery-spirited."

"Stop that right now. I'll climb back there and give you one."

"And so like you. The motor out of control. We will plunge down into the murk, to our watery deaths. Dead. Like Mummy and Daddy."

"Garnie, we know that they're not dead. How often must I tell you that? They might come waltzing in the door when we get home. Big as life."

Not as big as you. But I didn't say it. "They would hate the Terrible House."

"They would. Just as we do. But I worry about you. You must really stop this affectation. Affectation has its place."

You should know, I thought, but kept my pursed lips sealed.

"People talk. And we can't have folk snooping about our business. They might take you away from your Auntie Rye and then who would be your guardian? Off to an orphanage."

"Something out of Dickens." I read a lot. And Auntie Rye read to me as well. Not children's books, but Emily Bronte and Henry James and Mary Shelley. We liked a bit of horror in our lives. But we liked a little mystery as well. My own background was as shrouded as Holgrave's in *The House of Seven Gables*. "Perhaps I will become a daguerreotypist."

"I think not."

"What is a daguerreotypist?"

"It's why you can't become one. It was a person using a now antiquated photo technique developed in the early eighteen-hundreds. Daguerreotypists are all dead."

"You don't know that for sure. There could be a recluse daguerreotypist living in Nova Scotia."

"There probably is." She plunged the toe of her high heel to the clutch, shifted, and we rose up the incline of the suspension bridge. It rattled.

"You should buy this bridge." I was matter of fact.

"And why should I buy this bridge?"

"Because it rattles. It's a problem. And you forever and ever and always maintain there is no problem that if you throw enough money at it the problem will be resolv-ed." I pronounced the 'ed' in Shakespearean fashion. Yes, she read me that as well. *Macbeth* and *Titus Andronicus*. Oh, and *Richard the Third*. The snuffing of the lads in the tower. My favorite bit. "You have the money."

"And why is the bridge a problem?"

"It rattles." Did I have to repeat everything to her?

"I like the rattle. It's rhythmic." She hummed Mozart to the beat of the rattle. "There is no problem."

We rattled on. "I think you snuffed the mum and the da." I had said it before.

"Yes and walled them up in the cellar, no doubt."

"And stole all their money."

"But I have my own money."

"In the safe in the cellar in the Terrible House."

"In the safe in the cellar in the Terrible House. My money. Where would your mommy and daddy have gotten money? They always depended on your Auntie Rye."

"They robbed banks, I suspect. I have *always* suspected. Like Bonnie and Clyde. They were gunned down doing something naughty in the back of their Model A." I didn't quite know what the naughty was, but I knew it was naughty. I knew it had something to do with the dingy-dong and the woman's fluffy.

"An interesting image, but I doubt either had the imagination for it."

I had never posed the question before, but suddenly it occurred to me. "Where did you get your money, Aunt Penelope?"

"I ain't your Aunt Penelope. Auntie Rye — *wry*, like droll. But I got it in the crash. While everyone else was killing themselves, I made a killing. Never trust a bank. Particularly banks with the word 'trust' in the title." It was a saying of hers.

"Always keep your money in the safe in the cellar."

"Always."

We had crossed the Mississippi; we were in Wisconsin.

Auntie Rye wobbled off on her high heels to get beautified. The heels making her look only the taller. She was big. And she was forever having to shave: her legs, her face, her chest, her arms. She read to me; a book propped up on the music stand while she shaved her armpits, shifting from side to side, sometimes dripping on the page. She loved dialogue, mimicking the voice of Hester Prynne, the screaming of Fortunato as he was being mortared up, or the thumping of the tell-tale heart in a booming, high-pitched, voice. "I could have been an actor for Willie Shakespeare," she often repeated. How true, I would come to realize.

We had money. I didn't really understand that other people didn't. When a dollar would buy our groceries for the day with change returned, I would often have ten, fifteen, sometimes twenty dollars crumpled up in my pocket. "Buy," Auntie Rye would say. "They owe you that much." I didn't know who *they* were, but I suspected Mummy and Daddy.

But it was that day in Prairie du Chien that my future was conceived. Small things. I left Auntie Rye and watched as she wobbled off to beautification. I went searching for a soda fountain and a root beer float. Usually on our weekly crossing into Wisconsin I would go to Your Daily Bread for a raised sugar donut and a cream soda, but today I had a mind to slurp messy ice cream in root beer.

"Try Small's Drug Store," the old man puffing a meerschaum and sitting on the bench in front of Gracie's Girdles and Imported Shoes Shoppe responded to my question as to where I might get a root beer float. "It's just 'round the corner and down 'cross from the gas'leen station."

It was a gray morning. Later I would seek chiaroscuro, but on this day I had neither sense of the word, nor any idea how to spell it. A metal sign slapped in the wind. I took my index finger and thumb on each hand and made a frame, and through it saw the tottering red horse on the Mobil sign off its one hinge. Yet, it was strange. I suddenly didn't see the red horse as red. It was black and white as if in a photograph. I began at that precise moment to see the world quite often not in color but in black, white and numerous shades of gray.

The drug store was across the street. There was no traffic. The street was barren, not a person, as if the world had suddenly died and all that remained was the framed flying horse. I still held that picture in my frame. And it wasn't as if the world simply stood still in time like in a photograph, but as if this was an engulfing moment. I was only ten but sensed the world could be made to stand still, that time could be captured. I saw the man. Not a big man, but a stocky man with hair the color of coal. He stood behind the glass in the drug store door making a frame with his thumbs and fingers as I had done. Only he was framing me. And when he saw me seeing him, he dissolved back into the shadows of the store. I broke my frame and crossed the street. My eye was drawn to the drug store door, but shifted to the display window. There *it* was. I saw *it!* The Camera. There in the window. Below the painted, slightly chipping gold letters curved on the window: Small Drug Store. A folding camera. Its bellows open. Of course, I didn't know they were called bellows then, but that's what they were. Its blue face evident. I read the silver words engraved against blue, the face extended out from the black bellows: T B 25 50 Kodak No. BK — letters run together — and then below, Eastman Kodak Co. There was a handwritten sign beside the open camera: A no. 2A cartridge Hawk-Eye model B.

My life was decided. I would become a photographer. Not just *a* photographer, but a world-renowned photographer. The pictures in *Life* and *Look* would be mine. Pictures of Herr Hitler and Winston Churchill. And the king and the young princesses. I saw my world. It was entirely black and white. Next to the camera on the other side was another hand-painted sign: Film Developed on Premises. Reasonable Rates. Quality Prints.

I had to have that camera. There was a bell. It tinkled as I pushed open the glass door, also lettered in chipping gold: Small Drug Store. The place smelled of oiled sawdust and a slight lingering of chemicals. I was alone. Had I been taller I could have reached over the barrier behind the window display and grabbed the camera and been away. But I was ten and no taller than ten. My mind might be larger, but my body wasn't. A fact I deplored. I read in *Time* of a disease where people's internal organs aged faster than their outsides. I think I might have that disease of the mind. I had been told I was advanced. No. I think a mind disease. A soda fountain with chrome stools and black cushions stretched nearly back to the drug counter.

He appeared. The man. Stocky, curly black hair. He was wearing a white coat that he had not been wearing while framing me through the door window. He had big hands. "What can I get you, lad?" He had an accent and came out from behind the drug counter and put his large hand on my shoulder.

"I'll have a root beer float and that camera in the window."

"Not for sale. Just for show. 'Tis me own. I've got a nice Baby Brownie Special here for you, though. Just the thing for a handsome young lad of your age." He took a box from a shelf and removed an ugly little black square of a camera. "A snap of this white button and jazzo, a picture you got. No focusing, no nonsense and only a dollar twenty-five. Here, take a look-see."

"No. I don't want to. I want the camera in the window. How much?"

"It's not for sale, like I said. It was a gift to me, back in thirty-three."

"Anything's for sale. For a price."

"Sorry. There is no price what would let me part with that gift." He went behind the fountain counter and began concocting the float.

"How come you have an accent? Is it Irish?" I asked.

"It is, now."

"And how do you happen to be here? All the way from there?"

"'Tis a story and then some. I was a Jesuit. Taught out at the Academy. Don't tell many folk that, but you're a curious lad." He set the float in front of me and put his hand over mine. He took it away as I repositioned myself up on my knees. I didn't understand it, but I sensed it. And I sensed there was a way to get the camera and yet not clearly how. I reached across the counter to the large hand resting there and put my hand over the top of his with its bristle of black hair. His hand was really rough. He seemed pleased and smiled at me, a broad pleasant smile. "Why do you want a camera?"

"To stop time." I don't know why I answered like that, but I realized it was a good answer. That's what cameras did. I then posed my own question. "How come you left Campion?"

"We didn't see eye to eye, me and the Jebs. Are you Catholic, lad?"

I wanted to say 'aye,' but I thought he might think I was mocking him, so settled for a simple, "Yes."

"You live here in Prairie with your parents, I take it. You go to St. Gabriel's or St. John's?" My hand still rested across his and he made no effort to free his own.

"No, I live across the river in Iowa. My mummy and daddy are gone. I live with my Auntie Rye."

"I'm sorry," he said, moving his hand from under mine and putting it over my small hand. "When did they die?" He had very rough hands. Hands like a laborer's. Not like the hands of a priest. Father O'Tootle for all his Harley driving had the hands of a priest.

"Not dead. Gone."

"Gone?"

"Yes." I slurped the float and then sucked the air. "I suck good."

He smiled. "How old are you, lad?"

"Ten now. I was four then. One morning when I came downstairs.... It was a winding stair. We lived in the Opera House then. They were gone and my Auntie Rye was there. Had never seen her before, but there she was all big and bossy and took me away to live in the Terrible House."

"The Opera House? The Terrible House?"

"The Opera House because Auntie Rye said it reminded her of an ornate setting from a bad Italian opera. Or a New Orleans whore palace. I liked it. Floors of rooms with pretty wallpaper. Giant fireplaces and a grand, very grand, grand piano. As for the Terrible House, it's quite ghastly. The floors are Masonite. There's running water with a kitchen sink, but you have to go out to the outhouse to piss and shit."

"Those are not particularly nice words for a young lad."

"My Auntie Rye says piss is piss and shit is shit and calling it anything else doesn't much matter because it still is but piss and shit."

"Your Auntie Rye seems an interesting sort."

"Oh, she is that, all right. But she taught me to read and write before I ever started school, to play the piano, to play bridge, whist and poker, to speak some French, a smattering of German, even though she hates the Germans, a few Russian words, to draw with charcoal, paint with oil, to enjoy cuisine rather than food, though we mostly eat from cans, and we plan to take a world cruise, but I think not."

"You think not."

"The war."

"But America's not in the war."

"But it is coming."

"You think so, wise one?" He smiled and squeezed my hand.

"You're making fun of me."

"No. To the contrary. I find you absolutely charming. Delightful."

He let loose of my hand as the bell tinkled. A fat woman in a squashed yellow hat and white gloves swept in. "I need the usual," she said. She had a voice like a dying cow, I thought, or what I thought a cow might sound like if it could talk and was dying. I also noticed she had a large tear across the palm of her right glove. Still depressed by the Depression, no doubt. I would buy her a new pair of gloves if she were not so fat. At that moment I decided on a policy against fat people.

"I'll be with you in a moment, Mrs. Undershag." The man took my crumpled twenty. "Big bucks for a young lad." He turned the crank on the cash register and it clanged open. He handed me a sheaf of bills and some change. "You'll come visit me again?"

"I want the camera," I told him. I looked at Mrs. Undershag. There was a boy at my school, Pugmen Ugglefit, in the seventh grade. He was fat and mean as well. A fat bully with carrot hair. Perhaps all the fat people on earth should be lumped in one place, but then the earth would go wobbly and off its axis.

Mr. Small went over and took a box wrapped in plain blue paper from a shelf and pulled it down and handed it to the fat woman as I tinkled out the door.

Outside I stood staring into the window at the folding

blue Kodak and knew I would have the camera. I didn't quite understand it, but I sensed there was a way. I wanted to see how fast I could run and dashed to the cigar store: Mr. Jailanter T. Kruley, Tobacconist, purveyor of Cuban cigars and sundry leaf products. The words were painted on the awning. I popped in as a gentleman in a panama hat popped out. The store was laden with the heavy smell of tobacco and arrayed with pipes and cigarettes and boxes of cigars and tins of tobacco and rounds of snuff and stacks of newspapers.

"I would like a *Chicago Tribune* and an *American Herald*. And do you have a *New York Times?*"

"I do not have a *New York Times.*" It was the same every week and said with great definity. It was never "I do not carry the *New York Times,*" "I have never carried the *New York Times*" nor "It is not my intention to ever carry the *New York Times,*" but always "I do not have a *New York Times,*" as if the gentleman in the panama hat had just bought the last copy. I paid and took my three-day-old papers. The ink was dry. They arrived by Jefferson Line bus three days off the press from Chicago. The radio news was faster, but Auntie Rye said she preferred the unbiased news of print — ignoring the *Tribune's* bizarre spelling and its anti-Catholic tirades, and the fact that the radio station WGN stood for World's Greatest Newspaper and was owned by the *Tribune*. When I pointed this out to her, the response was as I suspected it would be. "That's simply the way the world is."

I went to the Ben Franklin store. I had thoughts of moving to Paris next week. I searched among the few caps and hats. None to be found. "Do you have any berets?" I asked the pox-faced woman whose spectacles were chained around the back of her neck. The chain links knotted below the upswept henna wisps were so thick that I wondered if they were a memorial to a dead chain-gang lover. I had read about chain gangs in the *Tribune*.

"No, no, no. You must go to Miller's Emporium to find the tams and berets."

So I went to Miller's Emporium and found a purple wool beret. "I will wear it," I told the screechy-voiced girl at the counter.

"You may not. It is not the policy," she screeched and popped the beret into a brown bag and stapled the top and then stapled it again and a third time, lest it attempt to escape. We had a stapler at school. I had not seen a stapler used like that in a store before. Miller's Emporium was obviously very progressive. Perhaps Auntie Rye should buy a stapler, though I didn't know what she might have to staple. Outside I tore open the bag and plopped the purple wool beret on my head at a jaunty angle. I peered into the window of Miller's Emporium and was pleased with the reflection of the French boy, *excusez-moi... garçon*, staring back. I looked at my oversized pocket Elgin. It had been my daddy's I had been told. But there were no fine engravings or messages inside the white-gold hinged opening, so I had to trust to Auntie Rye as I did in all matters of my personal history. I was early but went off to the Dodge and was standing there when Mr. Jailanter T. Kruley approached.

"Young Sir, I have received today's shipment of the *New York Times*."

My faith in the nation was restored. I dug in my pocket for the appropriate change, paid him; he handed me the paper and vanished. Or vanish-ed, as I noted silently. It was dated August 1, 1940. That was last Thursday. Today was Monday.

All the news that's fit to print five days old. I stepped up on the running board, opened the dark blue door and climbed in the backseat and read. The Duke and Duchess of Windsor were to sail from Lisbon on the steamship Excalibur and Under Secretary of State Welles denied any published reports that the ship was to have a convoy escort of British warships.

Auntie Rye approached. And while not visible to me, she no doubt had the usual pedicure and manicure, and she did have the quite visible new hairdo, a pageboy. She climbed into the driver's seat.

"Are you, madam, buoyed by ze pa-ag garçon you zo obtained?" I asked.

"I am, indeed, monsieur. So you are French? I see by your chapeau, you are the artiste."

"Oui, madam. And ze coiffure you sport iz quite chic, n'est pas?"

"The latest in styles, I am told."

"Let's hit the Seine, madam, and I have a surprise for you. The *New York Times*."

She backed the car away from the curb and pulled forward. "Read to me."

And I did. I forgot about being French and read of aerodromes bombed in Britain. Of Saks Fifth Avenue's final reduction summer clearances and laced corsets available for one dollar. Of Secretary of War Stimson advising the House Military Affairs Committee of a possible direct attack on the United States by Germany. Of Hanoverian royalty seeking a haven in Mexico. Of suede and lace kid gloves offered at Saks for a buck ninety-five. Of rolls and croissants being banned bread in Vichy France.

"No croissants in France? That is a crime of capital proportions."

"You have been to my France, madam?"

"Many times, monsieur."

I told her of the Duke and Duchess of Windsor and their sailing from Lisbon and the apparent problems about the convoy escort.

"They are parasites." There was vehemence I had not often heard in her voice.

"You always tell me you can't believe what you read in the press. Perhaps they are really really nice people."

"I know them. They are not nice people."

"You know them?" I was quite taken that she knew people whose pictures were in the *New York Times*.

"Met them in France. Jew-hating, Nazi-loving pustules that hopefully will drown in the crossing."

I was suspicious. They couldn't have lived in France that long. "When in France?"

"Back in thirty-seven. When I was gone those three weeks to my cousin Field Palmer's funeral and you stayed out on the Toddmans' farm."

"You never said that the funeral was in France. I thought you were in Chicago."

"You were only seven. I didn't see the need to upset you that I was so far away. Field was killed when a white owl came crashing through the windshield of his motor car when he was driving alone on a winding mountain road above Nice. The family should have brought him home to Chicago for burial."

"Why didn't they?"

"Because he was a little different." She rather whispered 'different.'

"He played with men's penises."

"Well, yes. I wouldn't put it that bluntly. Sometimes I don't know where you learn such things."

"Piss is piss and shit is shit," I quoted her.

"I hate it when you say that, but true enough I suppose. It's what I've taught you. Avoid the euphemism. Say what you are trying to say. Field had a special friend, a Fascist Italian count who had been one of Wallis Simpson's lovers. So she and the ex-king show up in Cannes at Field's funeral. They are a despicable pair of Fascists. And I have no doubt she is a Nazi spy."

I was not used to such anger in her voice. I quickly turned to the ads. I read about Sterns' new fall color striped dress with wide shoulders now offered at two ninety-eight. And famous shuffle-mate slacks and bush jackets at a dollar ninety-eight.

"I find pants unladylike." She called back over her shoulder as we rattled across the Seine. Her mood was still ugly.

I read to her of the Pan-American meeting on European dependencies in the Americas and the Havana Accord. Of a nice batiste blouse available for a dollar from Bloomingdale's. And of Paris having no part in blitzkrieg plans. "This is interesting, if incomprehensible." I practiced words. 'Incomprehensible' was a practice word. "'The FFC pledges help in television field.' What is television?"

"Pictures sent over airwaves that arrive in a box in the home."

"Whatever for?"

"Don't ask me. Sounds all a little too Flash Gordon."

"Or Buck Rogers." We drove down from the bridge.

"Or Buck Rogers." She was silent. "Garnie, I've been

thinking. We ought to buy a new Dodge. This one is getting a bit old."

"We could. Or a Buick," I suggested.

"Yes, or go all out and get a snazzy Packard. A bright yellow convertible sedan."

"That would be a humdinger."

"Or the big seven-passenger touring sedan."

"We don't know seven people. That is, seven people we could take touring. There is only us and Mr. Emblanci, and we never even take him in the Dodge." Mr. Emblanci was Auntie Rye's gentleman caller who lived in the county seat and drove over in an old Model A with one fender missing.

"But it wouldn't matter. Just you and me, my boy. In that Packard. We'd be real swells. It's time we drove to Chicago. We'll get a hotel suite on the lakefront and have lunch at the Pump Room. A ten-dollar lunch."

The thought of a ten-dollar lunch was staggering. Lunch at the Corner Café could be had for thirty-five cents. Or a dinner for eighty-five. I was mute for a minute or so, staring out at the cornfields beginning to yellow. "Auntie Rye. If we have so much money, why do we have to live in the Terrible House?"

"So as not to bring attention to ourselves."

"But wouldn't a big touring car do that?"

"I suppose. Maybe we will put in an indoor toilet. Would you like that, Garnie?"

"I would, ma'am. So very much."

We arrived in town. I won't give you the name of the town, primarily, I suppose, to protect the identity of those living there, although I am not certain from what they need protection. I could change all their names, but I shouldn't wish to needlessly confuse the reader or myself for that matter. In terms of population there were at the time, possibly even less now, only one thousand, one hundred and thirty-eight of them. The town, such as it was, was in northeast Iowa and not far from the Mississippi.

We arrived at the Terrible House. There was a driveway of sorts, a couple of ruts through the brown grass. There had been a tumbledown garage, but it had collapsed and been hauled away in pieces. I held the newspapers and some bags of cosmetics Auntie Rye had bought as she turned the key in the door. Most people in town didn't lock their houses. Auntie Rye did. People called her peculiar for the doing of it, but I knew it was because of the safe in the cellar. The cellar was reached through a trapdoor in the Masonite floor of the kitchen.

The kitchen had one window, a sink with running water and a kerosene stove with a top oven next to the burners. A copper boiler for heating laundry and bath water was propped against the stove leg. There was a four-year-old G.E. refrigerator with a monitor top that Auntie Rye had paid three hundred for new. The iceman no longer had to cometh. Oh, yes, Auntie read me the new play by the 'guilty Catholic Eugene' as she called him. It's no wonder my mind was advanced. There was an old ringer washer, a washtub for rinsing clothes and in which to take a weekly bath. Off the kitchen was a windowless pantry with store-bought cans of stuff. "We could turn that pantry into a toilet," but as yet it was only talk. Auntie Rye did no home canning like the other women of the town. She much admired *cuisine*, but we didn't 'et,' as Gertrude Hemps would say, much of it. A door from the kitchen went out to the sinking, rotting boards of the back porch.

The living room did not have a 'modern' Masonite floor. It had worn gray, tan, and faded red linoleum. There were two windows but the torn green shades were always kept down. No need for folk to see any business here. There was a couch that made into a bed, but it was never made into a bed as Auntie Rye never had visitors except for Mr. Emblanci. He never stayed but a few hours. An oil burner which heated the whole house sat in the center of the room. The stove pipe went up through a vented hole in the ceiling into my room above. It was surrounded by a kind of filigree 'register,' as Auntie Rye called it, that let heat come up into my bedroom. From it I could lay on the floor and peer down into the living room. It was how I first saw Auntie Rye's penis. I did not know at the time that a woman, that is most women, did not have a penis. I was quite shocked when Geraldina Lamtouse first exposed her thing, what she called her 'fluffy' to me. I thought her penis had been cut off and the awful slash, in which I had been allowed to insert my finger, was a remnant of her injury. Anyway, the large brown metal oil heater with front door panels occupied the center of the room. There was an upright piano, an ancient pump organ with missing knobs on the stops, two floor lamps, a music stand, an overstuffed chair, a pair of wobbly occasional tables, a Victrola, a Crosley radio with its inlaid cabinet and a cluster of bookshelves with glass fronts. You came directly into this room from the door leading to the front porch with its drooping green metal roof.

There was one bedroom off the living room on the first floor. That was Auntie Rye's room and *verboten* territory. Mostly it was filled with racks and boxes of clothes, shoes, belts, jewelry and assorted other accessories and junk. The house had no closets so it was all spread out, hung on wires, or shelved behind the mostly closed door.

A narrow enclosed stairway led up to the second floor. I had the big room over the living room with an iron bed and sinking feather mattress, paint-peeling dresser, wardrobe and chamber pot. Books were piled and strewn. I had few toys. They never interested me much. I preferred a universe of expanse and the miniaturized world of children never held an appeal. I thought stuffed animals stupid, dolls simply bizarre, toy cars and trucks worth no attention and children's board games infantile. From *Liberty*, *Look*, and the *Post*, but mostly *Life*, I cut out pictures, black and white photographs, of movie stars, baseball players, European battle scenes, aeroplanes, German tanks, Gestapo officers, RAF flyers, New York street scenes, Chicago restaurants, London waifs, Florida real estate investment tracts, dog shows, policemen, priests in full vestments and cowboys. These I thumb-tacked, without any discernible pattern in the array, on to peeling faded floral wallpaper. The only other room on the floor was the room on the left as you came up the stairs. It was for storage. Mostly the storage of things I suspected belonged to the vanish-ed — in Shakespearean terms — Mummy and Daddy.

I saw Auntie Rye's penis, not simply once but on a number of occasions when Mr. Emblanci came to call. I would often go outside during his visits, but in the cold or rain, I would simply go up to my room. Even in the beginning I was never asked to leave. I simply did. I did not much care for Mr. Emblanci. He was greasy. Bald and not cleanly shaven with a tiny moustache. He was effusive and waved his hands about when he talked. "Pay no mind," Auntie Rye said when I mentioned it. "It is the Italian way."

The first penis viewing was on a day about a year back. Mr. Emblanci came to call. It was raining so I made my way up to my room. I was bored and I lay there on the floor staring down into the grillwork of the round register surrounding the stovepipe. I could hear them talking, well, not talking just mostly groaning and grunting and making weird noises. I peered down and could see nothing and then they moved into my view. Mr. Emblanci was on his knees before Auntie Rye. She was naked from the waist down or appeared to be from my vantage, except for her high heels of course. And he took Auntie Rye's penis, kissed it and then stuck it in his mouth and began sucking on it. I think Mr. Emblanci was playing with his dingy as well, but I couldn't see down that well to be sure, but he was giving his right hand a lot of work, it seemed. I was terrified they would look up and see me and lay there frozen, as silent as possible and watched enthralled. Then Auntie Rye groaned more intensely and took her dingy all wet and dripping out of Mr. Emblanci's mouth and then he seemed to be pulling his dingy back and forth. There was a lot of unnecessary thrashing about, it seemed to me. He groaned. And then shortly after left.

It was after that I went out to the outhouse and played with my own dingy. I was thinking about how much fun it would be to have someone suck on it, or maybe I could suck on someone else's dingy-dong. Anyway, I kept jerking on it and it felt really good and then I had that special feeling. At the time, of course, I was too young to have an organism, but I had the sensation of having one.

After that when Mr. Emblanci came to call, I would spread out on the floor at the grill and watch. Auntie Rye never seemed to notice and if she did suspect, she never said a word about it. Perhaps she felt it was a 'necessity of my education.' So much of my life was explained as a 'necessity of my education.' When Abner St. Raymond-James had a stroke in the Jack Sprat store and fell head first into the pickle barrel it was, "That's just a necessity of your education." It was her refrain no matter how horrific. Like the time I came through the backyards of the neighborhood just after dark and saw Mrs. Dellatoast squatting up in her kitchen sink taking a pee, fully illuminated from her kitchen bare bulb. The Dellatoasts, like ourselves, had indoor water, but no toilet. When I told Auntie Rye of what I had seen, she simply replied, "That's just a necessity of your education."

Now at ten I was well practiced and was considering, as I sat in the outhouse and toyed with my own a bit, how I might like to see Mr. Small's dingy-dong, but then I heard Mr. Strapolet drive his cow into the barn. There is an old barn behind our property. It is no longer a farm, but Mr. Strapolet owns a cow and keeps some chickens. He sells milk and eggs. Sometimes when he milks the cow, named Eleanor deLacy, I wander over to watch. So I put my dingy-dong away in my underwear and pulled up my pants and left the outhouse. It had mostly stopped raining and was only a bit of a drizzle as I went through the dead garden patch. I entered the barn. Mr. Strapolet, who is a big man with a booming voice, was taking a piss in the gutter. He turned to me still pissing and in doing so displayed his very large dong. I am reluctant to call it a dingy-dong for it was far too fat and long to call a dingy. He shook it at me as he finished pissing. I couldn't help but stare.

"Careful, it will eat you up," he said, waggled his not-so-dingy dong at me and laughed with a boom.

I fled. Not terrified it would eat me, but terrified by my

own excitement. I went into the outhouse and played with my dingy until it felt good. If I had had the camera I could have taken a picture of Mr. Strapolet's thing. And I should like to see Mr. Small's dong, even if it wasn't a dingy. But I also had an idea. Not to become just a photographer, but I could become a world renowned dingy-dong photographer.

The following Saturday we drove the expanse of the Mississippi in the Dodge.

"You are very quiet today," Auntie Rye told me.

"I am thinking." And I was. The bridge rattled. I was in my thoughts. "I am thinking of becoming a world-renowned photographer."

"Despite Baudelaire's contention, photography is not an art. To paraphrase the great critic, 'let's leave it to Narcissus to gaze on his trivial image on a scrap of metal.'"

I knew who Baudelaire was although Auntie Rye felt I was not yet of an age ready for his poetry. My mind might be older, but sometimes not old enough.

"I think what you intend is admirable. To have goals is admirable, but you will need a camera."

"Yes. May I have fifty dollars?"

"Yes. That may be more than you will need."

"I know. But best to be prepared."

"Indeed," she said.

We rode in silence. But as she parked she said, "I have an errand to run after I am beautified. Can you occupy yourself for an extra hour and a half today?"

"I can," I told her. She handed me two twenties and two fives and I headed off toward Small's Drug.

I ran past the hanging red horse sign and stood for a moment looking at the Kodak in the window. Perhaps I could get it for fifty bucks, perhaps there were other ways. But I knew only that I must have a camera and not just any camera, but that particular Kodak with its blue face. The bell tinkled as I went in.

"I am happy to see you, lad," Mr. Small said. There was no one about the store. "Will it be a root beer float?"

"I should like to see where you develop pictures, if you will show me." And perhaps show me more. I had a plan.

"Why?"

"I want to become a photographer."

"I offered you a great little Baby Brownie. You didn't want it."

"I don't want to become that kind of snapshot taker. I want to become a real photographer."

"You need an eye."

"I have an eye." I held up my fingers and thumb making a frame of Mr. Small's face.

He smiled. "Perhaps you do." He made a frame with his hands with my face in the frame. "I will show you the darkroom. I will have to close up shop, though, to be back there any length of time." He went and pulled down the shade on the door, and turned the sign over to 'Closed' as he locked the door.

"I am called Garnie," I told him and offered him my hand.

"And I am Padric." He took my hand, held it for moment and then, with his arm about my shoulder, steered me beyond a curtain into the backroom of the shop. He really did have terrible, rough-looking hands. Blotchy and spotted.

He flipped a light switch near a door and then took me into a room, a very dark room, except for its red light. It had an unpainted wooden counter with metal trays and smelled of chemicals. It had a stained sink. Under the counter were large containers and brown jugs of chemicals. Black film strips held by clothespins hung on lines. There were things, equipment and packages of film in labeled bags and a bellows-camera-looking thing on a counter. He moved toward the counter with the trays. I reached over and tried to rub his dingy-dong through his pants.

"What are you doing?" He pulled away.

"I am going to suck your dingy-dong for you."

"You are ten years old! Wherever did you hear such things?"

"I watched Mr. Emblanci suck on Auntie Rye's dingy-dong."

"They let you watch?" He sounded horrified.

"No. I peeked through the floor register."

"Well, you shouldn't be seeing such things. And your Auntie Rye can't have a... well... a penis."

"She does and it's much bigger than mine."

"Garnie. Women do not have the same kind of privates that men do. They have what some call a muffin. It's a hole down there. It's all about making babies. Men put their dingy-dongs as you call them in the hole thing and shove it back and forth until they... well... have an orgasm —"

"An orgasm?"

"Yes, men release their seed into the woman's hole and then sometimes, more often than not, a baby grows from that seed inside the woman's tummy and then after nine months it, the baby, comes out the hole. Your Auntie Rye didn't explain this to you?"

"No."

"She should have. Let me show you how to develop film."

"Then why does Auntie Rye put her penis into Mr. Emblanci's mouth?"

"He probably gets pleasure from it."

"Mr. Emblanci?"

"Probably, but also your Auntie Rye. He gets pleasure from it."

"Auntie Rye is not a he."

"He, she, it, whatever gets pleasure from it."

"I would like to give you pleasure and suck your penis."

"You may not."

"Why? Don't you like me?"

"Of course I like you, but you are ten. It is improper, not to say illegal. I could be hauled off to jail for such."

"And were I twelve?"

"No matter."

"Say fifteen?"

"Garnie..."

"Sixteen, when I am sixteen."

"No."

"Seventeen?"

"OK, when you are seventeen, if that assurance will shut you up and keep you from raising the subject again. Now let's get to my explaining the nature of photo developing."

He turned on the regular lights. "Normally I would do this in the complete dark, not even the safe lights, the red lights, on, but since you can't see what I'm doing in the dark I will show you in the lights with some exposed film. Now before you turn off the lights, you take the reel." He took a metal reel from a wood bin on the shelf. "And this," he said, taking a metal can-like thing. "This is a tank, and this is its lid." He took a little film canister from a shelf. "This is thirty-five-millimeter film, probably not what you will be using, but the principle's the same. Now remember. It is totally dark when you are doing this. You can't see a thing." He popped the lid on the canister and took out the long roll of film. He took a metal reel-like thing from a bin. "Now, still in the dark, mind you, you wind the film on the reel like this." And he did so. "Now the first few times you do this in the dark, you would, if you were old enough, curse a lot."

"I could say, 'piss and shit.'"

"Yes, well. Once you have the film on the reel, you pop it in the tank like this and put the lid on like this. And you can turn on the safe light."

"It's got a hole in the top. How come the film doesn't get exposed when you turn on the red light?"

"This spout in the lid blocks out the light from getting to the film. Light can't travel around corners, Garnie. So, the film is still in the dark. Next take the developer, this bottle here. I've premixed this and the temperature has to be controlled. I keep it at sixty-nine degrees in here."

I looked up at the large round thermometer on the wall. The dial pointed to 69.

"Now you pour the developer into the tank, through the spout like this. Put this lid on and agitate it, by shaking it lightly like this, and turn it upside down and do the same. I always bump the tank on the counter a few times to get any bubbles out. This process takes a few minutes. This chemical I am using calls for five. You always need to watch the clock."

I looked up at a big clock on the wall next to the thermometer. "It's all kinda complicated, isn't it?"

"It becomes routine after the first one hundred and seventy-six times." He laughed. "Now you take the lid off and pour the developer down the drain and pour in the stop bath. It's that jug there, mostly water mixed with a bit of acid. Let it sit in the tank for half a minute. We pour out the water and pour in the fixer. We won't do that now, but we let the film sit in the fix for five to ten minutes. Then we pour the fixer back into the bottle to reuse it and take the lid off and pour in some cold water to rinse it again. We pour in some cleaning agent, put the lid on and agitate it for about five minutes, dump the cleansing agent back in the bottle and do another water rinse. After that, being careful how you handle the film, hang it with these clothespins on the line to dry."

"Those are the negatives?"

"Yes. And from them, using the enlarger over there, we make the prints, but we'll save that for another day. Think you are ready to develop film now?"

"No. I don't think I could do so much in the dark."

"In time. I'll let you come in here and practice, if you'd like."

"And if I mess up?"

"You're bound to. Unfortunately, in time, from all the chemicals you will have hands like mine. Come, I need to open the shop. There'll be folk dying for their drugs."

"Maybe they really are," I told him. "Outside the glass door on the stoop gasping their last."

"Maybe so."

We left the darkroom and stood in the back room outside it. He handed me an enlarged print. It was the hanging red Mobil horse, only the horse was not red, it was black and white as I imagined it. The bits of rusted chain were quite visible. But they too had no color, only black bits. "This is for you."

"I can keep it?"

He went over to the door and stared out the window. "I saw you framing the sign. Photography is mostly about the actuality of things. Having the eye to see the unreality of reality."

I understood what he meant. It was not the real world of color, or only seeing what was visible, but capturing it all. This was the world I wanted. The world that was all black and white. "It is beautiful, but yet it is not pretty."

"Precisely. And there is no story here. Photography, unlike painting, has no narrative."

"I understand, Padric," I told him.

"I believe you do. I actually believe you do. The art you will have to discover on your own. The technical aspects I can teach you. Shutter speed, aperture opening, film speed and using a light meter properly; these things you can learn from me. Your view, balance, the importance of immediacy and what you perceive as truth you will have to discover."

"Did you take this with the camera in the window?"

"No." He reached back to a table where we stood outside the darkroom and held up a camera. "I used this, my Leica. The Leica Three is perhaps the finest camera made. Takes thirty-five-millimeter. It has a slow shutter speed of one second and fast shutter speed of one-one-thousandth of a second." He set the camera back on the table. "Sorry," I know that means nothing to you, lad. But it will when I teach you how to be a photographer."

"I am smart," I assured him. "I learn easily."

"I have little doubt. I expect you'd make it big on Quiz Kids." He unlocked the door and went over to the window. He reached in and took out the blue Kodak and put it in the case that had been displayed in front of it. "This is for you." He handed it to me.

"Why?" I asked.

"Because I am very fond of you, Garnie."

"Why?"

"Because you remind me of Padric Small when he was a small Small."

"I can pay you. I have fifty dollars."

"No. It is a gift. It will do for now. We will get you a tripod for it and later you will learn to use the Leica."

"The finest camera ever made."

"Indeed, the Germans are the masters of technology. Perhaps the greatest geniuses of all ages."

"No," I said angrily. "The Luftwaffe are bombing London."

"Ah, so be it."

I scowled.

"Garnie, you must realize. I am an Irishman. The Irish hate the English."

"Why?"

"It is the way of the world. Everybody must hate somebody. Nations as well. Now, will you come next Saturday and I will teach you some more about the art of photography? How to use the enlarger and make prints. I will not sing *Deutschland, Deutschland Uber Alles* and you will not talk in that affected English manner. Will you come?"

"I will." I clutched my camera case and started out the door.

"Wait," he said. He handed me three rolls of film. "One-sixteen. It takes one–sixteen film."

I ran to the store of Mr. Jailanter T. Kruley, Tobacconist, purveyor of Cuban cigars and sundry leaf products. "I would like a *Chicago Tribune* and an *American Herald*. And do you have a *New York Times*?"

"Yes," he said. "You are later today. When you are later, I have the *New York Times*. It comes by train."

The Dodge was not parked where it usually was parked. I waited. Then a long yellow car pulled up next to the curb. Auntie Rye stepped out, the same pageboy, but newly set, and came around and opened the back door for me. "Our new Packard seven-passenger touring sedan," she said.

"Bright yellow." I stepped up on the running board and into the backseat with the newspapers and recently acquired Kodak in its case.

"Do you like?" she said as she pulled away and made a turn for the bridge.

"I thoroughly approve. You have my full approbation." That was a new word I had recently acquired from *Time*. "I have the *New York Times*."

"Read."

I read of President Roosevelt's meeting with Harry Hopkins and his vice-presidential candidate Mr. Henry Wallace. Of how Wendell Willkie proposed that federal officials list their assets. "You will be voting for FDR and not Mr. Willkie, I assume."

"I shall vote for neither. I support Earl Browder, the candidate of the Communist party."

"I support FDR."

"Well, it doesn't much matter a fart. You can't vote."

"Mr. Browder doesn't have a snowball's chance in hell of winning the election."

"Truth enough. And don't use such worn clichés."

"But why waste your vote?"

"Because I am a Marxist. I believe in the rights of workers. I oppose capitalism."

"But you have too much money not to be a capitalist."

"It's not about how much money one has. It's about the principle. Read me something else."

"Here is how you could spend some of your principal. A country garden apartment in Manhattan. Swimming pool, camera club, garden deck, playroom. From one hundred five dollars a month. Four spacious rooms, ample closets, bank, restaurant, all sorts of shops. Perhaps we should move to New York."

"Perhaps we should, but there is a war coming. New York will be bombed."

"There is — " I hesitated. "There is a picture of the king and queen looking at the homes destroyed by bombs. New York will look like London without the king and queen. The World's Fair has some interesting events. We should go to the World's Fair."

"And why not? Yes, why not? Before there is nothing left of New York. Next week before we go to Prairie we will pack. I will go have my hair and nails done as usual. You do what you do. We will leave directly from Prairie. Yes, drive to Chicago, park the Packard in a safe garage, take a taxi to LaSalle station, board the Twentieth Century Limited, a first-class bedroom of course, and traverse to Grand Central Station. In New York we will stay at the Waldorf and visit the fair."

"And I can take a lot of pictures with my new camera."

"You have a camera?"

"I do. It is my start in becoming a world-renowned photographer of illustrious proportions."

"And why not?"

"And why not."

And we did, though we did not take the train, we flew on United Airlines, the propellers revved up, and stayed at the Plaza and not the Waldorf. And we bought a *New York Times* which was not five days old.

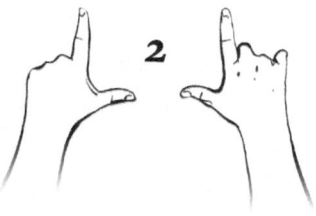

2

Developing

It was September. I moved from the south room to the north room of St. Ludmila's. Sister Mary Mildred was the benign ruler of grades one through four in the south room. Saint Mildred, her namesake, had been the daughter of King Merewald of Magonset and his wife Saint Ermenburga, or so we were told by Sister MM in credulous wonder. We called her MM because she mmm'd between every sentence. Saint Mildred had died in 732, but Sister MM lived on. As the fall of 1940 came I moved, along with the rest of what had been grade four and was now grade five, which consisted of myself and Geraldina Lamtouse — yes, that Geraldina Lamtouse without the penis — to the north room dominated by the tyrant, Sister Mary Saint Wulfhilda the Abbess. The saint, not the sister, was the abbess. The sister, not the saint, was the tyrant, but without a ruler. Instead she bore a leather crucifix with which she slapped us across the open palm, accompanied with the remonstrance: "In the name of Jesus, the scourged." As I said, there were two of us in grade five. There were six in grade six, four in grade seven and one in grade eight. But I was not there long, as I went away, but then I came back. More about that anon. Another of my Shakespearean usages.

The school was between the parsonage and the church and behind the three buildings were two cemeteries. St. Ludmila's and St. Patrick's, for while in life the Irish and the Bohemians might share a church pew, in death they must be segregated. There was only one other church in town: Erlöserkirche. It was Lutheran and in it they did not speak Latin, but German. Auntie Rye went to a funeral there for Gunter Hauswander, the owner of the IGA store, who fell from a third-story attic window above his store and splashed all over the sidewalk.

"You can't go to that church," I told her. "It's a mortal sin to go to Protestant churches or Jewish temples or Masonic — "

"I don't give a shit," she interrupted me, put on a large black hat with a large black plume that fell to the back and a large black veil which fell over her white-powdered face.

But, back to the cemetery. I stood on the hot fall day in my black cassock and white surplice holding the smoldering censer as not-so-old Father O'Tootle murmured goodbyes in Latin and they lowered Mister Hannigan, owner... well, late owner of Red's Tavern, into the rectangular hole, the opening draped in fake grass and piled with flowers, mostly yellow and orange mums. It was fall and mums were cheap. Auntie Rye, who, except for Sunday Mass, seldom appeared at any public gathering in the town, was drenched in layers of black chiffon and lace and stood heeled and tall, peering into the hole. Her face was veiled, but she had worn an enormously brimmed hat, not the one with the trailing black plume. "I have twenty-four black hats," Auntie Rye had once told me.

"To have more would be ostentatious. To have less would be imprudent."

I knew that she knew Hannigan and that on Friday nights while I went to the movies, she, dressed in red — sometimes rayon, sometimes wool, but always red, went to Red's, drank beer and played euchre with Hannigan, Tim Trum the trucker, Elton Brickenbrack the lawyer and Sleazy Slim who owned the Sinclair station. And while Father O'Tootle was spouting rhythmic wisdom in Latin, Hannigan's wife, Hilda Rose O'Shea Hannigan — and she was always called that for Red's had been O'Shea's Saloon before Hilda's father was snuffed by a falling full keg of Grain Belt — was spewing torrents of vehemence against the state of Iowa and the unfairness of its 3.2-beer-served-only liquor laws. which had killed both her dear father Shannigan O'Shea and that 'darlin' of a husband' Red. I failed to see how the state was to blame. Red had apparently passed out on the tavern floor after binging on the tavern's 3.2 and during the night choked on his own vomit.

"Hilda, shut up," Father O'Tootle ordered and took the censer from me and, with dramatic authority, rattled it over the grave in great sweeping movements. He took the aspergillum from Tilford Toddman, the other altar boy with ruly — if that is the antonym for unruly — red hair, and again with great sweeping gestures didn't simply sprinkle the casket below but wet us all. Cymbeline's words seemed appropriate for the event: "My tears that fall / Prove holy water on thee!" But Father O'Tootle preferred Latin to Shakespeare and implored, "*In nomine patris, et filii, et spiritus sancti...*" And then in a booming voice yelled out, "*Requiem aeternam dona eis, Domine.*" Tilford, being older — he was in the seventh grade, was allowed the response and mumbled, "*Et lux perpetua lucreat eis.*" "Don't whisper," Father O'Tootle yelled and boxed him across the ruly red hair. Dirt was thrown down into the hole and made a splashing sound as it hit the casket. It ended.

I went over to Auntie Rye. She adjusted her hat. "Filthy habit, that."

"What?" I asked.

"Throwing dirt on top of a brand new bronze casket like that."

Before I could remind her that shortly it would be pummeled with shovels full of earth, Hilda came over to her. "It's now O'Shea's Saloon and you and your kind are not welcome in any saloon owned and operated for the decency of the community."

Father O'Tootle apparently overheard and swooped over in his flipping vestments. "Hilda, you may not have paid for the funeral yet, but you need to keep your mouth shut. This is not the time nor place, poor Red barely laid to rest and you with an unChrist-like tongue. Here in this expanse of both Irish and Bohemian sainted dead departed. Appalling. You should apologize to Rye."

"Never. She is... she is... she is — " She didn't finish.

Auntie Rye tossed her right hand into the air in complete dismissal and then put the hand on my shoulder and led me out of the cemetery. "It may be time," she said and then left me there holding the censer and walked out to the street in front of the school to the yellow Packard. We lived only four blocks away and I walked to school, but she had chosen to drive to the funeral and burial. I went into the sacristy to remove the surplice and cassock. Tilford was already there and had removed his surplice. He pinched my butt and growled. "One of these days I'm gonna make you play with my wingy-wang."

"OK," I agreed.

"What do you mean 'OK'? Boys don't play with other boy's wingy-wangs."

"I was just trying to be nice, Tilly."

"Well, that ain't nice; it's disgusting."

Further conversation was interrupted by the arrival of Father O'Tootle. He was pulling the surplice over his head as he came in. "What's disgusting?"

"Garnie wants to play with my wingy-wang," Tilly told him.

"I never said that. He is misconstruing my words." Misconstruing, itself, was one of my words. Another new word I was trying.

Father O'Tootle unbuttoned his cassock. He wore a black T-shirt and dungarees with rolled cuffs. "We'll have no more misconstruing. Tilly, you get out of that cassock and get to school."

Father O'Tootle had huge arms that bulged out of his tight T-shirt and his huge thighs stretched his pants. I suspected in swimming trunks he would look like the pictures of Charles Atlas in sand-in-your-face ads from Auntie Rye's mags. "And Garnie, you put away the cruets and the missal. I have a last rites to perform out in Bohemian Valley. Old Mr. Lestina is dying. There may be another funeral before week's end. That'll be a Red Seal each. Here's today's." He handed us each a two-dollar red seal bill. "Off you go, Tilly. You get to class now."

Father O'Tootle folded his surplice and the black vestments from the Mass and placed them in large wooden drawers. He hung his cassock in the wardrobe and grabbed a leather jacket that had zippers everywhere and his black and white motorcycle helmet. "Always wear a helmet when riding a cycle, Garnie." With that he went out, zipped on the jacket and roared away on his brand new white and black El 1000 Knucklehead V-Twin Engine Harley-Davidson. When he traded in his old Harley, he explained to me in detail about the wonder of his new acquisition.

You could always tell when someone was dying in the countryside because for miles around you could hear the roar of his Harley, the old one of course before the new one, hours before the tolling of the bells of St. Ludmila's. Bells tolled the age of the newly Catholic dead, barely after the last rites had been administered. You would know who had died by the counting of the bells. For old Mr. Lestina the count would be ninety-two. I carried the big red missal to the sacristy.

Sister Mary Saint Wulfhilda the Abbess came in slapping her leather crucifix into her own palm. "Who was that person that spoke with you outside the cemetery?"

"Person?"

"Yes, the person in the disgusting black mess of fabric. Ostentation is a sin against the Jesus."

"Auntie Rye." I thought everyone knew Auntie Rye.

"Auntie Rye?" She huffed.

"My guardian."

"And your parents?" She slapped the crucifix into her palm. "Ouch."

"Gone." She should have known that.

"Dead?"

"Gone."

"Not dead?"

"Gone."

"I had heard rumors of this person. Talk amid the town folk. I don't listen to gossip. I don't repeat gossip. 'Tis a sin against the Jesus. Red is the color of the devil. But it doesn't mean I don't hear things." The latter she said like some sinister villain in a horror movie and then rather yelled or at the least said loudly: "May Day, May Day. Red is the color of vice." Perhaps it was some sort of prayer. She became silent and kept staring at me. Then she burst out with, "Ronnie!"

"What?"

"Your name is Ronnie."

"My name is Gardner. Garnie. You know what I am called."

"Ronnie McDonnie."

"Gardner Gardiner."

"You are Ronnie McDonnie. Your parents are Ebenezer and Lonnie McDonnie of Pleasant Hill Drive, Decorah. Five years ago they awoke and you were gone. Never has Winneshiek County had such a search. You were lost. Now you are found. Put away that missal and come to class."

"I have the cruets to do."

"After school we shall talk." She slapped the leather crucifix into her palm. "Ronnie," she repeated and slammed the door as she left the sacristy.

I put away the cruets, turned out the lights in both the sanctuary and the sacristy, and ran home.

"When I said it was time I didn't mean this instant." Auntie Rye looked at me as I came through the torn screen door that never did keep out the flies.

"Sister Mary Saint Wulfhilda the Abbess says I am the vanish-ed Ronnie McDonnie of Decorah."

Auntie Rye was still wearing black, but she was trying on

a yellow hat that looked like a Turk's turban. Peering in the cracked mirror with the brown spots that hung crookedly above the piano, she adjusted the tilt. "You have been many things from Nigel to Nicholas, but never were you, nor ever will you be, a Ronnie McDonnie. What a thoroughly disgusting name. But to ease your mind in its entirety, we shall drive to Decorah, find out about this Ronnie McDonnie, have a fine dinner in Decorah, come home, empty the safe and get out of Dodge."

"We shall leave town for a bit?"

"Forever."

"The Terrible House?"

"Burn it to the ground. Yes, blast it!"

"What hat will you wear, the yellow?"

"When we drive away forever? It would match the car."

"No. For Decorah." I really wasn't fond of the yellow hat, I decided.

"Oh. What do you think? I shall wear the sculpted purple gown with its draped pleats. I haven't worn it for a while. And the large swoop hat with the swans. What do you think, Garnie?"

"I think it would be sensational. The season for swooping, snooping swans."

"Indeed, my darling. Indeed, so, and if we're to pursue our inquiries into the assonant world of Ronnie McDonnie, the inquisitive swans are an appropriate choice."

She went to change. Auntie Rye, except for an occasional gown from New York or Chicago, had her clothes made for her by Jacques du Elanté of Austin. She would rip drawings of gowns she liked from ads in the *Times* and take them to Jacques, whose real name was Jack Carr, but he certainly wasn't built like a carjack. No heavy lifting for "no fat" Jack. Jack was skinny and, like a wired marionette, had long narrow arms and legs that flopped about. For forty hours a week he worked in the lard refinery at the Hormel meat-packing plant. The remainder of his time he drew, cut, stitched, sewed, finished and fitted 'apparel for the discriminating lady' as his embossed card read. However, his clientele was purported to be not as fully lady-ish as the attire into which he fitted them. His clients, big and tall, occasionally petite, sometimes with a bit of five o'clock shadow as I saw on a Mistress Brooks of Mankato and one deep-voiced colored woman, all the way from Kansas City. Women came in on the Hiawatha to Austin, of course to the Minnesota one and not to the Texas one, from Chicago and the Twin Cities and Omaha, and a huge burly woman from Denver. She was a bronco rider by occupation, working the rodeo circuit, she told me as I sat reading *Liberty* in the waiting room. "Look at those hands," she said. "Those are hands that get a solid grip. Also have some ribbons for riding the Brahmas. You haven't had an experience, my boy, until you have had a raging bull under your butt."

Jacques had been a Marine in the Great War and had fought at Belleau, but he had gone to Paris and, as he was wont to say, "my life, it was changed forever." He took, as he put it, "to bateau and the wrap top and the sheath and the illusion bodice and the dolman sleeve and the empire seams. I had a calling to the vendeusery or whatever one might call someone that wanted to be a vendeuse." He pinned Auntie Rye as she stood like a mannequin on the little revolving platform. "I spoke wonderful French. But I was told 'no' because I was a man. A man could not be a vendeuse. So I put on a gown, went back and said, 'see, I can be a woman.' The response was, 'but an ugly one.' No job. So I came home to Austin and Hormel. A man must eat, even if it's only Spam. There were quite obviously no positions in Austin, with its eighteen thousand three hundred and seven people, for a vendeuse. But fate. It's always fate, isn't it? It was getting ready to rain and I, in Chicago, ran from LaSalle Street on West Adams to catch my train, but alas I missed it. And there I found this Venus-in-search-of-a-dress-designer having a Rob Roy in the Flyer Lounge of Chicago's Union Station. We traveled together as far as Postville on the Hiawatha."

"The club car all the way," Auntie Rye chirped in.

"Indeed. How many Rob Roys? I forwent becoming a vendeuse. I became a designer and you my first client. Thanks to this discriminating lady, your auntie, who I would put on a pedestal if she wasn't already standing on one, I now create a Midwest facsimile of haute couture."

The Milwaukee Railroad had a direct train from Postville to Austin. I didn't always go with her to see Monsieur du Elanté, but when I did we treated ourselves to dinner at Spam on the Lamb, our Austin cuisine of choice. Auntie Rye always maintained that there was nothing like fresh Spam from the can, direct from the processing plant.

But today we would be merely driving through Postville on our way to Decorah. Before we left town we drove past Sleazy Slim's Sinclair. I heard the tolling and began counting. "It will be ninety-two. Old Mr. Lestina out in Bohemian Valley," I told Auntie Rye.

We reached Decorah. "A funny name for a town," I told her.

"Funny and misspelled. It's named for the Winnebago

chief D-e-c-a-r-r-a-h," she spelled out. "And funnier still, the old chief was a Catholic and this town is filled with Norwegian Lutherans."

In the Luther College library we found copies of the *Decorah Journal* dealing with the disappearance of Ronnie McDonnie. I looked at the picture of Ronnie McDonnie, age four.

"Is that you?" Auntie Rye asked.

"No. That is one ugly kid." I looked at the pictures of Ebenezer and Lonnie McDonnie.

"Is that your mummy and daddy?"

"I think you snuffed the mum and the da."

"Stop that. Is that your mummy and daddy?"

"No. They, too, are far too unattractive to have as parents."

"Then," Auntie Rye proclaimed, "you are not Ronnie McDonnie."

"I am not, nor ever will be Ronnie McDonnie." I looked down at the article. "Besides which my mummy and daddy were gone a year earlier than when Ronnie McDonnie vanish-ed. The house from which my parents disappeared was much bigger than anything you could ever find in Decorah."

"That's true. Even given that you were much younger and hence everything back then seemed larger. The main house on the estate in Barrington Hills —"

"Barrington Hills?"

"Yes. Illinois. That's where the Opera House was. It had twelve bedrooms and more bathrooms and that's not counting all the other rooms — the library, the billiard room, the servants' quarters, the playroom, the screening room, the wine cellar, and the chapel, the indoor swimming pool and the dabble room."

"You said *was*. Is it gone?"

"Probably. Do you remember the morning I came for you?"

"Yes. You said to me, 'Your mommy and daddy are gone and I am your Auntie Rye and you will come live with me.'"

"Yes. I said those very words and so you have. And I have taken the best of care of you. Have I not, Garnie?"

"What's a dabble room?"

"Where one dabbles in arts or crafts. Your mummy was a paintrix. She dabbled in oils."

"Wouldn't that be paintress?"

"I prefer the term paintrix. She splendored in her paintings of the nude model."

"Are they dead, Auntie Rye? Mummy and Daddy?"

"No, that I promise you. Just gone. You must always remember *just gone*, Garnie. Now. Come. Let's eat Chinese and make plans."

"Mr. Chang will like the swans. He will say you have a very fine hat."

Mr. Chang welcomed us to the Yung Pung Do with its red chairs and paper lanterns. "That is a very fine hat," he told Auntie Rye.

We had the wonton soup to start.

"Are you still destined to be the great and illustrious photographer?" Auntie Rye sipped her soup.

"With the help of my friend, Padric Small."

"He thinks you have talent, Garnie?"

"He says I have the eye. That I find a central problem and understand that the essence of craft is context."

"The essence of craft. You are developing the vocabulary of the artist." The waiter took away Auntie Rye's soup cup.

"A photographer must decide what must be included and

what rejected. Hence it is about where the edge must be, because you can't just take out a tree like a painter might."

"Padric's words?"

"Yes, I am paraphrasing him." What a lovely word paraphrasing was. It had a great sound. "He tells me I have much to learn but intuitively seem to grasp the basics. Yesterday at school I showed some pictures I took at the New York World's Fair. The picture of Mr. Sol Solomon when he jumped from one hundred and twenty feet in the air into that tank. The picture of Bobby Toomey when he drove his black sedan up the ramp and over the three trucks and crashed into another car and walked away."

"Those are great pictures, Garnie."

"No, they are not. They are fuzzy pictures. Padric calls them my fuzzy-wuzzies. The film was too slow and the camera was too slow and Mr. Solomon and Bobby Toomey way too fast."

"Are you trying to tell me that you need a better camera? Perhaps like Mr. Small's Leica, which you told me about?"

"I'm not ready for that. In time."

"But you may have it. You may have anything that money can buy."

"Yes," I said and finished my soup. But what money could not buy was Mummy and Daddy. And still when I thought about it, did I really want them back?

"You did not show all your New York photos?" Auntie Rye smiled.

"Indeed I did not." Padric had developed my pictures from the World's Fair, but there were other pictures of New York he also developed. These were not shown. Particularly the portraits. My artful photos of Madam Rodowckinski posing among us there in the studio. I, with Auntie Rye, had visited an artist friend of hers in the Village, Martin de Mecci.

"Children should be exposed to the human form in all its totality, all its imperfections and imbecility," Madam Rodowckinski said, her large hanging breasts on great display as well as her fluffy, which she exposed as she stood. You couldn't really see her fluffy, of course, but an enormous patch of coal-jet hair.

"May I take your photograph, madam?" I asked.

"Are you a photographer?"

"Not really as yet. I am but an immature novice at a skill for which I will become famous, an illustrious photographer, given time and experience. Or so Padric assures me."

"Then you must photograph me and my wallows of breasts and my great bush for posterity."

"Or perhaps an illustrious lexiconographer," Martin de Mecci suggested.

Padric had been somewhat more appalled at first rather than pleased as he developed my rolls of 116 film. "What is this?"

"That is Madam Rodowckinski in all her imperfections and imbecility."

"Yes. Well, I will give her credit for the latter. But I must say the lighting is good. Almost as if you used a reflector."

"I did. First I used the tripod Auntie Rye bought for me. I was careful with the aperture opening and the timing. Madam Rodowckinski was a model, so she knew not to move. Mr. de Mecci had great light in the studio and I saw this reflector which I had Auntie hold while I made the shot."

"I must say, you captured your subject's privates with great attention."

"I think the term a misnomer." Another new word I had acquired.

"What term?"

"Privates. That is plural and Madam Rodowckinski has only the one fluffy."

"True enough. What's this shot?" He was holding up the developed film strip and pointing to a particular frame.

"After our return from New York, I took a shot down through the register of Auntie Rye and Mr. Emblanci."

"While I might not approve your subject matter, you did not lie," Padric told me. "Your Auntie Rye does exhibit a penis and of quite respectable size."

The Chinese waiter brought our chop suey and chicken chow mein with hard noodles.

Auntie Rye sipped her green tea. "I suggest then in order that you may continue your training that we take up residence in Prairie du Chien. Let's face it, if it was good enough for Marquette and Joliet, it should be, couldn't but be, enough for us."

"But without trading in furs." I had been taught by Auntie Rye to use chopsticks and did so without difficulty. "And how will we live?"

"Unlike Father Marquette without bringing the natives to Jesus. He is on his own there. Here's the plan. We'll go to Chicago for a few weeks."

"How about school?"

"A few weeks off won't hurt. You are far brighter than any other child in that school no matter what the grade. I need you to take some pictures for me. And it is best we stay a little incognito to see how the winds blow after the big blow in the town. If all is well, we'll leave Chicago and go to Prairie and lodge at the Fort Crawford Hotel while we search for a house to buy."

"With a toilet?"

"A bathroom. A toilet and a bathtub." Auntie Rye picked a bit of chop suey from between her front teeth.

The waiter took away the bowls and plates and brought more tea and fortune cookies. I snapped the cookie and extracted the narrow paper and read to Auntie Rye. "The train leads somewhere, but not always where you think."

"Very mysterious. But we only ride the train to Austin and there isn't much mystery to our trips there."

"Le Train Bleu, perhaps. I might meet up with Katherine Grey," I suggested.

"And Hercule Poirot, *n'est pas?*"

"Oui. And yours?"

"'To burn is not always desire.' Well, that's most appropriate, isn't it?"

"To make a pun... that could be the terrible truth."

"Terrible, indeed." We got up to leave. "I want to phone Mr. Emblanci, but from here in Decorah. I don't want Astania Roms listening in with her big ears."

Astania was the local operator in our town. She listened in on all long distance calls. Everybody knew that.

"Why Mr. Emblanci?"

"I want him to take most of our clothes and things tonight in his Model A. I hope he has room for all the hat boxes. Of course, he must do it late when no one is looking. The rest we'll buy new. You want your pictures and stuff off your wall?"

"Some pictures from the wall. Not all. My new photos as well. I have them boxed. Clothes. My camera and film. Nothing else. Oh, but my photo of the Mobil sign."

"Yes. He can take that. We'll pack up stuff in the Packard as well. We can each take a suitcase with us. What we don't have but need, we can buy. We can't take a lot of suitcases. The money will take up room."

"The money?"

"We'll fill the trunk of the Packard."

"How about the Crosley?"

"No. We can always buy a new radio. Maybe a phonograph radio combo."

"And the upright?"

"So out of tune I can't stand to play it and I think it is beyond tuning. It will make good firewood. I will miss the old organ, but that will have to burn as well."

When we got back to town Auntie Rye began packing. I looked out toward the garden from the kitchen window. It was already getting dark but Eleanor deLacy was not in her enclosure. Mr. Strapolet must be milking her late. I decided to go over and watch the milking for one last time. I went in quietly, trying not to squeak in case Mr. Strapolet was taking another piss. He was not. There in his heavy boots, his overalls falling down about his calves, he stood on his toes on the three-legged milk stool, his bare hairy behind up and his big dong pounding away in Eleanor deLacy's ass. I slowly crept away.

"You look like you've seen a ghost." Auntie Rye patted her hand against my cheek.

"I just saw Mr. Strapolet with his dong up his cow's ass."

"Poor Mr. Strapolet. He must be a very lonely man. I should have been a better neighbor."

In the cellar, on some shelves in a dark area, Auntie Rye had nine metal cases, like suitcases but smaller and made of shiny metal. There was only a single bare light bulb in the cellar. She opened the big safe and I helped her take out neatly stacked and bundled bills and put them in the cases. Then Auntie Rye carried each case to the car herself. The Packard's trunk was like a giant suitcase itself and she put six of the cases in that. Then she opened the back seat and pulled and lifted the seat up and put three of the cases where the seat would go and put the seat back in place. She locked up both the trunk and the car tightly. We went in and she made some cocoa with marshmallows and we sat in the kitchen eating sugar bread and drinking cocoa.

"Do you have anything else to send with Mr. Emblanci?"

"No." I heard Mr. Emblanci's Model A with only one fender drive up. I went up to my room. I was not interested in the sucking and stretched out on the bed. I wondered what Auntie Rye needed pictures of in Chicago and why. Mr. Emblanci drove away and came back and then drove away and came back and drove away again and came back and drove away again. It must have been all those hat boxes.

The morning was a pretty fall day. I noticed the glass bookcases were empty. Auntie Rye was not a book burner. In the living room she took the can of gasoline that we had bought in Decorah and poured it into the metal scrub pail that was set next to the oil burner. She lit the oil burner and took the cap off its tank. She then arranged a candle in its holder at an angle at the edge of the oil burner. It was held by a piece of cord tied around the candle and, when it melted down to where it was tied, it would tip over into the gasoline. "Hopefully it won't blow out in the fall," Auntie Rye said. "Now get to the car and quick about it while I light the candle. Here's the car key."

I got out of there and in a moment so did Auntie Rye.

"What if it doesn't work?" I asked as she clutched, reversed out on to the street and then, in gear, drove up towards Sleazy Slim's Sinclair station.

"Then we go home and try again."

I regretted that I would not be able to see the Terrible House blow up.

"You're out early," Sleazy told her.

"Going to a friend's for a few days," Auntie Rye lied. "Over toward New Hampton."

"What do you need besides gas?"

"Check the oil for me. Should be all right, but you can't be too safe."

"Better be OK. It's a brand new car."

Sleazy charged enough for his gas, Auntie Rye always said. It was eighteen cents a gallon. He had just finished pumping when we heard the explosion.

"What was that?" Auntie Rye asked.

"Something blew up. I can see smoke now. There over the trees." The siren started to whine. "Got to go. A fireman. Your oil's probably fine."

"Of course you do." She paid him. He locked the door of his station; he, like Auntie Rye, perhaps had something to hide. He tore off in his Model T. Auntie Rye took some side streets until we reached the main road out of town to the south. We went in the opposite direction from New Hampton. We were headed east. The siren kept whining and I could see the black smoke was rising. "There goes the Terrible House."

"Must be a pretty fair fire, that," Auntie Rye said. "Pretty fair, indeed."

I sat in the back seat, chauffeur-driven as always. I had picked up an old copy of *Time* as I left the house. James Joyce was on the cover. "We never read Joyce," I told her.

"That's because he's a struggle. We don't read for struggle. We read for the horror of it."

"It says that *Ulysses* was considered baffling and obscure fifteen years ago, but is now accepted as a modern masterpiece."

"When you are forty you can read it as a classic."

I read *Time*. She drove. We arrived in Dubuque and had to take a detour. There was a sinkhole where the road had collapsed. "I blame it on Julian." She turned onto the side street as directed by the sign.

"Julian who?"

"Julian Dubuque, the namesake of this hole-y place."

"You are not saying it's holy because the Bishop lives here." We lived in the Dubuque diocese — well, probably no longer as the Terrible House blew up.

"I am not." She made another turn. "Julian discovered the Indians had their lead caves here and then spent years making more caves through his lead mining operations. He shipped piles of lead down the Mississippi back to Europe. Now the city is falling into the earth where it collapses into the holes."

"Lead is poisonous." Was it in a *Time* article that I read that? Couldn't remember.

"I am aware. Look for the dinosaur."

We drove across the Mississippi and into Illinois and then into Galena. It looked old Victorian, but shabby, as if the grand old lady had taken off her whalebone stays and

exhaled. It obviously had seen better days. I spotted the dinosaur. "Over there."

She pulled into the Sinclair station. "Ethyl," she told the
attendant in the greasy blue coveralls.

"You know that ethyl is lead," I pronounced. With great
authority, of course.

"You read too much."

"In fifty years we'll all be dead from the exhaust fumes of
ethyl."

"That's nineteen-ninety. I'll be dead anyway." She paid the
attendant.

"I shan't, well, at least mightn't."

She started the car. "Sure you will. From lead poisoning."

"I have to pee."

"We'll stop for lunch."

We went to the Corner Café located in an old Victorian
building that looked as though it might have been a bank
at one time. The scoured toilet reeked of strong chemicals.
There was no urinal. Only the toilet and a sink.

Auntie Rye sat in an uncushioned wooden booth. She was
drinking a beer from the bottle. A Tommy Dorsey sound
came from the jukebox. "I ordered you a cheeseburger, mustard, pickle on white buttered bread and a fountain cherry
Coke."

I sat and took a drink of water from the heavy tumbler
before me. "This town is a bit of a dump. Was there a Julian
Galena?"

"There might as well have been. Galena is the natural
mineral form of lead sulfide. The town used to be a big lead
mining center. No more."

"You'd think with all that ethyl gas." I toyed with the heavy tumbler. "And the water. I am being poisoned."

"Probably, but you can drink the cherry Coke."

"No I can't. The carbonated water will use local water."

The waitress, a girl of maybe fourteen, came with my burger and Coke. She set a grilled cheese sandwich and a piece of coconut cream pie in front of Auntie Rye.

"I'd like a chocolate shake," I told the waitress.

She looked at Auntie Rye. Auntie Rye nodded. "He will have a chocolate shake."

As the girl moved away toward the soda fountain, I stuck my tongue out at her.

"Behave." She took a drink from the beer bottle. "I have come to the conclusion that every town in America has a Corner Café."

"Perhaps it is an amendment to the Constitution," I suggested. "Is that beer you're drinking brewed here?"

"No, it is called Potosi." She exhibited the label to me. "I suppose because the beer is brewed in Potosi, Wisconsin."

We drove out of Galena. "Now I'm going to die." I crawled up on my knees and looked back on the town. It appeared more historical and less tumbling from a distance.

"We are all going to die." She shifted as the car moved up the hill.

In the Chicago Loop we drove up to the Palmer House. It was not my first trip to the Loop, of course, but my first to the Palmer House. On our last visit we stayed out at the Edgewater. "Careful of that, young man," Auntie Rye told the uniformed valet parking attendant as he got in behind the wheel of the Packard. All I could think of was the metal cases of money locked in the trunk and buried beneath the backseat.

The big automobile vanished. The porter took our suitcases into the hotel.

"This is a reconstruct," Auntie Rye told me. "The first Palmer House burned down in the great fire only thirteen days after it opened." I knew the story of Mrs. O'Leary's cow. I wondered if the fire had been put out at the Terrible House or had the whole town, like Chicago, burned down. Perhaps Mr. Strapolet's cow would be blamed for the Terrible House fire. Auntie Rye over-tipped the porter while I was helped by the uniformed doorman through the revolving door. I stared up at the most sumptuous ceiling of paintings. I was dumbfounded by the lobby. I had been to New York, had seen the Plaza, yet I had never seen anything as grand as the Palmer House. It looked like a great gold piece of jewelry and I was standing in the middle of it.

"Don't gawk." Auntie Rye brushed my hair with her hand.

"The ceiling paintings, monsieur," the monocled gentleman with the fastidious mustache said from behind the great counter, "are by Louis Pierre Rigal. The famed French Louis Rigal." He coughed delicately into both hands that he had formed in prayer fashion over his lower face, including the fastidious mustache. He removed his hands. "Welcome, Madam Gardiner, how nice to see you again. Is this young Gardner, perhaps?" He slid the guestbook toward her and handed her a pen.

"It is, Mr. Contreill. The Suite Claremont?" Auntie Rye did not pronounce the "t", being all very French.

"Of course, madam, as you requested."

I wondered when she had made the reservation. Sometimes Auntie Rye was a bit secretive. I admit that was an understatement. Auntie was often secretive. Perhaps it was

being a Communist and all. We followed the bellman toward
the ostentatious elevator. Auntie Rye must have been at least
six inches taller than the young man. He carried our suitcases
and my tripod. "This was the first hotel in the world to have
a public elevator," he told us.

Auntie Rye ignored him. "I would suggest, Garnie, you
do not take photos of the lobby. How would you capture in
black and white all that elegance of color?" and she slapped
the word 'elegance' as if she had just said 'fucking elegance.'
Auntie Rye never used that word, nor any variant of it, nor
would I expect it of her, but I had heard Jack Sprat use it on
more than one occasion. I had asked Father O'Tootle about
that word and if it was a mortal sin to say it.

"No. I am of the opinion that all language is but a social
contract. Nietzsche would have it so, as would Wittgenstein.
Philosophers you must read. When you are older, of course.
But what word is correct, God or Deo? Neither better than
the other; both words we have assigned letters to comprise.
In themselves the letters have no meaning. The Jew, he will
write G dash d. Why? By social contract with other Jews it
has meaning. Letters in themselves mean nothing, yet mean
anything. The letters G-o-d or D-e-o have no inherent
meaning, even as they comprise. And it is only by you and
me agreeing that they are given meaning as they are config-
ured into words."

"What of the second commandment?" I asked him.

"According to Saint Augustine that commandment reads:
'You shall not make wrongful use of the name of the LORD
your God, for the LORD will not acquit anyone who misuses
his name.' But what does that mean?"

"I don't know," I told him.

"And neither do I. And that's the point. It has to do with that nebulous nature of language. As for 'fuck', when I was in the Marines I used it all the time — adjective, adverb, noun and verb. It was not a word I recommend you regularly spout, but I don't see you going to hell for the use of it should an occasional 'fuck' slip from your lips."

"Were you a chaplain in the Marine Corps?"

"I was not. Marine chaplains are actually Navy officers. I was not an officer. Nor at the time was I yet a priest."

We stepped into the elevator. "This was once the largest hotel in the world," Auntie Rye said and took my hand as we rode up.

"It still is," the bellman said.

"I think not," Auntie Rye told him. Her voice was quite disdainful.

"Yes, madam. I'm quite certain you are quite right, madam."

We arrived on the eighteenth floor. The bellman placed our cases each in a separate bedroom, there being two of them off a living room. Auntie Rye gave him a two-dollar tip. I could tell she didn't like him. "Why did you over-tip him?"

"Because he was a little snot. And now he will have to grovel the rest of our stay here. Watch, he won't let another bellhop come near us."

"You are mean." But I laughed.

"I am a bitch. We shall dress for dinner. Yes, and go to Henrico's. First we shall take baths. We each have our own. Just like the Terrible House, nay?"

"I must break the bad news to you, madam. Like Walter Winchell, I tap the telegraph key," and I tapped on the lamp table. "Mr. and Mrs. America. The Terrible House with no bath, nor toilet whatsoever, was gutted by a giant explosion only this morning. Mr. Strapolet's cow tipped over a lantern."

"You heard that on WGN, no doubt. Woe are we. I am off to the bath."

"Why do you hate the beautiful lobby ceiling?" I asked as she went into her bedroom.

"Because the cost of it would feed all the Russian peasants for months. Potter Palmer had no compassion."

I wondered if that were true. I stood at the window of the eighteenth-floor hotel suite. Chicago was a world of sky-scrapers: the Tribune Tower, the great Merchandise Mart, the Sears Merchandise building, the Palmolive Building, the Wrigley Building, and all the others. But I could not find the individual buildings. Perhaps it was the eighteenth-story perspective or perhaps the directional view. Only the Car-bide and Carbon black stone structure with its golden cap was distinctive. "It is about vantage point," Padric had told me. Searching for the skyscrapers from this point of view, I had a better understanding of what he had meant. "Shooting pic-tures, depending on point of vantage, can obscure as well as clarify." I left the window and went in to have my own bath. I turned on the tap to let the tub fill, a luxury not experienced in the Terrible House. Back in the bedroom I retrieved the black herringbone suit from the case. It was wrinkled and I called down to have it pressed. Auntie Rye was right. The same bellhop appeared. I gave him the suit and my black shoes to be polished and a big tip.

"You're a precocious little fart, aren't you?"

"But I'm cute," I told him.

"I'll give you that." He laughed, took the suit, the shoes, his money and left.

I decided to bubble bath it and added the yellow liquid. I stood there, my hairless body naked, waiting as the water continued to run. If I could have a wish, it would be for pubic hair, masses of pubic hair. I also wished for a dingy, not so dingy, in fact the size of a giant cucumber and balls like Florida oranges, or even grapefruits. Privates I could be proud of it. Not this dinky little thing.

"Don't be so impatient," Auntie Rye had told me when I complained while bathing in the tub in the kitchen of the Terrible House. "You'll have them soon enough. And big."

"How can you be sure?"

"It's in your genes."

And what else was in my genes, I wondered. And how did my genes know to make my little dingy a big dongy?

We went to Henrico's. "You could feed the Russian peasants for a week on these prices," I told her as I perused the menu.

"Shut up," she told me. "Decide what you would like. Sometimes you are far too precocious."

"That's what the bellhop told me."

"He didn't."

"He did."

"I'll box his ears. The nerve."

"But he agreed when I told him I was cute."

"You are precocious."

"He was kind of cute himself."

"Sometimes, I swear, I think you are going to grow up to be a homosexual."

"Perhaps it is in the genes."

"Perhaps it is." She looked down into her menu.

The Swiss steak from prime rib with an onion sauce was

the evening special. I chose the consommé followed by the broiled whitefish maitre d'hotel with a bordure of rich mashed potatoes served on a plank of fragrant hickory and accompanied by garden salad. "A glass of wine is only thirty cents."

"Well, you shan't have one."

"Not for me, silly. For you."

"I already have the giant Manhattan. I shall be quite woozy."

"Not you. You drink like an iceberg."

"I find your analogy improbable. I doubt icebergs drink." We ate, not in silence. "Tomorrow, Garnie, I need to have some meetings. Do you feel safe roaming about downtown Chicago with your camera?"

"Cell meetings?" I remembered New York.

"Yes. There are organizational union problems with the meat packing industry. And the next day, I have some personal business that must be taken care of."

"I am not a baby." I sipped my consommé and did not slurp.

"No. You are not. You might be precocious, but I would suggest rather you have a maturity beyond your years."

"And might I say, Auntie Rye, it is a result of the fine education you provide me."

"At Saint Ludmila's?"

"God, no." Although I remembered Father O'Tootle's lecture on language. "No. It's the life experience you have provided me."

"I appreciate that you appreciate that, Garnie. My own life was far too sheltered and, as a result, far too traumatic."

The next day Auntie was off. I wandered around downtown. Marshall Field, the giant Merchandise Mart, not the man, allowed me to wander about although there was a huge galoot at the door apparently turning away those not dressed well enough to buy at such a fine establishment. I explored both sides of the river. I went to Sears with its pneumatic tubes and escalators. I took a taxi to Jackson Park and went to the Museum of Science and Industry. There, I explored the coal mine and was captivated. I went to the Field Museum of Natural History and took an impressive photograph, or at least it seemed so to me at the time, of the entrance, its grand pillars like some huge Roman temple. It was about vantage point. I laid on my back and took the pillars looking up, giving them distorted shapes. After, back near Jackson, I went to the impressive great hall in Union Station. Again, I laid on my back. This time on a massive wooden bench. Amid a bustle of suitcases and suitcase toters, perhaps heading for the Zephyrs or the City of Los Angeles, I took a shot of the glass ceiling that towered high above me. The hall was cavernous. With the help of a brown-suited man who fondled my unruly hair, I got route and timetables to Barrington Station. I hid them from Auntie Rye. That evening we dined at the Pump Room. I had the prime rib with horseradish sauce.

"Don't stare, but that is John Barrymore over there," Auntie Rye said.

"I won't stare," I assured her. "He is obviously drunk and being obnoxious."

She could hardly argue with me. He was loud. I hoped he would not stop at our table. But they often did. "The lad," they might say, "is such a handsome boy... or so cute... a young beauty." John Barrymore did not stop by. I admit I was rather put out by that.

"And your day?" I asked her.

"Hopefully the UPWA will be uniting. It was a good

meeting. Because of my familiarity with Austin and Albert Lee plants, I was able to provide some interesting facts. Next time we visit Jack, I will have you take some pictures of the workers at the Hormel plant."

"I should like that."

"But I do think it is time you had a more professional camera."

"I will talk to Padric about that."

"And your day?"

"I went to Sears and Marshall Field's and the Museum of Science and Industry and to the Field Museum. Marshall Field must be a very rich man." I was probing.

"Was. He's dead. Died back in aught-six. And he was a skinflint. He only gave money for the museum when he was coerced and more only when he was dead."

I probed no further.

The next morning we had breakfast in our living room. Eggs Benedict, a fresh fruit plate, and sweet rolls. And the coffee. I had the coffee as well. It was blended with chocolate and piled with whipped cream and a maraschino cherry atop it. Auntie Rye went off to attend to that personal business.

I took a morning train to Barrington. I had personal business of my own. At the station I asked the station attendant, who stood at the front of the brick structure puffing on a Lucky Strike and blowing smoke like a locomotive — I knew the brand because he held the pack in his hand, if he could direct me to the library.

"Well, there ain't actually a libury building as such. But over in the town center you'll find the nearest we gots to a libury." I walked in the pointed direction and wandered through the door into a large room piled with books. A large woman in a large dress, wearing large combs in a large pile of hair, let her large chained glasses drop to her large breasts and peered over a stack of books from where she sat. "Can I help yuh?"

"I was looking for back copies of the local newspaper. Nineteen-thirty most exactly."

"Ah... Well... That's not somethun' you'd find here, now is it? We're about books, you see. Just about books. Newspapers. They are to be found at the newspaper office. Now that's as it should be, isn't it?"

"I suspect so. And where might I find the newspaper office?"

"Ah... Well... That's easy enough, isn't it? You go out the door you came in and then you go to the right one block, and then to your right again one block, and there'll you'll be at the *Review*."

'Review' was printed in gold letters on the storefront window. I went in. It smelled distinctively of melted lead, ink, and newsprint. A young woman came to a front counter. Unlike the library lady she was small and wore no glasses. I had recently learned the word voluptuous and that's how I would describe her. In fact, she looked like she might work the nights in a strip club in Cicero. Where do I learn such things? How do I know about Cicero and crime? I simply listen. And I read. I read it all.

"Might I see a copy of the paper from August twelfth, nineteen-thirty?" I asked, looking across the counter at the voluptuous small woman.

"The *Barrington Review* is a weekly." She looked into a record book that looked like one an accountant might use. "I can give you the seventh or the fourteenth." Her voice smoldered with on-screen vampishness.

"I will take the fourteenth, if you please."

"Is that all you require, sir?" If I hadn't been so young I might have suspected by the tone of her voice that she was offering me other services.

I stood. She returned. Her cleavage was proudly displayed, her tits barely secured. And she bent over toward me with the newspaper, which she placed in front of me and turned. While I had my camera at hand and would have liked to take a picture of her exposed bosom, I did not.

She left me. I read. The big news seemed to be that a colored man had been hurt in a collision at a gap in Dundee Road and that the fifth show of the garden club attracted many. I turned the page. From the personal column I learned that Paul Fabor of Mendoto spent Friday evening with his aunt, Mrs. Ida Williamson, of 122 Waverly Road, and that Miss Marietta Wagner of Carpentersville is visiting Mr. and Mrs. Alvin Sempf of 432 Hough Street. But it was on page eight, the back page, that I found what I was looking for under BIRTHS. 'Mr. and Mrs. Riceland Gardiner announce the birth of a son, Gardner, on Tuesday past at Field House Estate, Barrington Hills. Mrs. Gardiner is the well-known artist, Millet nee Yarrow. Riceland Gardiner is a financier with Potter, Palmer, Gardiner and Field.'

And there it was. I was who I was. The voluptuous newspaper girl was occupied at a desk, writing. I took out my camera, held it very still and, without a wide-open aperture, took a photograph of the news article. That's for you, Sister Tyrant, and your Ronnie McDonnie theory.

I thanked the voluptuous young woman and walked back to the brick train station and found a single taxicab. The station guy was either again or still puffing smoke in the air.

"Could you take me to Field House Estate in Barrington

Hills?" Auntie Rye had implied the Opera House was no more. I wanted to see that for myself.

"Indeed, young sir." He was such a young cabbie, looked barely fifteen, but I was certain he must be much older. The automobile was a Plymouth and there was no meter.

He drove west out of the village, passed a movie theatre, the Catlow. The marquee announced: *Foreign Correspondent* with Joel McCrea. It was a Hitchcock film and hadn't arrived in our Iowa town yet. I guessed I wouldn't be seeing any more films at the Roxy and would be going to the movies in Prairie from now on. The countryside was rolling, but the road was straight and the only other vehicle on the road was a yellow car. It turned off ahead and then the cab driver turned as well; the street sign read Ridge. We were beginning to catch up with the yellow car. It was a Packard. As we neared I could see the Iowa license plate. "I don't want the driver in the car ahead to see me," I told the cabbie. He slowed. The yellow car turned and then stopped a short distance in front of large iron gates. Auntie Rye got out and went over to the gates, looked to be turning a key or doing something like that. I couldn't see all that well from my vantage point. But the gates opened and she got back in the car and drove up a winding lane that vanished in the trees toward the top of the hill. If there was a house there it was blocked by the trees. I had the driver round the corner and park. The street was Oak Knoll and I got out and walked the short distance to the open gate. I was afraid to step inside for fear the gates would close behind me and I would be trapped. Yet I needed to see. I tried to be calm. This was the Opera House. But why was she here? And what did it mean? I had my camera strapped about my neck. I simply stood there.

"Is everything, all right?" the young man called out to me.

"Fine," I assured him, although my voice perhaps revealed some apprehension. I chanced it and walked a short distance up the hill to get a view of the house. It was a sprawling mansion with turrets and windows protruding in all directions. It lacked any definition of period styling, or at least any I could recognize with my limited knowledge of architecture. Enormous seemed the dominant element of the house. I got pictures with assorted exposures and from slightly different perspectives. But I snapped quickly, finishing almost the entire roll of film, capturing not only the house but the grounds, the curving drive, the landscape. And I remembered. I had come down the winding staircase. She stood at the bottom. "I am your Auntie Rye. Mommy and Daddy are gone." Her voice was deep like a man's. Her hair was not deep auburn and luxurious as it was now. Black and more like a bad wig and the clothes didn't fit. Too tight. She wobbled in the high heels. My hand in her large one. And we went out the great front door and drove away.

I carried the camera and ran the short distance of the hill back toward the gate. As I approached, the gates began to close and I raced, escaping as they slammed shut.

At the cab I climbed in the back. "The house has been there a long time I take it?"

"Yes. Back into the last century, certainly." He started the engine.

"Field House. Is that who lives there?"

"Nobody lives there now, I'm told. The Gardiners did. But they're gone now. I don't know what happened to them."

"Take me back to the train station."

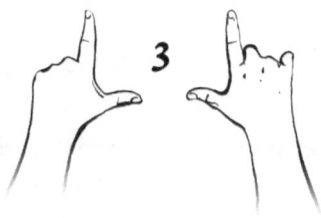

Out of Focus

BACK IN THE city I found the Cook County Courthouse without difficulty.

"I am sorry, youngster." He pronounced it like 'young steer'. "You are not of an age to have access to the birth records." He had a feminine flounce and a very splotchy explosion of pimples covering his face. The other clerks were occupied. And as they all disappeared through a door behind the counter, I laid a twenty on the counter and slipped it under a page of notepaper. "In Chicago," Auntie Rye had told me, "all wheels turn because all is well greased. A twenty will buy you anything." She was right.

"Exceptions can be made," Mr. Pimple-face said. "Riceland Gardiner, male, you say, Rye Gardiner, female, and Millet Yarrow, female?"

He found me a small out-of-the-way table in the corner and disappeared into the room behind the counter. When he returned he set a copy of a single record before me. It was the birth record of Riceland Gardiner. "I have no record of either a Rye Gardiner, female, nor Millet Yarrow, female, having been born in Cook County."

I read the single page. Riceland Silos Gardiner, male, born on February 22, 1906, Field House Estate, Barrington Hills, County of Cook, State of Illinois. Father: Colonel Carner S. Gardiner. Mother: Wheatley Fields, nee Palmer, Gardiner.

I returned the record, squeezed Mr. Pimple-face's hand and left the courthouse. Auntie Rye was in the lobby of the Palmer House, speaking with a large gentleman, dressed rather elegantly for the afternoon in a beige suit with a sporty plaid vest. She saw me, shook the man's hand, left him and came over to me. "That was Mr. Woolver Windlow. He's a draper, owns a drapery in Pensacola, Florida. I met him in the long bar."

"What's a drapery?" I asked.

"I'm not entirely certain. I suspect it must have something to do with fabric."

"Sounds British."

"Doesn't it? He kept talking about materials and textures. He has a very deep voice and a lovely tan. The bar in there is eighty-five feet long. And it is a bit rowdy. But then that's Chicago, isn't it? Did you have a good day?"

"Productive. Will you be seeing Mr. Windlow again?"

"Perhaps, who's to say? Shall we go up? I need to call Elton."

Elton Brickenbrack of Brickenbrack, Brickenbrack and Justbrack was Auntie Rye's lawyer as well as her euchre-playing friend. I did my English accent. "Your solicitor?"

"Indeed." She went in the bedroom to make the call.

Moments later she came out. "I have devastating news, Garnie." She dabbed her eyes with a handkerchief in exaggerated drama. "Our beautiful home exploded, was demolished, burned to the ground, is no more, kaput, easy come, easy blow as they say."

"All quite vanish-ed."

"Indeed, vanish-ed. And no insurance, so there won't be anyone snooping around."

"Whatever are we to do?" I asked.

"We'll go to Berghoff for a fine meal and celebrate. Go dress for dinner, Garnie."

And to Berghoff's on Adams we went. Very old country place, *sehr Deutsch*. I wondered how it would fare if there was a war. I ordered the onion soup to start. Auntie Rye had the miniature bratwurst. There were no waitresses, only tuxedoed waiters with white towels over their arms. Most, men of middle age.

"The bar here is all dark wood and masculine and does not admit women."

"How do you know what it looks like," I asked, "if women aren't admitted?"

She seemed at a loss for a moment and then smiled mischievously. "I snuck a peek in once."

I had sauerbraten, boiled potatoes and kraut. Auntie Rye had the wienerschnitzel and creamed spinach. She had a tall pilsner, foaming at the brim. "They make their own Dortmunder." She took a heavy slug of the beer.

We both had the cinnamon-apple strudel. I wanted coffee like Auntie Rye, but she insisted it was too late and would keep me awake.

Back at the hotel I went straight to bed. I stared up at the ceiling with its ornate molding and thought of my grandmother nee Palmer. Most certainly kin to the man who built this gaudy palace that I found hard to capture in black and white. But the heavy food had made me sleepy and I nodded off. I was awakened, however, by the sound of a deep male voice. I cracked the door to see Mr. Woolver Windlow in the sitting room. They left the room and went into Auntie Rye's bedroom. I went back to bed to try to sleep. But I hadn't yet fallen back asleep when I heard the deep voice yelling, "I had no idea. I never. What do you take me for? What kind of thing are you?"

All I heard Auntie Rye say was said softly. "I thought you surmised. And you being into fabrics, I also surmised. Wrongly I admit."

I went to the door and cracked it again. The deep voice was yelling, "How despicable. The very thought of such an experience." Mr. Windlow was running out of the bed-room, putting on his clothes and carrying his shoes and his plaid vest.

Auntie Rye stood in her bedroom door watching him. The door out of the suite slammed. Auntie Rye never even looked to see if I was watching; she merely said, "Go back to bed, Garnie."

The next morning she had the Packard brought 'round. I took my camera and tripod as directed. We drove south. Somewhere near Hammond, she pulled the car off onto a secluded street and checked the trunk and under the back seat. I stood beside the car watching. "It's all there." She was wearing a gown of the same yellow as the Packard and she rather melted into the car as she stood near the trunk. She also wore yellow driving gloves and a small yellow pillbox hat with bits of veiling. Only the cord cinches at her waist and the ankle-strapped heels were black.

We drove on to Gary and stopped at the harbor. I saw

the giant flat boats, piled like moving mountains, iron ore coming into the bleak Gary Harbor from the Hibbing, Minnesota mines. Perhaps because I was small, the mountains of ore looked enormous. I opened the camera, extracted the bellowed lens and affixed the camera to the tripod. Through the viewfinder I framed the raw ore, isolating it into pure mounds, only ore rising from a flat surface with a hint of the gray sky. I knew this was a really good photograph. I wasn't sure why. I knew, because I had read, how the ore in fire would be transformed, blasted, Bessemered into steel where the towering stacks billowed smoke. It was like magic. But the picture could not tell this story; the camera could only see the moment: the huge stacks and smoke spouting from them. I framed and snapped.

The Gary world was as black and gray as the prints that would be made. A bed of smoke spread above the city like a blanket, but it was too large for my lens and I was too close. It was not possible to contain so much within the frame. The smoke hurt my eyes and nose. That, too, was real but could not be captured in my picture. Padric had told me that I must always be aware of the limitations of the art of photography. I was beginning to grasp what he meant.

I knew that from these mills iron rails would be shipped on the iron rails that stretched out from the mill. The rails I could photograph, even artfully positioning myself to see the narrowing of the rails as they moved off, but where they went was beyond my picture. I knew the rails were a weaving web across the prairie in all directions. And so I shot these rails but nothing moved on them. I photographed the fenced black buildings that we were not allowed to go too near, not that Auntie Rye didn't try. "Too dangerous. No one is allowed to visit." I took shots of the steel workers moving forward like an army on offense as the whistle sounded and men poured out the gates into the taverns and saloons nearby. They laughed. They talked. They yelled. They hurried. Yet my army of steel workers never moved, never spoke. It was frozen silent in time by the lens. I began to understand at the age of ten what a photograph could do, but also what it could not do.

"Good work, Garnie."

"Perhaps, but it's not Alfred Eisenstaedt's squalor near the J&L plant."

"In time, Garnie. You may not be ready for *Life* as yet, but your photographs are quite sufficient for my needs." Auntie Rye began to speed. "Let's *in einem Engpass draufhalten*, as *die deutschen* might say."

"*Teufel soll das bedeuten?*"

"You shouldn't swear, and it means 'put the pedal to the metal.' It's what the Germans driving crazy in their Mercedes say on Herr Hitler's new Autobahn."

"Hell isn't swearing and you shouldn't emulate the Huns." I had been waiting for the opportunity to use the word 'emulate.'

"This coming from the mouth of he who wants a German camera." She did put the pedal to the metal and we sped back to the Loop and the car was given over to the valet.

We had the ten-dollar lunch with the flaming kabobs in the Pump Room.

After, we went to the huge Chicago Theatre on State Street. *Gone With the Wind* had returned for a reprisal from its June opening and the advertisement for live entertainment in the lobby was for Edgar Bergen and Charlie McCarthy. "I don't think Charlie is quite live entertainment. Do you?" I joked.

"Maybe we should sue for false advertising."

"Call Brickenbrack, Brickenbrack and Justbrack at once."

We went to our splendid seats in the red splendor of the amazing theater and ate our popcorn doused with real butter. The great organ cut loose and the show began. A man in a seat in front was making billowing smoke rings as he puffed on his cigarette. I watched the movie intently and cried a little here and there and then it ended. The winding staircase reminded me of the Opera House and the day Auntie Rye took me away.

I adjusted to the sunlight outside the theater. "Frankly, my dear, that was damn long."

"That it was. Did you like seeing Edgar Bergen and Charlie McCarthy?"

"I think they are better on the radio. Seeing ain't believing."

"Perhaps you're right. Where shall we dine? Your choice for tonight. Think about it. I'm going to pop into Poppa Barry's News to get a copy of the *Daily Worker*."

My WGN radio-listening kicked in. She came out with her copy of *Daily Worker*.

"How about the Blackhawk?"

"I doubt if they'll let you in," she said, "but..."

"Grease the wheel?"

"Nothing attempted, nothing achieved."

We went back to the hotel, dressed for dinner and made our way to the corner of Randolph and Wabash.

"I'm sorry, the kid." The doorman/bouncer, whatever he was, was a big guy, bulging in his ill-fitting tux.

Auntie Rye held out the twenty.

"Well, why the hell not? The kid's got a right to hear some great sounds."

The great sound was Bob Crosby and the Bobcats. The prices were cheap — well, cheap for Chicago. I had the whole broiled lobster for $2.25. And we jitterbugged with Auntie Rye giving me a whirl and a few pickups in her arms, raising me off the dance floor. She led and I followed. It sure beat sitting home listening to WGN's broadcast from the Blackhawk on the Crosley.

The next day I took photos for Auntie Rye of the conditions in the once "Utopian," as she put it, Pullman company town, and out near the stockyard — faces of colored women coming from the meat packing plants, faces that at some point might smile, but not here; faces frozen in a frame. Not all the faces, not all the women, only the select cropped by the limitation of the camera's view. Photography, as I was continuing to realize, never got the entire picture. Downtown, the camera recorded men in unemployment lines, a fact not fully obliterated by the New Deal. We stopped; I set up the tripod and shot colored slums, white slums, mansions along Lake Shore Drive, the great cattle-packed stockyard itself, and the massive rail yards. It was all about selection. I could have shot the clouds above the lake, the boats on the water, the trains on the El or the woman pushing the baby buggy, but I did not.

We spent our last evening dining in our suite, so as to get an early start for Prairie du Chien. "What a shame that they have turned that beautiful old Hotel Dousman on St. Feriole Island into a meat packing plant. Prairie must have been something back in the day; what a stay that might have been."

"How do you know it was beautiful?"

"I've seen pictures." She cut her steak. "Mnemonics — "

"What are mnemonics?"

"Memory. Memory is unreliable, but photos are not. They capture the real."

"Padric would disagree. He says the photographer may see the reality, but the picture he makes of it is limited by selection, the vantage point of the shot, the light or lack of it and limited by the frame."

"And you think Padric is right."

"I understand what he means when I take a photo."

"Sometimes I wonder if you are ten or twenty."

"I wish I were twenty. I wouldn't have such a little dingy-dong."

"You worry far too much about your penis and penises generally." She made reservations at the Fort Crawford Hotel in Prairie du Chien. I finished my prime rib and bread pudding and Auntie Rye read to me from Dostoevsky's *Crime and Punishment*. After, as I was stretched out in the big bed and heard the sirens of the city, I thought Chicago must be the greatest place to live. Even greater than New York. I went to sleep with pictures of Chicago in my head.

In the morning we were off early in the Packard. It was warm. Somewhere in the suburbs she stopped and checked the trunk and under the seat and opened some cases. "As right as mold in the Stilton." We began a game of movie stars. You gave the last name and the other player had to provide the first. We took turns. Auntie Rye was much better at it than I. At one bad point of the game I missed five in a row. Chester when she gave me Conklin along with Rod La Rocque, Conway Tearle and Linn Basquette. Auntie Rye's only miss was Wanda Hawley. I never saw any of her movies. She was a silenty, but I knew from the movie mags she had been in *The Young Rajah* with Rudolph Valentino. We decided to lunch in Janesville. As we drove in I pointed out, for I had read it on a sign outside of town, that Abraham Lincoln had stayed here in the Tallman House and that it was open to visitors.

"I doubt he's still here, so we may crop that from our list of people to visit."

"You think not."

"I think we will have to settle for lunch."

The streets of Janesville were like steps moving down toward the river.

"How about that old hotel over there?" I pointed to a Victorian-turreted building on the corner.

"Old London. Sounds too old and too musty." And she drove on down and turned onto one of the stepped streets. We passed the Woolworths dime store, another store with a sign that read 'Olin and Olson Paint' and that seemed to also house the facilities of 'Charles Pierce superior dentist for all your oral needs on the floor above.' I had a nasty thought. I mused whether or not he could service Mr. Emblanci's oral needs. Were such thoughts mortal or venial sins, I wondered.

"There's that place." She slowed the big car. The Monterey Hotel. She parked on the street almost directly in front. It was quite large, quite grand. In the lobby, she asked for the dining room. "There, madam," the room clerk told her and pointed to the right.

"And does the hotel service allow alcoholic beverages to ladies?"

"Yes, madam. In the dining room or the lobby, but the bar is restricted to male clientele only."

"We'll be dining," she said.

I followed. The menu was plain, rather uninspiring. "It ain't Chicago no more."

"No, Dorothy. We ain't in the Loop no longer. Oh, I suppose it is too early for a Manhattan or a Rob Roy."

"I can recommend the beer," I told her. "There is German-style beer from Winona, Oshkosh Special, Atlas All American, Jockey Club, Golden Drops Lager, Famous Milwaukee Pilsner, Düselager —"

"Enough. Whatever happened to Hamm's, Miller, Pabst, and Schlitz?"

"Look. Spam. I can order fried Spam with Kraft Macaroni and Cheese dinner."

"Garnie, you wouldn't."

"Sometimes I miss the Terrible House." It had been one of our staple meals.

"There's no place like home."

"You said it, kiddo," I told her. "There is no place called home, no more. I think I am going to have a round steak sandwich with grilled onions and a side of mashed potatoes with gravy. And a glass of chocolate milk."

The waitress came. She was a very large woman, heavy — oh, I must be honest, she was fat, the kind that could set the balance of the earth off its axis, but despite her girth, she wrote on a tiny green pad with teensy-tiny handwriting as she took my order. "Did you want your sandwich open-faced on toast?"

I was tempted to ask if it was tiny, but I did not. "No, closed-face on white bread."

"It's all we have today. We are out of rye and out of cracked wheat." Her pronouncement was said as if she was announcing the demise of all of Janesville, as if the great Janesville doom would encompass us all. It was true in a way. I suppose doom was upon us. The joyous escape had ended. We were returning to the world we knew — well, not quite the world we knew, but to the practicalities of life. The Chicago escape was over. I would be going back to school. A different school, I realized, but school nonetheless. The Terrible House was vapor, but no doubt there would be another terrible house. *Best to keep a low profile.* Wasn't that the dictum by which we lived and would we now have to find a terrible house in Prairie?

"I have decided," Auntie Rye said to me, as if reading my thoughts, and then turned to the fat waitress. "I will have the olive salad sandwich and a beer. You seem to have a very large selection. What do you recommend?"

"We ain't got most of those. We've got Schlitz, Pabst and Millers."

"I'll have a Miller."

"You want that straight from the bottle, with a mug or a pilsner glass?"

"I'll have the pilsner, thank you."

"I have decided," Auntie Rye said after the woman had waddled off, "that we shall have a nice house."

"Something with an indoor toilet."

"Perhaps two. One for each of us, and with baths. Real floors. A garage perhaps."

"No more Masonite."

"No more Masonite."

It was just turning evening as we arrived in Prairie. Before we even went to the hotel, Auntie Rye drove to Belle LaBelle's. The sign on the awning read *LaBelle de Salon Coiffeur Shampoineur Manicure-Nécessaire Pédicure.* Mademoiselle LaBelle came out from the front of the salon as we drove up. She was Creole, quite dark, and had enormous feet fitted into red high heels on which she tottered. She was from downriver somewhere near New Orleans. I suspected, now that I was somewhat more able to understand, though not fully understanding, that Mademoiselle might also have a penis. Her face, despite the shaving, by this hour of the day had the foretelling of a beard. "Around in the Alley," she told Auntie Rye. "Mr. Placard delivered the safe and installed it in the basement. Here's the instructions on setting the combination."

We drove around to the entrance of the alley and then up behind the salon. Mademoiselle stood at the open back door. "Garnie, you stay by the car." Auntie Rye went to the trunk and took out the first of the metal cases and disappeared in.

"Would you like a nice lolly to suck on?" Belle asked.

"Yes, ma'am. A chocolate, if you please."

I stood guard sucking on the brown lollipop as Auntie Rye made trips to and from the yellow Packard. When she was done, she kissed Belle on both cheeks and we drove off to the Fort Crawford Hotel on Blackhawk. The hotel was only three stories and had no elevator. Unfortunately, we were to be lodged on the third floor. We had the only suite the hotel had to offer, the Suite Versailles — two bedrooms, a single bathroom, and a living room with a mirrored wall, hence the Versailles, I suspected — I had seen pictures in the encyclopedia, and a utility kitchen. This meant we could have our favorite cuisines, at least mine. Either fried Spam with Kraft dinner or peanut butter sandwiches on Wonder or Campbell's tomato soup made with milk and served with grilled cheese sandwiches made with Wonder and real American slices. Not Velveeta.

It was September and hence school had started, but I was not yet enrolled. At breakfast in the hotel dining room, I had Post Toasties, a sweet roll and chocolate milk, while Auntie Rye had a coddled egg in a white porcelain coddler with a picture of a red sailing vessel on it, Melba toast, a broiled tomato and coffee. We talked about school, but I was not to enroll until we had found a house and were settled. There were four Catholic schools in Prairie. Campion and St. Mary's academies were high schools, boarding schools for boys and girls respectively. The Jesuits ran Campion; the School Sisters of Notre Dame ran St. Mary's.

"When you are older, you will go to Campion," Auntie Rye pronounced.

"What if I don't want to?"

"Why would you not want to?"

"Because only God can make a tree." It was a reference to Joyce Kilmer, the poet. Even at ten I thought the poem overly sentimental, or maybe I thought it overly sentimental because Auntie Rye thought it overly sentimental and voiced that opinion with great emphasis, raising her eyes and turning her head with a hand to the forehead like the imperiled Pauline getting ready to be tied to the tracks, as she recited Kilmer's lines. I should not wish to go to a high school that produced bad poets.

"One poet does not an academy make, plus we shouldn't speak ill of the dead." Kilmer had been killed during the war to end all wars, which wasn't exactly the case, the way things now stood in Europe.

There were two other Catholic schools, both parish schools, grades one through eight — St. Gabriel's and St. John's Nepomucene. Both were taught by the School Sisters of Notre Dame, but St. Gabriel's had been founded by the French and St. John's was German and Bohemian. There weren't a lot of French left and the Irish, Italians and others now comprised the parish membership.

"The Winnebago Chief Decarrah was a regular at St. Gabriel's." Aunt Rye crunched her Melba toast.

"How do you know? Did you sit in the pew behind him?"

"What an unkind thing to say to your Auntie, naughty boy. I read it in the brochure, 'Things to do, places to see in Prairie du Chien.' And I also read that St. Gabriel's is the oldest parish church in Wisconsin. I think St. Gabriel's should be the school for you."

"I shall become a Winnebago and wander along the river like Emma Big Bear."

"Here's something you didn't know, smarty pants. Emma is a descendant of Decarrah."

Emma Big Bear was an old squaw who could be seen along the river on the Iowa side, both in Marquette and McGregor, and the few miles between. She sold roots and baskets that she made from the reeds. I never spoke with her, but I had seen her, black blanket wrapped about her shoulders. Some said she could catch catfish in her bare hands. I ate my Post Toasties and asked for coffee.

"Little boys shouldn't drink coffee," Plowtee, the waitress said. She was an emaciated middle-aged woman who looked like she lived on coffee.

"Little boy," Auntie Rye said, "may have a morning cup of coffee, but half milk."

"His funeral." Plowtee flounced off toward the kitchen.

"In the new house, we should have a Silex." I did like such household gadgets. I wasn't quite certain of how the principle behind the glass vacuum coffee pot worked, but I had seen it in restaurants.

"Indeed," Auntie Rye said. "A Silex. What else is essential for our new house?"

"A darkroom. May I have a darkroom? And an indoor toilet."

"Of course the toilet, but a darkroom? We can have one built in a basement perhaps."

"It requires running water and a sink."

We talked some more of our dreams of a big house in Prairie du Chien and finished breakfast before Lucinda Latunda from 'REAL — the real real estate people, "We have your house'" — arrived in the lobby, "…looking for that person Rye Gardiner." Henna-haired Lucinda looked phony but sounded even more so, rather like a radio commercial on WGN. "Have I a house for you or have I not a house for you. River view, four bedrooms and two baaathes. Splendidly decoooored, wallpaper throughout, apple trees, a gayraaaage, coal heat, linoleum in the dining room as well as the kitchen, hot water heater, kitchen cupboards, basement."

"Splendidly décooor'ed,. I mocked her in my Shakespearean vernacular.

"Yes. And all this on a large ferteeile lot above the flood line."

Auntie drove off with Lucinda Latunda in her big red Hudson Great 8.

"Are you finished with that cereal?" Plowtee asked. "I'd like to clear."

I left the table and went into the lobby. I glanced at the front page of a recent edition of the *Times*. The New York State A.F. of L. was banning all Nazis, but also Communists, from holding office. I wondered what Auntie Rye might have to say about that.

I left the Fort Crawford Hotel and walked to Small Drug carrying my rolls of film to be developed.

"Garnie, lad. I missed you last Saturday." Padric gave me a big hug, locked up the store, turned the open sign around to closed and took me into the back to develop the film. When it came to things of photography he never seemed to care much if drug store customers were inconvenienced or not.

"We've been to Chicago and the house blew up. The Terrible House just blew up."

"You are homeless."

"We are living at the Fort Crawford Hotel and are moving to Prairie du Chien."

"I hope your Auntie Rye will find it welcoming here. The town is, how shall I say it, highly Catholic."

"That's all right then. My Auntie Rye is Catholic, never misses Mass, goes to confession a lot but does not accept the apparition of Fatima."

"She does not believe in the miracle of Fatima? Why not?"

"She says it is a Vatican plot to discredit Communist Russia. My Auntie Rye is a Communist."

"But you said she was opposed to Hitler. Germany and Russia are allies."

"She says the pact will never last. I need two sets of prints. One for Auntie Rye. Except for this roll. This is personal." I handed him the film.

"You been taking penis pictures again, lad?"

"No. It's just a house."

"Your Auntie Rye seems a bit of a paradox."

"I agree. Auntie Ryeadoxical."

Padric developed my film and left the photos hanging to dry, clothes-pinned to the line. Back out in the drug store, I had a root beer float and discussed the wonders of Chicago with him. He spoke of Ireland and his father, who had a different last name from Padric, because he legally had it changed to Biggs. "He suffers from the Irish disease."

"What is the Irish disease?"

"Alcoholism. Da's drinking will kill him one day." He then talked of France and California and Italy and of other places I must visit so that I might make pictures for posterity. Old Mr. Shombershill came in for his medication.

While he waited for Padric to fill the prescription, the old man turned to me. "My asshole is killing me. Damn piles. Pustules in the pooper, itching like a mosquito that don't quit the biting."

"I'm not sure, Mr. Shombershill, that is exactly the kind of image one wishes to conjure, nor one suitable for the young lad to be contemplating."

"Everyone needs to prepare for 'em. You live, you get 'em. Bloody doin's, I tell yah. Sooner or later, there they 'tis."

Padric handed him the prescription.

"Should've died in the Civil War, wouldn't have to deal with all this itchin' in the ass," he said and limped out the store, his cane flopping about.

"How old is he, Padric?"

"About ninety-five, I'd wager."

"He must have been a boy during the Civil War."

"Probably, a lot of the soldiers were, I'm given to understand. Come on. Let's make some prints of your negatives.

"Nice contrast. Too light. Lovely construction. Too dark. That face is phenomenal. What an eye, my boy. This is a bit

fuzzy. What a shot, Garnie! Again, on this one, a focus problem. What's this one?"

"From a newspaper. It's about my birth."

"Didn't your Auntie Rye tell you about your parents?"

"Mostly. But a sister where I went to school accused me of
being some ugly kidnapped kid from Decorah."

We left the darkroom. "Overall, Garnie, some nice work.
The steel mill pictures are strong. The difficulties with those
not so good is primarily the problem of the camera. The
old Kodak has limitation as does the film it uses. With the
Leica and thirty-five-millimeter film, you'd have had better
control. Better speed. I think you need to think about the
Leica."

"Am I ready, Padric?"

"I think you are."

"Can you order it for me?"

"Yes, but it's expensive."

"Money is not a problem."

"It never seems to be with you. Where does it all come
from?"

"Don't ask me. I'm just a kid." That wasn't something that
just came out. It was the answer I had been trained to give.
Auntie Rye had cautioned: 'Anybody asks you where all the
money's from, you just play dumb. You're just a kid; what are
you expected to know?'

"Because of the cost, I'd rather that you have your Auntie
Rye come in and make the purchase."

"OK," I said. "But don't mention the penis pictures."

"Of course I won't mention the penis pictures."

Mr. Austenette, the furniture store and funeral home
owner, came in. "Do you mind telling me why you were

closed? It's very stressful, your not being open when I have a need."

"Sorry, Austie, I was processing prints in the darkroom."

"I think you should develop after closing and tend to business during business hours. I am exceedingly stressed and have to get my prescription for my stress medication filled. Old Mr. Gedlilla's funeral was this morning and he was very heavy, must have weighed four hundred pounds."

"Surely you didn't have to carry the body."

"No, but I worried that the pallbearers might drop it."

"You worry too much, Austie."

"My God, it took a lot of embalming fluid. Fat people should be banned to Fatland and not be allowed to live among us."

I thought of my theory about the earth's axis.

"That's not very Christian, Austie."

"I'm not a Christian, at least not one of those holy-rolling kinky kinds. You know full well, Padric, I'm a Catholic, not a Christian, devout." He looked down at me. "And who are you, boy?"

"Garnie Gardiner."

"Oh, yes. The person's boy. I hear she's a Communist."

"She is," I said.

"Communists should be bound up in medical tape and shipped in boxes to Leningrad or Stalingrad or one of the grads."

Padric went back behind the drug counter to mix Mr. Austenette's medication. As I left the store I was wondering if they made colored medical tape. Certainly Auntie Rye would be bound in nothing less than something to match her ensemble.

I got back to the hotel before she did and was listening to the news from WGN in the lobby. Sixty thousand troops of the Army of Midwest were on maneuvers at Camp McCoy. That was right here in Wisconsin.

"Up near Sparta," the desk clerk said. He was listening as well.

Lucinda dropped off Auntie Rye. She came into the hotel, obviously excited. "I put an offer in on the house. They were asking thirty-four-hundred dollars. I offered the full asking price. Can't see any reason I won't get it. It's a nice house. It has everything Lucinda said it would have. We can take a drive up after we have some lunch and you can have a look-see."

I handed her a set of prints and she looked through them. "These are very professional, Garnie. These ones of the steel mills are particularly fine. And the women, the colored women, at the meat packing plant... well, they tell a story of cruelty and abuse."

"Cruelty and abuse?"

"Yes. The capitalistic exploitation of poor working women."

"Photography does not tell a story." Quoting Padric, I added, "It is a non-narrative art form."

Auntie Rye ignored me. "I will be sending these prints off to Madam Rodowckinski."

"Whatever for?"

"Because she asked for them."

"Whatever for?"

"Don't ask so many questions."

"Padric says I am ready for the Leica."

"I think you are. How much do you need? I will make a trip to LaBelle's."

"Padric says you must come in and order it."

"All right. It is time I met this Padric the Small."

"Just Small."

"I know, Garnie. I was being facetious. Now I must go up and change. A late summer white to meet your Mr. Small. What do you think?"

"I think that would be spiffy."

I sat in the lobby, listening to the radio with the desk clerk. Bing Crosby was singing and then he was singing with Mary Martin. I leafed through the hotel's copy of the Prairie du Chien *Courier*. There seemed to be a lot of nice houses for sale, but Auntie had already found one. There was to be a bake sale on the lawn at the Villa Louis sponsored by the Ladies Aid Society of St. John's Nepomucene on Saturday.

Auntie Rye, the lady in white, came down the steps. She was stunning. She wore an afternoon frock of starched and pressed white linen. The length fell to mid-calf, somewhat more of a thirties style, I thought, especially with the large white buttons that ran from her neck to down below the waist. She wore white stockings. Maybe they weren't so stunning. Only nurses wore white stockings. Her shoes were plain white, almost flat. About her neck she had wrapped a scarf-like shawl of white silk. Her hat was a white straw with a large brim and white lilies with white leaves. "Breathtaking," I said, but didn't add, 'maybe not the stockings.'

"Aren't I just." She smiled. "I thought as long as we were going to have to go by LaBelle's anyway, I might just have my nails done."

"Do they make white nail polish?" I asked.

"They should. Do you think that might accent the ensemble?"

"Magnifique, mademoiselle."

She had a white parasol with her and she was just about to
open it as we approached the lobby door to the street, when
Lucinda Latunda from 'REAL, the real real estate people,
"We have your house'" burst breathlessly into the lobby. "They
have declined your owffer." She spoke in her phony radio
commercial voice, and at the same time snapped both her
first fingers out from the thumbs in pointed emphasis.

"Why?" Auntie Rye was obviously surprised.

"I hate to say."

"Why?"

"In front of the boy and all."

"He will be told anyway. Tell us."

"It's you. I mean it's who you are. You know what I mean,
the unnaturalness of it all. I'm sure you understand. The
owners were worried about the neighborhood. It's a family...
a mother-father-four children-and-a-dog neighborhood.
They thought you... the words they used were 'disquieting',
'unnatural'. I'm sure you see their point of view."

"I don't." Auntie flicked her fingers in the air above her
hat brim.

"But I have another property. Have I a house for you or
have I not a house for you. The other side of tooown, four
bedrooms and two baaathes. Grape arbor, a gayraaage, oil
heat, lovely linoleum in the kitchen and adjoining breakfast
nooook, hot water heater, kitchen cupboards. All this on a
large ferteeile lot. I can show you the property at three this
afternoon."

We walked out of the hotel. "At three then," Auntie said
as Lucinda Latunda drove off in her big red Hudson Great 8.

Auntie Rye raised her parasol and we walked up the street

to *LaBelle de Salon Coiffeur Shampoineur Manicure-Nécessaire Pédicure.* There was a bit of a stir as we entered the shop.

A large woman with enormous breasts pushed back her hair dryer and stood up. "What a magnificent ensemble." She had a booming voice and gestured with a vast sweep of her hands.

Among the other ladies there was a round of ladylike applause, dainty but enthusiastic.

"You bring fashion to our modest town," a gray-haired matron said, not coming out from under her dryer.

"Thank you," Auntie Rye said modestly and then addressed LaBelle. "Just a manicure today. Do you have a white nail polish by chance?"

"Yes. Nobody has ever tried it," LaBelle told her.

"But in that fabulous outfit it must be white," the booming voice said and then sat and pulled the dryer back over her machination of curled hair.

The manicurist at LaBelle was a slight young man, Tomé, perhaps yet in his teens, who wore nail polish himself. His was a bright red. He spoke always with a French accent, which was terribly affected, and with the slight nuance of an Iowa farm boy, maybe left over from Tommy. "White will be so perfect, *ma cherie.*" He went to work on Auntie Rye.

I picked up a copy of *Ladies Home Journal* and began a supposedly shocking story about a young, well-tanned high school girl having an affair with a married man in his early thirties who sold insurance. I was not particularly shocked.

After, we walked to Small's Drug, my hand in Auntie Rye's left. In her right she carried the parasol, tipping it to those who stared — I assume in appreciation — as we passed along the sidewalk. "Mr. Small has a soda fountain?"

"Yes."

"Then I shall have a strawberry phosphate."

We entered the drug store. Overhead the fan whirred. Padric, in his white pharmacist coat, came out from behind the drug counter and moved to behind the fountain counter as we positioned ourselves on the stools. I did my usual kneel on the stool thing. "This is Miss Rye Gardiner, my aunt," I pronounced effusively and with a British accent. "Mr. Padric Small, Auntie."

"How do you do." Auntie folded her parasol and rested it on the counter.

"And you, madam." Padric rapped the tips of his fingers together. "Garnie, perhaps you could go get things ready in the darkroom, so that I might later show the facility to your aunt. I think she might like a private word with me."

I went off to the back but stayed within earshot. They spoke softly, but I had positioned myself so I could listen.

"I wish to assure you that I am not a pedophile. I assume that is your question."

"Yes. But you are an ex-priest."

"Yes. And the ex part of it may have something to do with sexuality, but I have no inclination for young boys."

"I am glad to hear that. I, too, have a sexuality denotation with which I must contend, but I also have my first responsibility and that is to this somewhat precocious boy. He is of blood kinship and will always be first in my life."

"Precocious is an understatement. But I do like the boy and would always have his best interest at heart as well. He has a natural affinity for photography, rare in one so young. He has an understanding of life well beyond his years."

"It's not just about life. He has an intelligence well beyond that of a ten-year-old. I've not had him tested. I would like his life to be as natural as it can be under the circumstances."

"Yes, the circumstances," Padric said. "He says you are planning on making Prairie your home."

"It is my intent, but I have already had a full offer on a house rejected."

"You will find this town, like all Wisconsin towns, liberal in many ways, but it is also an extremely Catholic sort of town."

"But I am Catholic."

"True but you have some other attributes, perhaps not quite as in keeping with the faith, and then I do hear you do not accept the miracle of Fatima."

"Garnie sometimes talks too much, but yes, I oppose belief in the apparition at Fatima because of its anti-Soviet stance. I am a voting Communist."

"I don't mean to pry, but you seem to have a great deal of wealth to have such a political affiliation."

"Well. I am a paradox, a mystery to be solved." She laughed. "But I can assure you the wealth is legitimate, old Chicago money. Inherited, if you must know."

"I thought no Chicago money was legitimate." He laughed.

"Let's talk about the Leica," she said.

I went into the darkroom and turned on the lights and tidied up a bit. Inherited wealth? That had never been mentioned by Auntie Rye before. It had always been a killing in the stock market during the crash. Did it have something to do with the house in Barrington Hills, I wondered.

I came out to a root beer float. Auntie Rye, her white-nail-polished fingers daintily displayed, was sipping her strawberry phosphate. We talked; Padric showed her the darkroom; she placed the order for the recommended Leica III, paid him, and we departed into the early fall sun. We stopped at Mr. Jailanter T. Kruley, Tobacconist and bought the newspapers, including the *New York Times* and walked back to the Fort Crawford Hotel. We sat in the lobby and read a bit before Lucinda Latunda from REAL came by. She physically steered Auntie Rye out the door and took her off in her big red Hudson Great 8.

Over dinner in the hotel dining room, I asked Auntie Rye about the house.

"Same as the last one, pretty much. I put in an offer, four hundred over the asking price. Let's see them get out of this one."

The desk clerk came into the dining room, where I was a having a T-bone steak and French fries. "You have a phone call, ma'am. You can take the call on the phone in the lobby."

I cut my steak and made a moustache as I drank chocolate milk.

Auntie Rye returned. "My offer was declined." She sat down to her French fried shrimp and mashed potatoes, teensy salad and side of creamed corn.

Henna-haired Lucinda appeared in the lobby at ten the next morning. "Have I a house for you or have I not a house for you," she commercial-voiced to Auntie Rye. "River view, five bedrooms and two baaathes, Victorian. Crab apple tree, a double gayraaage, wrap-around porch, coal heat from a cellar furnace, linoleum in the kitchen, electric hot water heater, kitchen cupboards and a butler's pantry. All this on a large ferteeile lot above the flood line." Auntie drove off with Lucinda Latunda in her big red Hudson Great 8.

I took pictures of the bridge from the Wisconsin vantage

point and of the pontoon rail bridge as well. I would not be using this camera much longer. Still I took care with my aperture settings. I was seeking contrast in the afternoon sun. The way the light flickered across the leaves in the trees along the river. From the river I walked to the establishment of Mr. Jailanter T. Kruley, Tobacconist where the air was heavily laden with the perfume of Cuban cigars and sundry leaf products. I picked up the three-day-old papers and the even older *New York Times* and went back to the Crawford. Auntie hadn't returned. I stayed in the lobby and read the *Tribune*. On the front page was an announcement that before the end of the year, Sears would discontinue selling its homes ordered through the mail, first offered in 1908.

I didn't get any further reading done. Auntie Rye bustled in. We had lunch. Lucinda came to tell her the offer over the asking price had been declined but had she another house. "Six bedrooms and three baaathes, Victorian wrap-around porch. Pine trees, gayraaage, coal heat, linoleum in the kitchen, hot water heater, kitchen cupboards and basement. Under four thousand. All this on a large ferteeile lot." Auntie drove off with Lucinda Latunda in her big red Hudson Great 8.

After dinner we sat in the lobby reading the papers and waiting for the call. The desk clerk gave a nod and Auntie Rye went over to the table with a lace doily beneath the phone and lifted the receiver.

"That was Lucinda. The offer on the house was declined."

And so it went for three more days. Two houses seen per day; two house offers declined per day.

On the fourth day we had finished breakfast when Lucinda Latunda arrived in the lobby. "Have I a house for you or have I not a house for you —"

"Not." Auntie Rye interrupted before she could go further. "I will not be sold a house in this town."

"That is true," Lucinda assured her.

"Because —"

"You are a Communist," Lucinda interrupted. "This town will tolerate just about anything, but not that. This town has a long memory. When the meat packing plant was here, there was turmoil, unrest, brother against brother, son against father. There was even a related murder. The Communists were involved. We need no more of it."

"And when you put in my offers you told them I was a card-carrying member of the Communist Party."

"I did. It was my responsibility to the people of this community. It was not a falsehood, was it?"

"It was not. Good-bye, Lucinda."

Lucinda Latunda drove off in her big red Hudson Great 8.

"I am afraid, Garnie, we are going to have to go back across the Mississippi. My Red leanings are not welcome here. This is a Catholic town and the Catholics are opposed to the Communists."

"Probably because Stalin murders them all."

"That's not true. Where do you hear such things?"

"I read about it in a *Catholic Review* that I found here in the lobby."

"You'd better stick to the *Times* and all the news that's fit to print."

"We can't go back to the Terrible House. That is a certainty."

"No. But I have a thought. We own a lot. A vacant lot."

"A big hole in the ground more like it," I told her.

"Cut down on the cost when they are excavating the basement."

"Not a cellar? But a real basement?"

"Yes," she assured me. "Not a cellar, but a real basement. A basement with a darkroom, plumbing and all. A basement with a real furnace, coal stoker perhaps. And a room for the safe. I will have them put in a secret room for the safe." She paused for a moment and then added with solemnity, "I plan on buying a Sears house."

"From the catalog?"

"Yes. And a very nice house at that. This afternoon I am sending away for the Sears Modern Home Division catalog. Next week we will go over to the town, see the hole, and see what's to be done. I thought we might live in tourist cabins outside of town at the Texaco station while they are building the house."

"Tourist as in 'Bear Lantern Tourist's Relaxing Rest with coil boxed springs on all the beds and toilets in every room?'"

"The exact place."

"There is a problem," I told her.

"What, with the 'Bear Lantern Tourist's Relaxing Rest with coil boxed springs on all the beds and toilets in every room?'"

"No, with the Sears house. I read in the *Tribune* that this is the last year they are going to sell the modern homes."

"You read that in the *Tribune*?"

"Yes."

"Then we had better act quickly." Auntie Rye went over and took some stationery from the desk in the lobby and wrote the request for the Sears Modern Home Division catalog and put it in a hotel envelope. "I will need a regular Sears catalog to get the address. Rodney, do you have a Sears catalog about?"

Rodney Relent was the desk clerk on duty. "In the back, ma'am, I think. I'll look for you."

After he brought the catalog, Auntie Rye wrote the correct address on the envelope and we were off to the post office. "The house doesn't come built?" I questioned.

"No. And don't lollygag. We have to go to Chicago this afternoon. No, the house comes in pieces, the wood frame, the walls made out of some new material called gypsum, the electrical, the plumbing and we have to have it put together."

"Not you and me?"

"Of course not. I thought I would employ Mr. Grungedagger."

"Eddledorf Grungedagger? He stinks. He has such terrible B.O."

"What will that matter to us? He's a fine carpenter and we don't have to be around him except outside in the air. For the sake of our future we can handle a little B.O."

I made the foghorn sound from the radio commercial. "He needs some Lifebuoy." But I shut up then. I didn't want to spoil the mood. We reached the post office. Auntie Rye posted her catalog request to Sears. Then we went to *LaBelle de Salon Coiffeur Shampoineur Manicure-Nécessaire Pédicure*, where Auntie got money from the safe. "For Chicago," she said as we made our way back toward the hotel. But it was a lot of money. She was carrying one of the metal cases.

"Why are we going to Chicago?"

"I have," she spoke emphatically, "decided to vote for Franklin Delano Roosevelt."

"But Earl Browder?"

"I am no longer a Communist."

"Just like that, you are no longer a Communist."

"Yes. It was causing us too many problems. The whole Trotsky business was a fiasco, and Stalin making a pact with Hitler, of that I certainly didn't approve. But the main problem is that it is causing *us*, personally, difficulties. I can't buy a house here in Prairie because of it. Frankly I was far more concerned that it might be for another reason, and that seemed to be of no concern at all."

Because you have a penis, I thought, but I didn't say it.

"And what does that have to do with us going to Chicago, you might ask."

"I might yes, but I didn't let my curiosity get the better of me, as you see."

"Very patient of you, Garnie, and I commend you for your restraint. Before I sever my connections with the party, I have a promise to Madam Rodowckinski which must be kept. I need you to take some pictures for me."

"Why?"

"Because I ask it. Is that a good enough reason?"

"Yes," I said. "But I won't have the Leica yet."

"The Kodak will have to do. We will be gone four or five days, maybe even a week. You must drop by now and tell Mr. Small. I will explain to Rodney, the Relentless —"

"His name is Rodney Relent," I corrected her.

"I know, silly. I was just being clever. I will explain we will be gone for a few days and that our suite is to be retained as if we were here. Now run off to see Mr. Small. I'll pack us a few things, make some phone calls and then we'll be off. We'll open all the windows and drive off into the wind. A bit of speed and we will have a lovely late dinner in Chicago."

But we didn't make it to Chicago. We ended up spending the night in Lake Geneva. "Wright," Auntie Rye said.

"Right what?" I asked.

But as she turned into the parking lot, she didn't need to explain. There it was. A building one could only describe as horizontal. Long, low, stretching and horizontal with its great overhanging eaves. The structure had to be one designed by 'the immense ego,' as Auntie Rye had described him to me, or as she also called him, the 'Maestro, the Beethoven of architecture,' Frank Lloyd Wright. She had met him, of course. "Vain, haughty, the most narcissistic human I have ever encountered, but also, perhaps, the one true genius." She spoke of him almost in whispers as if he was listening and might upbraid her for what she was saying. She showed me pictures and I cut and tacked them to the wall, of Fallingwater, of the towering lily pads of the Johnson Wax building, and of the Wingspread house. And here we were. I simply stood in awe by the Packard in the parking lot of the Lake Geneva Hotel. Auntie didn't yell at me for lollygagging as she walked ahead toward the entrance, apparently in awe of my being so in awe. We went up the right side of the steps to the lobby. Auntie Rye called it the 'loggia.' There, as she spoke to the desk clerk, I gawked. The fireplace with globular andirons was a semi-circular design. There were no suites and we were each to have a separate room and bath.

"You are impressed," she said as we followed the bellman to our rooms.

"I am impress-ed," I assured her.

I had a corner room with art glass windows on two full sides of the room. I gently touched the angled lines across the glass. Windows actually designed by Frank Lloyd Wright, and I realized even the bed, the dresser, the lamp stand and the carpet were his designs. I took out the camera and took pictures of the room from every angle. I let the room embrace me as if I knew that for the rest of my life I could brag that I had spent the night in a building designed by Frank Lloyd Wright.

I was to meet Auntie Rye in the loggia and, arriving before her, went to the cigar store and purchased more film. As I waited, I stood looking out.

The hotel stretched along the lake. Some bathers were on a piece of beach and in another direction small boats were at anchor. I took pictures that would be lined with the art of the glass windows. Auntie Rye arrived completely in puce.

Dinner was fine, not so fine as we would have in Chicago, but certainly acceptable. Auntie Rye began with the Manhattan priced at thirty-five cents. "During Prohibition, it is said, there was gin-running at the hotel, and that there is still a tunnel leading down to the boats that were for the arrival of booze and the escape of the drinkers." While she sipped her Manhattan we ordered our appetizers. The menu was typewritten for the day and we both chose the fresh shrimp cocktail rather than the tomato juice or fruit cup to start.

"There is something so basically American about Wisconsin," Auntie said. "I am talking of the land itself and yet, despite that, there is a singular wild beauty so distinctly Wisconsian in the tree-covered rolling hills, the green valleys, the many lakes, the wandering streams. I can understand Wright's attachment to it."

"We were to be Wisconsinites," I reminded her.

"Indeed we were. But alas now Iowans again." She sounded wistful.

The broiled fillet of mackerel or the ham cold plate dinner was $1.50, the country fried chicken $2.00, thick pan-fried or broiled pork chops $2.25 or the blue ribbon steak $2.75. Auntie chose the mackerel and I the fried pork chops. A chunk of iceberg with Thousand Island dressing was set before us after the iced bowls for the shrimp cocktail were removed.

A gentleman in evening dress, wearing spats, approached our table. He had the look of Adolph Menjou — suave, moustached and obviously meticulous. "I thought," he said, "what a perfect pair you are, the mysterious lady and the attentive young dinner companion."

"Well, thank you." Auntie Rye batted her eyelashes as she cut her lettuce with her fork.

"May I introduce myself? I am Admiral Saturnious Feltmore, United States Navy, retired."

"Miss," and she punched the 'Miss,' "Rye Gardiner, admiral, and my ward, Gardner Gardiner."

"So pleased. This is such a pleasant place. The Wright place, so to speak."

"How clever, sir." Auntie Rye giggled. It was so fake. She almost sounded a parody of herself. I thought I might gag.

"Perhaps after your young gentleman dinner companion has retired for the evening, you might join me in the bar for a drink."

"I would enjoy that, admiral, but I recently had a misconstrued drink with a gentleman and I am twice shy as you might expect. I would like you to fully understand, sir, that I am quite tall and I would not wish there to be any misconception."

"Indeed, madam, no misconception." He twisted his Menjou moustache between his fingers. "Nor conception either, I would suspect." He smiled profusely. "Later then, madam."

"He was certainly a phony," I said biting into the garlic bread.

"Oh, I don't know," she spoke pensively. "The world is never quite all it seems."

Our entrees arrived and were accompanied by mashed potatoes and corn on the cob. The meal was pleasant if not spectacular. "As you are going for a drink, I would like to take my camera and the new flash Padric gave me and take some night shots of the lake." We finished with cake à la mode.

"Enjoy yourself," she said, headed toward the café bar. "Don't use up all your film. Lots of pictures tomorrow."

I used the entire roll of film. Only about a quarter of it in the evening darkness, but I got up early and took pictures in the daylight. I shot the hotel and the lake from every perspective and vantage point. It's not every day that you have an opportunity to photograph a Frank Lloyd Wright building. I also had taken pictures of the Yerkes Observatory against the night sky. It was said to house the world's largest refracting telescope and was owned by the University of Chicago. This according to the postcards for sale in the hotel lobby. I bought more film at the cigar shop. Auntie herself rose relatively early. We both had slices of Canadian bacon and cheese-and-green pepper omelets before heading off.

"Slight change of plans," Auntie Rye said as she pulled away. "We are going to visit the Great Lakes Naval Training Station and you are going to take some pictures for me."

"I think military bases are secure. What if they don't let us drive on?"

She waved a paper at me. "Admiral Feltmore gave me a pass. But that's not our only change of plan. We are driving on after Chicago."

"To where?"

"To Manhattan."

"We are driving to New York City? Driving?"

"Yes and you, my precious friend, will have an opportunity to take pictures all along the way."

I was being used. An underage photographer-slave. Had she never heard of child labor laws? I knew I was being silly and did not voice my ridiculous thoughts. After all, the prospect of taking all the pictures — that was a humdinger.

"So onward to Great Lakes."

I only had to surmise that the admiral had not gone screaming off into the hallway, carrying his shoes. We drove east toward Kenosha and then along Michigan south to the Naval Station. She had me take pictures of everything — the ships, the building with the tall tower, the navy recruits marching on a parade field, and brick building after brick building after brick building. They all looked the same to me, yet she continued saying, "Take that one and that one."

We had lunch at the Edgewater Beach Hotel. The visit to Great Lakes had been unplanned and if she had any schedule she didn't seem bothered by time. In fact, over lunch she said, "I have a great idea. Let's not wait for the Sears Modern Home Catalog to arrive. We'll go to the Sears store and get one." So we went downtown. "Might I have a Sears Modern Home Division catalog?" she asked the important woman at the important information desk.

"Customer Service, on the second floor," the important woman said with restrained importance. The collar on her dress reminded me of the antimacassar on my upholstered chair in my room at the Fort Crawford Hotel. When she retired from being the important woman, perhaps she might become an upholstered chair. She had the posture for a very upright chair.

"Garnie, stop staring and quit your lollygagging. We are late. We should have been well on our way to Cleveland."

"What Cleveland?" The plan was all new to me.

"Ohio," she said back to me as she stepped on the escalator.

"I know where Cleveland is. I'm not stupid."

We arrived in Customer Service and Auntie Rye asked about a Sears Modern Home Catalog.

"I can give you one of course," the tall woman at the counter said, "but if you are planning to order a home, it might be advisable to speak with Mrs. Albertatoss." She turned to the woman next to her. "Mrs. Albertatoss, this personage is inquiring about a Sears Modern Home."

"Then I should speak with the personage."

The tall woman at the counter turned to Auntie. "Mrs. Albertatoss will speak with you."

Mrs. Albertatoss took a clipboard with a form on it and came over to Auntie. "Might I have your name, madam? It is necessary for all inquiries at this time. The mail order Modern Homes are being discontinued after this year."

"Miss Rye Gardiner," Auntie told her.

Mrs. Albertatoss stared at Auntie. "You are *the* Rye Gardiner, the famous Rye Gardiner?" She wrote on her clipboard form.

"Or infamous, as the case may be," Auntie told her.

"Of Barrington Hills?"

"Formerly, now of Iowa." And Auntie Rye gave them the name of our town.

"You would like a complete, already cut and fitted house?"

"Yes."

"What a delight. A Gardiner would like one of our already cut and fitted houses." Mrs. Albertatoss wrote the name of our town. "Do you have rail service into the town?"

"Yes, the Milwaukee Railroad."

"The homes are precut and fitted and shipped from our mill in Cairo." She pronounced it KayRo. "Might I assume you will want Honor Bilt construction? That is our traditional top grade and most popular construction."

"Yes."

"And being that you are one of *the* Gardiners, might I assume you will not be requiring a mortgage of Sears."

"I will pay cash," Auntie Rye told her.

"Would you like to select a home now?"

"We would like some time to look at the various models."

"Of course." She brought out a catalog and presented it to us with a gracious lifting of her hands and the admonition that while all models were currently available, Sears was discontinuing the sales of its homes.

We rode down the escalator. I was still somewhat perplexed that Auntie Rye was some famous Auntie Rye and yet, considering she seemed to know everyone from the Duke and Duchess of Windsor to Frank Lloyd Wright, I shouldn't have been. We got in the big yellow car and headed away from the Windy City on Route 20. Auntie Rye handed me the Sears Modern Home Division catalog. I leafed through and went back and forth from page to page. I had found it! The house! But, of course, it was the most expensive.

"Well, don't keep me in suspense. Have you found the one?"

"Well, there is the Cape Cod." I spoke without enthusiasm. "It is eight hundred and eighty-six dollars. It has two bedrooms, a bathroom, a kitchen and a living room."

"No dining room?"

"There is an upgraded model that has a dining room, but that is one thousand and ninety-seven dollars."

"What else do they have?"

"The Brentwood. It is about the same arrangement of rooms for eight-sixty-nine, or you can have it with wide shingle siding for nine twenty-three."

"But you don't like either of those, do you, Garnie?"

"No, ma'am."

"You like the most expensive house in the catalog, don't you, Garnie?"

"Yes, ma'am. The Torrington..."

"Tell me about it."

"Well," and I read: "'Men are concerned about the ruggedness of construction — with the quality of material and in an economical plan to finance the home — women are too. But women are also interested in other things as well — in beauty and style. They are concerned with the convenience of room arrangement; with features that add to the appearance of interior and exterior; with the many modern-day improvements that help to lighten the task of housekeeping.'"

"Are you the practical man here, Garnie. Is it all cost and construction for you?"

"Oh, no. The women's point of view here is essential."

"I agree, Garnie. Read on."

"Here is the woman's point of view: 'This beautiful colonial design is planned with outside walls of siding and brick. The gable ends and front and back walls of the wings are of face brick while the center portion is of white siding. Not only has careful thought been given to the front entrance, dining room bay, well balanced dormers and exterior details, but the floor plans are ideal for a house of this size. The first floor. Entering the main stair hall you have a large arched opening into the dining room on the left and living room on the right. Size is fourteen feet by twenty-two feet with three exposed walls, the living room lends itself to many happy arrangements of furniture with the fireplace as the pivot of interest.'"

"A fireplace. Wouldn't that be nice, Garnie? To have a fireplace."

"Oh, yes, ma'am." I read on, "'Just one surprise after another as you continue to study the plan. The back hall or passage contains an additional closet and lavatory — '"

"A lavatory on the main floor, and there is an upstairs, I take it?"

"Indeed, Auntie Rye. 'There is a dining alcove with space for china cases; the most convenient kitchen you would ever hope for; attached garage and cellar entrance'...well, let's make that a basement entrance..."

"Indeed we shall, and I was thinking maybe even a wine cellar in that basement."

"Like the cask of Amontillado."

"We could hole up the widow Hannigan, Hilda Rose O'Shea Hannigan."

"Or Tilford Toddman."

"I thought you liked Tilford."

"He told me that he was going to make me play with his wingy-wang. And I was just trying to be nice so I said OK and then he yelled at me for saying OK and said that boys don't play with other boy's wingy-wangs."

"And you hate him for that?"

"No. I hate him because he told Father O'Tootle."

"And what did Father say?"

"That Tilford shouldn't misconstrue my words."

"Well, Father was right. After all, you didn't ask Tilford to play with his whatever you call it, did you?"

"No. But I wouldn't have minded any."

"I suppose not with your penis obsession. Well, never mind. Read on."

"Well, there is '...the cellar entrance next to the rear door. The porch at the front of the garage has a French door entrance from the dining room.' Now for the second floor: 'There are four large bedrooms, each with two or three exposures, fine wall space and good closets will be just to your liking.' That's what it says. 'The master bedroom, located over the dining room is planned for a private bath but could be rearranged with a door into the hall if so desired.'"

"By all means a private bath. I should like that. I take it there is another bath in the hall for you."

"Oh, yes, right at the top of the stairs."

"That would be handy for company."

"But there is a lavatory downstairs for company. There are pictures of two bathrooms. The Fairview has a shower and shower ring with a curtain in the tub which has feet. The sink hangs off the wall. The other, the Chippendale, has no shower, but a fancier tub without feet, a sink that stands on a pedestal-like thing and has toilet paper. There are also stools in the pictures."

"I am assuming you mean wooden stools."

"Yes, ma'am." I understood her joke.

"I doubt either really come with toilet paper. OK, tell me. How much?"

"I hesitate to say," I said softly.

"Hit me with it."

I spoke quickly. "Three thousand, three hundred and thirty."

"A dinger! That is two Russian squirrel capes, a mink stole, an ermine jacket and a muskrat coat. Fur deprived, I will be. And we will have the added cost of excavation and construction. But, there will be the darkroom, the safe room..."

"And the wine cellar," I added.

"Costly yes, but we will have a much newer, much bigger house."

"It says here that the kitchen where most women spend practically two-thirds of every day is strictly modern in every respect."

"Well, I'm not spending two-thirds of my day in any kitchen. I think we are going to have to think about a hired girl or housekeeper-cook or both." She slowed the Packard. "There's a Standard Oil up ahead and we need to tank up."

She pulled off under a huge white canopy: Standard Stations, Inc. It was a big station. The attendants wore white uniforms with white caps and there were three gas pumps. "I need to pee," I told her.

"Go ahead. Hand me the catalog. I'll take a look at the floor plans."

I ran to the toilet. It was very white and very clean and as I went up to the urinal, this really big, really fat, really old man came out of the stall and stood in the stall door. He was standing with his front to the stall and his really big fat butt turned toward me. I was trying to pee and he was making me nervous.

"You want to see my really big, really long and really fat prick, kid?"

"No," I told him, trying to pee.

He turned and showed me his really long, really fat, really big thing.

I was terrified. I stopped peeing in mid-stream and ran out of the toilet, my pants still unbuttoned. I wanted to say a really bad word. I wanted to say 'fuck' so I whispered it. I still had to pee and I couldn't go back in there. So I went into the ladies. Nobody was there and I finished peeing in a regular toilet and went back to the car.

"Is something the matter?" Auntie Rye asked as I climbed in the back.

"No," I said weakly. "Where are we?"

"Indiana. Why do you ask?" She started the car and pulled out into the traffic.

"No reason. Just curious."

"Are you sure you are all right? When you got in the car, you looked like you'd seen a ghost."

"No. No ghost." I did not add that I had just seen a really long, really fat, really big thing.

"I have decided we will buy the Torrington." She handed the catalog back to me. "Seven rooms, two baths, garage and a dining room. We have no alley, so we will have to have a drive that curves around and comes in from the back."

"From where the weed garden and the outhouse are now."

"Yes, exactly. And we'll have bushes and shrubs and a little arbor like the one in the picture."

"It says here," and I read to her: "'Miss E.L. Meyer, recognized throughout the world as one of the greatest feminine home authorities, also suggests the most effective way of landscaping the various houses to bring out their individuality.' How long do you suppose it will take to build?"

"Maybe we can get in before Election Day?"

"Before you vote for FDR."

"Yes, and we can have Thanksgiving dinner in our new house instead of going to a restaurant."

"Do you know how to cook a turkey?"

"No, but I can learn… or we can have the housekeeper-cook roast it. Of course, who knows when Thanksgiving is. FDR keeps changing the date."

"It's a wonder the Indians don't protest." In the back, I was looking at the house in the catalog.

We continued on highway 20 in Indiana heading for Toledo.

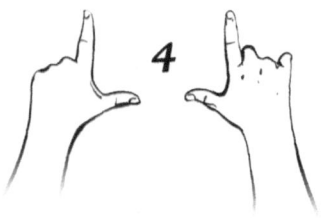

Black and White

It was near Toledo that my world again became black and white. I no longer saw the world about me in shades of lime and pink and mauve and peach, but through the eye of the camera, which was framed in black and white and all the shades of gray between. It was appropriate, I suppose, for the time. The lights, as the song would have it, were going out in Europe, if not yet in America. The world was being framed by the black and white photos on the pages of the *New York Times*, in the rotogravure section, and war pages of the photo magazines. Life was not in color. War, death, mayhem, inhumanity, destruction and terror were black and white. But war was not in my thoughts as we drove to the outskirts of Toledo on a warm fall day. My black and white was about viewing Toledo and the rest of my world through the lens that saw everything in black and white.

There was a billboard for Put-in-Bay, an Island Resort. I tried to throw aside the color picture on the billboard and see the beach and sky and boats as if in a black and white print.

This was not easy and would take some practice, I realized. "Put-in-Bay," I said.

"Put-in-Bay," Auntie Rye echoed. "I remember Put-in-Bay as a young bo — child." Auntie Rye drove toward the center of Toledo. "We shall go. We can take the ferry boat across. We will stay the night on the island and in the morning you shall take some pictures of Toledo. We will drive to Cleveland, take some pictures there as well and spend the night."

I spotted another billboard. This one advertising Ford trimotor flights to Put-in-Bay. "We could fly over."

"I saw that billboard, too. Why not?"

We found the airport and flew in the three-propeller plane over a bit of Lake Erie to the island.

"The Victory Hotel?" Auntie Rye asked the pilot after we landed.

"Burned, but the other hotels are still here. Spending the night?"

"Yes. Can we get an early flight back? And will my car be safe?"

"Yes, I'll put your car in a hangar if you give me the key."

We walked to a nearby ungraceful Victorian structure, a hotel, the name sign badly faded. "Is this the best hotel in Put-in-Bay?" Auntie Rye asked the desk clerk as she stood in the shabby decrepit lobby.

"There ain't no best no more. Not in Put-in-Bay. It's all gone to seed. But you won't do no better than this, nor worse probably."

Auntie Rye got us two rooms. The toilets and bath were down the hall.

We met in the lobby to promenade, as she put it. "The *fin*

de siècle Put-in-Bay exists no more but we shall imagine it has not disappeared."

I took shots of Auntie Rye. Her blue gown and blue hat and blue shoes would now be captured forever in shades of black. "What is *fin de siècle?*"

"The cultured world in the turn-of-the-century years before the arrival of the Great War."

"The war to end all wars," I said.

"Yes, that apparently didn't. This was once a place of ornate Victorian hotels and persons of prominence promenading along the boardwalk, cyclists and bathers, boaters and boats and oars and sails. All a colorful mélange. An American depiction of that painting you like so much at the Art Institute — Georges Seurat's 'A Sunday on La Grande Jatte.'"

"Now," I said, "it is bleak and decrepit and empty. I see it in black and white."

"An apt metaphor."

We promenaded and I took pictures of the hotels, and boats, some of which were rotting, and snaps of the few tourists. I took pictures of a handsome man, perhaps in his twenties, in belted bathing trunks. I took five pictures of him and he saw me and he stopped and flexed his muscles and posed and I took more shots.

"Haven't you taken enough snapshots of that man?" she asked.

"Yes," I said and took one more. The man walked away. He seemed to have disappeared near the public toilet.

"I have to pee," I told Auntie.

"Yes."

I, too, disappeared into the public toilet. There he was. In totality. He had removed his trunks and stood posed. "You may take my picture," he said.

I did. Then he turned and modeled his butt side, and when he turned back he had made his penis hard and big. "You like this." It was not a question so I did not respond. I took more pictures. He even allowed me a close up of his penis and balls. I found it all quite thrilling, but I realized I had not captured the tanned body, the golden hair, the blue eyes. What I had taken were gray images in a decaying public toilet. He put on his trunks, arranged his privates, a still hard penis, and readied to leave. I took a final picture of the hard image in the black trunks and he left. I forgot to pee and left as well.

I found Auntie Rye down at the edge of the water. "It's all so sad." She extended her hands out in a gesture of dismay. We walked along the water. I took some shots of rusting boats and a rotting breakwater.

Supper was canned mushroom soup, Lake Erie perch, mashed parsnips and coleslaw. I had a Coke but fingered some foam off Auntie Rye's mug of Buckeye Beer.

"Thief," she said. "But anything to kill the taste of dinner, right? If they had cooked that fish any longer it would have been like eating wood chips."

After a strawberry Jello-banana dessert with whipped cream with not enough sugar in it, Auntie retired and I went out into the evening air and took carefully timed night shots of the hotel, the beach and the empty boardwalk. It was so still out, neither breeze nor creature in motion. I wondered what had happened to the man who liked to have his picture taken. I finished off the roll photographing the black trees against a dim heaven. Back in the hotel I put in a fresh roll of film for the morning. I got into the creaking iron bed with the sheets that smelled of strong soap and, in the morning, we left on the first tri-engine back to Toledo, with the same pilot. Once in the Packard we drove to the Champion Spark Plug factory and then the Willys-Overland auto plant, where I took photographs for Auntie Rye. I had bite marks, little red blotches on my arms and I could feel the itch on my legs.

"Why do you want pictures of this factory? Nobody buys Willys."

"Because Madam Rodowckinski wants them."

"Why?"

"You ask too many questions."

"Sorry," I pouted.

"Don't be like that, Garnie. And why are you scratching?"

"It's just that I could take better pictures if I knew the purpose. I have mosquito bites."

"If you must know, Willys-Overland has a contract to make a vehicle for the Army. A tough car, they call it."

"Thank you," I said. But it still didn't make a lot of sense to me why Madam Rodowckinski wanted pictures of the Willys-Overland factory or the Champion Spark Plug company, but I began to have my suspicions. Bolsheviks were always pictured blowing things up. I had no idea why Madam Rodowckinski should want to blow up the Champion Spark Plug factory.

"Let me see your bites." We were waiting at a rail crossing for a passing train.

"Good Lord. Those aren't mosquito bites. Those are bedbug bites."

We drove out of Toledo and off toward Cleveland on Route 2, traveling along the Lake Erie coastline. We had 'escaped' as Auntie Rye put it, before they could serve us something resembling breakfast or I got any more bedbug bites.

She stopped at the Port Clinton Hotel in Port Clinton and, after some discussion with the desk clerk over check-in time and check-out time, of appropriate time and inappropriate time, and a pointing to the clock and the examining of Auntie Rye's pendant watch and, finally, a Chicago twenty, I was given a room with a bath. She went out shopping while I bathed. I thought I had bathed enough, but when she came back she scrubbed me with medicated soap and then dried me and put a lotion all over my body. Her hands were large but she rubbed the lotion on gently. She laid out clean clothes and underwear and put the clothes I had been wearing into the brown paper bag that came with her purchases. While I went into the dining room, she took the bag outside and set it near the car. I had ordered for us both, bacon and eggs and toast and fried potatoes and coffee and sweet rolls. We ate and talked but there was no mention of bedbugs. Afterward Auntie Rye checked out and I bought a copy of the *Toledo Blade* and an Ohio tour book at the newsstand. There was a man burning leaves in a vacant lot next to the hotel parking lot. She walked over and, without asking, threw the bag with my clothes onto the fire. Although I never saw any of them, I hoped the bugs all sizzled.

We continued our route along the lake and as we came toward Cleveland from the West, I read from the tour book. "Cleveland is the sixth largest city in the United States."

"I know," she said. "What's in the news?"

"The headlines. Center of London battered by heavy bombs. The Cleveland Indians battle Detroit Tigers for American League pennant."

"Are they playing in Cleveland?"

"Yes. Detroit tonight under the lights, it says. Bob Feller is to pitch."

"We will go to the ballgame," she said.

Auntie Rye loved baseball. Most people in the town in Iowa followed the St. Louis Cardinals, but not Auntie Rye; she was a Sox fan. I had asked her once, "Why not the Cubs?"

"My father was a Sox fan and when I was hardly older than you are now, he took me to see the Sox play in a World Series game at Comiskey Park. Nineteen-seventeen, it was. I've seen all the American League teams play, but that was a long time ago."

There was a lot of interest in our town — well, our former Iowa town — in high school baseball. Because the town doctor, Dr. Von Hunggor, who was head of the school board, thought football too brutal, the town high school played fall baseball as well as spring. We continued driving, sometimes along the lake and sometimes a distance from it. Now I thought about who her father was. Was his name Carner? Was it the same as Riceland Silos Gardiner's father, Colonel Carner S. Gardiner? Was she Riceland's sibling? But I did not ask.

"I think you snuffed the mum and the da."

"What made you bring that up?"

"I was thinking there was no cellar left to wall them," I lied to cover my thoughts about the Gardiners. "We could stay there." I pointed as we drove past the tall Westlake Hotel and continued over the bridge into Lakewood.

"We could, but we won't. We are staying at the Cleveland Hotel on Terminal Square."

"Ah, yes, I see," I said, looking at my tour book. "The

Cleveland Hotel is adjacent the Terminal Tower, the largest
skyscraper outside New York City."

But we didn't go there immediately. Instead of crossing over
the high bridge into downtown and toward the towering gray
Terminal Tower, looming above in a gray sky, she drove down
into the Flats and had me take pictures of river boats and
barges along the Cuyahoga. The tour book stated that in 1936
the water was so polluted that the river caught fire. Cleveland
was a black and white city. A film of smoke hung over the vast
steel mills as we crossed the river and approached the stacks,
and I took more pictures of them and then of the oil refineries blowing flames in the air that would not appear orange
in the photos. We drove up away from the mills to the near
east side where I took more pictures, some of a chemical plant,
Harshaw, and then changed film before we drove through
downtown and to the west side where there were more
factories — paint factories, aluminum product factories, and
electric product factories and factory after factory until I
thought everybody in Cleveland must work in a factory.

"Can you shoot that factory for me?" Auntie Rye asked.

"You want a picture of Sapirstein Greeting Card Company? The film roll is finished. Wait until I change the roll."

"Never mind. I thought that was National Carbon. It's
around here somewhere, but that's enough for today. I didn't
realize it was a greeting card company."

We headed east again over the high bridge and approached
Terminal Square. A valet took care of the Packard and the
doorman ushered us into the hotel. The grand staircase
and grand lobby with its vaulted ceiling and fountain made
me forget that I should be seeing in black and white as I
had through the flats and industrial areas. Here in colored

splendor we sat in a plush red booth in a plush red bar and I had a Nehi orange soda as Auntie sipped her Rob Roy. Then we went to Higbee's Department Store around the corner, just past the entrance to Terminal Tower. She bought me new clothes and underwear to replace the burned ones, a new blue cardigan and an Indians cap to wear to the game.

"You wouldn't happen to carry White Sox caps?" she asked the woman waiting on us.

"Of course, madam. For all our out-of-town fans."

Auntie Rye teetered in her heels and I held tight to her hand as we made our way down the concrete steps to our wooden seats in Municipal Stadium. Even though it was not yet dark, the bright tiers of lights were on and the batters were warming up.

"Boo," a man said and pointed to Auntie's cap.

"Up yours," Auntie Rye said with a laugh, but she did not raise her middle finger as I had seen her do before. The man returned the laugh. I ate hot dogs with mustard and Auntie Rye drank Carlings Black Label and Bob Feller pitched a winning game and Hank Greenberg drove in a run for the Tigers. "Feller pitched a no-hitter opening day," she told me. Auntie Rye knew her baseball and talked to me about sacrifice flies and the reason for bunting and she talked a lot during the whole game, and while I knew I would become a baseball player, perhaps only on the high school team, I would not become a pitcher. It was far too much work while the rest of the team could stand around scratching their crotches, a fact I did not miss; I thought I should have brought my camera. I was, however, getting sleepy and was glad when we made our way back to the hotel and I was in the splendorous room with the splendorous bed and heard the siren sounds of the

Cleveland night. I hoped there were no bedbugs in the Cleveland Hotel.

In the morning, we went off immediately after breakfast. Near Ravenna we stopped while I took photos of an auto assembly plant. In Youngstown we stopped while I took photos of more steel mills. In Pittsburgh it was more steel mills and aluminum plants. Outside Pittsburgh near Irwin, the new Pennsylvania turnpike with two concrete lanes running in each direction and tunnels through mountains was getting ready to open, but that was a month away, or so the signs stated, so we continued on the twisting, turning Lincoln Highway and spent the night in tourist cabins, each with our own, outside of Bedford. The next morning Auntie Rye inspected me for bedbugs. And the rest of the morning I mostly slept, curled in the backseat as we wound our way through the treed mountains of southern Pennsylvania until we reached Gettysburg. I looked at my pocket watch when we arrived and when we left. We did not tarry long. Auntie Rye seemed bored by the battlefields.

"There is a sameness about battlefields," she said.

"Sameness?"

"Yes, emptiness except for the monuments."

We went to York and Lancaster and she didn't stop so I had no record of the Amish and their black buggies, which we passed along the road, and the white barns that flashed by through the car window. It was a black and white world, this world of the Amish, and I was sorry that I had taken no pictures of it.

"I am tired of it all and tired of the driving," was her excuse.

Being practical, I reminded her that we still had to drive back home after we went to New York.

"I have a thought on that," she said and drove on. We left the Lincoln Highway and drove south to Wilmington where I took photos of the chemical plants and docks and refineries and storage tanks. We went on to Philadelphia and it was the shipyards and factories and plants, and then into New Jersey and more plants and factories and factories and plants. And I was bored by all this black and white sameness and knew my work was getting sloppy.

"You can put your camera away," she said as we approached the Holland Tunnel.

"Where are we staying?" I put the camera back in its case.

"The Waldorf." She crossed over to and up Park Avenue. The Art Deco-ish Waldorf hyphen Astoria loomed ahead.

In the lobby, the giant clock with Queen Victoria and the presidents glaring at me assured me that it was long past dinner hour. No wonder I was hungry. There were no suites available, but before going up to our rooms Auntie Rye met with the concierge, a mellow man with the looks of a young Nelson Eddy — I expected him to burst into a deep baritone rendition of the "Indian Love Call." His voice was appropriately deep baritone. "Well, sir — "

"Ma'am," Auntie Rye corrected him.

"I was about to say well sir-ree, ma'am. I meant no disrespect, ma'am. But it's not an easily achieved request and very expensive."

"Well, the money is of little concern or I wouldn't be stopping here, would I? But it can be done?"

"Yes. It can be done. I will have the car — "

"Packard."

"Yes, Packard touring car, yellow, as you said, shipped by rail to Chicago the quickest way possible."

"And I will need to book a drawing room on the 20th Century Limited for Chicago on Saturday for the two of us."

Auntie turned to me. "The fastest train in the world, Garnie."

"Yes," Nelson Eddy look-and-sound-alike assured her. "Nine hundred and sixty miles in nine hundred and sixty minutes. Or so they advertise."

Auntie Rye had our dinner sent up to her room. She had a baked oyster dish; I settled for chicken Kiev. After she sent me off to my room to sleep and she had disappeared — down into some cauldron of a bar off the lobby, I suspected — I slipped up to the floor that was occupied by the Starlight room and hung about in the Starlight lobby listening to the Benny Goodman Sextet. A burly man in a tuxedo with hands like an iron worker's — perhaps he was by day — policed the door. He winked at me and found me a well-cushioned chair behind a potted plant near the entrance where I could listen to the music and not be too conspicuous. Occasionally, he would ask, "Are you all right there now, young gentleman?" and I would assure him that I was. In the lobby there were individual pictures of the sextet in frames: Benny Goodman, of course, Charlie Christian, Lionel Hampton, Johnny Guarnieri, Artie Bernstein and Nick Fatool. I listened until I got sleepy, thanked the iron worker-bouncer man and went down to my room.

In the morning we had breakfast down in one of the dining rooms. Fresh fruit 'picked yesterday in Florida' and Eggs Benedict. Oscar, as in Veal Oscar and Waldorf Salad fame, dropped by the table to compliment Auntie Rye on her hat, a thing in itself that looked as if the fruit 'had been picked yesterday in Florida,' although this fruit was constructed from assorted fabrics. There was a Carmen Miranda silliness about the hat and the fruit on top was just slightly crushed from the traveling.

"How have you been, Rye?" he asked.

"Well, Oscar, and you?"

"Amazing, quite so. I will be in Chicago next month. Perhaps we might have a drink."

"I'm there so little now," she told him. "Garnie, you see. School."

"Of course. Millet has a show. In the Village. Have you seen it?"

"No and probably won't."

Oscar looked at me. "I understand, of course."

I realized that Millet, the artist with a show, was probably my mother. My gone mother. I pretended not to be excited, but if she had a show, she was undoubtedly not dead, *truly* not dead, just gone, *truly* just gone.

After breakfast, in the lobby, I surrendered my rolls of film to Auntie, that is all the rolls except the one with the bathing-trunks guy and night photos of Put-in-Bay. I was sorry I had not taken photos of bedbugs. "I thought you weren't a Communist anymore."

"I'm not, and what is the connection with my being a Communist and Madam Rodowckinski?" she said in a loud whisper.

"The film, the pictures are for Madam Rodowckinski because she is a Communist and a Russian spy," I pronounced.

"Sometimes your imagination gets the better of you. Russian spy, really! Yes, the film is for Madam Rodowckinski, for her collection on the American worker and the industrial places of work. And yes, I am no longer a Communist. Yes, I am going to vote for FDR and no, I will not be voting for Browder." We went out into the wind. She turned to the doorman. "Could you hail us a cab, please?"

She held on to the fruit cluster on her head as she bent and got in the cab. I climbed in after and she gave the cabbie the address on Bleecker.

"Do I have to go to Madam Rodowckinski's?"

"No, of course not. She thinks you a darling, but it might be easier for me to speak to her if you weren't there. Madam Rodowckinski thinks you are the most beautiful of all children. And that because of it your life will be charmed. She has a theory that beautiful people have everything given to them. And the more beautiful, the more they are given. But don't let it go to your head. One woman's beauty is another's ugly. Now, if you don't go to Madam Rodowckinski's, what will you do?"

"Shop or window shop. Just people look. I think walking the streets of New York is one of the most exciting things in all the world to do." Then I added rather pompously, "Perhaps it is my photographic eye."

"Don't be such a twit. But exciting people in the Village? Strange, different, unconventional, but *exciting?*"

"Yes, in the Village, too."

"Promise me you won't take any pictures of men in bathing trunks."

"I promise, but it's highly unlikely that I'll be seeing any men in bathing trunks."

"In the Village, all is possible." She dug about in her purse and took out a small map. "Here, you'll need this. It's a map of the Greenwich Village area."

I left her at the address on Bleecker with a promise to meet her in two hours. When she disappeared inside, I examined the map. Seventh Avenue looked like a busy street and I ran over to it and found a newsstand. *What's Doin' in the Village*, the paper was called. It was free and in it I found the listing of the exhibit: Millet Yarrow current exhibit — *Sex, as Close as It Gets*. Gorley Gallery. Exhibiting daily 9 to 7. The address was right on Seventh and I walked to it.

As I tried to enter, I was immediately stopped by a skinny woman, almost emaciated, in a gypsy costume that seemed to hang far too large on her, rather than being simply worn. She had shiny black hair that spiked up and then fell down like water streams from a fountain. Her long nails, which she pointed at me, curled over and were polished black. "This is not an exhibit for youngsters of your age. I am sorry. Shoo."

"I am an acquaintance of the artist. She suggested I come here."

"And where would you know the artist from?"

"Chicago. Barrington, actually. And I am not as young as I appear. I am developing late. I am thirteen."

"I see. Well, then, if Miss Yarrow insists, then you must. Would you sign your name in the guest book, please?"

I wrote Gerome du Pleseant. It seemed such a pleasant name. I then approached the pictures. They were all huge. Seven or eight feet high and nearly as wide in most cases. The first was an oil, but entirely black and white. I could relate to that, though I hadn't been seeing the world as much in that light since my arrival in New York. I stood and stared at the thin lines of black against the white. The painting was entitled, "Lady of the Bush." I suddenly realized, as I stared intently at it, what it was, what it had to be. It was a woman's fluffy. The painting could have been of Madam Rodowckinski's fluffy. *Sex Close* now made sense to me. The next painting was called "The Floral Center." It was an oil. There was a flower, an iris, and it was pink, but in the center, in reds, was what looked like torn skin, like a wound. The next painting I immediately identified. It was called "Ball Gown." It was a testicle hanging in a see-through piece of lace or gauze-like material. I looked back at "The Floral Center" and suspected what it might be, but my lack of experience did not offer me certainty. The next oil was a more square-shaped canvas, perhaps five-by-five in size. It was entitled "Head On" and as I looked at it I realized it was the head of a penis, the piss slot with bits of moisture on it like dew on a leaf or flower. Next was another penis painting, "Head of Class," followed by another called "Cone" and then what appeared to be the last of the penis paintings, a huge oil entitled "Mushroom." Next was a series of three paintings, each about six-by-three. They were clustered like a Russian triptych I had once seen at the Art Institute of Chicago, but, unlike the triptych, I couldn't make them out. They were all three shades of reds and oranges and kind of like wounds, but I recognized nothing. The first was called "The Button," the second different but similar to the first was called "Zee Clit" and the third, "The Man in the Boat," looking much as the other two. The next oil could have been a girl's fluffy for, as it was hairless, it looked a bit like Geraldina's slash thing. The thing that was not a penis. It was called "Labia Lazuli, the Precious Jewel." Yes, that's what it was, I decided, a girl's fluffy part, but hairless like Geraldina's. There were two other similar paintings — "The Big Dipper: Vulva Major" and the "Little Dipper: Vulva Minor."

"And did you form an opinion?" the emaciated woman with the hair asked as I came back to the front of the gallery.

I gave my voice a tone of authority. "Mostly unpleasant."

"Not to your taste." She was mocking me.

I didn't care. "The penis ones were acceptable, but the others, well?" My voice carried a strong note of disapproval.

She glared at me. "Perhaps your tendency is more toward the penis."

I didn't respond. I knew what she was suggesting. I walked proudly from the gallery. At the corner I found a uniformed policemen. "Could you tell me where the library is?"

"A ways, young man, up Fifth Avenue at Forty-second."

Time for ingenuity. "A used book store?"

"Just around the corner, middle of the block. Can't miss it."

In the dusty book store I found a dusty set of Encyclopedia Americana. In the C volume, I didn't find clit but instead discovered clitoris and knew I had the found the right entry when I also found an illustration and additional illustrations, those of the vulva and labia. I understood my mother's paintings, but it gave me no understanding of my mother other than to make me think I might have come by my artistic talents as inherited ones. Perhaps also my interests in the privates. I could hardly fault her for the penis paintings. I had taken photos of the man in the belted bathing trunks without the trunks. And then there was my artistic photo with the carefully reflected light of Madam Rodowckinski's fluffy. Yes, perhaps it was an inherited talent. I had found my mother. Where was my father? I tossed *What's Doin' in the Village* in the trash and stood waiting for Auntie on Bleecker. A small ragged looking dog trailing a leash ran by. I wondered what had happened to the owner. Dead, perhaps. Dropped over dead walking his dog. Maybe it was an old lady. Her dog. She dropped over dead. There would be no bell tolling for the dead of the Village, I suspected.

"I thought we might go see a show tonight," Auntie Rye said as we walked back over to Seventh to hail a cab. She carried a section of the *Times* with her. In the cab she read to me. "There is *Tobacco Road* with Will Geer, *The Man Who Came to Dinner* with Monty Woolley. Bert Lahr in *DuBarry was a Lady*. Oh, and Al Jolson and Martha Raye in *Hold on to Your Hat*. But that's just opening tonight. We'd never get tickets. Oh, there's a new play by A.J. Cronin. He wrote the novel *Keys of the Kingdom*."

"You never read that to me."

"Not enough gore for your taste. The play *Juniper Laughs* is with Jessica Tandy and Alexander Knox. Should we give it a whirl?"

Whirl was certainly the wrong word. It was boring. *Juniper Laughs* was not a laugh. "Sonorous," Auntie Rye pronounced and we left at intermission. "What shall we do tomorrow?" It was more an internal musing than a question to me as she stood hand in the air waving to an approaching cab.

"The Empire State." I was enthusiastic. I had yet to go up into the building which stretched into the heavens. To go up into the tallest building in the world.

We sat in the back of the cab. "Perhaps not tomorrow," she told me. "Perhaps the day after. I am no longer a Communist, but I want you to understand what drove me to become one. That is important. Tomorrow we will go up to Harlem. It is time you met Miss Lilith. Miss Lilith Anderson, formerly of Chicago, now of Harlem. And I want you to take your camera."

"I thought you were done. That you needed no more pictures."

"These are not for me. These are pictures you will want to take."

After a heavenly breakfast of crepes and melon balls and slices of ham sautéed with fresh pineapple, we left the kaleidoscope that was the Waldorf-Astoria and rode the subway north to West 125th Street. Through the turnstile and up the steps and into hell. Harlem was not simply a ghetto, it was a slum. It was filth and rot and decay and strong odors of corruption and faces of despair, but most particularly the faces of children of despair. It was boarded buildings and broken windows, uncollected trash and dirt. There was no color here, a bleak black and white. I stopped and took photos and Auntie Rye waited with complete patience as I circled about capturing the panorama of gray. It was a collection of no hope. I indicated I was ready to move on and, without verbalizing, she walked and I followed through alleys of trash and more streets of burned out buildings and vacant stores without glass in the windows.

"The riots of thirty-five. Nothing changes." She walked on ahead of me. She wore a brown suit with a fur collar and a plain brown felt hat. Little girls in once-white-now-yellowed-from-bleach dresses stood staring; little boys in torn suits and shabby shoes stood staring. It was a world of children looking out. Wishing, it seemed, for something that wasn't there. I followed her into a tenement, the plaster broken, its lath exposed and the dark green paint peeling. I stopped and took a picture. Then up three flights of creaking steps, through hallways of broken balustrades until she stopped and rapped on a door.

A woman's voice responded. A black woman's voice that carefully articulated the few words. "Who is it?"

"It is Rye, Miss Lilith. I have young Garnie with me."

The sounds of bolts being unbolted preceded the opening of the door and the tall elderly woman stepped back. The voice was melodious. "Do come in."

We went in. In contrast to the outside, here all was immaculate. The woman moved back and stood by a rocker. She had a cane, an elegant cane with an ivory handle upon which she leaned. She wore white, an elegant white dress, the long skirt coming to her ankles, the sleeves stretching the full length of her long arms to points at the wrists, a pendant of an emerald-colored stone hung from a heavy gold chain about her neck.

"I would like to take your picture."

"You may," she said. Her hand now held the back of the chair.

"You look well, Miss Lilith," Auntie Rye said.

I took Miss Lilith's picture. Advanced the film and took another.

"I am well, Rye. For ninety I am exceedingly well, but it's due to your kindness that I am well. I have faith, even some hope in this place where hope seems to have vanished and, of course, your charity. Please, both be seated."

"Charity meaning love only. For that is what it is… love." Auntie Rye sat on an ornate Victorian chair.

I chose to sit on a matching ottoman, not taking my eyes from the commanding presence of the towering dark-skinned woman in white.

The woman sat, not in the rocker but in a large overstuffed horsehair chair. She resembled a queen on a throne.

"You were hardly more than a baby when I saw you last, Garnie."

"Before Mummy and Daddy were gone," I said. "In Chicago. In a big house with a winding staircase." It had been just days since we had seen *Gone With the Wind.* "It was like the staircase in *Gone With the Wind.*"

"Yes, the staircase was like that. The movie was racist, however."

"You saw it?" Auntie Rye seemed surprised.

"It played here in Harlem. I thought there would be more riots. But it was mostly met with silence."

"You get out then?"

"A great deal. I go on the subway or by cab to the Village with some regularity. Old Negro women are made to feel welcome in the Village. I go there for a cocktail or for dinner. I went to see Millet's gallery opening. Have you seen it?"

"No," Auntie told her. "How did you find it?"

"She has an enlarged view of things, and I mean things from a purely euphemistic perspective. I thought it overblown, if you will excuse a bad pun. I am not a prude, as you full well know, but some things are inherently ugly and I am not certain lend themselves to wall displays. I can't imagine staring at one of those paintings as I was trying to get my dinner down. I shouldn't be so pejorative; she thought enough and was kind enough to invite me to the opening, and the champagne and the array of New Yorkers assembled were first class. The Little Flower was there." It was only later I realized she had been referring to Mayor LaGuardia.

"And Millet is well?"

"Yes."

"And you are managing?"

"Oh, yes. Gladys comes in mornings and, if I haven't died during the night — and as you can see I haven't mastered that yet — she tends to my needs. I usually go out for dinner or she prepares something for me to pop in the oven. But enough of me. I am glad that Garnie has come to meet me. You see, Garnie, I was the housekeeper at the Field House even before your father was born."

"My gone father. What is the Field House?" I pretended ignorance.

"The Field House Estate in Barrington Hills. The *Gone With the Wind* staircase. Your grandfather the colonel, who survived the great crash of twenty-nine, only to plunge to death in a crash of his own making a year later, had married Wheatley Palmer and, being not too bright, she, the fool, was in the aeroplane with him. They plunged to their fiery deaths. Your great-grandfather on Wheatley's side was one of the Fields of Massachusetts, but kin to Marshall Field."

"The department store? I should have asked for a discount," I told her.

"You never would have gotten it. He was so cheap. I worked for them before the Gardiners. He used to give me a pair of gloves from the store as a Christmas gift."

"Grandfather was an aviator?"

"Yes. Does Rye tell you nothing?"

"Nothing," she responded.

"I suppose under the circumstances it takes less explaining. Not even the basics?"

"Particularly not the basics."

I pumped the old woman for information. "And Palmer? You said my grandmother was named Palmer."

"Yes." She got up out of the chair. "You guessed right. The

Palmer House. I suspect you have stayed there. Rye, will you have a cup of tea or coffee? It is too early for whiskey. And Garnie?"

"Coffee with lots of milk."

"Marcella LaMonta brought me back a can of Nescafe from Switzerland. It is called instant coffee. It is quite terrible. I won't make you endure it. I have a Silex."

"May I watch?" I asked and I did.

The three of us sat drinking our coffee. Mine with half top milk. "When did you come to New York?" I asked her, stirring the sugar in my coffee.

"When your mother and father went away."

"When they were gone."

"Yes. I came to Chicago in eighteen-sixty-three. The year of emancipation. I was born a slave and was one, well, until I was thirteen."

"Tell Garnie the story, Miss Lilith. Begin with your free ancestors."

"All right. It is a story he should hear. Back in the twenties, Garnie, that's the eighteen-twenties, my father was a free Negro living in Delaware. His ancestors had come over into the Jamestown Colony, not as slaves, but before slavery, as indentured servants. When the indenture had been served, he was able to buy a bit of useless land deep in Indian territory that Captain John Smith had explored and that became the Colony and then the State of Delaware. And for nearly two hundred years, my ancestors farmed the same farm in Delaware as free men. But then came the infamous Patty Cannon and her son-in-law, Joe Johnson. They and their gang, mostly made up of other relatives, would kidnap the free black folks and take them from Delaware to Maryland, into Patty's house, where it was said they were shackled. Even though it never seceded, Maryland was more a slave state and the Mason-Dixon Line didn't just go east and west between Pennsylvania and Maryland, but north and south between Maryland and Delaware. My mother, as she told it, was shackled in the attic in this house and then taken in a wagon to Sharpstown and then down the Nanticoke by boat to a ship anchored in Tangier Sound, where the rivers flow into the Chesapeake Bay. There were many Negroes on the ship, all shackled, all now chattel, and the ship went all the way 'round to a slave market in New Orleans. There she, mother, was bought by the agent of a Mississippi plantation owner." Miss Lilith's voice was strong and unwavering. "My mother was taken to a plantation near Vicksburg and trained as a house slave where my father was already a house slave. I was born into slavery in what must have been eighteen-fifty, thirteen years before emancipation. But then the war came and the master of the plantation left to go off and be a major or something in the Confederate Army. The mistress, one Miss Lydia as we called her, was a sickly, swooning sort of woman and she moved into the town of Vicksburg to be near the doctors. My mother and I went with her to this big house on the bluff. My father went off with the major to the war. I never heard from him, nor saw him again."

"Not even after the war?" I asked.

"No, not even after the war. In those days, it was not easy to find out what happened to people, and, of course, I had left, but I am getting ahead of my story. My mother and I tended to Miss Lydia and her many visitors' needs, but, as she got more sickly, she moved north to be with her sister in Tennessee. She took the other slaves but left my mother and me to serve the new tenants of the mansion house. She had rented it to a Mr. Anderson Miller and his wife, Dora nee Richards, of San Croix in the West Indies. Mr. Miller was from Arkansas, a lawyer. And she, too, Miss Dora, had lived there when they married. I never quite understood his position. He worked for the Confederate government doing something in administration and came to Vicksburg in that capacity. But he was secretly opposed to slavery and so was she, perhaps even more so. The slaves in San Croix, it was a Dutch Colony, had been freed in eighteen-forty-eight before I was even born. Dora spoke perfect English, but she never considered herself an American." Miss Lilith finished her coffee and poured herself another cup from the Silex pot. She drank it black without sugar.

"Dora was good to me and my mother — I did cleaning; my mother did cleaning and cooking. Dora loved to read and she read Charles Dickens to me for she particularly liked Dickens. My mother was a great cook, and while we ate left-overs, they were great leftovers. My mother knew where and how to buy the best and Dora trusted her with the money to buy the best meats, the freshest eggs and cheeses. Mr. Miller purchased quantities of wine, both in casks and bottles. The house had two cisterns of fresh water and a garden tended by a day Negro, so there were always fresh vegetables during the season and the place had fine fruit trees and my mother canned both vegetables and fruits for the house, but there wasn't much canning that summer for the Millers had not been there many months when General Grant and the Union troops, the Army of the Tennessee, arrived and the battle and then the siege of Vicksburg began. The shelling came in the early spring of sixty-three. Because the mansion was up on a hill, high above the river, it was obviously a perfect target. Many of the white folk took to the caves and the Millers did for a bit, but they couldn't buy a cave and couldn't find one to rent, so they mostly stayed in the mansion, and when the shelling commenced each day, as it did every day, we all went and huddled in the cellar. It was there, perhaps only to cure her boredom and maybe to counteract her fear, that Dora Anderson taught me to read. The shelling was continuous and became more intense and longer each day and often into the night. Part of the house walls were blown away. Lamps, if they had not been destroyed in the shelling, were of little use as there was little oil. They gave way to crude candles, not the beautifully made tapers, but the crudest of brown candles with bad wicks that barely lit.

"March moved into April into May. Food became more difficult for my mother to get. There were no longer dogs or cats about. I had seen dried rats hanging in the meat stalls. Our food staple became cornbread. Dora hated cornbread. She allowed one cistern to be used for the scraggly soldiers that came by and ordered cornbread scraps be provided them. More parts of the house blew away. Dora was nearly killed when a ceiling above her gave way. Mule meat was sold in the market. Dora found it more difficult to find books, yet she continued to read to me and to teach me to read. We, my mother and I, were allowed wine, which was unheard of to give to slaves, but it was plentiful at the Millers', said to be curative, and there were casks of it, but we were told to keep this fact hidden from the soldiers.

"May became June and the shelling became even more intense; practically every piece of crockery was broken. My mother came from the market to tell of the girl there whose leg had been torn off by a shell. And then the next night was the terrible night. My mother had barely found scraps to make a soup and some corn mush and was cleaning a pot when a shell tore through the house. It hit her directly. I ran to her, this bleeding pile of flesh that had been my mother. 'She is dead,' Dora said and led me away. Dora held me as if I had not been a young Negress, as if I had not been black-skinned and a slave. A few days later there was one huge explosion, a shell into the caves in the hill and then absolute quiet. It was July fourth. I knew of Independence Day. Was this suspension of war in celebration of the holiday? 'No,' Mr. Miller said. 'The Confederate Army has surrendered.' He also told me then that Mr. Lincoln had freed the slaves.

"I was no longer a slave. I sat down and cried, there in the silence of the ceasefire in the shelled house with a partial roof. I did not cry for my mother. I cried because I did not know what was to become of me. Freedom was a terribly frightening thought. It was Dora who spoke to me. 'We have some greenbacks. Confederate money would be useless. You can sew some money in your skirt. We will give you some money so that you may take a riverboat north to St. Louis. The Yankees control the river now. You will be safe, or at least as safe as a Negro can be in this terrible time. After St. Louis you can find a boat to take you up the Illinois and to Chicago. My sister there will find you a job. This letter will introduce you.' And so it was."

"You lived happily ever after," I told her.

"Not quite. Now I live in this trash heap called Harlem. It's little better than the shelled-out mansion in Vicksburg."

"Why doesn't Aunt Rye give you enough money to move out? Why don't you, Auntie Rye?"

"And there is your answer, Garnie, as to why I became a Communist. Miss Lilith can't move out. She can't live anywhere else."

"Why?"

"Because she is colored. The New Deal may be doing great things for White America to recover from the Depression, but nothing for the Negro. That is why I wanted you to see Harlem. I could as well have taken you to Brooklyn, to Bedford-Stuyvesant. It's called redlining. The banks, the insurance companies, the real estate companies are not simply encouraged to prevent Negroes from moving into areas but directed by law to do so. Mayor LaGuardia, Roosevelt, and particularly Robert Moses, while giving mouth to anti-segregation, do nothing about redlining. Only the Communists have been vocal against it."

"So why then have you stopped being a Communist?" I asked her.

"Because they embrace Stalin and he is no better than Hitler."

"Segregation is a terrible thing," I said to Miss Lilith. "I mean it."

"Yes," she said. "Always remember me living here. I am not alone. We are a silent army of black faces. I fear one day that army will explode. Jesse Owens was given a ticker-tape parade, but at the reception after in the Waldorf-Astoria, where you now stay, he could not ride the elevator up to the reception in his honor because he was colored. He had to go up in the freight elevator. That was the hotel's segregation policy." She paused for a moment as if to catch her breath. "You take pictures."

Auntie Rye told her of my intense interest in photography.

"You use your art to change the world, Garnie," Miss Lilith told me.

I did not forget her words.

That night we went to see a revival of Lillian Hellman's *The Children's Hour*. Because of my earlier visit with Miss Lilith I understood the damage people can do to one another. Mary was not a mean child. She was an evil one. The next day we went to the Natural History Museum and I stood in awe at the great skeleton of the Barosaurus. The day after, it was the Statue of Liberty, and while Auntie Rye waited below, I was allowed to climb up inside. And the day after that it was the Metropolitan Museum of Art; it was wonderfully fascinating but too much for one day and so we spent two. I saw for the first time the work of Alfred Stieglitz, Edward Weston, and Paul Strand and, just by looking at the black and white images of those artists, I knew what it meant to be not only a photographer, but also an artist. And when I rode back in the subway I tried excitedly to explain this to Auntie Rye.

"I understand," I told her, "that in Stieglitz's portraits of Georgia O'Keeffe, he is exploring the fragmented nature of self."

"You read that at the museum."

"I did, but that doesn't mean I didn't understand it. I would like to photograph you, the fragmented Rye."

"You are only ten. How can you grasp the idea of a fragmented self?"

"I'm not yet fragmented. I am too young to be in parts, but I see it in old people."

"Are you saying I'm old? I'm not old."

"You know what I mean. For someone my age everybody

over twelve is old. And people aren't just one thing. Padric is a photographer, but he is also a druggist, an Irishman and ex-priest, a man with hands blotched from the chemicals and one who is prejudiced against the English."

"I may not let you see the fragmented me. At least not all the fragmented me, but I am proud of you, Garnie, even though sometimes when you talk I realize you are not simply precocious but perhaps a genius. Your age is ten. Your mind is more twenty."

"Am I a genius?"

"Yes, I am afraid you might be."

"Isn't that a good thing?"

"Not entirely. But I suspect together we will deal with it. And at other times I am glad you are yet the young boy. I love you, Garnie, more than I love anything in life. You must always remember that. You are first in my life and, when I forget that, you must remind me."

After breakfast the following morning, we took the subway to midtown to our destination, the Empire State Building. Auntie said before we entered, "Al Smith was one of the men responsible for this fine but unfortunately unrentable-for-the-most-part edifice."

"He was Catholic. Irish," I told her.

"I know," she said.

"It's why he didn't get elected. People are afraid of Catholics, I read. But no one seems afraid of me. I guess it's only old Catholics people are afraid of."

"It's simple ignorance. More bigotry. See, it's not just the Negroes that are victims of prejudice. It's the Catholics, too."

"And the Indians. I read about that, too. Indians can't drink liquor. It's against the law."

"I know."

The elevator just kept going up and up. I had the uncased camera, heavy as it was, draped about my neck. No tripod, but I planned to take photos of New York from on high. There was the man in an Empire State uniform talking about the wind speeds of a previous day getting up to 94 miles an hour and how they had closed the observation deck. And the man to whom he was talking seemed to work there as well, and he talked about bats flying into the building and how it was inexplicable, as if their antenna, or whatever it was they had, didn't work.

It was cold on the deck despite being warm down on the street. And it was windy and I stood on tiptoes, holding tight to the camera as I took pictures of New York below. The frame was so much more expansive than I was used to and in the distance, looking south, I could see what might be the towering Woolworth skyscraper, so diminished in size in the frame.

There were five sailors but not many others up there. And one of the sailors held me up to the binocular thing and he put money in and I saw this island called New York in smaller frames closer up. Not so distant now, it was clear that it *was* the Woolworth building in all its gothic glory. I remember seeing a photo, perhaps in a rotogravure section, I'm not sure, of when the 'great cathedral', as they called it, was being built back before the Great War. In the picture there was something like a narrow board sticking out from the steel girders and a shirt-sleeved man was dangerously perched there, large in the frame, with a big camera shooting the city below. That photo frightened me. It frightens me to think about it now. It was not a photo I would want to take. And who took the photo of the photographer? Where was he to get such a view?

"Ain't that sumthin', kid?" the sailor said, pointing out at Manhattan stretching to the Battery. "Ain't that just sumthin? Where you from?" he asked. "I heard you talkin' to the lady. You sounded like you're from England or somewhere."

"That's all fake," I told him. I looked over at Auntie Rye where she stood talking to the uniformed Empire State man. "I'm really from Wisconsin." Well, I was now, wasn't I? Not Iowa again, yet.

"Ain't that sumthin' else. So am I." He called out to his buddies. "This kid's all the way from Wisconsin, too."

"Prairie," I told him.

"Prairie du Chien? No shit... I mean no kiddin', kid. My old man runs the shoe store. Betters and Betters. I'm one of the Betters in the sign, but, of course, I ain't there these days. Johnny Betters the name."

"Next to Small's Drug," I told him.

"Yeah. Mr. Small, well he's..."

"My friend," I told him. "He develops all my photos for me and is teaching me how to develop film as well."

"Well, speaking of Small, it's a small world, kid. And you say 'Hello' to Padric for me. You tell him Johnny Betters is doin' better than Betters. That the Navy's the right place for Johnny. This here uniform fits me to a tee."

And it seemed to. So I took a couple of quick snaps of him in blue bell bottoms and jaunty angled white cap. "For Padric," I told him.

"Here then, get one more." He put his arms around two of his buddies. They all three looked a bit cocky and I snapped the framed shot. The other two got in the picture as well, putting their arms around the guys on the outside. I took a photo of all five.

After the sailors left I took some more pictures of the city from this height. A few people came and went, but Auntie Rye seemed to be patient as long as I was taking photos. And then the clouds came in and the city below disappeared. It began to rain lightly.

"We'd better go down," Auntie said. "I think we are about to get soaked."

And then there was a sharp crack of lightning that hit the rod atop the tower far overhead. Thunder followed. "Did you ever? Just a moment, Auntie." And then there was another shot of lightning, only this time I was ready and hit the button on the camera.

"We need to get out of here now." She took hold of my shoulders.

Another attendant came up and began herding the few of us left on the observation deck back toward the elevator.

"That was amazing. The most amazing thing I have ever seen in my life." I was enthralled as we rode otherwise silently with the others down the elevator.

But that turned out not to be the highlight of the trip. That occurred the next day, the day before we were to leave on the 20th Century Limited. She didn't tell me in advance. "A surprise," was all she said. So I draped the Kodak about my neck just in case the surprise lent itself to photography. We went into a building — the letters on the glass door read "509 Madison" — and we took the elevator to the seventeenth floor. It was a gallery, the American Place it was called. We went in and I stared in awe. Here were walls of the paintings of Georgia O'Keeffe, of Arthur Dove, of John Marin, and more walls of the photography of Ansel Adams and then the Stieglitz photos, amazing black and white, and there were photographs of O'Keeffe and other photo portraits. One of John Marin. And there at the end of the exhibit stood the man himself. I immediately recognized him from his photographs. He was like a black and white of himself, wearing glasses, standing slightly bent in a black suit and black tie, like some mourner readying for the funeral.

Mr. Stieglitz stared at me. "It is not nice to stare," he said. "I am an old man, seventy-six. Old men should be forgotten, not stared at." There was just the slightest hint of a German accent in his speech.

"This is my Garnie." Auntie Rye stood tall behind me. "He wants to be a photographer, Alfred."

"Why?" He moved closer as if to inspect me.

"So that I might understand." I don't know why I answered this way, but it was true. Somehow through photography I knew I was already learning, but would learn more. Learn to live.

"Yes," he agreed. "Are you any good?"

"I am only ten."

"That is no answer to the question. I was only eleven when I started. In Berlin, I was only eleven and I was good. I was very good."

"I am very good." I spoke with a positive, strong voice.

"You need a European-made camera. Not an American piece of shit."

"I have a Leica Three on order."

"A Leica Three? Rye must be getting richer."

Auntie Rye answered for herself. "It doesn't matter much whether I am or not. What the boy needs for his art, he will have."

"Next to the not-necessarily-fine-but-good camera, what

an artist needs most is a patron. You have the patron, in Rye. Would you like some advice? Advice of a photographic art nature?"

"From the master himself, yes." I knew what he told me would be worth keeping.

"From the maestro, yes. Don't rely too heavily on the tripod. My own is very old and in very poor shape. The camera in your hands is immediately accessible; the subject may vanish in a moment. Never go without your camera. Don't over-worry about shutter speed. A fast-moving body is more moving with a slight blur. Lines and lighting are of greater importance. Wait if you must but look for balance. Capture that perfectly framed moment. You are the god. You are the stopper of time, all time. This means patience, but it also means chance. You may fail. What the shit! It doesn't matter. Film is expendable; the final frame is not."

He looked over at Auntie Rye. "I would not have known you from the old days. If you had not called and said you would be here, well, I might well not have recognized you."

"I suppose not." She turned to look at a photograph. "Do you disapprove?"

"It's something I don't understand."

"I don't expect you to. And Georgia? Where is she?"

"Here," he pointed toward several nudes and photos of hands and arms and body parts, "and in New Mexico at her Ghost Ranch. She needs the sun for her art, greater than she needs me at times. She will probably not come back."

"You don't believe that."

"No, but it makes me miserable to think on it. And I enjoy being miserable when Georgia is there. A joy in being old is being miserable."

"Do you not go out there?" I asked.

"My heart. The elevation takes my breath away, literally. I cannot survive in the thinness of that beauty. All that color, the sun. It is so overpowering. Perhaps it is less the air than the color. I am so all-encompassing black and white."

Auntie Rye looked directly at him, almost through him. "You are far too nuanced for that. And I doubt you would ever miss a woman, even Georgia. I remember your maxim: 'A woman is just like an empty freight car. The yard simply pulls in another.'"

"That was then. This is now. I no longer exist without Georgia. I am old. I tend to fart a lot. Can't seem to control it. And I quit taking photographs."

"Why?" the question was mine, not Auntie Rye's.

"A writer can write as long as he can vomit words, a painter paint as long as he can find the paint on the palette, a sculptor carve as long as he has memory and a musician compose, even when he has gone deaf. But a photographer needs amazing eyesight and the steadiest of hands and when those have left him, he must quit. Photography is an art with parameters and limits. And it's not just control of the camera, it is the physical requirements of developing, of printing. Steady hands and eyes that perceive." He turned from me and spoke to Auntie Rye. "I saw Millet's exhibition."

"How was it?"

"Ghastly. If she's going to reproduce those things, she should simply use the camera. She would get a far better reproduction of what it seems she's attempting. Perhaps your young friend here could take up the art."

"I would hope not."

They didn't realize I knew exactly what they were talking

147

about. I was a clever boy, I thought. A genius, perhaps. And why not? I decided, then and there, staring up at the big man in the dark suit and round glasses, and hoping he did not fart, that I would be a genius as well as a great photographer. Was Stieglitz a genius?

"I simply hope none of them are of Georgia."

"Her flowers…." Auntie Rye suggested.

"Her flowers are that; they are flowers, not vaginas. Not vaginas no matter what the stupid critics say."

Stieglitz and Auntie Rye talked of people and the past. I gazed, examined, and looked intently at the photographs and for a few brief moments forgot the two of them. But when I turned back, Stieglitz was standing somewhat apart from Auntie Rye. I took the camera from the case and shot a dozen or so sequentially — another of my new words, quick frames of Stieglitz looking intense at the art about him.

"You took my photograph," he said.

"'Never go without your camera, a wise man once told me,'" I told him.

He smiled. It was the only time I saw him smile. I wished I had captured that moment as well.

That was the day, the one I carry with me. I know it cannot be taken from me and until I am old and start to fart without control I can keep that day, recall it, marvel at it and know it shall not leave me. Stieglitz and Auntie Rye again talked of people and the past; I turned back to the hanging photographs. It was only his work that I saw, not the others. I also knew that as great as Stieglitz's art was, it would not be my art. It was pure. It was beautiful. It was magnificent. But it was not the world I would photograph. In isolation, he could capture the soul of a beggar, but he did not capture the beggar's need, his plight. Precocious, perhaps, but even at ten I saw this, understood this — no, perhaps more *felt* than understood, but then as I proclaimed, 'I was a genius.' But it was genius with a social conscience. Photography, I knew, would be my world, but not pure art. It had to be with what I had heard called 'the human condition.'

On Saturday we walked to Grand Central. The black porter wheeled the luggage behind us. I hoped Auntie Rye would give him a Chicago twenty tip. I had so much, and there in Harlem there was so much want.

She said, as if reading my mind, and she tended to do that at times, "I was watching you examining the photographs. And you saw Stieglitz through his work. You must not feel guilty, Garnie. If Mayor LaGuardia, and Franklin Roosevelt and all his New Deal programs cannot solve the problem created by the Great Depression, you should not expect more of yourself."

"But there is such great inequity."

"Yes, but you are ten and you might be a genius or not, but you can't solve the problems of the world."

"And through my art?"

"Through your photography you will bring attention to inequity where you find it, but you must not ask more of yourself. You are rich, not just in promise but in fact, and you must not tear yourself apart with worry when there is nothing that you can do about a situation. And you must be content at times to enjoy the pleasures that wealth brings."

"How," I asked, "with what we saw in Harlem?"

From behind me the porter spoke. "It ain't my place, but I

tell you, young gentleman, you listen to the lady. She knows. I am segregated and there ain't much you can do about that to get me un-segregated. You have some fun."

"Thank you," Auntie Rye told him.

We arrived in Grand Central and it was that, truly grand. The ceiling was towering, so far overhead. Auntie Rye had the tickets provided by the concierge and we walked to where three representatives in the uniform of New York Central sat. One quickly examined her tickets and motioned us toward Gate 20. We walked through to the awaiting famous, fabulous, fashionable Train 25, 20th Century Limited Westbound. As we stepped through the iron gates, we stepped onto a rolled-out length of red carpet. The carpet was woven with the 20th Century logo with its stripes. We moved beyond the rounded end of the train, the observation car.

"In the old days," Auntie Rye said, "it used to be open, a real observation platform with chairs, like a balcony trailing behind."

"Must've been damned windy," I responded.

We moved along the red carpet, the porter with our bags wheeling along behind but off the carpet. We reached the car, the Glen Anna. Auntie Rye simply pointed and moved toward the awaiting uniformed conductor.

"I want to see the engine," I told her.

"Glen Anna," she reminded me.

"I will tend to the tip," I told her.

"Fine," she said.

As the porter was attempting to enter the car with our bags, I handed him a Chicago twenty.

"That is too much," he said.

"No, it is not."

"You perhaps don't know how much that is, young gentleman."

"I know," I told him and headed for the front of the great blue and gray stream of cars, keeping to the red carpet until it was no more. The engine was massive and looked like a spaceship from Flash Gordon or Buck Rogers, its single center light like a giant's eye. I was impressed and opened my camera and took pictures of the great monster from outer space. Behind the engine was the mail car and, in New York, you could have your mail stamped by the 20th Century Limited and it would arrive in Chicago in sixteen hours. I should have mailed a letter to someone. Maybe Padric. It was too late.

I went back to the car and found the drawing room. Auntie Rye was sitting in a chair near the window with a copy of *Time*. Orchids were in a vase high up on the wall and dripped down. "I like orchids," I told her and made myself comfortable on the couch, near the window. "I wish I had sent a letter so that it could have been stamped with the 20th Century Limited stamp."

"You may dictate a letter to the steno and you can mail it here on the train. Who do you want to send a letter to?"

"Padric, I think."

Shortly, the train moved so smoothly forward that I had the weird sensation that the world outside the window was moving and we were standing still.

"It is all war and politics," she said and put *Time* aside. "Mr. Willkie seems destined for defeat as it is claimed that Roosevelt is not running against the Republican candidate but Herr Hitler. We shall forget both war and politics, and I shall read you Voltaire's *Candide*." She took a book from her large purse and stood, readying to histrophize or otherwise dramatize and went into her 'I could have been a great Shakespearean actor' mode, reading with careful articulation and great pronunciation. "'In a castle of Westphalia, belonging to the Baron of Thunder-ten-Tronckh, lived a youth, whom nature had endowed with the most gentle manners. His countenance was a true picture of his soul. He combined a true judgment with simplicity of spirit, which was the reason, I apprehend, of his being called Candide...'"

"It sounds like a fairy tale."

"It is. Yes, of the beautiful Miss Cunégonde and wondrous Candide."

I listened as she read and watched the train leave the security of the great rail yards and the great city and move up along the Hudson. It was a cloudy bleak day, easier to view as black and white. And while I saw it all only in black and white, it was quite beautiful. As Auntie Rye read, and I looked out the window, I came to conclude Dr. Pangloss was right. It must be the best of all possible worlds.

Later as we sat in the observation car, where Auntie Rye enjoyed a Manhattan and I a Coke, I watched the posted speedometer as it hovered around the seventy-miles-an-hour mark. The woman sitting across from me — she was making herself conspicuously inconspicuous — was, I knew, Constance Bennett. She conversed with some man with a frilled shirt, who had an obnoxiously effeminate, high-pitched voice and waved about an elongated cigarette holder with lit cigarette like some sparkling magical wand. He gave me a look of utter disdain and I wandered to the back of the car and looked out the curved windows at the four parallel lines of receding railroad tracks.

A woman came up and stood beside me. She was wearing a green dress and her hands were quite carefully manicured but without rings, and she wore no bracelet either. "What do you see?" she asked. Her voice was distinctive and I didn't immediately identify it.

"Black and white," I said. "Four lines of tracks becoming narrow and smaller and then disappearing behind the bend, along with the river."

"Like a photograph," she said.

I did not have to look up; I now knew the voice. "I am a photographer."

"But not yet famous," she said.

"No, but I will be. Perhaps when I am famous, like you, you will let me take your portrait."

"Perhaps I will," she said and walked away.

I stood there watching the tracks fade as dusk crowded about. There was a slight mist over the river, visible in flashes between the trees. I felt Auntie Rye's hand on my shoulder. "We should dine now," she said.

Katharine Hepburn, sitting in her green dress, smiled at me as I walked past. Perhaps someday she would let me take her photograph.

The dining car was modern, though perhaps not as Art Deco-articulated — I loved thinking in big artistic words — as the observation car. We were seated at a table for two. The white linen cloth had been set with finger bowl in place, two forks, knife, soup spoon, butter knife, bread plate, water glass, cup and saucer and, to the side, a dessert spoon. There was a silver water pitcher on the table.

The waiter in tuxedo took my order for steak with Irish mashed and Auntie Rye had squab. Some pickled things were brought to the table. "The famous watermelon pickles," Auntie Rye told me.

I ate one and decided they must be an acquired taste.

"And what did Miss Hepburn have to say?" Auntie asked.

"That I might, when I become famous, take her photograph."

"Great contracts are signed, great contacts are made, wheeling, dealing, and careers are all made on the 20th Century Limited, Garnie. And the world is but a telephone call away while in a station."

I had the famous 20th Century Limited ice cream and we left the dining car.

"Would you like a haircut, Garnie?"

"Not while we're moving at seventy miles an hour," I told her.

"Men have shaves."

"Do they live to tell about it?" Auntie Rye had read me a story, "The String of Pearls," about a barber in nineteenth-century London who slashed the throats of his customers and then his accomplice ground them up for meat pies. "Do they have meat pies on the train menu?" I asked.

"Garnie! You are thinking of Sweeney Todd. Let's hope not."

I dictated my letter to the stenographer and we went back to our drawing room. Auntie Rye continued reading *Candide* to me. And then the porter came and made up our beds. He was the tallest man I had ever seen. I could have walked between his long legs without bending. I woke just once in the night as we sped through a city. I lay there watching the lights flicker by and wondered if it were Cleveland.

Dodging and Burning

"SHOULD WE PRAY?" I asked as we stood above and gazed down into the hole below. The air was still. Eleanor deLacy swatted a few fall flies with her tail, but otherwise the world about us was immobile.

"Only in thanks that the Terrible House is gone." Auntie Rye gaped down into the hole.

"It is a crater," I said and I took a picture. Within the frame of the viewfinder it didn't look like what it was, the remains of a house after an explosion. It looked more massive, more grand. Then, letting the camera hang down around my neck, I peered into the actuality. "Not as grand as the Grand Canyon nor as crater-ish as Crater Lake."

"The excavation will be a job, but we'll turn this into a basement." Auntie Rye teetered at the edge. "The question is: cement block or poured concrete."

I looked down into the crater. "The Jerry's done did us in, luv." I was in Nigel voice. "While we was huddled in the underground the Luftwaffe wiped us out, destroyed it all. 'Tis all we had and now it's gone. Kaput."

"Not quite all." Auntie Rye pointed down into the hole where the safe rested on its side, burned but intact, door open.

"We could've asked," and I added a lisp to my accent, "Thybil Thnowdon of Thouthampton to lodge us on her eth-tate, but we can't."

"And why is that?"

"Thybil was chasing and screaming at a German recon-naissance plane, Focke-Wulf FW One-Eighty-Nine. It was flying low over her 'ethtate.'" I'd been reading about German aircraft in *Time* magazine. "Well, she was yelling for the 'damn flying piece of thhit —'"

"Garnie —"

"Nigel," I corrected her.

"Nigel, then, watch your language."

"I was thimply quoting Thybil. Anyway, she was chasing this plane and looking up and she ran smack dab into a tree, an elder I believe. And she was taken to hospital and hence can't be hospitable."

"Sometimes I worry about you."

"Don't worry about me. Worry about poor Thybil Thnowdon."

"Of Thouthampton, I believe."

"Yeth."

"Let uth leave thith hole. Now you've got me doing it." Auntie Rye preceded me back to the car, as I raised up the camera and snapped another shot. She stood by the driver's door. "Let's get in our big yellow touring car and tour to Bear Lantern Tourist's Relaxing Rest with... you know the rest."

I climbed into the backseat of the Packard and Auntie Rye pulled away from where the Terrible House once stood. But it was more than the loss of the house, more than just the house being blown away. Auntie Rye had changed. It began with our arrival back in Chicago's LaSalle Station on the 20th Century Limited. There was no red carpet. The porters teetered the luggage behind us to a taxi, and from there we went straight to the Palmer House. The Packard had not yet arrived. And that's when the difference began. It was about money. Auntie Rye had carried and kept a close eye on the metal case she had taken with her from *LaBelle de Salon Coiffeur Shampoineur Manicure-Nécessaire Pédicure.* But now, Auntie Rye, who claimed not to trust banks, went to the LaSalle Bank in a towering skyscraper appropriately called the LaSalle Bank Building. I took pictures of the Art Deco lobby while Auntie Rye sat, beyond the glass but still in my view, at the desk of a manager type. Here in the lobby, near the elevators, was a photograph of a stern looking Potter Palmer, a more stern looking Marshall Field, and a third seemingly indifferent face, labeled 'Levi Leiter.'

"I have opened an account," she said, sailing out of the bank into the lobby in her green suit with orange buttons and wearing an orange hat tilted rakishly to the right. She rather tossed about the obviously now empty metal case.

"You don't trust banks," I reminded her. "Not even ones with *trust* in the name, as I recall."

She ignored my statement completely. "I deposited the money from the case and liquidated some assets and we now have a large checking account with the largest bank in Chicago." I didn't for a moment doubt that she had family ties to the Fields and Palmers in the portraits. But perhaps financial connection to Levi Leiter and LaSalle Bank as well? "We are going to Sears to buy the Torrington House."

We passed by the important woman at the important

information desk with the antimacassar dress collar looking upholsterly upright and went up the escalator to Customer Service. Auntie Rye asked the tall woman at the counter if she might speak with Mrs. Albertatoss, and the tall woman turned to the woman next to her and said, "Mrs. Albertatoss, this personage wishes to speak with you."

"Then I should speak with the personage."

The tall woman at the counter turned to Auntie. "Mrs. Albertatoss will speak with you."

"Miss Gardiner," Mrs. Albertatoss addressed her. "You have decided on a house?"

"We have, Mrs. Albertatoss. We have decided on the Torrington."

"An exquisite choice, Miss Gardiner. Did you fill out the tear-out form at the back of the catalog?"

"I did not, Mrs. Albertatoss. I have so many questions and need some expert advice on choices."

"Of course. Let me take you back to Mr. Plexipere, who is an expert on all things Honor Bilt Modern Homes. His office is this way."

Auntie Rye followed Mrs. Albertatoss and I followed Auntie Rye to a windowed office. A man stood as we entered. I mean really stood. He must have been nearly seven feet tall and had thighs like chimneys. All the Sears clothing on him seemed too small, too tight.

"Miss Gardiner, whom I spoke to you of, Mr. Plexipere." And Mrs. Albertatoss completed the introductions, including me. I was not certain how she knew my name. And then, handing the man the form, she left.

"Miss Gardiner, you have questions?" He had a slight Minnesota accent. Perhaps Norwegian. He certainly resembled my idea of what King Olaf or King Canute might have looked like. I pictured him in horned helmet, carrying a shield and wielding an axe. "I take it your questions are not about the purchasing or the price."

"No, I have technical questions of which I have so little mastery." I think she was batting her eyes at the Norwegian king.

"Of course, ma'am. Men understand these construction details, but it's not expected of the gentler gender. Please have a seat. And you, too, young sir." I had the urge to go sit in his big lap. I thought there would be great security in that, although I don't know from what I was seeking security. The world for Nigel might not be safe, but for Garnie there was no war, there was no great fear in the world. And now Auntie was about to buy the very best house that money could buy, at least from a catalog.

"Column one." Auntie pointed to the form. "I assume I would check 'as shown' as it is both brick veneer and wood siding. But my answer to other questions are not so easy. Do I want warm air or steam heat?"

Mr. Plexipere's response took fifteen minutes. Our answer thirty seconds. We settled on forced warm air. And then it was storm window and door choices, bathroom choices, hardware from the various design offerings, should it be cedar rather than asphalt roof shingles, the hi-glo light fixture and chandelier choices, the tub and bathroom designs, the choice of kitchen cabinets and the color, flexible conduit, hard conduit or knob and tube, the mantel, which was the best for us, and kitchen paint, what color enamel, and Auntie consulted me on all choices. Mr. Plexipere seemed to approve of that and would address questions to me as well as Auntie when he gave his lengthy answers to our quandary of choices. And there were extra charges for some of Auntie's and my choices. Mr. Plexipere big-fingered a big adding machine with a crank handle that came down with noise. And there were more extras to be cranked: the utility sink for the basement, the window shades, the built-in ironing board, lighting for the basement and the wallpaper selected. The crank was yanked again and again. In the end he tore a piece of paper from the adding machine and handed it to Auntie Rye. It well exceeded the book price listed for the Torrington Model 3355.

She wrote a check from her new checkbook. Mr. Plexipere gently took her hand. I thought he might bend and kiss the hand with the painted nails, but he did not. It was determined and pronounced that the house would be shipped on two rail cars on the Milwaukee Railroad to our Iowa town. "You will be pleased with the quality of all the materials," he assured her.

We started down the escalator. The vacuum tubes bumped overhead. "What a way to buy a house," Auntie chirped and the hat seemed to tip even more rakishly as we passed the upholstered-chair lady. I wondered if one of the cylinders banging overhead carried our order and Auntie Rye's check for the new house. We left the big Sears building.

And now we had to remain in Chicago awaiting the Packard.

"Who needs Lucinda Latunda from 'REAL, the real real estate people…'?" My question was less of a chirp and more a musical pronouncement.

"Who, indeed, needs that beluga Lucinda, that rotunda Latunda." Hers was not a question.

I had trouble developing the image, so I suggested quietly, "She isn't exactly fat, you know."

"She has a fat mind."

"Yes." I was pacified.

We spent the rest of the day at the Art Institute. As Auntie Rye wandered the galleries, I concentrated on a small space, the single gallery allocated to photographic art. I discovered Berenice Abbott. It was more than discovery; it was kinship. I looked at the street scenes of Manhattan and knew what Abbott was about. There was a little brochure about her in a little wooden pocket on the wall, and I took a copy and read that "Abbott's project, the one exhibited here, is primarily a sociological study imbedded within modernist aesthetic practices. She has sought to create a broadly inclusive collection of photographs that together suggest a vital interaction between three aspects of urban life: the diverse people of the city; the places they live, work and play; and their daily activities."

I understood Abbott. I continued reading: "Abbott is critical of what the machine and its age wrought and the inhumane effects that the age had upon those working the machines." It was something I hadn't previously given any thought: the inhumanity of the machine. I read on. "These photographs illustrate particularly what that mechanization had done to Manhattan." Abbott was an advocate for urban planning. I understood her photos because of my own photographs of Harlem, of the Negro children. They were victims of the mechanized society.

I was only ten. I knew that, but that didn't mean I couldn't understand. Before Harlem I never could have thought about machines this way. Machines did good things — the Frigidaire that kept things cold, the mangle that could iron clothes,

the airplane... but now I also understood that the machines
had to be worked. Dickens wrote about it in novels and the
women who died in the fire at the Triangle Shirtwaist Company were victims of machines. As to Abbott's photography, I
knew I didn't understand the aesthetic, I barely knew the word,
the nature of art, but at least I grasped a sense of balance, the
essential necessity of light, some things about nuances and
that my work, like all art, must be something seen not quite
the way anything had been seen before. This was Abbott.
Looking at things differently. It was heavy stuff, and I didn't
grasp it all, but I did see the importance of originality to art.

We walked, searching for supper after leaving the museum.
It was windy in the Windy City and Auntie Rye held onto
the rakish hat tightly as I told her about Berenice Abbott.

"Abbott was a friend of Djuna Barnes." I knew Djuna
Barnes because Auntie Rye had read me bits and pieces of
Nightwood, which had made absolutely no sense to me at all.
I wondered if Berenice Abbott had read *Nightwood* and, if
she had, if she had understood any of it. "I met Abbott once."

I was impressed. "In Manhattan?"

"No. In Paris."

I had not known before her revelation about the Wind-
sors that Auntie Rye had ever been to France.

"This was not when you went to the funeral."

"No, this was much earlier. I spent some months in Paris.
Man Ray introduced me. You must see his photography.
Abbott was his pupil."

The name was new to me. "He was a famous photographer?"

"Not *just* a photographer. He was an eclectic artist. Paint,
collage, film. He knew everybody and everybody knew him.

He was close to Dali and the surrealists, but he himself was more of a Dadaist."

I didn't know what a Dadaist was, but I didn't display my ignorance. I would check the encyclopedia later. "I'm hungry."

"I have just the thing to cure your condition."

"What?"

"Surprise," she told me and pulled me along to the El. We took the train to the South Side and walked to a little bar.

"Grittani's," I said, reading the printed letters on the glass window.

"Better known as the 'Home Run Inn.' A ball from the ballpark over there came through the window."

The place smelled of beer and pungent Italian spices. We sat at a small wooden table. "I need to introduce Garnie to pizza, Vincent," she told the dark-haired man in a red-stained apron who came over to the table.

"Pepperoni?"

"Who's Pizza?" I asked.

"Yes," she told Vincent. "You shall see," she told me.

I could see the rather open kitchen from my table and watched, fascinated, as a man tossed dough in the air and rotated it and thinned it out. I couldn't see what, but he put stuff on it and then with a big wooden paddle put it into a blackened brick oven.

Auntie Rye drank her beer and I my Coke and then the hot sloppy thin pie arrived and I tasted my first pizza.

"You will always remember the taste of your first pizza," she told me. "And it will never be equaled."

That would be my last night in Chicago for a while. Life was to become far less cosmopolitan. No more museums, no more grand hotels, no more pizza.

The Packard arrived the next morning at the Palmer House and we started almost immediately for Prairie. But when we arrived there she drove right through and up onto the suspension bridge.

"Where are we going?" I was in a slight panic.

"To arrange our lodgings, and I need to see Eddledorf Grungedagger."

"To see him or to smell him?"

"Don't be crude."

"I can't help it. I am being kidnapped."

"No. You are being dramatic."

I was quiet for a moment and then asked, "May I have a set of encyclopedias?"

"We have too many bedrooms."

I didn't understand the connection.

"We don't need four bedrooms. Look at the diagram of the Torrington."

I picked up the catalog and opened it to the Torrington page.

"There are only two of us. A bedroom for you, a bedroom for me, a guest bedroom for God knows whomever—we don't have houseguests, and then that bedroom over the living room… that will be our library. A to Z, from Aakjaer's novels to Voltaire's *Zadig*."

"And a set of encyclopedias."

"Two. We shall have the *Britannica* and the *Americana*. We shall have atlases and gazetteers, almanacs and dictionaries."

I would look up Dadaist. "And books of photography?" I would press for it all. "Stieglitz and Weston."

"And Man Ray, perhaps?"

"And Man Ray, perhaps."

During our library litany we not only arrived on the Iowa side of the river but in town, and we parked to gape at the great hole in the ground.

Now we had seen the hole again and we were on our way to the Bear Lantern Tourist's Relaxing Rest. It had been formerly the Kastle Kourts until it was purchased by Steed Enstead. Steed and his three girls, Floskie, Moskie, and Daralinda, ran the establishment. His wife, Trinda, referred to by Steed as Trashy Trinda, had run off with the popcorn machine salesman from Blue Earth, Minnesota.

We entered what Steed referred to as the 'grand lobby' of the Bear Lantern Tourist's Relaxing Rest. It was intended to be grand. There was a spiral staircase that rose to the ceiling, but was of little use as there was no second floor to the structure which Steed and his daughters occupied. "It's going to be grand, but we are still in the looking-to-the-lodge-ahead stage. When the second floor is added, this will be a fine hotel, perhaps among the finest between Chicago and the Mayo Clinic."

Steed went behind the fold-down counter at the little room that had once been a closet and folded back down the counter. "I can't rent to you." He pointed to the sign on the wall just to the side of the fold-down counter: 'We do not rent to locals.' "Locals would come here for the fling-flang, a bit of afternoon nastiness. I can't have it. I have a fine moral compass, by which I am fully directed."

"But, Steed, you know that is not my intent," Auntie Rye told him. "I need a place to live. I have ordered a Sears house and am having it built on my lot where the Terrible House used to be. This is the only lodging in town."

"I know that, Rye, and as much as I would like to, I have posted the rules and must abide by them. Beside which, I have a personal rule about renting to Communists."

"On that score, you will be much relieved to know that I have disowned the Communists and am voting for FDR."

"I think you should post a sign on your building site, stating that fact. You will find yourself much more welcome in town."

"I will do that. Now may I have two rooms?"

"Still have to abide by posted rules."

Auntie Rye thought for a bit. "You still may. You see, Garnie and I are not technically locals at the present and won't be until the house is built. We are residents of Prairie du Chien. Out of town. Out of state even."

"So you are."

"Do you have any units adjacent?"

"I do. Numbers Forty-two and Eight Hundred and Sevety-five are next to one another."

"How come such numbers? You only have ten cabins."

"Lodgings. I call them lodgings. It's all about expansion and planning. When we become the finest hotel between Chicago and the Mayo Clinic these two will be adjacent. It's all about planning. Daralinda, show Miz Gardiner accommodations Forty-two and Eight-Seventy-five, please."

Auntie Rye inspected, accepted and paid a month's rent by check from her new account at the LaSalle Bank, and we headed off to see Eddledorf Grungedagger.

I breathed through my mouth. Eddledorf Grungedagger's living room reeked of Eddledagger Grungedagger.

"I don't build for Communists, though I do beg your pardon for that inconvenience," he told Auntie Rye.

"On that score, you will be much relieved to know that I have disowned the Communists and am voting for FDR."

"You have become a New Dealist?"

"I have."

"But, do folks know that? I don't care much one way or the other if I build for Communists, but it's how other people see it and how that affects my business."

"I plan on posting a sign on the building site, stating that I am no longer a Communist and that I will be voting for Roosevelt. May I show you the plan of the house?"

"Please." He took the catalog and looked at the open page. "Gypsum. I've never worked with gypsum before."

"Will you be able to?"

"Oh, yes. Far less work than lath and plaster. I shall think of it as a challenge. *Leben ist eine Herausforderung.*"

"*Ich stimme zu,*" Auntie Rye responded.

"*Der Bibliothek.*" I was showing off, I knew, but then I'm a precocious child.

Auntie Rye smiled. "I won't forget to discuss the library."

I asked to be excused and went out into the air as she talked with Eddledorf Grungedagger. I can only assume they talked about the excavation, the basement, and the construction of the house itself and the library. There would need to be library shelves.

"Yes," she said, "it is settled. Eddledorf will begin the excavation as soon as the blueprints arrive." We sped off to downtown which was four blocks away. First stop, the Ben Franklin 5 and 10 where Auntie Rye bought some crayons from Miss Ridley, the proprietress and sole clerk, then to 'Ludwig Undercutt's, the finest meat cuttery 'tween Elgin and Omaha,' where she was given some free butcher paper, and lastly to Abraham Littletuff's 'Emporium of tools and hand implements,' where she purchased some stakes and a hammer. We drove back the four blocks and spread the unrolled paper on the sidewalk in front of where the Terrible House once stood and, with crayons, made the sign: 'Rye Gardiner has disavowed the Communist Party. She embraces the New Deal and will cast her vote in the election for Franklin Delano Roosevelt.

"Maybe you should add 'So help me God!'" I suggested.

"Probably not appropriate for signage."

We staked it up, stood back and admired our work. We then drove back the four blocks to the Corner Café for a 'respite' as Auntie Rye called it. I had a Coke and a bowl of potato chips; Auntie had coffee and a sweet roll. The place was fairly empty except for the O'Brien twins, Jimmy and Johnny, who preferred to be called James and John, but nobody ever did. They were named for Christ's apostles James and John, but nobody ever considered that preference and they were pretty much stuck with Jimmy and Johnny. They were eighteen but had different birthdays. Jimmy was born two minutes before midnight on the sixteenth of June 1922 and Johnny was born a few minutes after midnight on the seventeenth of June 1922. They looked so much alike nobody could tell them apart. It is a wonder they could tell each other apart. And apart they never were. I had never seen one without the other. People thought them a bit strange. They seldom talked to other people, only to each other. And when people did ask a question of them they both gave part of an answer. They held hands in public and some claimed to have seen them kiss on the lips. I never saw that, but I often saw them with one arm about the other. They were huddled now, animated, and had direct eye contact oblivious to either Auntie Rye or myself. I wondered what they talked about all the time so intently.

Auntie paid Sharlotte Shenandoah, the waitress, and gave her a fifty-cent tip. Auntie Rye was the only person in town who ever tipped the waitresses and the one waiter, whose name I could never remember; it was Remblehondras or Rembleondor or something like that, but everyone in town just called him 'the fruit.' Auntie Rye scolded me when I would refer to him that way and so I had come to calling him 'the waiter.'

We got in the yellow Packard and drove back toward the Mississippi. I was too tired to be Nigel and just sat in the back silent.

"You are unusually quiet," Auntie Rye said back across her shoulder.

"I am thinking," I told her.

"Musing and cogitating."

"Yes. Contemplating. I am thinking I do not feel whole."

"What do you mean, you don't feel whole? You mean fragmented like Georgia O'Keeffe?"

"No, more like part of me is missing."

"Count your toes and fingers," she said back. "They all seemed to be there the last time I looked. You still have your genitals, I assume."

"As little as they are. No, it is more like there should be more to me. I quite think I had a twin that was abducted at our birth."

"Absolutely ridiculous. You did not have a twin. You never had a twin."

"How do you know? You weren't there."

"I was," she said.

"Oh." I was again silent but for a different reason. Why had Auntie Rye been at my birth?

We rattled across the bridge, to Prairie and the Fort Crawford Hotel. Rodney Relent was the desk clerk on duty and welcomed us back. He handed Auntie Rye an accumulation of mail. Most of it was business mail and magazines, but the copy of the Sears house catalog had also come. Didn't need it now. Already had a house being shipped.

Plowtee, the waitress, came into the lobby. She was examining her watch as if the numbers might be vanishing. "If you'll be wanting food, I suggest you order now. We will be wanting to close the dining room."

"I think we will be having Chinese over at Willy Wong's," Auntie Rye told her.

"Your funeral." Plowtee flounced off toward the kitchen, once again.

We freshened up and were off to Willy Wong's. 'The best Midwestern style Chinese Cuisine in the America' it read on the menu cover. We had the best chop suey, best chow mein, best egg foo yung, and best egg roll in 'the America' and went back to the Crawford to have an early evening. I listened to the news on the radio in the lobby, *Fibber McGee and Molly*, and perused *Time*. "At 7:57 one night last week after 76 hours of debate, the Senate passed The Burke-Wadsworth Compulsory Military Training Bill, 58 to 31." In eight years I would be drafted. And war was coming. Perhaps I would be killed, maimed for life or shot down over Germany. I should learn more German. It was not a pleasant thought, being shot down, maimed or killed. I turned the page. Married. Scarlett O'Hara. It didn't say that. It said "Vivien Leigh, 26, cinemactress, and

Laurence Olivier, 33, cinemactor, in Santa Barbara, California."
I read down. A Negro lawyer, a friend of John D. Rockefeller
and the first Negro to be elected to judicial office in a northern state, was killed in a motorcycle accident at age 95. He had
been a slave. Why was he riding a motorcycle at age 95? Oh,
Auntie Rye would love this one. "At a Nassau cocktail party
the Duchess of Windsor chatted about mosquito bites and
showed a guest great lumps on her arms and silk-clad legs."
And Auntie Rye thought the Duchess was the parasite. She
was the victim. Poor bitten Duchess. I fell asleep dreaming
of a man in a *Time* magazine suit bathing a nude Duchess in
calamine lotion while the Duke of Windsor, wearing a crown,
read to her about Vivien Leigh's wedding.

After my breakfast, including the Plowtee disapproval of
'it's the young boy's funeral' cup of coffee, half milk, I was off
to deliver my film to Padric, but I did stop for just a moment
at the shoe store next door.

"Mr. Betters?"

The man was balding, slightly paunchy, but I could see the
resemblance to the son. "Yes."

"Mr. Betters, I was just in New York and went up on the
observation deck of the Empire State Building and this sailor,
he held me up to look through the telescope and he told me
that he was from Prairie, too, and that his name was Johnny
Betters."

"Well, he ain't Betters. No more Betters."

"Sir, he told me his father ran a shoe store right here in
Prairie, right next to Small's Drug Store."

"And I told you he ain't no longer my son. And I don't care
for people saying that Betters and Betters is next door to
Small's Drug. Ain't nobody's business what's next to."

"Johnny said he was one of the Betters in Betters and Betters."

"Well, I'm thinking to have it changed to just Betters, if it weren't so expensive."

"I'm sorry to have bothered you, sir. I'm off to Small's to have Padric develop my film."

"I'd be cautious, if I were you. That ain't all he is off for developing. Ask him about Johnny and developing. Just ask him."

But I didn't, at least not immediately. I was excited about Padric developing my film and what he would think, and forgot about Johnny Betters as I ran into the drug store, the familiar bell tinkling behind me. "Padric," I screamed and ran to where he was filling prescriptions.

He put down a vial and gave me a rough hug in his rough hands. "I've missed you, lad."

"I've got film." I handed him a brown bag that said Macy's on it. It contained the boxed rolls of one-sixteen. "Some surprises."

"Surprises, uhm? Well, I have my own surprise for you, Garnie." He went to the back and came out with a box. On the box in big letters was the word *Leica*. "You read the instruction manual. I will develop your film." He seemed to forget the prescription he was filling and went back to the darkroom.

There were other words on the box besides Leica. All in German. I hoped the instructions were in English. Padric had opened the carton and I put it on the soda fountain marble counter and crawled up on my knees and lifted out the camera. How light compared to the Kodak. There was a rough texture to the finish. I ran the palm of my hand over it. What a beauty. It was mine. I held it. I turned it about. I examined it. I set it on the counter. I touched it. I picked it up. Then I set it down again on the counter and took out the instruction manual. It was in English.

I read: "The architecture and shape of the Leica represents the essence of 35mm rangefinder photography. Each interchangeable lens features an inner cam ring which interacts with a sensor arm within the camera body. Note the placement of the independent viewfinder between the two rangefinder windows. The Leica III includes an extended range of slow shutter speeds. With the Leica III the shutter speed selection range is from between 1/500th of a second to 1 full second."

There was an illustration of the camera with numbers indicating the parts of the camera. I was examining it when Padric hurried in from the darkroom.

"What did the man do to you?" There was panic in his voice.

"What man?" I set the instruction manual on the counter.

"The young man in the photographs. Nude and with an erection and whose penis and balls are in a close-up in another frame."

"He did nothing. He asked me if I wanted to take his picture. I said I did and I did."

"He didn't touch you?"

"No."

"But you touched him."

"No. He wouldn't let me. He wanted to be photographed, nothing more."

"You got that close without touching him."

"He wouldn't let me. I would have liked to. He had a very pretty penis."

"I'll give you that." Padric picked up the Leica. "It's a beauty, the Leica, I mean, isn't it? Garnie, you have to be careful. You can't do this. Someday, the man won't just be an exhibitionist. He will do you harm."

Exhibitionist. That was a great word. That's what the man was all right. I didn't say that to Padric. Instead I told him about the fat old man exposing himself in the Standard Oil station toilet.

"That's what I mean. Did you tell your Auntie about the fat man?" He put the camera down.

"No. She would have gone in and killed him."

"Maybe she should have."

"No. I was scared, but I got to thinking about it later. I feel sorry for the man. He was old and fat and ugly and nobody wanted to see his dingy-dong. Someday maybe I will be old and fat and ugly. And I'll probably fart a lot." I was thinking of Stieglitz.

"Sometimes you think too much. And other times not enough. Promise me you will be more careful."

"I promise," I said and picked up the instruction book.

Padric went back to the darkroom.

I read the instructions again and again. Padric came out and made me a root beer float and I told him about the trip, but not about Miss Lilith, nor Stieglitz. And I didn't tell him about meeting Johnny Betters. I wanted him to be surprised when he made the prints.

He finished the prescription he had been working on when I had come in and then I went with him to the darkroom. In the red safelight I watched as Padric made the prints. He held one up.

"That's the Hotel Geneva," I told him, "We spent the night there."

"It looks almost like a Frank Lloyd Wright building." He examined the print for flaws.

"It is."

I had impressed him. He made some prints of the hotel, of the observatory, and night prints of the hotel and the lake. "Good work. These night shots took some patience and you used the flash."

"I did."

He held up another print. "What's this?"

"Put-in-Bay. An island in Lake Erie. Near Toledo."

"By the sequence I gather it's where you took pictures of the nude man. The place looks pretty run down." He examined a photo of the hotel.

"I got bedbug bites in that hotel," I added. "The *fin de siècle* Put-in-Bay is gone."

"The words you come out with. A bit pretentious, wouldn't you say?"

"I am precocious, you know."

"I'll give you that. But you didn't take any pictures between Geneva and Toledo?"

"Lots but they were for Auntie to give to Madam Rodowckinski."

"Ah, Madam Rodowckinski of imperfections and imbecility."

"Yes."

He printed the pictures of the nude young man. "Despite the situation, these are extremely good photographs."

"Yes, but the guy was golden tanned with the bluest of eyes. That couldn't be captured in these photos."

"But you have something better." Padric looked at various prints as he made them. "There is something really sad about these photos. The self-absorbed young man, exhibiting, strutting his body in this hideous setting. I can see what looks to be urine or urine stains on the floor and the graffiti on the dirty walls. The contrast between the man and the background is striking. Dare I say 'good work'? But no more of this kind of picture-taking, promise?"

I said, "Promise." But I crossed my fingers behind my back.

He made prints of the Harlem negatives. "These are exceptional, Garnie. But this one is amazing." He showed me a print of Miss Lilith, superimposed over the Negro children. It was a double exposure. "Quite beautiful."

"It was an accident. I forgot to wind the film forward."

"A happy accident." He examined the print carefully. "With the Leica you can experiment and do all sorts of innovative photography using double-exposure techniques. Sequential moving of autos or runners or boys on a sled in the winter snow moving down the hill. That's kind of the photo version of Duchamp's painting, 'Nude Descending a Staircase.'"

I wonder if my mother painted pictures of women's fluffies descending stairs, but I didn't voice the thought. Instead I told him about Miss Lilith and being a slave, as he printed out more photos. He interrupted my story. "This looks like a kid from Prairie… Johnny Betters." He examined the print carefully.

"It is Johnny Betters."

"You met Johnny Betters in New York? At the top of the Empire State Building? This is the top of the Empire State Building, I take it."

"He held me up to look through the binoculars. And when

I told him where I was from and how I knew you and that the drug store was next to Betters he told me to tell Padric that the Navy fit him like a tee."

"Ain't that a wonder! You meeting Johnny like that. Sometimes truth is stranger than fiction."

"I stopped to tell his dad. He was rude as could be. He said I should ask you 'bout Johnny and developing. What did he mean?"

"Johnny used to sweep up the place for me after school and take out the trash. He was a good kid, Johnny, but, well…"

"Well, what?"

"Well, nothing. Here, let me show you how to dodge. I take this opaque paper." He reached up and took some white shiny paper that looked more like cloth off the shelf. "You cut it like this and then, as it prints, the background stays darker as it burns more and the Johnny here in the picture becomes lighter because we covered him. He pops out from the background, see."

I had a sense about things. "What about Johnny?"

"What do you mean, what about Johnny?" Padric rinsed the print.

"Did he want to touch your dingy-dong?"

"If you must know, yes. He was much older than you, nearly seventeen at the time, and I didn't let him, but I understood. Old man Betters never believed that, of course, and when he confronted us, Johnny told him that I never touched him, but that he wanted me to. Mr. Betters called him a queer, disowned him. Said he was no Betters. Johnny stayed with me in the apartment upstairs for the month or so he had left to finish high school. I suggested he join the Navy."

"Why the Navy?"

"So he could meet some other fellows like himself."

I was beginning to understand more. I was beginning to understand about boys, about men, but I needed to understand more. I braved the word, but softly. "Homosexuals?"

"Yes. Now let's get to making prints."

"Are there homosexuals in the Marines? Were there when you were in the Marines?" I thought of Jack Sprat. Jack must be a homosexual.

"Yes. Enough." He went back to the printer.

"I think I'm a homosexual," I told him.

"I think you're too young to know what you are. My God, I didn't realize it looking at the negative. This is Stieglitz. You met Stieglitz."

"Auntie Rye knew him. It was a surprise for me. She took me to see him in this building on Madison — "

"The American Place, was it?"

"Yes."

"And he let you take his photograph."

"I didn't ask. I just took it."

"He looks sad." Padric simply stared at the print.

"He is sad. He no longer takes pictures. He said that a photographer needs amazing eyesight and steady hands. He no longer has them."

"That is sad. Did he tell you anything else?"

"That American cameras were pieces of shit and that I needed a Leica. To always have my camera ready, not to worry about shutter speed, that lines and lighting were more important and that a fast-moving object can have a slight blur. Oh, and he told me that it was about capturing time."

Padric showed me the technique of burning, which was just the opposite of dodging, where you make things in the picture darker. He made some extra copies of some of the prints, like the ones of Miss Lilith and of Stieglitz. We left the darkroom. He boxed up my prints and my Leica with some 35mm film in canisters. "Another float?" he asked.

"No, but I could use a Coke." I told him about leaving Prairie and how Auntie Rye and I were moving into the Sears house when it was built.

"I will miss you, Garnie."

"I will still come to Prairie on Saturdays. I have much to learn about developing and printing."

"You do," he said. "You have much to learn. No more penis photos," he yelled after me as I tinkled out the door.

Two days later Auntie Rye and I packed up and left the Crawford Hotel for the less accommodating Bear Lantern Tourist's Relaxing Rest. It wasn't the Versailles Suite at the Crawford, but it was better than the Terrible House. Auntie Rye bought me a large cork board and I thumb-tacked some of my prints on it. Most prominent of these was Padric's photo of the Mobile horse hanging on one chain in the wind. Before I went back to school, Auntie Rye imposed her tall self upon the parsonage and met with Sister Mary Saint Wulfhilda the Abbess and Father O'Tootle. "There will be no more Ronnie McDonnie business," she told me upon returning.

I entered the four-classes classroom, grades 5 through 8, and Tilford Toddman with the ruly red hair was sitting there with the three other seventh graders in the seventh-grade row. Behind Sister Mary Saint Wulfhilda the Abbess's back he grabbed his crotch and jiggled it at me and whispered, "I'm gonna make you play with my wingy-wang."

I stood at my seat behind Geraldina Lamtouse. All four classes recited five Hail Marys in monotone unison and afterwards slapped into our fold-down seats affixed to the desks behind. The desks with iron legs like Singer sewing machines were bolted to the floor. They were marred and carved and had holes for inkwells, but we were modern and used pencils and fountain pens. The first lesson for the fifth grade was to write out all the states and the capitals. I knew all forty-eight. Geraldina got only twenty-two right and that made her cry. Sister Mary Saint Wulfhilda the Abbess told her to stop her whimpering and spend less time crying and more opening the book and learning her states and capitals.

At recess Tilford Toddman with ruly red hair pushed me behind a bush and told me he was gonna make me play with his swell wingy-wang.

"I never want to see or hear about your wingy-wang again. You are an awful person, Tilford, and I bet you have an ugly little dingy-dong that nobody wants to see."

"Yeah. You don't know. I am overdeveloped, that's what Dr. Von Hunggor said. My daddy took me to be checked-up and I heard Doc talking to Daddy over at the West Union base-ball game when they didn't know I was listening and Dr. Von Hunggor said, 'Tilford is overdeveloped for his age, Ernie.' He always calls Daddy Ernie. 'I've never seen such a big schwantz on a twelve-year-old.'"

"That don't sound like medical talk to me. You're a liar, Tilford."

"I ain't not. He don't talk medical talk to my daddy cuz they play euchre together. Jeepers creepers, you don't know everything, smarty pants. And you ain't gonna call me a liar when you see my wingy-wang. You're gonna say, 'Golly gee, I ain't never seen a wingy-wang so big.' You're gonna wanna play with it and I might as not let you."

"Don't want to anyway." The bell rang. That was a lie that I told Tilford. I wanted to take a picture of his wingy-wang, but I'd have to wait until I had my darkroom. I had promised Padric I wouldn't take anymore penis pictures.

I was smarter than the other kids, even the eighth graders. I'm not bragging. It's just the way it was. I couldn't help it if I was a genius any more than I could help being a ten-year-old and, no doubt, a homosexual. Things were what they were. So, sometimes Edna, an eighth grader, couldn't answer her algebra question and I would leap up with the answer, and Sister Mary Saint Wulfhilda the Abbess would clench her fist and her face would turn red, but she never told me I was wrong, only glared until I sat down. I bet she wanted to pull her hair, but I suspected she couldn't. We were told — I don't know if it was true or not — that beneath the wimple they had shaved heads.

Father O'Tootle, who conducted our religion class, all four grades together, never objected when I answered or interrupted. Like the day he was talking about Papal Bulls.

"*Sicut Judaeis,*" I responded.

"Do you know what it means?" Father asked me.

"It provides protection for the Jews who suffered from the hands of the first crusaders."

"Yes. It was issued by Pope Callixtus the second in the twelfth century. Why is it important in this age? Can anyone other than Garnie tell me?"

Nobody could, which didn't surprise me. I waited and then answered. "Because of Hitler's persecution of the Jews. The Roman Catholic Church will come to the aid of the Jews."

"*Der Geizhals.*" Sister Mary Saint Wulfhilda the Abbess frowned.

"Sister," Father O'Tootle scolded. "That's perjorative."

"*Vergib mir, ich sprach falsch. Ich mein zu sagen Juden.*" She made the sign of the cross hurriedly and looked down, fingering her leather crucifix.

"Of course, Sister. And, Garnie, we can only hope that Holy Mother Church will come to aid of the unfortunate Jews," Father said.

The school days passed in an endless series of questions and answers, not all of them satisfactory, and then the great day came. The excavation had been completed. It had been debated between Auntie Rye and Auntie Rye — that is she argued with herself over the matter — should it be cement block or poured concrete? She decided on cement block. The basement foundation was completed by Eddeldorf block by block. You could always tell the days he worked, which was most days, by the odiferous residue in the air. Each day walking home from school, I stopped by the place where the Terrible House once stood to inspect. Usually Eddeldorf had finished by the time I got out of school, but sometimes he was still there and the smell was particularly bad. But the foundation and basement were finished, complete with drains and plumbing.

And then the day came. It was as if the carnival were coming to town. A great crowd gathered. Mr. Illefdonner, the town railroad station manager and the telegrapher, had called Auntie Rye to report the impending arrival time of the freight train. Astania Roms, the telephone operator, called everyone in town to give them the news. Short, tall, fat, skinny, lame and well, the town gathered in anticipation. The diesel engine powering the Milwaukee Railroad freight train pulled on to a siding, jerked and stopped, unhitched and pulled forward, leaving two flat cars, their freight covered in a blanket of tar paper. Tim Trum the trucker came with his truck. He had borrowed a kind of tractor thing he called a forklift from a friend up Luana way. The tarpaper was lifted off and there was much consternation at the sight of all the lumber and cartons. Tim rode the forklift and, with the help of Asker Neice, who worked for Eddledorf — Eddledorf said he "warn't too bright, but was strapping," unloaded the lumber and all the boxes of nails and fittings and shingles and stacks of gypsum wallboard and fixtures and toilets and bathtubs and sinks. Auntie Rye beamed. There it was: the Sears Torrington House in all its bits and pieces. Another set of blueprints and instructions in a huge bound binder were there as well. At the end of each length of lumber was printed a number.

"It's like a giant Tinker Toy," Eddledorf pronounced, examining it and supervising Tim and Asker as the Sears Torrington House, Model 3355, in parts, was loaded onto the truck bed.

"It's a wonder," Father O'Tootle declared and with flicks of the aspergillum splashed water which blew in the wind about the moving lumber.

Hilda Rose O'Shea Hannigan came over to Auntie Rye. "I saw the sign. I'd be much pleased if you would come to the beer saloon on Friday night and play euchre with Tim the trucker, Elton the lawyer, Sleazy Slim and me."

"I thank you," Auntie Rye told her. "I'm much obliged and I will be there in red."

"Perhaps another color might be better."

"I get your point," Auntie Rye said. "And I will make certain *not* to wear red."

Connecting the numbered pieces, each piece of 2 × 4 or 2 × 6 numbered at the end, the frame rose as Eddledorf, with Asker's help, carefully followed the instructions. I took pictures. Then the roof boards were affixed. I took pictures. The cedar shingles were hammered. The rooms were framed and I went from room to room taking pictures. The doors and windows went in. I took pictures. The electrician, wiry Fidelius Foxe, strung the conduit and put in switches and outlet boxes and fixture boxes. I took pictures. Willieford Waters came and installed the furnace and ran the plumbing pipes as he bent over turning his wrench. I took a picture of the crack of his butt exposed by the droop of his pants. How was I to know it was a cliché? I was only ten.

Election Day came and Auntie Rye went to vote for Roosevelt. She told me the ballot was as big as a tablecloth with at least twelve presidential candidates. And Election Day went by and we still weren't moved in. I went from space to space in the framed rooms and could see from one end of the house to the other. The outside siding was hammered in place. But the house still wasn't finished when the first snow came. It was cold and Eddledorf Grungedagger wore a big coat as the innovative gypsum was attached to framed open studs dividing the rooms and then the electricity was turned on and the heat was turned on and the water turned on and Thanksgiving arrived. We were still living at the Bear Lantern Tourist's Relaxing Rest. We had Thanksgiving dinner at the Corner Café. Just us, the owner-cook Elda and 'the waiter.' As we finished our pumpkin pie and coffee, mine half milk, of course, and stepped out into the snow, Elda pulled the shade and locked the door. We stopped by the house and sat on the floor in the empty living room, imagining a roaring fire in the fireplace.

"By Christmas," Eddledorf Grungedagger told Auntie Rye.

After school, I went as always to the house; sometimes Eddledorf wasn't even there, but the house smelled like him. He had started to paint and paper the walls. The oak flooring was hammered into place on the first floor and the pine boards on the second. The staircase went in and I no longer had to climb a ladder to get up there. The bookshelves were being erected in the library and the darkroom was being constructed in the basement near the toilet that had been installed extra. The front door was always locked now, but the key was kept in the garage and, after inspecting the house, I put it back in its place and walked in the snow, leaving my tracks to the Bear Lantern Tourist's Relaxing Rest.

I stopped to make a snow angel. Auntie Rye came to the door of her cabin and watched me. "I have to go to Chicago on business," she told me as I took off my overshoes and went into her cabin.

"I will look after the Torrington House," I told her.

"No, I want you to stay with the Toddmans the week I will be gone." That was Toddman, like Tilford Toddman with the ruly red hair.

"I don't want to stay with the Toddmans."

"Like it or not you will. You can't stay here at the Bear Lantern Tourist's Relaxing Rest by yourself."

"What if some life-changing experience happens to me at the Toddmans?" I was thinking of Tilford with the ruly red hair beating the crap out of me.

"The least likely thing to occur. Pack what you need. I'll

drive you out. You can ride the school bus in with Tilford in the morning."

Auntie Rye skidded on the snow-slippery roads as we made our way out of town toward the Toddman farm. We drove up the snow-filled ruts of the drive toward the weathered barn and gingerbread-y Victorian white house. I was scared of Tilford with the ruly red hair, but at least I would have my own room. I did last time I had to stay here when Auntie was off to France. I was much younger then. The Toddmans didn't have electricity back then. But now because of the REA they got electricity through the local co-op.

The heat poured out as Glydece Toddman opened the side door and urged us in. It was getting dark but it was light and warm in the Toddman kitchen. Glydece's hair was a flaming red and pulled into braids that turned around the back of her head in two big loops.

"So good of you to do this, Glydece."

"Not a problem, Rye. Garnie will have to bunk in with Tilford, however. Morden left her husband and came home to stay for a spell. Yamerdel took up with some yokel from up Yellow River way."

Forgive the bad word, but Oh shit, I thought. 'Bunk in' meant staying in the same bed with Tilford. He was going to kill me. I knew it. Auntie Rye kissed me on the forehead and left. She'd be sorry to come and find me bruised and beaten.

Glydece went to help Ernie with the milking and Tilford and I played Monopoly while Morden, who had strawberry hair, alternated between listening to sad country music on the radio and drying her eyes with tatters of white Kleenex. Tilford was as nice as pie to me and I began not to worry. Ernie and Glydece came in from the barn. Both wore bib overalls, only Ernie's were much larger. He was a big man with unruly rather than ruly red hair. I won or nearly won as we quit Monopoly and went to the dinner table. Glydece had fixed home-canned beef and gravy, mashed potatoes, home-canned corn and home-canned carrots and home-canned pickles and homemade bread and homemade pumpkin pie with whipped cream. The whole family drank tea with the meal, so I did as well. Hot tea that was not Chinese was a new experience for me. Padric sometimes had a cup of tea while he worked, but he put milk in it. I chose to have it without.

We listened to the radio after dinner while Morden helped her mother with the dishes and dried her eyes on the dish towel. "It's time for bed, boys," Ernie said. "And Tilford, you be good to Garnie now. He's a little boy and you're over-developed."

"I'll show you my wingy-wang," Tilford said as we got out of our long johns and into pajamas. He turned about. "See. Get a look at that." He hadn't been lying. He was definitely over-developed. I hadn't seen such a big wingy-wang before on boy or man, except for the fat man and he didn't count because I was scared. "You can touch it if you like, Garnie." I did like and I did. "You can put it in your mouth, Garnie."

"I don't think it will fit," I told him.

"Sure 'twill."

And I did. And it did.

"Do you like that, Garnie?"

I could only nod. And then I got this stuff in my mouth.

"What?" I gagged.

"It's only jizz. That's the part what feels good. When you get to be twelve like me, you'll have it too."

I crawled under the comforter next to Tilford. I didn't say it, but I knew, despite what Padric might tell me — I was a homosexual.

Glydece was the correspondent for the *Waterloo Courier*, the *Cedar Rapids Gazette* and the *Des Moines Register*. The next night we had to go to the town's high school basketball game so that she could call the scores in after the game. Ernie, Tilford and I went to the Corner Café for hamburgers and Cokes when the game was over, while Glydece went up to the telephone office to call the newspapers. When we got home and went to bed, Tilford explained to me how to suck better. And on the third night, he told me he was going to corn-hole me.

"What's that?" I asked him, admiring his hard wingy-wang.

"I'm gonna stick my wingy-wang up your butt hole."

"That will hurt," I protested.

"Maybe a little, but you'll like it."

It did and more than a little and I didn't like it. I cried.

"Don't be such a pansy."

"I ain't crying cuz it hurt," I whimpered. I remembered what Padric told me about the seed. "I'm crying cuz I don't want to have no baby."

"You are a baby. Don't be so stupid. Men can't have babies." I was much relieved, but on the fourth night I wouldn't let Tilford do any corn-holing to me. I took pictures of Tilford's wingy-wang and his balls. He displayed them proudly for me, but I knew I couldn't have Padric develop these shots for me. I had promised him no more pictures of dingy-dongs or wingy-wangs and would have to wait until I could develop them in my own darkroom.

On the fifth day, Auntie Rye came home from Chicago and

drove up through the rutted farm lane to pick me up. There had been a change in the weather, and for a few brief days the snow turned to slush and the rutted farm lane to mud. The Packard was loaded with packages. All sorts of things for the new house, and then other stuff came to the post office from Sears Roebuck, Montgomery Ward, and Spiegel. Every day, more packages, and we didn't walk to the post office but drove and loaded up the yellow Packard. The *Britannica* and the *Americana* came from Menington Book Store in the Loop, along with boxes and boxes of other books. There was bigger stuff—furniture from Sears delivered by truck.

A week before Christmas, furniture also arrived from Austenette's furniture store and funeral parlor in Prairie du Chien. There were beds, not iron, which was thought to be more sanitary, but real beds with wood headboards and matching dressers. Lamps and end tables and a pair of matching sofas that Auntie Rye placed facing opposite each other near the fireplace, rather than pushed up against the wall like most sofas were. A special truck came all the way from Chicago with the Baldwin Baby Grand piano. A Hoover vacuum was delivered by the traveling man that Auntie Rye met over at the Crawford lobby on one of our Saturday trips to Prairie. We still went on most Saturdays, me to continue learning how to develop film and Auntie to get beautified. Auntie Rye bought the dining room set from Austenette's, which was no longer owned and operated by anybody named Austenette. Austie had croaked over a corpse and Austenette's was now operated by Winifreder Riley, Austie's much maligned son-in-law, who was the only mortician in town, his bifurcation — one of my more recent new words — had to be endured.

Christmas was coming. We finally moved in and we got a great Christmas tree from out at the Toddmans'. Ernie cut us "a beauty," as he called it. We bought presents for each other in Prairie and for others as well. I bought Tilford a jock strap with an extra-large hard athletic cup. Auntie Rye planned a great Christmas dinner which she was going to prepare herself since the hired woman, Nancilette Nardo — who had great enormous tits, a cackle laugh, and a voice that sang Catholic hymns mostly in Latin and quite constantly — had her own family to be with on the holiday and would not cook for us. We went to midnight Mass. Tilford and I served and after Mass I gave him his present, suggesting he open it when others weren't about. Then the following day, Mr. Strapolet trudged through the snow, careful not to step in cowshit; Mr. Emblanci arrived in his Model A, puffing exhaust into the cold, the fender still missing; LaBelle rode over from Prairie with Padric; and Father O'Tootle barreled up on his motorcycle after the last Christmas Day Mass. The fire roared and Auntie Rye cooked. I think she cooked everything she could think of in case most of it didn't turn out. It wasn't bad. It was not the best, but it wasn't bad. The goose was a little greasy, the turkey a little dry, the mashed potatoes a little lumpy, the dressing had a bit too much sage, the ham was a bit too salty, the yams a little hard, the squash a little too mushy, the homemade donuts a bit too hard, the corn not hand-canned, the cranberries not fully un-berried, the candied carrots a bit raw, the Waldorf Salad obviously not prepared by Oscar of Veal Oscar fame, but the pimento-stuffed olives just near perfect out of the jar.

We had a really 'nice little red wine,' as Father called it, a French Bordeaux from our new, but as yet not too well-stocked, wine cellar. After dinner in the living room, Auntie Rye played the Baldwin and we all sang Christmas carols and opened our presents.

"A merry and blessed Christmas," Father O'Tootle said, raising his cup of eggnog and brandy, having opened and put on a black cashmere sweater that Auntie had ordered from Marshall Field's. He offered a Lucky Strike to Padric, who took and lit it and the priest's with his new silver lighter from Tiffany, a gift from Auntie Rye. "I think nineteen-forty-one will be the best of years," Padric predicted.

The others raised their cups as I did mine, sans the brandy. Padric snapped his Leica. LaBelle had her own cigarettes, Chesterfields, and lit up. Auntie didn't smoke. She thought it a filthy habit. "It stains the fingers and the teeth. I see no point in puffing on a piece of paper with burning weeds inside."

I looked around me and came to the realization that I was truly happy. What more could any boy ask for? I now had the daily luxury of exploring all thirteen volumes, along with the supplement, of the Oxford English Dictionary — the OED, as everyone 'in the know' called it — filled with nothing but words. Their wrapping paper was still strewn about the volumes. Everyone was happy, a bit tipsy with their tippling and a bit clouded in their smoke. Professor Pangloss was right. It was the best of all possible worlds.

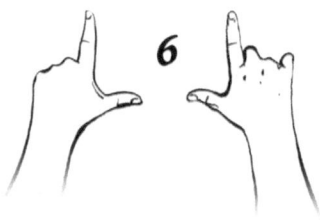

Out of Focus

And yet…

In this same room less than a year later, it was not, after all, the best of all possible worlds.

Auntie and I had finished a reheated Sunday lunch left us by Nancilette Nardo, who had taken to singing the entire requiem Mass so that it was peaceful when she was gone. Sunday was her day off, otherwise she was here from eight in the morning until seven-thirty or so at night, forever vocalizing. Auntie was half reading Edna Ferber's *Saratoga Trunk*, not to me as was usual with novels, but silently to herself amidst strewn pages of the Sunday *Des Moines Register*. I was listening to Sammy Kaye's Sunday Serenade on our new General Electric radio-phonograph with Superheterodyne Circuit, built in Beam A Scope, 12-inch Dynamic speaker, illuminated Visualux dial, G-E tone selector with automatic tone compensation and the automatic record changer with permanent sapphire needle. I was about to change the station because the University of Chicago Roundtable was coming on; then the message came, "President Roosevelt says that the Japanese have attacked Pearl Harbor from the air."

"Turn it up." Auntie Rye set *Saratoga Trunk* open on the sofa, spilled the *Register* pages to the floor and came over and stood above where I was spread out on the Persian rug on my stomach, legs extended and feet crossed in the air. I reached up and turned up the volume. It was about 1:30 Central Standard Time when the news first came. We listened to the reports throughout the afternoon and evening, having our supper in the living room.

The next day we listened to President Roosevelt speak. "Mr. Vice President, Mr. Speaker of the House, members of the Senate and the House of Representatives, yesterday, December 7, 1941 — a day which will live in infamy…the United States of America was suddenly and deliberately attacked by naval and air forces of the Empire of Japan."

It was definitely not the best of all possible worlds. My life changed. Not just in the usual 'for the duration' sort of way, but in a morbid, black-and white-graphic preoccupation with the violence of death sort of way.

On December 7, 1941, when the Japs 'deliberately and without warning attacked the United States,' they attacked me as well. It was not a sudden *epiphany*; I had previously only thought of that word as a church holy day. And not one of the obligation days because it was always Epiphany Sunday. No, it was my eleven-year-old mind coming to grips with the reality that death not only existed in the tolling of the bells for the old but in the violent ending of life for young men. 'Our Boys,' they were called, but they weren't boys, they were young men like Harmon Benson. Harmon Benson was killed at Hickman Field the day Pearl Harbor was bombed, but we didn't know that on December 7. We also didn't know that the Philippines were invaded by the Japs until several days later.

On the Wednesday after war was declared, Auntie and I went 'to show,' as we called going to the movies in our town, to see Joel McCrea and Laraine Day in *Foreign Correspondent*. I didn't mention to Auntie Rye, actually couldn't mention to Auntie Rye, about having seen this film on the marquee in Catlow on that day I first saw the Opera House. The movie was, appropriately, about impending war in Europe, which, of course, was no longer impending, but it was the newsreel which really captured our interest. I was enthralled to see the bombing of Pearl Harbor; Auntie was angry. She was picking a bit of popcorn hull from a tooth as we walked out. "Pure fluff. That was lousy," she said.

"The movie?"

"No, the newsreel. No facts. Not how many battleships were sunk, nor cruisers, nor how many planes were shot down, how many sailors or soldiers were killed. Pure propaganda crap to get us riled up. Well, it got me riled up but not in the way that was expected."

"I'm not sure I want to know," I told her as we began the walk home.

"It's important, always, to know," she told me.

And so it began, my having to know, my record-keeping of the war on the wall in my room from articles in the *Register*, *Courier*, *Gazette*, *New York Times*, *Chicago Tribune*, *Life*, *Time* and *Look*. I cut and tacked up on my wall-to-wall cork board the devastation and horror of war. And the war was not just in Bataan in the Philippines; it was in Malaysia, in Singapore, in Thailand, in Shanghai and Hong Kong. There were attacks on Wake Island. The war continued between the Soviets and Germans and Rommel's tank battles with the Brits in North Africa.

Auntie examined my wall. "You're becoming obsessive."

"Yes," I agreed.

The Japs took 300 American soldiers prisoners in Guam. But the worst pictures were those of the dead. And while all in black and white, the blood was still evident. Headless corpses, torn limbs, guts spilling out: Yanks, Brits, Chinese and Aussies. Dead.

"Why are you wearing that thing on your arm?" Sister Mary Saint Wulfhilda the Abbess demanded. She was referring to the black armband I had wrapped and safety-pinned above my right elbow.

"To remember the dead."

"Well. Take it off. It's morbid," she ordered.

"No," I told her and took my seat.

I asked Auntie for a map of the world. She ordered one from Chicago. The big map was delivered along with a portable cork board on wheels. She thumb-tacked the map to the board, which we set up in the library. She had also ordered Moore map pins. These were round-headed little pins in many colors. I decided on orange for the Japs, yellow for the Chinese, black for the Nazis, red for the Soviets, white for the Americans, blue for the Brits, green for the Free French and pushed in the rounded pins on the big map and created battle lines. "Appropriate choices," Auntie said. But once the pins were in place it was obvious the Nazis and the Nips — as the Japs were now sometimes called, from Nippons — were winning; it was depressing.

The Japs launched attacks in Borneo; Rommel continued

to battle the Brits in North Africa; the dead continued to pile up. Geraldina Lamtouse's father, Abner, joined up. General Nimitz was appointed to command the Pacific Fleet. The rotogravure section of the *Register* had photos of mutilated German bodies from the Eastern front. I tacked them on my wall. Dr. Von Hunggor's brother, Elert, a pharmacist in Calmer, joined up. Italian midget subs sank the British battle-ships *Queen Elizabeth* and *Valiant*. Mr. Illefdonner, the town railroad station manager and telegrapher, joined the Navy. Astania Roms called everyone to tell them: then her mother, Hilda Roms Border, who knew telegraphy, became the sta-tion mistress. Hitler took over the command of the German army himself. I cut out the picture of Der Fuehrer and tacked it up through his moustache. Arnst Eggledorf, who ran the Jack Sprat store, joined the Army. His wife, Benevola, took over running the store. Tim Trum the trucker left for the Marines and Alison Neblitz, his fiancée, the dry cleaneress, took his place at Friday night euchre at Hilda Rose O'Shea Hannigan's. The battle of Wake Island continued and there were more pictures of dead bodies, which I cut and tacked to the walls. Eddledorf Grungedagger's helper, Asker Neice, signed up with the Navy recruiters in Waterloo. Churchill met with Roosevelt in Washington. The Americans surren-dered to the Japs on Wake Island.

And then Christmas arrived. There was no snow. Padric had been wrong. 1941 had not been the best of years. The tree was a little scraggly; Auntie Rye's decorations a little sparse. LaBelle rode over with Padric, and Father O'Tootle walked over after the last Christmas Day Mass. Even though ration-ing had not yet gone into effect, there was a sense of the war all over our celebration. Mr. Strapolet came bearing both milk and eggs. Mr. Emblanci still hadn't replaced the missing fender. The turkey was smaller but just as dry, the cranberries from a can, the squash undercooked, the potatoes too milky, but the pimento-stuffed olives just near perfect out of the jar. A bottle of wine was opened after dinner.

"To all the dead," I said and raised my small wineglass.

"*Requiescant in pace*," Father O'Tootle declared and downed his wine.

"Aren't we being a bit morbid?" LaBelle asked.

"It's a time of great sorrow," I told her.

"But not the end of the world," Auntie Rye said and went over to the Baldwin.

"Perhaps it is." I fingered the black armband on my sleeve.

Before the New Year arrived, General MacArthur fled but said, "I shall return," and Robbie Bratten of McGregor was rounded up with the rest of the Americans in Manila along with his Uncle Raymond with whom he had been staying. They were being held at a makeshift prison created at the university by the Japs. It was shown at the Roxy in the newsreel when we went to see Ann Sothern in *Maisie Was a Lady*. I didn't see Robbie in the newsreel. He was eleven, my age, and I only met him once at a Catholic picnic for county parishes. I watched him pee so I could see his dingy-dong, which was really skinny, but long.

In 1942, the world and everything in it seemed black-and-white, including the movies we saw, and we went 'to show' a lot. With Auntie I saw *The Little Foxes* with Bette Davis. We watched Errol Flynn "die with his boots on." *That Hamilton Woman* had both Oliviers. And we sat through *Major Barbara* with Wendy Hiller, and a lot more. But it was the newsreels and the war that we ended up talking about as we left the smell of popcorn and wandered down the closed-stores street away from the lights of the marquee.

"Errol Flynn is just about the handsomest man in the whole wide world," I announced.

"Yeah, and about the wildest. More 'woman trouble' than he needs, and there's talk of a rape. I guess the expression 'in like Flynn' isn't just words."

I would let him rape me, but I didn't tell Auntie that as we continued home in the cold. Sometimes I went to the movies without her. I saw lots of westerns, like Roy Rogers in *Bad Man of Deadwood* and Gene Autry in *Back in the Saddle*. I went with Tilly — that's what I started calling Tilford Todd-man — on Friday nights, but Tilly always went to pee during the newsreels. He wouldn't talk about the war. It was as if it didn't exist for him. When he came to my house and was up in my room, he made me cover my 'war wall' as he called it with a sheet. And there were getting to be lots of photos on the wall, mostly photos of the wounded and the dead. I also started clipping Ernie Pyle's columns about the war and was compiling a scrapbook of his war writings.

"This is getting to be an obsession," Auntie said. "I worry about you."

"I think a lot about death," I told her.

"That's not healthy for someone your age. I think you should take off the armband."

I did, but I still thought about death. In the Arctic, a Soviet sub was sunk by a U-Boat. I thought of the dying men who all drowned. They must have screamed a lot. I could hear the screams in my head and the screams were in Russian, or what I imagined Russian screams would sound like. I wrote to Robbie Bratten in care of the Red Cross. I hoped the Japs had not killed him and sent it to him. There were pictures of dead and wounded Australians from the battle at Batu Anam. I advanced the orange tacks on the wall map where Malaysia was. With Rommel on the offense, I had new pictures of dead Brits in the desert. What happened to corpses in the desert? I couldn't find anything helpful on the subject in the *Britannica*. The first American soldiers arrived in England. The Japs attacked Bataan and it was bloody. Bataan was in the Philippines and made me think of Robbie again. Had the Japs butchered him? They did that to people they held as prisoners — hacked off their heads with swords. Auntie made me take down one of my head-chopping photos. "That's too gruesome to have to sleep in the same room with."

"You ended your sentence with a preposition," I said.

She simply glared at me. Auntie was all about the home front, which was beginning to consume our lives. She bought war bonds and I had a ten-cent savings stamp book and pasted in it. In January the O'Brien twins, Jimmy and Johnny, who preferred to be called James and John, joined the Navy and went off arm-in-arm to Great Lakes Naval Training Center. Pictures torn from the *Times* of Rommel's tanks on the offensive from El Alamein driving toward Tobruk were tacked next to *Life* shots of the Yanks arriving in Great Britain. I decided I would go to Oxford after the war, if I wasn't killed or maimed or blind. It was what Nigel would do. I was in a particularly affected stage and spoke almost entirely in an upper-class English accent. "Stop that!" Auntie would yell. Sister Mary Saint Wulfhilda the Abbess would slap me across the palm with her leather crucifix. "Enough," Padric would demand and Father O'Tootle boxed me across my cute head. Still I persisted. It seemed the right thing for me to do. Brit kids suffered. I needed to suffer. I could now be a real victim of the Blitz. I often slept the night huddled in the tube station.

Up in my bedroom, my war wall sheet-draped, I let Tilly corn-hole me. And in my great imaginative world the bombs of the Blitz were falling around us. I came up out of the tube station shelter unscathed. The next Sunday Tilly and I served Mass. Sometimes Father O'Tootle took Saturday and Sunday off and Father Petroff from McGregor came up and said Mass. Tilly said that Father Petroff was screwing his housekeeper, Cushinda Leonard, a somewhat big-titted, youngish woman who always wore pink pullovers. I told him that wasn't true because priests were celibate and did not have carnal — another of my new words — knowledge of womankind. Tilly said I was nuts and full of shit and that priests were men and all men screwed women. The next Sunday Father O'Tootle was back, and while Tilly and I got into our cassocks, I reminded him that it was good he was not a man, because he wasn't screwing women but corn-holing me. Tilly told me he had pretty much made up his mind to quit corn-holing me and take to screwing girls. I told him he'd have to find a girl first to let him and he told me he had a mind to screw Geraldina Lamtouse, and I told him Geraldina was a virgin and that she would have to be such in order to get married and for her to screw him would be a mortal sin, and he reminded me that getting corn-holed was also a mortal sin, so I didn't go to communion.

"You didn't take communion," Father O'Tootle said as he took off his vestments.

"I couldn't," I explained. "I didn't go to confession. I'm not in a state of grace."

"So I shall hear your confession."

"Now?"

"Why not? We can't have you going around not in a state of grace."

With trepidation I followed him toward the confessional. The loud slam of the little window-opening gave me the willies and I stared through at the distorted image of the priest. I was in an utter state of panic. "Bless me Father…" I whispered.

"Speak up."

And I went through the rest of the ritualistic part and then quickly added, "And I let Tilford corn-hole me."

"No names," the priest reminded me.

"I let this other boy corn-hole me."

"And what other sins have you to confess?"

"I sucked his wingy-wangy and I said piss and shit twenty-seven times."

"And anything else?"

"No."

"Say five hail Marys and five Our Fathers and now make a good act of contrition."

"That's it?"

"That's it," he affirmed and then in Latin mumbled the absolution. I had expected a lecture on the terrible sin of sodomy. I did know the real word for corn-holing and had explored the dictionary and the *Americana* and *Britannica*. I was certain the terrible penance for such horrific sins would probably be stations of the cross twelve times and that I would still be genuflecting from pew to pew until the church was empty and everyone had left gossiping of what terrible sins I must be guilty.

Major Vidkum Quisling was appointed head of the Norwegian Nazi government. If I were in Norway, I would be in the mountains on skis as part of the resistance and probably be shot by Nazi snipers and lay bleeding in the snow; in black and white, of course, because I would take a picture of myself as I lay dying. I wondered if Robbie lay dying. Had the Japs killed him? The British troop transport *Empress of Asia* was sunk by the Japs. I asked Sister Mary Saint Wulfhilda the Abbess if we could pray for the dead Brits. She said, "No, they aren't Catholic." The United States declared war on Thailand. There were a lot of frozen corpses, both German and Soviet, in Belorussia. The photos, while black and white, were predominantly white. The Brits surrendered in Malaysia. I cut out a picture of two Brits in shorts carrying flags. "The number of British that died in Malaysia is staggering," I told Auntie. "A hundred and thirty-eight thousand."

"Enough! You've got to stop dwelling on death. This war..." But she didn't finish her sentence.

"This war is all about death," I reminded her.

I found myself crying over the dead. But I muffled the sound of my sobbing in the pillow so that Auntie Rye didn't hear me.

"You need to focus on life," Auntie told me and walked that day to school with me. It was to comfort me, I suppose. I still thought about the war.

I asked Sister Mary Saint Wulfhilda the Abbess if we might pray for Robbie Bratten of McGregor who is Catholic.

"And why does he need our prayers?"

"Because he is a prisoner of the Japs at Manila University."

"That is not *just* a university," she said. "That is the Pontifical and Royal Catholic, Santo Tomas University of the

Philippines. We shall pray for Robbie Bratten every day for a month and we shall all write letters to him and tell him in our letters that we are a friend of Gardner Gardiner who is his friend, won't we students?"

"Yes, Sister," they answered in unison.

"And send them to him in care of the Red Cross," I added.

"Yes," she said and then began, "Oh, Jesus, Mary and Joseph, remember thy Catholic child, Robbie Bratten of McGregor, imprisoned by the pagan, yellow rotten Japs at the Pontifical and Royal Catholic, Santo Tomas University of the Philippines... Hail Mary, full of grace..."

In addition to Sisters Mary Mildred and Mary Saint Wulfhilda the Abbess, there was a third nun of the Presentation Order at the school. She was Sister Mary Leonardo da Vinci and she was the music teacher. I wanted to ask her how she could be Leonardo da Vinci because it was not a saint's name, but I never did.

"Garnie needs a new focus. He will learn to play the piano," Auntie Rye told her.

"But you already taught me to play," I said.

"But not correctly. Sister will teach you properly."

So I took piano lessons. Sister was partial to Mozart, but Auntie insisted on Bach as well, so from scales to Mozart to Bach, I, being the gifted child that I was, learned to play quite beautifully as well as correctly. We had a Hammond electric organ in the church loft, and as Auntie had insisted on Bach, Sister Mary Leonardo da Vinci insisted on the organ as well. So, within a short span of time I could roar out Bach's *Toccata and Fugue in D minor*. It vibrated and the windows of the church rattled, and as I finished, Father O'Tootle, who had apparently been listening below, applauded.

"Don't encourage the child," Sister Mary Leonardo da Vinci called down to him, but I could tell she was pleased.

Auntie said that Leonardo da Vinci was hardly a saint and wondered why sister had such a name.

"I thought it strange, too. And when I asked her she said a nun often took the name of her father. She told me her late father had been Leonardo da Vinci Frantinelli."

"She is very tall for an Italian," Auntie said, "and very pale-skinned."

U-Boats sunk seven tankers near Aruba. The week after *that* confession, I played with Tilly's organ as well as the one in the church and I let him corn-hole me, and while he was about it I talked of the horrors of the Blitz in my fake British accent. "Will you shut up," he screamed and came and I reminded Auntie after he had left of my intent to go to Oxford.

"Why Maudlin?" That was the way Auntie pronounced Magdalen.

"It's where Oscar Wilde went after Trinity. He was a homosexual."

"Yes, I know."

"I plan on being a homosexual," I told her.

"I should not be surprised, but then one never knows."

We went to Wednesday night show. It was a strange double bill with Nelson Eddy and Rise Stevens in *The Chocolate Soldier* and Orson Wells in *Citizen Kane*. But it was the newsreel we talked about after. There on the screen had been General MacArthur in sunglasses vowing to return. "A total ass," Auntie said. "It's his fault that the Philippines fell."

I rather admired the General, so I changed the topic. "The popcorn needed more butter."

German losses in the Soviet Union were reported to be one and a half million.

"That is a good thing," Auntie said.

"Is any death a good thing?"

"War is about death," she said. "And only when all the Nazis are dead will it end."

I did not disagree. German U-Boats were spotted off the East Coast. The Japs bombed Darwin, Australia. I bought more stamps. *Time* reported that Nancy Kelly and Edmund O'Brien got divorced. Was that a mortal sin? With names like that, they had to be Catholic. Roosevelt turned sixty. I tore Jap General Yamashita off the March cover of *Time* and put the thumbtack through his eye as I stuck him to the wall. The Yank and Philippine troops were getting ill because of short rations. I decided to quit eating for the duration.

"Eat," Auntie ordered.

"Why?"

"To keep your strength up for the war effort."

I ate my Quaker Oats. The Japs invaded New Guinea with hardly any opposition. I had to buy more orange-colored Moore tacks. I had a picture of the Brits, just their backs, as they retreated on bikes from Prome. I would have given them my Schwinn but didn't know how to get it to them. The Japs landed at Bougainville. The map was getting an awful lot of orange tacks. The Yanks and Filipinos surrendered in the Philippines. I wondered if Robbie still had his head. There was word of a hundred-mile death march of prisoners.

"Put on your heavy coat. It is cold out," Auntie ordered.

As I trooped to school I wondered what it would be like if I suddenly dropped over dead from exhaustion. I batted away flies that weren't there and was choking from the heat despite the real temperature in my hundred-mile march. I collapsed on the sidewalk.

Fat Pugmen Ugglefit waddled up to me. "Why are you lying on the sidewalk?"

"It's a scientific thing," I lied as I got to my feet, bruised from the beating I had taken from the Jap guard.

We had a late spring snow. The daffodils were popping yellow through the soft snow. It only lasted a day and most of it melted. The Nazis were still bombing the Brits, and I, as Nigel, took shelter in the tube station, but the RAF were bombing back with two-ton bombs on Essen and really pissing off Hitler.

"Don't say pissing off," Auntie ordered. "Especially in that fake accent."

Helmer Neisson, the Chevy dealer, didn't join up. He was 4-F.

"He has enlarged testicles," Tilly told me.

"How do you know?"

"I just know."

I wished I had enlarged testicles. Back home in London, Rear Admiral Lord Mount Batten was appointed Chief of Staff of Combined Operations. I knew Dicky would do us Brits proud.

"The news is good," Auntie told me when I came in from school. "Colonel Jimmy Doolittle just bombed Tokyo today."

"Were there a lot of dying Japs?"

"I suspect so, yes."

"I hope it was slow and painful." I was angry with the Japs for what they had done to me on the death march in the Philippines and for what they had done to Robbie, though I wasn't certain they had chopped off his head.

Things in England were looking bad. Both Bath and Exeter

were bombed. I wondered about the state of my acquaintance, Lady Dalrymple, and was she yet in Bath? And the Elliots, how were they faring? I decided that I would visit Bath after the war. The Philippines fell on May 6 when General Wainwright surrendered Corregidor. I went to bed, hiding it from Auntie, but in tears. There was little doubt any longer. The Japs had killed Robbie.

Gasoline rationing went into effect. Three gallons a week. There was no more rubber, so galoshes and tires were in shortage. That gas rationing cut down on our travel. We went to Prairie only one Saturday a month. "My hair looks like shit," Auntie told me.

"Don't say 'looks like shit,'" I told her. School ended at the end of May. Auntie gave me a war bond as a reward for taking piano lessons, and I continued over vacation, except when Sister Mary Leonardo da Vinci went to Dubuque. Roosevelt expanded selective service. I knew at eighteen I would be called up and killed. I would not live long enough to be the world's great photographer.

I missed seeing Padric every week; still I was learning to develop film even though I wasn't taking a lot of pictures. One thousand Brit bombers blasted Cologne, leaving some 45,000 Huns homeless. My first pictures of Tillly's big wingy-wangy got a bit messed up in the developing, but Tilly obliged me with another shooting opportunity. "All the rotten Japs here are being rounded up and sent to camps," Tilly told me, displaying his hard wingy-wangy as I snapped my Leica from various viewpoints. I was surprised he said anything about the war, but I suppose rounding up American Japanese was not exactly war news. And then he did surprise me. "We will join up. The Marines."

"Yes." That excited me.

"You'll have to learn to shoot. To use a gun."

That did not excite me.

"Have you ever gone hunting?"

I didn't even lie. "No."

"We'll go squirrel hunting. Take the twenty-twos and hit the woods."

We did. It wasn't all bad. I shot a squirrel and brought it home.

"Ugh," Auntie Rye squealed. "Get that thing out of the house."

My hunting days were short-lived.

I had Dorothea Lange's photos of the internees being hauled off to camps on my wall. They told the story despite what Padric said about photos not having a narrative. They looked so destroyed. "You shouldn't call them that. They are Japanese-Americans, not Japs, and shouldn't be in camps," I said.

"They're all slant eyes. All the same. And they all got little dicks."

"You are a bigoted" — a recent new word — "son-of-a-bitch," I told him.

"Take that back, Tilly."

"Will not."

"Then I'm gonna corn-hole you." He came at me and pulled down my pants.

"No, you aren't."

But he did. I let him and it was OK because I was training to become a homosexual.

Auntie Rye said Hitler was rounding up the Jews and sending them off to camps.

"I didn't read anything about it in the *Times*," I told her. "But it's just like Roosevelt is doing with the Japanese, isn't it?"

"It wasn't in the *Times*. Madam Rodowckinski wrote me about it. And it *is like* what Roosevelt *is* doing with the Japanese."

"Could I go to one of the Nissei camps and take pictures?"

"I would let you if I could," Auntie said, "but I'm more than certain the government would never allow it."

"If I knew a Japanese-American boy my age I could go visit him."

"But you don't know any Japanese-Americans, your age or otherwise."

"No," I said. I wondered if I did know a Japanese-American boy my age if he would have a little dick.

At the Battle of Midway the American Fleet was successful over the Jap Navy. Perhaps the tide of the war was turning, though the British were routed in North Africa near Tobruk and just hanging on in Malta. The Allies were being beaten in Burma and the Soviets struggled on the Eastern front. Perhaps the tide was not turning. Tobruk fell to Rommel and 30,000 Brits and Free French were taken prisoner.

"Three million rations and 500,000 gallons of gas were lost to the Nazis at Tobruk," Auntie Rye read aloud from *Times*.

I cut out more of Dorothea Lange's pictures and tacked them up on my wall. Auntie Rye and Nancilette Nardo planted a victory garden, but Auntie Rye didn't do the weeding. Nancilette did and sang Catholic hymns as she weeded. I began to play the same hymns on the piano in the living room and Nancilette learned to sing her hymns to match my playing. Rommel was made a field marshal by Hitler. It was a shame we didn't have a Hammond. "Can we have a Hammond?" I asked Auntie.

"None available. I had thought about it." She added, "Hammond is making communication transmitters for the war effort, I am told."

Steed Enstead, a veteran of the Great War, went back to war. Axis troops invaded Egypt. Floskie joined the WACS. General Eisenhower was appointed to command the Allied forces in Europe. Germany began its summer offensive against the Russians. Moskie went to Cleveland to work in a factory. In North Africa, the New Zealanders destroyed nearly an entire Italian division. Daralinda ran the Bear Lantern Tourist's Relaxing Rest without any other family help. The Army Air Force struck German air bases in Holland. I was nearing twelve and discovered a black pubic hair. My very first. My very own. Two Japanese carriers were sunk in the Pacific. Chiang Kai-shek made the cover of *Time*.

"He's apparently pissed with General Stilwell, or the other way around."

"Don't say pissed."

I tacked up the Generalissimo's picture, but not through the eye. It was the Fourth of July. Nancilette made potato salad which Auntie Rye took to the town picnic in the town park and the high school band played *Stars and Stripes Forever*. Auntie drank Hamms, but the can was kept in a brown paper bag. And there were no fireworks due to the war effort.

Nancilette made me a sugarless cake for my birthday. I took a picture of it and developed it. Even with imperfections in the printing technique, the picture looked better than the cake tasted. There were twelve candles. Matches were getting scarce; we, fortunately, had pilot lights on the gas range.

British General Gort was killed on a flight to Cairo and Montgomery took over. The Marines landed on Guadalcanal. "Forty-two is a tough year," Mr. Strapolet said, when he joined up. Eleanor deLacy went off to the Toddman farm for the duration. The chickens were made into chicken soup. There'd be no more fresh eggs from Mr. Strapolet's chickens. A U.S. sub sunk a Jap cruiser in the Solomons.

"Prince George, the Duke of Kent, was killed when the plane he was flying — a Short Sunderland flying boat — crashed in Scotland," I read to Auntie from the *Times*.

"I know," she said.

"What, did you hear it on the radio?"

"No. I spoke to Lilith last evening when you were out biking with Tilly."

"Should I go to the funeral, do you suppose?" I asked in the best of British accents.

"I suspect you won't want to when I tell you a bit about the King's brother. First off, he was probably homosexual."

"That's hardly a reason not to go."

"Of course not, and it was claimed he was bisexual, though I'm of the opinion he was a total homo."

"You've met him?"

"Yes. Anyway, as you say, that would not be a problem. One of his lovers, however, may have been Louis Ferdinand, the Prince of Prussia, heir to the German throne. Be that as it may, Prince Louis probably doesn't have much use for Hitler. But the Duke, Prince George, was good friends with his brother and sister-in-law, the Nazi sympathizers, the Duke and Duchess of Windsor —"

"Whom you hate," I interrupted.

"Yes, well an artist friend of Lilith's told her that she heard from someone in the British community in Lisbon that it was common gossip that Prince George was trying to arrange a separate peace with the Nazis and was going to meet with them and maybe even meet with Rudolf Hess."

"Isn't Hess in jail?"

"Somewhere. But in Scotland most likely. The Duke was apparently going to Iceland when his plane crashed. Who knows who he was going to meet with there, or in Scotland? There are rumors that the SOE may actually have been responsible for the crash, the plane sabotaged."

I wondered if the artist who had told Lilith the news had been my mother. "What is the SOE?"

"Churchill's secret army, the Special Operations Executive."

"I didn't know Churchill had a secret army."

"He does."

"You know so much," I said in admiration. "Perhaps I won't go to the funeral." I still kept the British accent.

"Probably for the best," she suggested.

The Brits were beginning to slow Rommel down with mine fields. The Marines still held on Guadalcanal. School started. Geraldina Lamtouse and I were now in the seventh grade, but we had a third student, a transfer from St. Michael's in Brooklyn, New York. His name was Rupert von Totten and he was Dutch, but spoke perfect English.

"He is a Jew," Sister Mary Saint Wulfhilda the Abbess whispered to Father O'Tootle.

"I know he is a Jew," Father replied so that the entire class could hear.

Sister dropped the whisper. "Then what is he doing in a Catholic school?"

"He is a child of God, foremost, but his grandfather

smuggled him out of Amsterdam to England, where he stayed for awhile. He is a displaced person. He came to live with his great uncle in Brooklyn, who recently died. I knew the family. They contacted me and felt the boy would be safer in Iowa. I brought him here to live with the O'Briens for the duration. And he is to be made welcome at St. Ludmila's. Is that right, students?"

"Yes," we all responded.

The leaves on the trees were turning. Nancilette began canning peas, green beans and tomatoes. We would save ration points: 16 points for a can of tomatoes, 14 points for green beans and 16 for peas. Another 16: the Germans were 16 miles from Stalingrad. Spam and tuna fish were both rationed. Saturday came and I went to go to confession but learned Father O'Tootle was out of town and Father Petroff was hearing confessions. I decided to wait a week until Father O'Tootle was back. I walked back from the church and Auntie Rye drove thirty-five-miles-an-hour as we made our way over the rattling bridge to Prairie for the not-so-weekly beautification. There was a Harley parked in front of Small's Drugs. I tinkled in and Padric came out from the back. Father O'Tootle, small duffle bag in hand, was behind him.

"Hi there, Garnie," the priest said and ruffled my unruly hair.

"I didn't go to confession," I blurted.

"Next week. Time enough," the priest assured me.

"I hope I don't die during the week."

"We all hope that, Garnie." The priest turned back to Padric. "I'll be off then, Padric."

"See you soon, I hope, Marty." Padric was smiling.

The priest tinkled out the door and the Harley kicked

over, revved up, and roared out of town. I could hear him almost all the way to the bridge.

"I've been sent a cablegram from Ireland." Padric showed it to me. 'FATHER BEATEN OVER HEAD WHISKEY BOTTLE STOP DEAD STOP COME HOME.'

"Is that why Father O'Tootle was here?"

"No." He didn't elaborate.

I resented his meeting with the priest other than at our house but didn't know why I resented it. "Are you going home to Ireland?"

"No. I couldn't if I wanted to. Travel on any liner is too risky. Besides, I am not unhappy the old bastard is dead. He makes Mr. Betters look like a saint." Padric had a blue star for Johnny hanging in his store window where the blue-faced camera had been.

It took Auntie Rye longer to get beautified these days and I spent most of the day with Padric. He had been taking pictures of river boats and barges on the Mississippi. Like the freight trains that passed through our town, the war effort was being shipped. By rail and by barge, tanks and troop carriers, bazookas and bombs were heading for the coasts. I saw it on the newsreels. But Padric saw it all in shadows and light and explained the importance of capturing the light, on the leaves, across the water on the reflection of ship's metal surfaces and its war cargo.

In New Guinea the Aussies were driven back by the Japs. Sunday was the new big movie night at the Roxy and Auntie and I went to see *Mrs. Miniver* with Greer Garson. The theater was out of butter and put corn oil on the popcorn. I didn't care. Auntie said 'ugh' and gave me hers. While I had become somewhat inured, the latest photos from

Guadalcanal, from Bloody Ridge, made me ill. I went up to my room and hid under the bed. I had to escape the Japs. The war was going to last and I would be eighteen in six years and I would be dying at Guadalcanal amidst a pile of screaming bodies. Auntie came to the door of my room. "Are you all right, Garnie?"

"Yes," I replied.

"Why are you under the bed?"

"I am practicing in the event of an air raid."

She seemed satisfied and left me.

The next day, not under the bed, I read that Stalingrad was surrounded.

Habor Liechtner, the postmaster, was an officer in the Marine Reserves and was called up. Tiffy Ambacher, the postal worker, took over and the odds were that Roosevelt would appoint her as postmistress, though the official title for a woman was still postmaster.

"Maybe Roosevelt will appoint you," I suggested to Auntie Rye.

"I haven't been a Democrat long enough. Tiffy has apparently been a Democrat all her life. She will get the appointment." Auntie had a letter from Madam Rodowckinski. She read to me. "The Jews have been taken from their homes in Opoczno in cattle cars. Opoczno is Poland."

"Where were they taken?"

"To their deaths, I assume."

Tuesday and Wednesday were bank nights at the Roxy. First there was the Movietone newsreel and it was about the Aussies on the offensive in New Guinea, the Brits advancing on Tamatave, the capital of Madagascar, and General Rommel flying home to Germany for unspecified medical treatment. This was followed by the double bill. The first movie was *Blood and Sand*. Tyrone Power was a bullfighter.

"Tyrone Power is the handsomest man in the world," I said as they were getting ready to draw for the dishes.

"I thought you said Errol Flynn was."

"I was wrong."

"'Tyrone might be a beauty in his toreador pants, but those dishes they are giving away are really ugly," Auntie said. "They look like they came out of a cereal box."

"We didn't win them," I told her. "Anister Rabar, the beautician, did."

"Thank God."

The second film was John Payne in *To the Shores of Tripoli*.

"Talk about Payne in pain. This may be the worst movie of the year," Auntie said.

"Or ever," I suggested.

"Should we leave?"

And we did. I went home and thought about Tyrone Power and played with my dingy-dong. The rainy season started in Guadalcanal and the Marines were mired in the mud. It rained in town as well and I trudged through the mud to school. Geraldina Lamtouse was standing outside the school door protected from the rain by the overhang.

"Why are you walking so funny?" she asked.

"I am trudging through the mud."

"There is no mud. The sidewalks are washed clean."

"I know," I told her.

"Sometimes, Garnie, you are very strange."

Nancilette Nardo left us. Her husband, Elmer, the John Deere salesman, was drafted and went off to Fort McCoy and Nancilette moved to Detroit to work in an aircraft plant.

But she wasn't a riveter. She sent Auntie a postcard with a picture of Detroit's Ford plant, which wasn't in Detroit but in Dearborn, and on the non-picture side she wrote that she boxed plane replacement parts. 'Nancy, the Neverivetter,' Auntie called her.

Auntie ignored the garden. The weeds took over, but it was fall and didn't matter. I stopped playing hymns on the piano.

The tractor factory in Stalingrad was under constant siege. The tractor plant looked grander than museums in Chicago. Hitler ordered all prisoners taken in commando raids be shot immediately. Were I eighteen, I probably would have been a commando, as I am adventurous and courageous, and would be shot by the SS. I stretched out on the living room like a corpse.

"Why are you just lying there like that?" Auntie came in from the kitchen carrying her cup of tea. Coffee was becoming scarce.

"I have been shot by a firing squad."

"Well, don't get blood on the Persian." Auntie moved the Sunday *Register* and made room for herself on the sofa.

I got up off the floor and picked up part of the *Register*. The battle on Guadalcanal raged on, but the Marines were holding. The death toll was astronomical. It was hard to imagine that many dead bodies. There must be piles of them. All those rotting corpses. Did the souls go to heaven? I hoped there was room. Or were they all in purgatory? "Will you join me for an evening rosary for the Marines dying on Guadalcanal?" I asked Auntie.

"I am not big on home religious services. That's the reason we have churches. Religion requires ritual, pomp, ceremony and lots of Latin. It needs theatricality to be effective. Don't you agree?" Auntie took a section of the *Register* and began reading.

She was right, of course. Father O'Tootle was greatly theatrical with sweeping gestures and intoned Latin in a deep baritone voice. I gave up on the idea of the home rosary, and from the rotogravure section cut out a photo of British soldiers huddling down around a tank near El Alamein. I cut out a photograph of a German soldier in his distinctively German helmet on the Eastern front. He was not particularly handsome, but the photographer had captured both the man's mad intensity and the fact that he was obviously weary. I cut out a photo of the Allies exploding German mines at El Alamein. The photo was not about war; it was about the balance of elements within the frame. And the variance of grays in the explosion most particularly intrigued me. I cut out a picture of an Aussie in New Guinea. There amidst the rubble stood this soldier. He had a certain swagger about him captured even in this still photo. Sometimes it wasn't about the war. Sometimes it was simply about the art of photography.

It snowed a lot in November. The Republicans won seats in both the House and Senate. The Yanks landed in North Africa. The battle on Guadalcanal raged on. Seaman Asker Neice, Eddledorf Grungedagger's helper, was killed in action in a naval battle off Guadalcanal. Astania Roms called everyone to tell them. I put on a white shirt, my black suit and polished black shoes. I knotted my black tie and went down to the kitchen where Auntie had apparently made us lunch and was taking a casserole from the oven.

"And?" Auntie asked, looking at me.

"I am off to pay my respects to Mrs. Neice."

"I don't like making condolence calls," Auntie said, "but you shall take this tuna noodle casserole with Campbell's mushroom soup and topped with crumbled potato chips with you. I will drive you but not go in, and you can walk home."

There was already the replacement gold star flag in the window. I turned the crank on the doorbell and Mrs. Neice motioned me in. "I've come to pay my respects." I handed her the Pyrex dish casserole.

After, I walked home. "You paid your respects," Auntie said as I came in. "And how did you find Mrs. Neice?"

"Somber. She said to me, 'Asker was a good boy even if he wasn't the sharpest nail in the coffin.'"

"I find the metaphor totally inappropriate," Auntie said and stifled a giggle.

"As did I, Auntie. Totally." I put my hand over my mouth to keep from laughing.

In Tunisia the French Vichy generals were switching sides and joining the Allies. Tilford and I went on Friday night to see Gene Autry in *Star Dust on the Sage*. Geraldina Lamtouse went with us and Tilford tried to feel her up and she slapped him and left and missed hearing Gene Autry's song.

We went to the Toddmans' for Thanksgiving dinner. I was also out there the day before and took pictures as Glydece Toddman whacked the head off the turkey, and took more pictures as the bird ran about the gravel drive with its head chopped off. In the Toddman living room we listened to the radio after dinner. The Soviets had launched Operation Uranus.

"Up yours, Herr Hitler," Ernie said. "Up yer anus."

"That's not nice," Glydece said. "Especially on Thanksgiving."

"But it's funny," Tilly said.

I wondered if Tilly wanted to go up mine.

We had a treat with our pumpkin pie — coffee. After we drove home, it snowed heavily. Abner T. Instern, who was retarded, came the next morning to shovel the walks and driveway.

"I need to hire a girl," Auntie said and did. Sooturn Babjak was a Slovak from up Yellow River way. She was certainly no Nancilette Nardo.

"Sooturn, you are slow," Auntie told her.

"I got As in school," Sooturn told her.

"I didn't mean slow in the head. You are just slow. It takes you hours to do the simplest chore."

"It's my pace."

"I know it's your pace. You need to pick it up."

But she didn't. She left early the second day she worked for Auntie, but had left us Spam baked with canned pineapple slices for dinner with lumpy mashed potatoes and home canned carrots. I don't know how many points canned pineapple were, but I bet it was plenty.

A couple of days later Auntie said, "The slovenly Slovak left early today. Probably because she came in late." I helped Auntie wash the dishes. After, Auntie read to me from her newspaper how Jap General Horii drowned in a retreat across the Kumusi in New Guinea.

"I bet he gurgled in the damn river. A river filled with body parts and blood and floating guts. I wish I could have taken a photograph of it. Maybe in color for greater effect."

"Sometimes you are unnecessarily gruesome, Garnie."

The American Navy took control of the sea and supply lines around Guadalcanal.

Arnst Eggledorf, who had run the Jack Sprat store, was killed in New Guinea. I dressed in a clean white shirt, my black suit and put on my newly polished black shoes. Auntie made a tuna casserole with Campbell's mushroom soup and potato chip crumbs on top. This time she added home canned peas. I went by the Jack Sprat store on my way to the Eggledorf home and was surprised to see Benevola standing near the pickle barrel.

"I've come to pay my respects." I offered her the casserole. "I did not expect to find you here at the store and was going to the house."

She put out her cigarette in the ashtray on the counter and took the casserole dish. "Life must go on. People still need to buy toilet paper. That is, if there isn't a shortage. Because of the war effort there seems to be a shortage of most things." She was somber, but not crying nor anything.

"She sounded very stoic," Auntie said when I reported on my condolence call.

Word came to Auntie from someone in New York. She didn't say who. The Germans herded all the men, women and children from the ghetto in Poland into a large barn and murdered all 888 of them. "You must invite that young Jewish boy Rupert over," Auntie told me.

The Red Army had entrapped hundreds of thousands of Germans at Stalingrad and encircled a Romanian division as well. The Greek resistance fighters in occupied Greece, with the help of the S.O.E. agents, blew up a railroad viaduct on the route that carried supplies to Rommel in North Africa. I cut out a picture of the French Fleet scuttled by Admiral Labrode at Toulon when the German Panzers barreled into the city. Three battleships, seven cruisers, sixteen submarines, along with other smaller craft, went down. The tipping angles of the ships' masts made for a particularly interesting photo. The Japs dropped supplies by air on Guadalcanal but less than a fifth of the supplies actually were said to have gotten to the Jap soldiers. There was support in Congress for a Jewish homeland in Palestine. The Yanks bombed Naples. On Christmas Eve in Algiers, Admiral Darlan, Admiral of the Fleet of the Vichy government, was murdered.

Christmas came and only Padric was there, and then Father O'Tootle came to dinner after last Mass. We had a ham, mashed potatoes, home canned peas and a sugarless apple pie Auntie Rye had concocted, which we left on our plates. The Jack Sprat had been out of olives. After dinner I played carols on the piano and we sang and then we sat by the fire. Auntie, Padric, and Father O'Tootle drank eggnog and I had some without brandy. And, perhaps because it was snowing heavily, Father O'Tootle spent the night as well, though I couldn't see how it was that big a thing to walk through the snow the few blocks to the parsonage. For Christmas Johnny and Jimmy O'Brien came home on leave in their bell bottoms, walking arm in arm from the Jefferson bus. German troops marched into Vichy France. Padric did not say that 1942 had been the best of years or that 1943 might be.

My wingy-wanger was getting as big as Tilly's and I had masses of black public hair and hair in my pits. I felt sorry for Rupert. He was Jewish and that meant being discriminated against. I was always nice to him, even when he was not nice to me. I wondered what his wingy-wanger looked like. No doubt he was circumcised, but then so was I. It was almost the Feast of the Circumcision and that seemed the weirdest holy day of obligation. I invited him over to play and thought I might ask him to show me his wingy-wanger.

"I like to ice skate," he said as he came in the house. "But why wouldn't I? I'm Dutch."

"I like to skate," I told him.

"But you're probably not as fast as me." He looked about the house. "You've got a nice enough house. Not what like my family had in The Netherlands. My Grandpere was in the diamond trade. He sewed some in my coat when he sent me to England."

"I guess the Nazis took your big house?"

"Yeah… and my parents as well. They're probably dead."

I took him to my room. He looked at my wall. "This is too much war. You're extreme. Moderation is better. Remember that."

I was beginning not to like Rupert. "What do you think of Johnny and Jimmy?" Now there, I thought, are two extreme characters.

"I think they are goddamn incestuous cocksuckers. Never seen the likes. Cocksuckers, I betcha, the pair of 'em are."

"You didn't see the cocking or anything?"

"Naw, but they kiss like a man and woman would."

"And cocksucking is a bad thing?" I asked.

"The worst goddamn thing in all the world. Cocksuckers are the most unnatural people in the entire world… the solar system, maybe the universe."

I didn't ask Rupert to see his wingy-wanger and was glad when he went home.

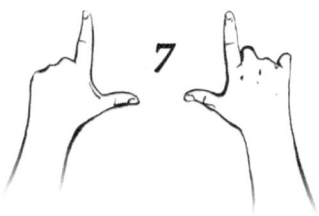

The Picture Changes

In January of '43 the *Waterloo Courier's* front-page picture was of the five Sullivan brothers killed when their ship, unnamed because of wartime security, was attacked. The little flag in the window at the Sullivans' house on a quiet street in Waterloo with five blue stars was removed and a new little flag with gold stars took its place. That picture was also in the *Courier*. There was to be a new policy against siblings serving in the same command. I wondered what would happen to the inseparable O'Brien twins. The *New York Times* had a story that $50,000 worth of cigarettes were stolen from the Army by some American truck drivers in Liverpool, England. There was no picture, but I cut the article out and put it in my Ernie Pyle scrapbook as a reminder of the horrors of war. It was a terrible act, depriving the fighting troops of their cigarettes. Soviet troops, breaking out of Stalingrad, killed or captured 140,000 Huns. I cut out a picture of Red infantrymen moving forward in heavy coats, ready to fire through the snow. It was coffee-stained; Auntie had a tendency to set her cup on the newspaper. The age of enlistment was cut to 17. Was I going to be killed, maimed, blinded, or become a war hero? There was no end in sight. The duration, as we called it, was going to be long. And I was getting older.

In February the widow Benevola Eggledorf, who was Lutheran, closed the Jack Sprat on a Saturday — the big grocery shopping day for the farmers — and went to Prairie du Chien, and in a civil ceremony married Helmer Neisson, the Chevy dealer, who was 4-F and divorced. Astania Roms called everyone in town to tell them and announced that the couple was honeymooning at the Crawford Hotel. I wondered if Helmer with the enlarged testicles was doing the thingy with Benevola in my old bed in the Versailles Suite.

I carefully cut out an excellent photo of two crouching Russian soldiers, weapons pointing down, as they crept through a debris-strewn field with billowing smoke in the background. No photographer was credited. I wondered if he was an American on the Eastern Front or a Soviet. Photographers should be credited. Another photo I cut out with equal care was of a transport plane, swastika prominently displayed, plane cut in half. Empty, bombed out buildings formed the background. Another particularly good picture was of a snakelike, endless line of Axis prisoners bundled and marching through the Russian snow. I had an idea. It was six a.m. and still dark out. I dressed and bundled in my mackintosh. Careful not to wake Auntie, I took my Leica and trudged through the snow to the dark downtown. I stood and waited, staring across at the vacant lot between the Jack Sprat and the post office. I was waiting for first light to capture the snow. It was the shot I had been thinking about. But then, just as the first light of day appeared, a figure in a heavy coat and ear-flap hat moved from the alley toward a side rear door of the post office. I caught the dark figure with a finger touch; stopped him in motion. I snapped a second shot and then he disappeared into the post office. It was serendipitous, a new word for me, this figure in my photograph. Later when I developed and printed the photo, I had more than achieved my intent. I had not just captured a scene on the Eastern Front in the two black buildings and snow-piled lot, but the dark, bundled, Soviet figure in morning light added to the authenticity of my war photograph.

"I need another cork board," I told Auntie. "I want to do my own war photographs on another wall."

"Your own war photographs?"

"Yes." I didn't explain.

"Ludwig Undercutt has been named by Roosevelt to be the new postmaster."

"Tiffy will be pissed. And who will run the finest meat cuttery 'tween Elgin and Omaha' and, if it closes, what will we do for meat?" I asked.

"Don't say 'pissed' and I doubt it will close; and besides, we get most of our meat from the Toddmans' locker anyway.

"Why Ludwig?"

"Ludwig is on the state Democratic Party Committee. I am not surprised by the appointment."

I realized Ludwig must have been the Soviet figure in my photo.

I cut photos of Churchill, Roosevelt, General DeGaulle, and General Marshall from the *Times*. They had been meeting secretly in Casablanca. I had seen the movie. I wondered if they visited Rick's Café Américain. Sometimes it was difficult to separate fact from fiction. Auntie Rye so often spouted,

"Of all the gin joints in all the towns in all the world, she walks into mine." It was one of Auntie Rye's favorite movies.

The cork arrived for my new war wall. Auntie had Ernie Toddman affix it to the space between the windows in my bedroom. I tacked up the first of my photos. There between two black buildings, perhaps burned out, in the snows of Russia, a figure stood in the early morning light. I wrote out a caption: 'Early morning on the Eastern Front.'

Auntie Rye received an anonymous gift in the mail. Wrapped in plain brown paper was a framed engraving. Actually, a copy of an engraving, as Auntie pointed out. It was an eighteenth-century noble woman.

"Who sent it?"

She examined the paper. "It was posted in New York. No return address."

"Who is she? The woman in the engraving?"

"Copy of an engraving. She is the Chevalier d'Eon."

"I thought a chevalier was a man."

"She was *le Secret du Roi*, a spy for Louis the fourteenth. She lived the first part of her life as a man and the rest as a woman. She was virulently anti-homosexual and I mean in a malignant sense."

"How can that be?"

"She wore dresses, actually developed breasts and stuck her penis, well, I'll be coarse about it, in vaginas."

"You want me to throw it in the trash?"

"No. We will hang it in the basement and you can use it for a dart board."

I was pushing a lot of red pins against the black ones. The Germans were surrounded at Stalingrad and retreating in the Caucasus, but the place names were strange, all those 'grads' and 'vsks' and 'kovs' and it was hard to find the places on the map.

The Eastern Front was very big, but so was my wingy-wang now. I pulled it out hard and big and showed it to Tilly.

"Would you look at that," Tilly said. "Just look at that."

"Yeah," I told him and whacked off until I had pumped a shot of jizz all over his pants leg.

"You stupid shit!" Tilly swore. "What's my mama going to say?"

"Tell her you spilled your ice cream cone. Vanilla."

"I never order vanilla. She knows that."

The war was going better. Auntie read to me from the *Register* over breakfast that the RAF launched their first daylight raid over Berlin with Mosquito Bombers. When we went to see Mickey Rooney in *Andy Hardy's Double Life*, the news-reel showed Field Marshal Paulus surrendering the southern half of Stalingrad. Everyone in the Roxy applauded. A British sub sank an Italian tanker near Palermo. The audience applauded again. The Japs evacuated from Guadalcanal. Everybody clapped a third time.

Several days later there was news in the *Gazette* that the Germans had lost Stalingrad completely. I moved pins. And in the days following, the Soviets advanced along the Eastern Front and drove the Germans back. All the lend-lease to the Soviets was having a positive result, an editorial in the *Times* declared. But the battle for Kharkov was a long one. The city kept going back and forth, black pins to red pins, red pins to black pins, black pins to red pins. Norwegian resistance soldiers parachuted in from England and damaged the Norsk Hydro power plant that had something to do with heavy water and atomic research, whatever that was. I had no color for the New Zealanders who were fighting the Italians in Tunisia so I had to use Aussie pins. The Aussies themselves had only had their own teal pins a few months.

"They probably won't mind," Auntie assured me.

"I know. It's just the principle."

Tilly came over and we played with the new darts Auntie had bought me and we punctured the Chevalier d'Eon until she looked like she had innumerable — a word that meant lots of — scars from the small pox.

"The trouble is," Tilly told me, "that no girl wants to let me screw her."

"You could always fuck Eleanor deLacy."

"You shouldn't say 'fuck' and I ain't fucking no cow."

"I'm going into the Marines, so I figure I need to practice saying 'fuck.'"

"Me, too. I'm gonna join the Marines. So I guess I should start practicing to say 'fuck', too. We can join the fucking Marines together, Garnie."

The USAAF bombed the Japs in the Aleutian Islands. I understood why they called it a world war; it seemed to be all over the world at once. I hoped the U.S. wasn't invaded. Roosevelt announced wage and price freezes. The Axis continued to retreat in Tunisia and I moved the pins. The slovenly Slovak took a week off and went to Chicago with little explanation. In the mail I received a surprise box of purple pins Auntie had ordered for me and I used them for the New Zealanders. An airplane carrying the Commander of the Jap fleet was shot down and Admiral Yamamoto was killed. There was a small article in the *Times* about the Jews in the Warsaw ghetto rising up against the Nazis, but no pictures and few details.

There was a night fire at the abandoned grain elevator down near the rail tracks and I grabbed my Leica and took a series of shots of the fire, including several where I lay on the ground looking up. Large numbers of planes attempting to get supplies to the Axis in Tunisia were shot down. The war was going well in the Pacific, in New Guinea, in the Aleutians, in Tunisia and on the Eastern Front, but badly for the Brits in Burma. I cut out a picture taken from a plane window of massive numbers of Axis troops surrendering in Tunisia. It reminded me of air shots of the crowds at the New York World's Fair.

It was reported that the SS took many Jews out of the Warsaw ghetto to camps away from the city. "They are dead by now," Auntie said. I developed my photos of the elevator fire and selected the best of them, the very best being the one taken when I was on my back shooting up. I tacked it up on my own war wall. The caption read 'R.A.F. blow up S.S. Headquarters in Warsaw.'

Tim Trum, the trucker, came home and I served Mass at his wedding to the white-gowned Alison Neblitz, the dry-cleaneress. The RAF dropped 2000 tons of bombs on the Ruhr. A postcard with a picture of the stockyards came from the slovenly Slovak. "Deer Garny and Rie. Meet a sailer at dance from Grate Lake. We is gitting murried and moving to Mobule Ala. It is raening hear. Wont be back. I am fine hop your the same. Miss Sooturn Babjak."

"Well if she got As in school, as she claimed," Auntie said, "it sure wasn't in spelling."

I tacked up a picture of G.I.s in the muck of Attu. But there was as much rain in Iowa, and there was massive flooding along the Illinois and the Missouri rivers. Yugoslavian resistance fighters under Tito were attacked by German, Bulgarian, and Italian forces. There was more rain and flooding along the Mississippi River now as well. Auntie Rye went to McGregor and Marquette and helped fill sand bags. The sewers backed up in McGregor and the railroad tracks along the Mississippi were torn up by the water. Prairie du Chien, too, was flooded. I took pictures of the torn-up tracks, printed and captioned them as bomb damage in the Ruhr Valley, and tacked them to the cork board. The Pope appealed for humanity in aerial bombing, but none of the countries paid much attention. Some 150,000 were said to be homeless from the floods. Auntie started a new campaign to put up an honor board, a roster of all our boys in the service. She put in a hundred dollars toward the project which was to be built on the vacant lot between the post office and the Jack Sprat.

School was out for the year. Tyrone Power became a Marine flyer. He looked so sharp in his aviator uniform. I tore off the magazine cover photo but didn't tack it up on the wall. I got a frame for it from the Ben Franklin store in Prairie and kept it on my little bed table. I went by myself to see him in *A Yank in the R.A.F.* He did it all, getting the plane to England and joining the RAF for Betty Grable. I might just join the RAF. Tilly thought Betty was a good beat-off, as he called it. I didn't give two hoots in a nut for BG. I ran home after the show forgetting all about the bombs dropping and buildings bursting into flames of the newsreel and took the picture of Tyrone Power in his uniform and held it in one hand and whacked away at my dingy-dong with the other.

Geraldina Lamtouse's father, Abner Lamtouse the third, was missing in action. "Do I make a condolence call?" I asked Auntie Rye.

"Absolutely not. No death, no condolence call. It would seem to the family as if you thought him dead. No tuna-noodle casserole, either."

Except for Tyrone Power movies I preferred the newsreels, the real stuff, to the made-up stuff. Moving pictures of the war were not like the still war tacked to my wall. The bombs dropping were much more real and the guns firing more terrifying. I wondered if I should produce movies as a career rather than still photos. I could make art films. Of course, I never saw any art films. They were mostly foreign. I read about them, like Eric Portman's *A Canterbury Tale*, but they didn't come to the Roxy.

Auntie Rye gave me a picture of the Warsaw ghetto sent to her by Madam Rodowckinski. Madam Rodowckinski wrote Auntie that on Passover, more than 2000 Waffen SS soldiers under the command of SS General Jürgen Stroop attacked the ghetto with tanks, artillery and flame throwers. Twelve hundred Jews, armed with smuggled-in pistols, rifles, a few machine guns, grenades and Molotov cocktails, fought back. I put the picture up on the wall. That was in April. But the postcard wasn't sent until June. Later in June, she wrote Auntie that the ghetto had been destroyed and that more than 56,000 Jews were killed in the process. In occupied France the Michelin tire works was blown up by resistance fighters. I cut out the picture of King George visiting the Brit troops in North Africa. He wasn't a particularly handsome man. His brother, the air-crash-dead George — there were too many Georges in that family — Duke of Kent was better looking. The Yanks had great success against the Japs in New Georgia in the Solomons.

Tires were hard to get and when the tire store in Prairie

caught fire, it made the shortage in the area greater. I took my Leica along on the following Saturday to Prairie and took close-in photos of sections of the burned-out building and the few remains of the tires, which mostly burned. After I developed and printed them, I selected the best and captioned them 'Michelin plant in France attacked by Resistance Fighters.' Massive tank battles between the Soviets and the Nazis raged in the Kursk Salient. Salient was a military term for a bulge in the line. I lined up the red and black pins around the bulge. In July the allies invaded Sicily and caught the Italians and Germans off guard. I had a picture of an American Cruiser being blown up.

"Why?" Auntie Rye asked. "Why that photo? It's depressing because it's an American vessel."

"It's not about the content. Well, content in a normal sense." I knew my voice was a shade pedantic. But at least I knew what the word pedantic meant. "It's about the structure of the photograph. The intensity of the cloud of the explosion, of the ammunition ship and the positioning of the ship and the other great cloud of smoke in the upper section of the frame."

"It's about art," she said. "That's what you are saying."

"Yes. Like the photo of the Marines on Guadalcanal over there."

"And your picture of Tyrone Power in his Marine outfit? Is that art?"

"Maybe that's pornography."

"I wouldn't allow you to have pornography."

Jap positions at Mubo in New Guinea were overrun and the Japs wiped out. I removed the orange pins from that position. Auntie examined the placement of the blue, white, green and black pins about Catania in Sicily.

"Ah, the *Teatro Massimo Bellini.*" She squeezed the tips of her fingers together in Italian fashion. "*Fantastico. Bello!*"

"You've been to Catania."

"*Sì ho e la musica è squisita.* And the opera house itself is simply *così bella.* After the war we will go to an opera at the Bellini, something very Italian. Verdi, perhaps, and at some point drive to Taormina for a dinner. There is no better food in the world."

"If it isn't all shot to hell in the war."

She said nothing about my use of the word 'hell'. "The Italians will throw in the towel before they let that happen."

"The waiter's towel at some *squisito ristorante*, perhaps."

"Precisely."

When Montgomery's eighth army moved into Tripoli, I tacked up the picture of palm trees and tanks and G.I.s. Pictures of bombed-out Hamburg made it look like there was not a window left in any building in the city. Strips of metal foil had been dropped by the RAF in the bombing and it confused the German radar.

We went to see Roz Russell as an ad exec and Fred Mac-Murray as her secretary in *Take a Letter, Darling.* "That was a silly little piece of fluff," Auntie said as we walked home in the humid night air.

"It was nominated for an Oscar."

"For cinematography," she scoffed.

"Movies would be nothing without the camera. And you should be happy we saw the Brits had secured Catania. Your opera house is safe." The newsreels had been all good news. The Soviets took Belgorod. Three Jap transports were sunk in the Solomons. Yank bombers blew up oilfields in Borneo. Again, everyone in the Roxy clapped.

The war was changing. Perhaps it would end before I was of age. Perhaps I would not be blinded, maimed or killed. There was a picture of a Lt. John F. Kennedy of Massachusetts rescuing one of his men when their PT boat was rammed off the coast of some remote atoll in the Pacific. The Brits took Taormina. I hoped they stopped for dinner. John and James, Johnny and Jimmy, O'Brien were 'killed in action in the Pacific Theater.' Astania Roms' mother, the telegrapher Hilda Roms Border, told Astania and she called everyone to tell them and the whole town probably knew before Seamus-Sean, who was never called that, but 'Hence' instead, and Nieve O'Brien, the twins' parents did. Father O'Tootle announced at Sunday Mass that on the following Saturday there would be a Requiem Memorial Mass for the O'Brien twins. Although there was no report of where they were killed, it was known it was aboard a cruiser that had not been sunk but had taken a lot of fire. I don't know how the O'Briens learned this, but that's what everyone was told by them. I suspected it was in the Solomons.

"What would Emily Post recommend, do you suppose? Two casseroles or one?" Auntie asked.

"I don't know about Emily, but I think two would be correct form."

And so Auntie made two tuna-noodle casseroles with Campbell's mushroom soup and peas, with crumpled potato chips on top. She added black olives. She had been keeping a hard-to-come-by can for a special occasion and they were pitted and she chopped them and added them to both casseroles. In my black mourning outfit I rode in the yellow Packard with the casseroles on my lap. I had to make two trips from the car with the casseroles.

"Thank your auntie twice for me," Nieve said. I offered my condolences to Nieve and Hence, who were receiving in the little front parlor with the lace curtains and doilies on every conceivable wooden and upholstered space. They had two large photos of the uniformed twins on easels. I couldn't tell which was which and, as the easels were separated, couldn't recall ever having seen the twins that far apart.

"It's not a funeral; there are no bodies," Father O'Tootle told the O'Briens in the sacristy after Sunday Mass. "A memorial, but we'll sing the Requiem Mass, just the same."

"Hence, the boys' favorite hymn was *Nearer My God to Thee*," Hence O'Brien told the priest. Hence inserted 'hence' into almost every sentence, though he didn't speak many. "Hence," Hence said, "you gotta have that hymn."

"It isn't a Catholic hymn. So we have a bit of a problem." Father turned to me. "Garnie, get Sister from the choir loft to come down here if she will, please."

I did and Sister Mary Leonardo da Vinci came into the sacristy and the priest explained the dilemma.

"I'm sorry," Sister Mary Leonardo da Vinci told the O'Briens. "I'm forbidden by the rules of the Presentation Order from playing a non-Catholic hymn in church or on consecrated grounds."

"Hence, you're saying we can't have these poor dead heroes' favorite hymn. They heard it was sung at the sinking of the Titanic and hence took a great hankering to it. Hence, Nieve and I want to honor our boys, strange as they were and we know they was strange. Hence, there ain't no argument there."

"Is there anyone else who could play it and if so, Sister, have you any objection?" Father asked the nun.

"No objection. It's just that I can't play it. Garnie could."

Sister Mary Leonardo da Vinci decided it would be best if she simply went to the Mother House in Dubuque, so Father asked me to play the organ for the Mass, not just the hymn. Nieve O'Brien took to keening during the service and sometimes it was hard to hear Father O'Tootle over her outbursts. When I was playing I simply drowned her out. The requested hymn was saved for the "grand finale." I not only played the organ but I sang the sad words of the sinking ship in a clear tenor voice. *Nearer My God to Thee.* And it was only after I finished that the tears streamed down my face. I looked up to see Sister Mary Leonardo da Vinci, who was supposed to be in Dubuque, standing there at the top of the loft. Her face was beaming as she handed me her large, white handkerchief. After I dried my eyes, she helped me pack up the music and I left the choir loft.

Rupert stood outside the church door, leaning against the church in a cocky fashion. He whispered as I went by, "Dead or not. They were a pair of incestuous cocksuckers."

I raised my arm, clenched my fist and belted him a hard one right in the nose. It bled and he whimpered.

"Garnie," Father O'Tootle came over to me. "You may sing beautifully, but this was uncalled for. This is hardly the time and place."

"It was called for and this is the time and place." I walked down the sidewalk, still angry, to where Auntie was waiting.

Rupert was holding his nose and crying, and Father O'Tootle gave him a handkerchief.

"Why?" Auntie asked and I told her.

"I should go back and give him another pop," Auntie said, but she walked me away from the church.

Fall was coming. I would be going back to Catholic school,

but Tilly was fourteen and would be going to public high school.

More pubic hair and my dingy-dong was getting wingy-wangier. I was thirteen and could proudly shoot a load of jizz up to my unruly head of hair. I went to confession. "I poked a guy in the nose — "

"I know," the priest responded.

"And I jerked off — "

"Masturbated," Father O'Tootle corrected me.

"I masturbated thirty-four times."

"Isn't that a bit excessive, Garnie? In a week's time."

"Aren't I supposed to be anonymous?"

"Yes, of course, lad."

"I think I have a hormonal imbalance." I had been reading about hormonal imbalance.

"Perhaps," the priest agreed. "Say five Hail Marys and five Our Fathers and make a good act of contrition."

General Patton arrived before the Brits in Messina. The Germans escaped to the Italian mainland. More than 100,000 Italians were taken prisoner. After unrest in Copenhagen the Germans took full control of the Danish government and declared martial law. I tacked up photos of overturned burning cars and Danish ships being scuttled. The Soviets continued pushing the Germans back on the Eastern Front and I moved a shitload — but didn't say that aloud for Auntie to hear — of black and red pins. The Allies invaded the Italian mainland with little resistance. Someone set a fire out at the scrap metal yard near the stock car racetrack in Calmer. There were no races during the duration. The metal was being collected for the war effort.

"We need to go to Calmer," I told Auntie.

"Pictures?"

"Yes."

"You are hard on my gas allocation." But I knew she didn't really mind.

"And the importance of that picture?" Auntie asked, examining the Canadian soldier examining a captured German MG 34 machine gun.

"According to the caption," I read to her, "'This weapon has a rate of fire of up to nine hundred rounds per minute; it is significantly faster firing than its Canadian army counterpart, the Bren gun.' But that's not the real reason I cut out the photo."

"And the real reason?"

"Is because that Canadian is the best-looking man in any of the photos. He is a real humdinger."

"I won't disagree," Auntie said. "But that is a rather homosexual perspective."

"True," I told her, but I did hanker after that Canadian soldier.

At the scrap yard in Calmer, a Chicago twenty and an explanation about the photographs convinced the guard to allow us in the fenced area of the still-smoldering, ruined piles of vehicles. "Arson," the guard told Auntie.

"Could it be sabotage?" I asked.

"Always the possibility, though I ain't seen any Japs or Nazis about."

I found some excellent photo possibilities amid the burned-out vehicles and got some great pictures. The printed photos chosen for my war wall were captioned 'Burning vehicles on the streets of Copenhagen.'

Sister Leonardo da Vinci and I got back to my piano

lessons. She had big feet and wore high-top black shoes which tapped away at foot pedals when she played the Hammond in the church loft. "I heard you gave Rupert a black eye."

"No, it was a bloody nose."

"Did you hurt your hand?"

"No," I assured her.

School started. Geraldina Lamtouse, whose father was still MIA, Rupert von Totten and I, as expected, comprised the eighth grade. Rupert avoided me as much as possible. I tacked up pictures of the 503rd parachuting into Nadzab to link up with the Aussies from Tsili Tsili. I found the names of these places in New Guinea weird. General Badoglio announced the Italian surrender in Rome. It meant only that Italy was now occupied by the Nazis. German glider bombs attacked Italian ships as they tried to reach Allied ports. The Germans held Rome. Geraldina was developing large tits. "Your sweater is too tight," Sister Mary Saint Wulfhilda the Abbess told her. "I know," Geraldina responded, "but because of the war effort it's hard to get new sweaters." Mussolini was rescued from the Italians in the Abruzzi Mountains by the Nazis and taken to Germany. In Peking, Chiang Kai-shek became Chinese president.

"Sometimes this map changing gets confusing," I told Auntie. "The Germans are fighting the Italians in Greece. The Soviets on the Eastern Front are advancing faster than I can move pins. In Naples, the civilians have risen up against the Nazis. What kinda pins should I use for that?"

"Maybe you should give up this obsession with the war," Auntie suggested.

Maybe she was right. I didn't think so much about death anymore. Auntie and I went to see *Cabin in the Sky*. There were a lot of Negroes in the movie. There were not only no Negroes living in our town, there were none living in the county.

Rupert came up to me at recess. "I want to talk to you." He had an abrasive — a lovely new word — way of speaking.

"Well, I don't want to talk to you."

"I am a prick." He spoke less abrasively.

I did not say, "I would like to see your prick," which I wouldn't mind, but instead said. "Yes, you are."

"I say things I don't mean. I don't have anything against cocksuckers."

"Then why did you say it?"

"Because when you are a Jew everybody picks on you because you are a Jew, so you have to find someone to make the butt, excuse the pun, of your anger and hatred. So I chose the cocksuckers."

"Well, nobody picks on you here because you're a Jew. Except maybe Sister Mary Saint Wulfhilda the Abbess, and I think she's Adolf Hitler's sister."

"But they will in time. Is she really Hitler's sister?"

"Of course not. And you're right about people picking on you. They will if you keep acting like you do."

"Forgive me, Garnie."

"Yeah, and you forgive me for popping you in the nose."

"Can we be friends?"

"Yeah," I said. Down deep I knew it would be difficult to be Rupert's friend, but somebody had to be.

I came home from school to find that Auntie Rye had been crying. "It is Lilith. She is seriously ill and has been taken to Metropolitan Hospital in Harlem."

"Are we going to New York?"

"It will have to be by train. To Chicago, and then on to New York. There's no gas for driving." She never questioned the 'we.'

The Third Marines made an amphibious landing on Bougainville. The French resistance fighters set off bombs in the Peugot factory where tank parts were made. Kiev, the capital of the Ukraine, was liberated. Auntie was having difficulty trying to get train tickets. I accidently cut off the caption of a great photograph. The palm tree was blown to bits. A bare-chested Marine squatted in the sun. There was so much light in the photo. And I couldn't identify the location. It had to be in the Pacific, but where? It was frustrating. A week went by and Auntie, despite offering amounts over posted prices and trying various Chicago travel agencies, still couldn't get train tickets. Tarawa in the Gilberts had fallen and while 1000 Marines died, only 17 of 4800 Japs were left. "Perhaps I should try chartering an airplane," Auntie said. The Italian campaign continued. Roosevelt, Churchill and Stalin met at Tehran.

In the end it was too late. A telegram came. Lilith was dead.

Auntie Rye cried and tossed the telegram down on the kitchen table. I was certain that everyone in town had learned of the contents before Auntie received it, so I picked it up and read. "LILITH DIED A.M. STOP WITH CASKET TRAIN TO BARRINGTON. STOP SENDING DATE TIME ARRIVAL STOP MILLET.

"We are going to Barrington?"

"Barrington Hills, yes."

"And I may come as well?"

"Yes. It is time. You are old enough now."

Old enough for what, I wondered.

"I will cancel Christmas. Obviously, we will be in Chicago."

She called Padric to tell him and also told Father O'Tootle. He said he would remember Lilith in his prayers. The big problem was gas. We were going to need the car. There was to be no sugarless pie. To avoid the Astania-Roms-Hilda-Roms-Border public announcement system, Auntie neither sent wires nor made long distance calls locally. We drove to Postville. I mostly sat in the car outside the telephone office or the Postville train station from which she sent telegrams. It seemed there were a lot of arrangements to be made. Ernie Toddman told her we could have some tractor gas.

So, with mostly black clothes and a trunk with cans of gasoline, we headed for Chicago. Auntie had packed many black hats.

"I hope we are not attacked by bombers," I told her as she plowed along at thirty-five miles an hour. "With all that gas we'd be blown to bits."

Despite the slow speed we drove straight through. Fetally curled up with a blanket and pillow in the backseat, I slept through much of the slow ride. I was not awake when we arrived at the gates of Field House Estate in Barrington Hills. In fact, I was still half asleep when I was led up the Gone-with-the-Wind staircase by Auntie Rye and put to bed in one of the twelve bedrooms. I awoke in the luxurious setting, somewhat alarmed. I was in my own familiar pajamas, but not in my own bed. The more I awoke, the more I realized where I was. I went to the heavily draped window, held a drape back and looked down at the stone terrace, the swimming pool frozen over. Across at the tennis court and, beyond, were probably gardens, but they were now buried beneath snow. There was a frozen pond. The outbuildings were of brick and stone, including a stable. There was a corral, but I saw no horses. Just before the woods there were cleared walks leading to a mausoleum with a tall stone cross and a stone dead Jesus hanging from it. There was a rap on my door.

"Yes."

A servant with a large crooked nose, but not a Negro as might have been appropriate to the Gone-with-the-Wind setting, came into the room. "Would you like some breakfast, sir?" He went over to the windows and pulled open the heavy drapes. He stoked the fireplace that I hadn't even really noticed before and it flamed up. Then he put little rounded biscuits of coal on it.

"Yes, please."

"Breakfast is laid in the dining room. May I bring you up some coffee, sir?"

"Yes, please."

The footman, that's how I thought of him, bowed. Footman, yes; I was feeling very country English in these surroundings. After he left I peeked about. Next to the bedroom was an adjacent sitting room with books and copies of the Chicago papers, this morning's and last night's, neatly arranged on a small lamp table. In the other direction, a heavy oak door led to a bathroom. All tiled, it was luxurious, with separate shower and tub. I took a piss then beat off thinking of the Canadian soldier even if I didn't have his pictures. My coffee arrived. I felt so English I should have asked for tea. There was milk in a pitcher and a bowl of sugar cubes.

"May I run you a bath?" the footman asked.

"I will shower," I told him.

"Very good, sir. Your clothes have been unpacked and you

will find them in the drawers or hanging in the closet. May I
lay something out for you, sir?"

"I'll be fine, thank you. What is your name?"

"Exeter."

"Exeter what?"

"Just Exeter, sir." He left. I did not make my coffee half
milk and coffee, but instead drank it with a bit of milk and
six lumps of sugar. Apparently the rich didn't worry about
rationing.

I went down the winding staircase and into the dining
room. Breakfast was in chafing dishes on a sideboard. Bright
cold morning light poured through tall windows. Auntie
Rye, in blue housecoat and seemingly quite at home, was at
the long dining room table drinking coffee and reading the
morning paper.

"It's much like having breakfast at Lady Rochester's," I said
in my British accent. "The ambience of the place so much like
her country place. What was the name of her country house?"

"I haven't a clue." Auntie never looked up from her paper.
"And you really haven't seen the ambience, have you? You have
the whole morning. You can have a good look about on your
own. At twelve-seventeen Lilith's body will arrive at the Barrington Station. We will meet her train. I think a black suit
appropriate."

After French toast, scrambled eggs, sausage, Post Toasties,
orange juice, and milk, I explored. None of the eleven other
bedrooms were as large as the suite I occupied. I thought that
strange. Auntie Rye's room, despite the array of clothing she
had brought, had no sitting room and only a bath without a
separate shower. All the bedrooms, however, had fireplaces
and telephones. The decor in each bedroom was distinct

from the others. My room was predominantly red; Auntie Rye's blue. On the same floor as the bedrooms was a nursery with children's toys that seemed both like antiques and as if they had been played with yesterday. There were two sitting rooms on the floor and a kind of sewing room with an unfinished quilt stretched across a table. A stairway led to the floor above, but I had been told not to go up there as it was where the servants lived and it would be improper.

On the sprawling main floor there were hallways and doors that seemed to go everywhere. There were several drawing rooms, another room filled with morning light that, in my best English fashion, I designated the morning room, a billiard room, a library towering with books, many leatherbound, and a music room with two grand pianos. I was sorry there was no organ. At the end of a long hall was a glass conservatory that rose two stories and some plants, trees of some sort, actually, that rose nearly to the glass ceiling. The room was furnished with white wicker chairs and tables that were a striking contrast to the green plants. Very Oscar Wilde-ish, I thought. Off the conservatory, perpendicular in one direction, was an artist's studio. This was the 'dabble room', I gathered. In the other direction there were heavy, carved wooden doors that, when opened, revealed a chapel with stained-glass windows. There was an unlit red sanctuary light. It was obviously Catholic. What intrigued me most was not the marble tiled floor, painted ceiling of biblical stories, nor the heavy wood pews, but the organ. A real pipe organ, with pipes that rose in the loft at the rear of the chapel. The console was huge and in an alcove off the sanctuary. I resisted playing it now, but knew I must. I went back out into the hallway from the conservatory. I had found no kitchen. They were cleaning up the breakfast things in the dining room; that is, several maids, a footman and a towering man with imposing shoulders who was obviously in charge, were removing the accoutrements — I dropped the 't' in my French thinking of the word.

"Sir?" I approached the imposing man.

"I am not 'sir'. Sir, I am Anderson. I am the butler." His accent was Swedish or Norwegian.

"Anderson, I can't find any kitchen."

"It is downstairs, sir." He pointed in the direction of a back hallway.

Downstairs, there were cooks and other people in white working in several kitchens. There was a laundry facility. And a room where I saw my own shoes being polished by the crooked-nose footman. "Are you a footman?" I asked.

"No, sir. I am the master's valet."

I did not need to hunt for Auntie Rye — I heard her attacking Cole Porter's *De-Lovely* on a piano and headed for the music room. She finished and turned to me. "Well?"

"Who lives here?"

"Nobody. Well, nobody but the servants."

"When's the last time anybody lived here?"

"When you and I walked out the door when you were four."

"And so just the servants live in this sprawling mansion."

"They take care of it. What servants do probably isn't living in the house the way you and I would think of it. And there are not as many as there were before the war. Some are in the military. The furniture is covered and the public rooms and bedrooms shut down when no family is in residence. So, it's been, more or less, unoccupied since nineteen-thirty-three."

"Who pays for this? My dead, missing or otherwise vanish-ed parents?"

"No, Garnie, the trust. I will explain the trust to you later. At the moment, you need to change to meet the train."

"Will I be allowed to play the organ in the chapel?"

"It is not a matter of being allowed. You can do whatever you wish in this house. It's at your command."

My polished oxfords had been returned to my room. A new black suit — a three-piecer I had never seen before — a white shirt with cuffs for cufflinks, a slightly patterned black tie, and black socks. The crooked-nosed valet entered and proceeded immediately to help me dress. No one had dressed me since Auntie Rye used to when I was little. He had large hands and I got a bit of a hard-on when he began playing around with my pants and suspenders. All this dressing me would have been awkward had I not been British and of the class where such attention was expected. He put in the cufflinks, put the vest on me, buttoned it, and slipped me into the suit coat and led me over to a full-length, hinged, free-standing mirror. It was a good fit. "You look fine, sir. I believe, yes, quite fine."

I stared at the going-on-fourteen bonny lad, as Padric might say, and thought, that's an understatement. The boy in the mirror was damned cute. No other way to put it: 'damned cute.' I went down the staircase. Exeter stood waiting with an overcoat held out for me. It was a new black coat. Wool, cashmere, perhaps. I didn't know, but it felt like fabric that should have been banned by the War Production Board. I was handed a black felt fedora. I had never worn a hat before, only caps. I realized I was growing up. A moment of panic. The war felt closer — me... maimed, blinded or killed.

The car was at the front entrance, but it was not Auntie Rye's Packard. It was a black Mercedes limousine. A uniformed driver got out and opened the door for Auntie and me. I held the fedora and felt dwarfed in that large back-seat. Despite being raised amid the British gentry, I was beginning to feel slightly intimidated by it all.

We sat there silently, as if silence was mandated by the occasion. Auntie Rye wore a small black hat with a tiny veil drawn across her forehead. Her coat was not black but a snow leopard, so she called it. I had not seen it before. I had put on the fedora as we got out of the limo. I tilted it slightly at a Sinatra-ish angle and stood immobile, posing perhaps, awaiting the train. The stationmaster stood equally immobile with a whistle in his mouth. I wished I had brought my Leica. The black hearse pulled up to the brick Barrington station and parked at the end of the platform. A woman in a red suit with no coat held a red suitcase in one hand and an open red umbrella in the other despite there being neither rain nor snow. The train, with blasting whistle and puffing steam, pulled into the station. The stationmaster blew his whistle. A conductor appeared and a Marine in dress uniform, two sailors and then the woman, quite imposing, hatless, her auburn hair brushed back by the slight wind, took the conductor's hand and stepped down. She wore a black mink coat, beneath which she wore black flaring slacks, actually a one-piece outfit, like coveralls. Behind her was a man bundled in a heavy coat with a large fur collar and a fur hat. The woman came up to us carrying only her black purse, followed by the fur-collared man.

"This is Millet Yarrow, Garnie," Auntie Rye said.

"You are quite grown-up, Garnie," she responded. "That is good. I am not particularly partial to children." She turned to the man and said to me, "Garnie, this is Prince Jablonowski."

The prince snapped his heels together in Prussian fashion and looked at me. He spoke in a heavy Polish accent. "So nice of you to have me as a guest, Gardner." Then he turned to Auntie. "Field House remains unchanged, I hope." Train porters unloaded Millet's luggage and the prince's and piled it near us. "I was with Lilith when she died," the prince said. "It was peaceful."

"That was your mama's coat," Millet said to Auntie.

"It was. And none the worse for no wear."

The limousine driver came and toted away the luggage, making several trips. "Thank you, Nestor," Millet said to him as if she had seen him only yesterday.

"And your family, Jabby?" Auntie Rye asked the prince.

"Ah… well… so many killed by Nazis, of course. A few in exile in England and how many still in Chicago, I will have to discover."

"You are wearing slacks, Millet?" Auntie asked.

"Hardly slacks. I would think with your fashion sense you would know. This is a siren suit. They are the rage."

"They don't look very siren-y to me," Auntie Rye told her.

"Not that kind of siren. No, like in air-raid siren. Something to wear over your pajamas in case you have to make a quick dash to the shelter."

"Were you afraid the train was going to be attacked?"

"The Germans wouldn't dare attack the Twentieth Century Limited. No. I wear them so lecherous men can't be trying to look up skirts and see my vaggy."

I thought, yes, as if a great many haven't already seen many of your vaggies. I looked directly at her. "You said you were not fond of children. Do you have any?"

"No. I had a child once. I lost him." It was said as if the

child had been some not-too-favorite handbag she had misplaced. I thought of Miss Prism.

So, there I stood between what I had come to assume were the vanish-ed parents: the mother in her siren suit who didn't like children, the auntie-father in his mama's snow leopard coat. At what point I realized Rye was my father I was uncertain, but it grew on me. And I had learned Millet was my mother from the bits of New York conversation and the birth announcement in the newspaper.

Black-suited men removed a bronze casket from the baggage section of the train and put it on a church truck and wheeled it off to the hearse. We followed like mourners. "What shall I call you?" I asked her as we waited for the men from the funeral home to put the coffin in the hearse.

"Millet, please. 'Miss Yarrow' would be far too formal."

I took off the fedora and got in the limo. It pulled out from the station following the hearse, which moved at a dignified pace through the Barrington downtown. *Tortilla Flat* with Spencer Tracy was playing at the Catlow. "I saw your vaginas."

"Garnie!" Auntie Rye gasped.

"I did… in exhibition."

"In New York?" Millet seemed more pleased than taken aback.

"The gallery on Seventh Street," I told her.

"Good God! Where was I?" Auntie asked.

"With Madam Rodowckinski and I've seen her vagina, or at least I saw a thicket of black pubic hair."

"Oh, God!" Auntie Rye repeated.

"He's going to be fourteen. It's time he saw some vagina," Millet said.

"I preferred the penis paintings," I told her.

"Perhaps that's genetic," Millet said.

The prince changed the subject. "I understand the archbishop will be saying the Mass."

"Yes."

The closed casket was placed on the bier in the chapel, in the aisle just before the sanctuary. A simple but large cross of white roses was set on top. I was glad the coffin was closed. While I had seen thousands of pictures of dead, sometimes mutilated bodies, I had never seen a real dead body and did not wish to see one now. Flowers arrived throughout the day. Sometimes I went to the chapel and knelt alone and prayed. Sometimes I was not alone. Auntie came to kneel and pray, as did Millet, and the prince and some of the older servants.

A Requiem Mass was sung the next day in the chapel. A choir of maybe ten and an organist accompanied Samuel Alphonsius Archbishop Stritch. His Grace had not known Lilith, but she was Negro and the archbishop was a supporter of Negro causes. And he did know the Gardiners and they were rich, very rich, and Millet said he often went out of his way to oblige the rich so that he could fund his causes: the plight of Negroes and children. He was not an old man. Before the Mass Auntie Rye had friendly conversations with him in the conservatory. The archbishop patted me on my unruly hair. "Thank you for having me in your home," he said. Millet was frowning after he put on his vestments, saying that he was too condescending to the rich, even the homosexual rich, and she thought him a hypocrite. "You are either for the church's position on homosexuality or not. Not this wishy-washy stance."

Many came through the conservatory as I stood there between my vanish-ed parents. Willa Beatrice Brown, a

Negro, was introduced to me. Millet told me after she passed through that she trained pilots for civil defense and that she'd known Lilith. There were a number of politicians there, among them Mayor Kelly of Chicago. "He's a crook," Millet said after he went by. "But I guess you have to be to be mayor of Chicago." He hadn't known Lilith. Marshall Field IV was there in his ensign's uniform. He was a handsome man and gripped my hand. He had known Lilith. "Used to play here with Rye when we were children." He had a deep pleasant voice. "I like the name of your home." He let loose of my hand. The writer Nelson Algren was there. He, like Field, used to play here as a child.

"Do you have a passion in life, Garnie? Everyone should have a passion in life."

"Photography," I told him.

"Sin is mine. Never underestimate the fun of sin." He *arrived* more than simply entered the chapel.

"I hope they don't seat him close to the mayor. Nelson is a muckraker and I think he's writing about Kelly." Prince Jablonowski, who had stood rather silently with us, said. "Algren is a Pole-bashing bastard." Auntie and I had not read him.

The chapel was packed, the organ roared, the Mass was theatrical and my favorite, the *dies irae*, was spectacular. It screamed of wrath and made my spine tingle. The elegy was delivered by Auntie Rye as a loving tribute. The mourners followed Archbishop Stritch, the acolytes and casket on the snow-cleared walk to the family mausoleum where Lilith was, in the words of the archbishop, 'put to rest.'

Later in the larger drawing room there were piles of food consumed and drinks drunk. There were cocktails of every variety. When final condolence had been spoken and the last limo and car had driven off, I sat alone with Millet and Auntie Rye in the library. The prince, or Andrzej, had gone into Chicago to meet with some Polish kin.

"If my parents don't own Field House, who does?" I asked.

Millet looked over at Auntie. It was Auntie Rye who spoke. "It belongs to you. It's yours, Garnie, but it is administered by a trust. Millet and I are the trustees. And, frankly, it is for you to decide. Do you wish to remain here? It is your house, after all, your home. Or would you rather return to Iowa?"

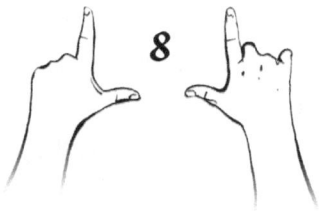

8

Different Angles

"I WOULD LIKE to go home to the Torrington House," I told them.

"And leave all this?" Millet asked.

"You did, Mother," was my reply.

"So may I assume you believe that?"

"Yes."

"Fine. But I would prefer you call me Millet."

"Yes, Millet."

"Frankly," Auntie Rye said, "I'm relieved by your decision. Your decision to return to Iowa, that is."

We had Christmas at Field House. The trees were huge. One in the grand entrance hall and another in the large drawing room. I had a plethora — I adored that word — of gifts. The decorations throughout the house were ornate and extravagant. It was hard to believe that there was a war on. Auntie Rye gave me a brochure and a voucher for a Hammond and two first-class tickets on the City of San Francisco, date and time to be established. "When the war ends," she said.

Millet gave me a baseball mitt and a bat. "You should take an interest in baseball," she said.

"I already have an interest in baseball," I replied. I did not add 'watching, not playing.'

"Are you afraid I will become a homosexual?" I asked her.

"You will be what you will be, Garnie. We all are that. Nothing more."

Archbishop Stritch's small gift was beautifully wrapped in a brocade fabric rather than paper. It was a black-beaded rosary blessed by the Holy Father. Ensign Field sent me a gift of 82 rolls of 35mm film. Nelson Algren sent me an autographed copy of his novel, *Never Come Morning*. Inside, the inscription read, "For Garnie. You'll discover the world ain't all that pretty a place, Kid. But don't die without taking in Lottie's. Nels Algren." "What's Lottie's?" I asked.

"That book is hard to come by in Chicago," Auntie Rye said. "Mayor Kelly has banned it from the Chicago public libraries."

Millet, sipping her coffee, looked sternly at me. "I am opposed to book banning naturally, but if a book has to be banned, probably *Never Come Morning* isn't a bad choice. And Lottie's is a despicable pub in Bucktown."

"Zagorski's Tavern, officially. Zagorski is Lottie, a meaner-than-hell transvestite," Auntie added.

"The place is a hangout for gangsters and crooked politicians," Millet said. The prince, who was spending Christmas in Polonia, as Auntie called it, gave me a light blue necktie with the darker blue and gold Jablonowski crest and a brown leather-bound edition of *Leaves of Grass*.

In all it was a fine enough Christmas, with a huge dinner eaten in the splendor of the dining room and snow falling beyond the beveled glass of the mullioned windows. But I missed the traditional Christmas with Padric, Father O'Tootle, and the others. I missed the apple pie nobody ever ate and lumpy mashed potatoes. And the olives were bulk olives stuffed with blue cheese, not the pimento jar olives. The truth was I missed home.

On the thirty-five-mile-an-hour drive back, Auntie and I sang songs: "Comin' in on a Wing and a Prayer," "Taking a Chance on Love," and "Pistol Packin' Mama."

"What did you think of Millet?" Auntie asked me.

"Personable."

"That's a bit cold."

"So was she. She hates children and I think she hates queers."

"You're wrong there," Auntie said.

"Why do you say that?"

"Because her constant companion is Jablonowski."

"The Prince is queer?"

"Yes, and I wish you wouldn't use that disgusting euphemism. Homosexual. Use homosexual."

"Was it Millet who sent you the copy of the Chevalier d'Eon etching?"

"It was not. I asked."

I didn't sleep much on the long drive and I was glad when we reached home. I went up to my room, looked at my walls of war and whacked off, as I now called it, looking at the photo of the Canadian soldier.

Millet wrote Auntie Rye: "I would suggest Campion Academy for Garnie."

Had I any thoughts of Campion I knew for certain I would never go now. Millet had no right to make any decisions about my life. I knew I should like her — she was my mother. And while I was happy with my life with my father and would want it no other way, I could not forgive Millet for abandoning me. I said nothing of this to Auntie Rye.

I saw Rupert out at Cowper's field at the edge of town where the ground had been flooded and frozen to make an ice rink. "This is lousy ice," he said. I didn't disagree. He skated with great speed and flair. He did whirls and jumps and leaps and skated backward.

"Hey, you are one helluva skater," I said.

"I know." But you could tell he was down in the mouth.

"What's wrong?"

"It's the O'Briens. Everything is so sad there. All they talk about are the dead twins."

Padric and Father O'Tootle came over for New Year's Eve. I invited Rupert, not that I really wanted to be with Rupert, but to cheer him up and so he wouldn't have to spend New Year's Eve at the O'Briens.

Auntie Rye popped a bottle of French Champagne. "From Garnie's stash at Field House Estate."

"Garnie has an estate?" Padric sipped his champagne and looked a bit odd.

"He does. A mansion with everything a mansion needs: stables, tennis courts, swimming pool, conservatory, chapel," Auntie told him.

"And a mausoleum. Field House is like an enormous English country house," I added in my English accent.

"Must you be fake English?" Padric sipped his champagne.

"The Blitz is getting worse. Every night, now. I mostly stay out of London."

"I bet you do." Padric could be sarcastic.

"Well, let's hope you have no need for a mausoleum for a long time to come," the priest interjected.

"All that wealth. Maybe I should be nicer to him." Padric laughed and addressed his comment to Father O'Tootle. Auntie handed him the jar of pimento-filled olives that we would have had for Christmas dinner and he poured them into a dish.

"I think huge mansions are really important," Rupert said and managed to put three olives in his mouth at once. "The most important thing in the world. To own a big mansion means you are somebody." Rupert and I each had a glass of champagne. The others had more. Midnight came and with it 1944. There were no other women to kiss, so we all awkwardly kissed Auntie Rye.

Rupert slept in my bed with me. He was nude. "I always sleep naked," he said, "even when it is as cold as shit out. And I have a great body."

He did have a nice body, although I don't know what that had to do with sleeping in the nude. I noticed also that he had a very nice wingy-wang, circumcised and all.

"I think, Garnie, that Padric and Martin are cocksuckers."

"There you go with the cocksuckers thing again."

"I don't mean there is nothing wrong with it. I'm just stating what I think."

"Father O'Tootle is a priest, Rupert, for God's sake."

"Well, I'm a Jew and I don't buy into that Catholic shit."

I knew he was probably right, but kinda thinking it and saying it — well, they were different things.

"You ever sucked a cock, Garnie?"

"Of course not," I lied. "Have you?"

"Of course not, but it might be better than beatin' off. We

should probably give a try." He threw back the sheet with
which he had covered his lower half and displayed his wingy-
wang, now very hard and good-sized. Not as big as mine, of
course, which he went on about after he saw it. "I don't know
if I can put that big thing in my mouth," he said. "You go first."

"No, you first."

"OK, both together," he said.

And so we sixty-nined, as he called it. He claimed never
to have sucked a cock before but I could tell he had. He was
very good at it. After blowing his load as well he spoke softly.
"We're not queer."

"Of course, we're not."

In the morning I showed Rupert how to throw darts and
we made more scars on poor Chevalier d'Eon. We joined
Padric, Father O'Tootle and Auntie Rye for a New Year's
morning breakfast of eggs and bacon brought back from
Field House. Four cocksuckers and an Auntie, I thought, as
I looked about the table.

"What are you smiling about?" Auntie asked.

"Just happy."

The Soviets advanced into Poland. I clipped out a photo of
ragtag Chindits who operated as special forces behind enemy
lines in Burma. But I decided to take real pictures of the real
town's war effort. I photographed the Jack Sprat ration points
signs printed and affixed to shelves of canned food. I shot
an 'out of gas until Tuesday' handwritten sign at the Sinclair.
Auntie's endeavor to have an honor board succeeded and land
had been cleared and as soon as the ground thawed the foot-
ers were to be poured. I took a picture of the cleared lot and
planned to record the work as it progressed. I photographed
the 'what to do in case of an air raid' instructions posted next

to the men's toilet in the town hall + fire department building. And inside the toilet, the sign that read 'Help our boys. Use less toilet paper.' I photographed 'Uncle Sam Needs You' and 'Buy War Bonds' posters hanging next to 'Strain and reuse your frying oil.' I finished off one of the 82 rolls with a quick shot of a sign posted outside O'Shea-Hannigan's that read: 'Sorry No Beer Today.' That was just for strangers and tourists. Hilda Rose always had beer for the locals. Auntie Rye still played euchre most Friday nights.

This would be my last year at Catholic school. In the fall I would start high school. I had this great photo of a 240 mm Howitzer of Battery B from the U.S. 697th Field Artillery Battalion ready to fire into German-held territory near Cassino, Italy. I found two chest hairs. The Germans dropped 3,000 tons of bombs on Hamburg. I whacked off, looking at the photo of the Canadian soldier. I dodged and burned my own prints just as Padric taught me. I cut out a picture of an elephant being used to load air transports to supply the garrison in Imphal India on the Burma Road.

Spring came early. The Supreme Court ruled that Negroes had the right to vote in Texas. That was in the morning *Register*. "Even so, we're never going to live in Texas," Auntie said over her morning tea. We were out of coffee. "In fact, I would not feel safe even driving through Texas." I didn't remind her that we didn't have the gas to drive to Texas, let alone across it. I went off to school. Our first prayers in the morning were for 'our boys at the front' and that the 'Holy Father not be butchered in the fall of Rome.' Sister Mary Saint Wulfhilda the Abbess, when speaking of the pontiff, 'our holy father,' would close her eyes and, in a loud reverent whisper, proclaim, "His Holiness the Pope, Bishop of Rome and Vicar of

Jesus Christ, Successor of Saint Peter, Prince of the Apostles, Supreme Pontiff of the Universal Church, Patriarch of the West, Primate of Italy, Archbishop and Metropolitan of the Roman Province, Sovereign of Vatican City, Servant of the Servants of God. May he not be butchered in the fall of Rome."

When I told Auntie of our prayers for the pontiff, she said. "That's shit. The pope's doing nothing to help the Jews."

"I didn't say anything about the Jews. You shouldn't say 'that's shit.'"

"Well, it is shit. Millions of Jews are being killed by Hitler."

"You don't know that for an absolute fact."

"I do. You do as well. That picture I gave you from Madam Rodowckinski represents only a fraction of what the Germans are really doing to the Jews. They are being taken en masse — women, men, children — to these horrible concentration camps and gassed in ovens."

Auntie had read me *The Bridge of San Luis Rey*, so when the movie came to the Roxy, we went to see it. The newsreel was about the border being heavily patrolled between Northern Ireland and Eire, as they called the regular Ireland, and the security in traveling between the two Irelands. All international phone service to Ireland was cut off. I wondered what Padric thought of it. It was to keep spies from getting information about the invasion of France that everybody talked about.

"The invasion is coming," Alison Trum the drycleaneress said and handed me Auntie Rye's paper-bagged violet suit with the large purple buttons. Then she started to cry and I didn't know what to say. Tim Trum, the trucker, was in England. Everybody in town knew that even though in his letters to Alison, which she read to everyone, he always wrote, 'I can't tell you where I'm at.'

"Eisenhower has told the resistance fighters to be ready for the invasion," Ludwig Undercutt, the postmaster, told Madame Szabolcs, the dowager, as she was called, as I waited behind her in line to pick up the mail, including the days-old *Times*. "I read it in the Gazette."

"I would have been a resistance fighter myself had I stayed," she replied in her indefinable European accent. The dowager, who had moved into the big old empty Bambard house at the very north end of town, the last house on the road out of town, was mysterious. She had moved in during March and was called the dowager because she introduced herself as such: "I am Madame Szabolcs, the dowager."

May came. There were May Day riots in Nazi-occupied areas. "It says in the *Times* that a hundred WACS were sworn in during a mass induction ceremony in Times Square. Jane Powell sang "The Star-Spangled Banner." I was reading from all the news that was fit to print, five days old.

"I should not want to be a WAC. The uniforms are so ugly."

I didn't say, 'you couldn't be a WAC,' but said instead, "Jane Powell is only fourteen. Imagine that. I'm nearly as old as Jane Powell."

"Rosie O'Neill, creator of the Kewpie doll, died." Auntie looked up from her section of the *Times*.

"That's not really newsworthy." I thought the Kewpie dolls and the comic script were stupid.

"This *is* newsworthy," Auntie said. "The *Times* is now reporting that back in nineteen-forty-three, forty-eight thousand Jews in Greece were taken by the Nazis in box cars to extermination camps in Poland. That's the word they use, 'extermination'. Finally, there is recognition of what Hitler is doing. The invasion can't come soon enough."

I thought the war must be getting better. The American Legion, according to the *Times*, was calling for a 'freedom of the air' policy after the war. 'After the war,' what a wonderful thought. Perhaps I would escape being blinded, butchered or maimed. And meat, except for steak, was removed from the ration list. Perhaps it really *was* getting better. School ended for the year, as did the necessity of praying. Tilford wanted to teach me how to throw a football. I was terrible at it. "You throw like a pussy." He kept throwing the ball at me hard, and it hurt. I kept throwing it back at him. "Pussy," he screamed and threw it hard and I got angry and threw it back and hit him hard in the stomach with it. "That's a boy," he screamed back at me. I kept throwing and he kept throwing and I learned to throw a football 'like a real man,' as Tilford put it. Later in my bedroom, as Tilford was shoving his wingy-wang in my mouth, he announced, "I'm gonna stop doing this and take up with girls." I took it out of my mouth, "Yeah, cuz they have tits," I said. All the while Pope Pius XII from a cut-out-cover of *Time* was looking down on us.

I didn't cut out as many pictures of the war now as I had. I became even less concerned about death. I tried to teach Rupert to throw a football, but he refused. "I'm not good at American sports," he said. "If I can, you can," I assured him. "I ain't fuckin' interested," he told me. "You shouldn't say fuck." "You do." "Yeah, but I'm training to be a Marine." But perhaps the war was going to end and I wouldn't have a chance to be a Marine.

"I'm glad to see you are less obsessed," Auntie told me.

But then Rome was liberated and I got out my scissors.

June 5. The first news was on the radio. The evening papers
came with pictures. And then we listened to Roosevelt's fire-
side chat. "My Friends. Yesterday, on June fourth, nineteen-
forty-four, Rome fell to American and Allied troops. The
first of the Axis capitals is now in our hands. One up and
two to go!"

I went to my room and moved pins on the map, which
I had been neglecting. But perhaps I would have given up
cutting out pictures after Rome if the next day hadn't been
D-Day. With great enthusiasm I pushed an array of colored
and white pins into France. Days later, when the Sunday
Times arrived, I cut out the cover of the magazine section:
Eisenhower and Montgomery. And then a group of soldiers
that were more walking than marching. It was the determina-
tion in their faces that the photographer had captured. There
was the picture of the gaunt children — European eyes and
such hunger in them.

My prick, as I called it now, was getting humongous.
Auntie said the cows had been invaded as well. "Cows?"

"Yes, the Channel Islands. Jersey and Guernsey."

I read in the *Times* that the funeral for Kermit Roosevelt,
the son of President Teddy Roosevelt, was held, but that he
had died a year ago in Alaska. I wondered if he had been
kept frozen for a year. I cut a nicely constructed photo of
General Omar Bradley watching the landing assault at Normandy, another of planes overhead, and another of the landing assault itself. 'Attack on Bayeux' the headline read and I
thought of pictures I had seen of the Bayeux tapestry and
the Viking ships woven in fabric. I set up my camera on the
tripod and, with the timer, took photos of my prick from various perspectives.

In *Life* and *Look* there were more pictures of the landing at Normandy. A June cover of *Time* was of four-star General Eisenhower. I cut and tacked up the magazine photos and the cover of *Time*, but the photos I had taken and developed of my prick I hid in one of my dresser drawers. The Reich capital was set afire. I cut out a picture of Major General Julian Smith and tacked him on the wall. He was the Marine commander at the battle of Tarawa.

"Why do you have his picture up there?" Tilford asked.

"Because he's a swell looking fella."

"Sometimes I think you are going to be a queer."

"Sometimes I think I am. Nothing wrong in that."

"Yes, there is."

"Why so?"

"Cuz people hate queers."

I cut and tacked up two pictures of Cherbourg. One of a dead German soldier who was said to be one of the "last stand" defenders of the city and, looking down on him, was the G.I., a Captain Earl Topley, who led one of the first outfits into Cherbourg. The other photo was of French refugees: a happy-looking woman, but the two children in the photo looked sad, as if it didn't matter that they returned to the city. It was the light that gave the photo its beauty, but I also realized it had something to do with the contrast between the woman and the children. The *Times* had an article about doughboys taking Numfor. That was somewhere in the Pacific, but I didn't know where. I went to check the *Britannica*.

Tilford again decided he didn't want to corn-hole me any longer and this time he didn't. "I am going to screw girls."

"Why?" I asked, knowing the answer.

"Cause they have big tits."

"Not all of them. Geraldine has little tits." I was ready for him this time.

"They'll get bigger."

We played tackle football, and when I tackled him I grabbed him in the crotch.

"Stop that," he ordered. "I ain't queer and you ain't goin' be a queer neither, if I have to whop it out of you."

Tilford tried to teach me to throw a baseball. There had been no pictures of the young guy in the *Times*, but there was an article about the high-school pitcher in New Orleans who received a $15,000 bonus and signed with the Red Sox. How did he escape the draft? I wondered. Tilford had two mitts and made me wear one, even though I had my own, the one Millet had given me. He threw the ball at me and I ducked. "Pussy," he called. I was worse at throwing than catching and was barely able to get the ball halfway to him. "Pussy, pussy, pussy," he kept yelling, and I kept throwing, and it took a few days, maybe a week, but I got the ball further and further and I began to catch it. "You ain't no homosexual, Garnie. You don't throw no more like a homosexual. You gots to stop taking peter up your ass or suckin' on it."

"I ain't never done that with no one else but you," I lied.

"And you ain't gonna do no others. Nor with me neither. You ain't no queer, Garnie."

After, I went to my room, looked at the photo of Tyrone Power and whacked off.

"If you are going to be starting high school in the fall, you need to learn to play another instrument," Sister Mary Leonardo da Vinci pronounced. "I think you shall take up the bassoon."

"Why the bassoon?"

"First, because I am particularly proficient at it and, secondly, I have learned that the current bassoonist just graduated, a girl named Alice something-or-another, and she is off to Iowa State Teachers College in Cedar Falls. Tell your Auntie she needs to buy a bassoon."

We, Tilford and I, began playing baseball with the other guys in town or from the country near town. Most of these guys all went to the public high school with Tilford or would be going with me as they were eighth graders. We played with Danny and Kenny K and Bob and Don and Dick Von Hunggor and Kenny M mostly. And Joe, he was the superintendent's son and he came home from camp and played. There was the handsomest player of the group, Charles, but he drove to high school in the county seat, Elkader, so that he could play football, and wouldn't be playing with us once school started. I was a big hit with the baseball players, not because of my catching or throwing abilities, but because I could hit that ball. Nobody in the group could swing a baseball bat like I could, nor send the ball sailing so far.

I tried to get Rupert to play catch. He wouldn't. "Jews don't play baseball," he said.

"Hank Greenberg. You're forgetting Hank Greenberg."

"He's an exception."

"An anomaly," I offered.

"You and your damn big words. Let's go up to your room and play with another kind of balls," he suggested.

On the Fourth of July we went to a picnic out at the Toddman farm. Ernie and Glydece never worried about meat rationing like we had to at home. And even though most rationing was over, there was still a scarcity, but not for the

Toddmans. They wanted pork? They just butchered another pig. So we feasted on barbecued pork chops and Glydece's potato salad. The Toddmans, like Auntie Rye, were avid Democrats and more leftist than most. While we ate out on the picnic table, they spent a lot of time complaining about rumors that Roosevelt was going along with the dumping of Henry Wallace as his vice president 'for this Truman fellow.'

"I ain't against the fourth term or anything," Ernie said. "We shouldn't change horses in midstream, but he shouldn't dump Wallace."

"Truman's a nobody," Auntie said, "a product of machine politics. We know we can trust Henry, and let's face it, Roosevelt isn't a well man."

Wallace was an Iowan, but it was his policies toward the Soviets that Auntie Rye both approved of and worried about. She supported maintaining good relations with the Russians after the war, but hated Stalin and thought him an anti-Semite. She spoke to them of her concern.

"You are Catholic, ain't you?" Glydece asked Auntie.

"Yes, why do you ask?"

"It's just so often you seem so concerned about the Jews. I was wondering if you had been a Jew."

"No. Though I have many Jewish friends in New York and Chicago. No, it's that all minorities need our protection. I consider myself a person of minority status…"

I thought, yeah, a minority of one.

"…and any abuse toward any minority should be considered abuse to all minorities."

"Does that mean the coloreds?" Ernie asked.

"Particularly the Negroes," Auntie responded.

"I've been to Harlem," I announced, but nobody seemed

to care. They just went on talking about Henry Wallace. So I got out my Leica and took pictures of them all. All, that is, except Tilford.

I was putting my camera in the case over by the Packard and Tilford came up to me. "You didn't take my picture," he said.

"I'll take a picture of your wiener."

"Suck on it and I'll let you."

I wanted to, but instead said, "Not in a dumpling's year." But I took the Leica and snapped a picture of Tilford sticking his tongue out at me.

Maybe I wasn't homosexual anymore, but I cut out the *Time* cover picture of Marshal Novikov because he was handsome and tacked him on the wall. By the end of July the news from France was bad. General Montgomery's drive east of Caen had come to a *halten*, as the Germans might say. Mark Clark was having better results in Italy. The Nazis were in peril in Russia. I thought of Charles and whacked off. I took pictures of the guys playing baseball, but I took special pictures of Charles when he was by himself. I took one of him when he was changing his shirt, and he caught me at it but only smiled. I didn't put it or the others of Charles on the wall. I didn't want Tilford to see. They went in the drawer.

I was now introduced to basketball. Tilford took me over to the high school gym. I loved the pungent smell of the locker room when we changed. I was not really tall enough to be a basketball player, but I soon discovered I had an affinity — lovely word — for it. Almost immediately I could out-dribble and out-shoot Tilford, who tried his damnedest to guard me. "You are really good at this, Garnie," he told me without envy. "You sure as hell ain't no goddamn queer. I'm telling you. No queer could shoot like that." He was immensely pleased and willing to play often. though I always got the better of him. Mr. Peterson, the baseball and boys' basketball coach, came in the gym one day in late summer and stood watching us.

"You're new here," he said as we took a breather.

"Yes, sir, Coach Pete," Tilford told him. "This here is my best friend Garnie and he's a real whiz at basketball… and baseball, as well. He's real manly-like and comes over from St. Ludmila's like me and will be a Bulldog come fall."

"Well, we'll see you at baseball tryouts and basketball as well, I take it."

"Yes, sir. I will be there." I stared after him. Mr. Peterson was one of those jazzy guys — built like Charles Atlas and with a deep voice that made you want to just lay down and let him stick his dong up your hole. I had seen him before, when Auntie and I had gone to the high school for baseball games, and thought him something then, but I had never seen him so close up nor talked to him before, though I guess I did very little talking. Not being homosexual was going to be a great deal more difficult with Mr. Peterson being around.

Auntie had a birthday party for me. My fourteenth. She gave me a $500 war bond and promised to teach me how to drive and let me have a party. I invited Tilford and Danny and Kenny K and Bob and Don and Kenny M and Joe and Charles. And Rupert, too, of course. And we played baseball in the backyard, everyone, that is, except Rupert. And we smoked cigarettes, Lucky Strikes that Danny had stolen from his dad's carton, and we lit up out behind the garage and we split three quarts of Hamms. Charles didn't smoke or drink. "Training for football," was all he said. Rupert didn't play ball, but he did smoke and drink.

"Sometimes I wonder about you," Auntie said after all the guys left. "Smoking and drinking. I thought I raised you better."

"To be a queer?"

"I hate that word."

But we didn't discuss it further.

I found a picture of Mr. Peterson in an old copy of the local paper, the *Leader*, and cut it out and tacked it on the wall. I could tell Tilford it was just because he was the coach. 'The great coach,' the local fans called him. So what the hell that I whacked off at the picture? Tilford didn't need to know.

Paris was liberated. DeGaulle led the parade through the streets, but German prisoners were paraded as well. And Nazi sympathizers — women had their heads shaved. I had pictures of all of it there on my wall. We celebrated the liberation of Paris. Auntie spoke French and made the best French cuisine she could muster considering the rationing and her cooking skills. Father O'Tootle came to dinner. He, too, spoke French and I added to the conversation with my limited French vocabulary. I spent the summer playing baseball, taking pictures, going on Saturdays to see Padric and playing the piano and sometimes the church organ. I practiced the bassoon, and as with everything else I did, I became more than competent at it. Auntie Rye had taken to playing duets with me. She on the piano and me on the bassoon. "We should give a recital for all our friends," Auntie suggested. I agreed, but we never did. I had dreams of inviting Mr. Peterson to the recital and then bringing him up to my room to see my wall and maybe my big wanger.

At the end of summer Madame Szabolcs, the dowager, telephoned. I'm sure all five on the party line listened in. They always did. Auntie repeated her conversation to me. "She said this is Madame Szabolcs, the dowager. Although she pronounced 'this' as 'dis' and 'is' as 'ist' and 'dowager' as 'dovager.' 'I wonder if I might call upon you on Thursday next, Miss Gardiner?'"

"I am Madame Szabolcs, the dowager," she announced in her German accent as she swooped into the living room like some giant crane and landed on the sofa without being asked to sit. "I am grossa troubled, so sorely filled with pain of exceeding heartache and I need your intercession."

Auntie served tea and petit fours which she had concocted, using corn syrup instead of sugar. Even though it was August and hot, Madame Szabolcs, the dowager, wore a red-fox wrap with heads and tails and nibbled on a petit four, which she didn't finish. "Tasty. But I have so little appetite. Herr Szabolcs, my husband Ludovic, is a Jew. There were some two hundred thousand Jews in Budapesh." She took a sip of tea. "So many Jews. So, so, so many Jews."

I sat stiffly in my chair, sipping my tea in what I thought a proper British fashion, the eyes of the foxes staring directly at me.

"You are not a Jew?" Auntie offered another petit four which was declined with a nod.

"No, I am an Aryan. It is why I am here alive and my poor Ludovic is now behind barbed wire in the ghetto, in the *shul*, in Pesh. Yet, I believe alive. The Arrow Cross, you probably know, is the Hungarian equivalent of the Nazis in the *Deutschland*. The Arrow Cross was bad enough, but we could still live in the big house in Buda. My husband's family, although Jewish, had been the von Szabolcs until the dissolution of the Hapsburg nobility. They were bankers, unlike

America where there aren't any Jewish bankers, there were many Jewish bankers in *Europe*. The Szabolcs were very rich — as Ludovic used to say, 'as rich as poodle-doodle in Paris.' I met and married my beloved Ludovic in Paris."

"You have children, Madame Szabolcs?" Auntie asked.

"None that lived and, though I mourn their premature deaths, I am relieved that all have escaped the terror of the SS. When Miklós Horthy tried to make a deal with the Soviets, with Stalin, the Nazis invaded Hungary and the Jews that had not been killed by the Arrow Cross were arrested and taken to the *shul*. My beloved Ludovic among them."

"But you were not?"

"I was. But when we arrived I was separated from Ludovic to the *frauen* gallery above and there behind the rose window sat my cousin, SS-Obersturmbannführer Adolf Eichmann. I pleaded that Ludovic and I be sent home. 'Nein,' he said and told me that 'der pestilence, der Jüdin must be exterminated and der erde cleansed.' I shrieked at him. I called him *strafverfahren und mörder* but nothing would move him. When I asked to be sent back down to be with Ludovic, Adolf tells me 'nein' and that, because of my mother, I was to be saved. He said that when he was a child and first moved to Linz with his papa, after his mother had died, that my mother bared her breasts to him and told him that 'the breasts that had nursed her children were as if they had nursed him and that he would be her child as well.' When I continued to shriek at Adolf a doctor came and an injection by needle was jabbed in my arm. I was kept heavily sedated and apart from Ludovic. I was held under guard and taken by *ausbilden* — how you say it?"

"By train," Auntie told her.

"Yes, by train to Lisbon."

"Not to Austria?" I had listened to her story with amazement.

"No. Adolf knew. He knew I would prove an annoyance and maybe even a danger to him and his high and mighty status if I was to speak of how the wife of *der Judin* banker was let go. So I was not sent to Linz nor to *der Deutschland*. In the Lisbon hospital, I was visited by an American envoy and told I would be transported to New York."

"Strange he would send you to the enemy… to the United States." Auntie offered more tea.

Madame Szabolcs, the dowager, indicated no more tea with her hands. "It was the safest place. The Americans don't seem to believe, or if they do, don't care much what is happening to the Jews in Hitler's Europe."

"How the devil did you end up in this place, in our town?"

"A Rumänish frau I met in New York."

"Madam Rodowckinski," Auntie said.

"Yes. And so I came here and bought the house at the very edge of town so that when the SS arrive I can more easily escape."

"Well, I doubt we will have to worry about the SS coming to town, but you said I might intercede for you."

"Yes, I have written out in the best English I could. I write better than I speak. I wrote out all that happened to *der Judin* in Budapesh. I need President Roosevelt to know this. You known Erzbischof, uhm Archbishop Stritch. He is a friend to the Jews and he speaks with President Roosevelt."

"I will write Archbishop Stritch and forward your document," Auntie told her.

"Danke," she said and shortly thereafter the staring eyes

of the fox disappeared and Madame Szabolcs, the dowager, drove off in her 1929 red Cord Phaeton. Auntie wrote to the archbishop.

And then the fall came. The big change came. Perhaps it was even bigger than the duration being over, which wasn't yet, of course. I started high school! I was a Bulldog, "and my ears were made of leather and they flapped in windy weather. We are Bulldogs, we are Bulldogs..." I sang that with the guys, but that wasn't all I sang. "You have a lovely voice," Miss Sanderwelt said and I joined glee club, mixed chorus, the octet and, in a short time, was singing solos.

Madame Szabolcs, the dowager, came to call again, bearing pictures from an abandoned extermination camp, Majdanek in Poland. "The U.S. government dismisses these," she said, "as Soviet propaganda. There will be more, no doubt. The world will see."

I auditioned for the band. I was lined up with the newbies. Not all were freshmen; there were public-school seventh and eighth graders there as well. Mr. Henvenderson was a graduate of Luther College, had been a Marine non-commissioned officer and a bandleader, but he had been given early release to go back to teaching. He walked like a Marine should walk and he barked like a Marine should bark and it was said he had designed new band uniforms that would be made after the duration, but they looked like Marine uniforms, at least the collars did. I only knew this from hearsay, from Don who played the cornet in the band. Another baseball player, Joe, was also in the band, but he played percussion.

"What's your name?" Mr. Henvenderson barked.

"Gardner Gardiner. I am called Garnie." I held the cased bassoon, tightly.

"Well, Garnie, perhaps I can interest you in percussion. You could start on cymbals if you can count and bang two pieces of metal together and then, in time, learn the drums."

"I play the bassoon," I told him and motioned to the case I was holding.

"The bassoon? That is a coincidence... or is it? Where did you learn to play?"

"At St. Ludmila's. Sister Mary Leonardo da Vinci taught me."

"The great nun, the *vunderkinder* of the Catholic music, the great da Vinci herself taught you? Then you must no doubt be the genius." I wasn't certain whether he was being fully satiric or a little complimentary to the Sister. "So, genius, play for me."

I uncased the bassoon, assembled the parts and put the double reed in place and brought my lips to it, woefully blowing my wind the nine feet down to the base and up and out in a Bachian dirge I had practiced for the occasion.

"Eureka," Henvenderson yelled out. "We have a bassoonist." For whatever reason, I never thought of him as Mr. Henvenderson from that moment forward. He was too large for the title; just Henvenderson seemed more appropriate. "The great da Vinci has come through for me again." I half expected him to say, 'Bless her,' but he did not. I sat through the other auditions and, admittedly, most were bad.

"Do you play any other instruments?" Henvenderson yelled at me.

"The piano and the organ," I told him.

"We will expand your musical range. You will be taught the tymps, the baritone perhaps, and maybe even the flute or the string bass." The band had a string bass, uncased, which was standing in the corner. "You have your own bassoon — it is yours and not the great da Vinci's, I assume? The school bassoon is like a piece of dog diddle and should be left on the lawn as such." The room giggled in response. "There will be no giggling at my analogies in the band room," he pronounced, but he smiled when he said it.

I assured him the instrument was my own and then packed it up, parked it and went off to Miss Swinettag and English class. From there it was typing and algebra. Typing was just typing with Miss Smiley, but algebra was elation. Mr. Peterson taught algebra and I sat gazing at him as I listened to the deep voice explain the equation. I would be *the* best for Mr. Peterson. The best at algebra as well as baseball. Then I noticed the girl, her name was Arletta Kweever, and she was staring at me the way I was staring at Mr. Peterson. Oh, shit! After class I escaped an approaching Arletta and ran home to have lunch. I went home to steaming canned tomato soup with a spoon of butter on top — despite rationing, Auntie always managed to save enough butter for tomato soup — and a tuna salad Miracle Whip sandwich. I started a full disclosure of my morning at school when I realized Auntie Rye had been crying.

"What's wrong?"

"It's Emblanci. He was killed in action." She dried her eyes on the dish towel.

I never particularly liked Mr. Emblanci. When I heard the derogatory term 'cocksucker' I thought of Mr. Emblanci through the floor register, but he was Auntie Rye's friend and I felt sorry for her and went over and put my arm around her waist. She had either gotten shorter or I had gotten taller; I realized it was the latter. That would be great for basketball.

I looked quickly at the *Des Moines Register* before heading back to school. The Soviets had liberated the abandoned extermination camps of Belzec, Sobibor, and Treblinka.

After lunch was shop and I soon discovered it was a subject not really attuned to anyone intending to practice homosexuality. I knew I would not be at home with the saws and drills and hand-sanding techniques that we were informed would be our course of instruction. I lacked the teaching and guidance of non-homosexual approaches to shop, what with Tilford not being in the class, as he was a sophomore and already involved in sophomore shop and its expert training in tractor and auto mechanics. After shop was history and physics. Mr. Peterson taught physics, but not at the freshman level, which was instead taught by the principal, Joe's father. I soon realized I probably knew more already about freshman physics than Mr. Benson, whose main insistence from that day forward was to reiterate at almost every class meeting that 'we should do one thing in life better than anyone else.'

At the end of the class sessions came the period for which I had waited all day. Tilford and Danny Swinert and Kenny Kelner and Bobby Schmidt and Don Hoovner and Kenny Mister as well as Joe Benson and Johnny Moore and Dick Von Hunggor were there in their varsity practice uniforms. I was given some gray sweats to put on. I had been warned by Tilford to bring a jock strap with a hard cup insert. Auntie had bought it for me from the Sears catalog. She was somewhat surprised by the size requirement I needed, but then added, "I always told you not to worry about your dinky dingy. Didn't I? It's all genetic." Arriving late for practice were Ronnie Lestina, Donny Drahm, Tibert O'Brien, Donald Von Hunggor and Wilson Holt. There were fifteen in all.

"Sorry, Coach Pete, Mr. Benson kept his class late," Donald Von Hunggor told him.

So there I was in sweats and my bulging hard cup, bat in hand, waiting my turn at tryout. I blasted the first and second pitches deep into left field and the third over the schoolyard fence.

"I told you, Coach Pete," Joe Benson said to Mr. Peterson, "the kid's got a bat."

I didn't do as well at throwing and catching. "Well, we'll need to give that mitt a workout, that's for fuckin' sure," Mr. Peterson said. Nobody much batted an eye when he said 'fuckin', but I had not much heard it before. Perhaps Mr. Peterson had been in the Marine Corps. Even Tilford, who planned on going into the Marine Corps, never used it that much, and he swore like a drunk pig at slaughter time.

"Yeah, we'll fuckin' need to work on that," the coach told me. "Normally, I would put you on the freshman team, but with a bat like that I need you on varsity. So you're on the team. Garnie, is it?"

"Yes, Mr. Peterson," I said.

"You call me Coach Pete, Garnie. All my guys do."

I was one of Coach Pete's guys. Tilford was all smiles. But I garnered more than smiles in the locker room. I took off the sweats and with a little fanfare removed the jock strap and the bulging hard cup. And there it hung, my mostly soft but giant dong proudly on display.

Don Hoovner just looked down on it and then pointed. "Hey, Garnie, that's one big prick. Hey, guys, get a gander. That thing hard must be as big as a stovepipe."

I only smiled.

"My God," Joe Benson said. "What horse did you steal

that off of? Wait 'til Eleanor Greatsinger gets word of it." I knew of Eleanor Greatsinger. She was the daughter of the Lutheran minister. Tilford called her 'the town pump,' and though he hadn't screwed her yet, he knew that he always could. Eleanor let everybody screw her. She was Tilford's desperate-time screw.

"What's the commotion?" Coach Pete asked, coming in the room.

"It seems, Coach Pete," Don told him, "that Garnie is hung like a horse."

"When you said he had a big bat," the coach responded, "I didn't know that was what you meant." Everybody laughed. I was pleased that the coach took a gander at the object of the conversation, but then he ordered us all to shower and to get dressed so that we could talk about the upcoming fall season. Fall baseball was played by the big high schools in the state that had both fall baseball teams and football teams and by the smaller schools that had no football. Dr. Von Hunggor called the latter "a barbarous, dangerous sport, if you can call it a sport." Others said it was only because both his sons, Don and Dick, were good at baseball but lousy at football.

"Rules first, as always," Coach Pete said in his deep voice as we gathered around. What I wouldn't give to see his dong. "No smoking until after season ends, including, we hope, all the way to Davenport for the state championship. But then no smoking for anyone on the basketball team until spring, because there's no smoking during spring baseball. No beer drinkin' until Christmas and none after New Year's. Absolutely no fuckin' and no staying up past ten o'clock on nights before games. Cut the overeating, especially fat foods, milk shakes and crap like potato chips. No tobacco chewin' during games, the state's got rules on that one, not mine, and no swearing during games, particularly don't say fuck or god-damn or refer to anybody's mother in a derogatory fashion. You travel to the out-of-town games only on the school bus and no messing about with the cheerleaders or pep band players. Any questions?"

"None, coach," Donald Von Hunggor immediately responded.

"Donald's the team captain," Tilford told me after.

Arletta Kweever sent me a note saying that if I went out with her, she would let me play with her tits. "You can nibble my niples," she scrawled. Her penmanship was terrible and her spelling atrocious — such a wonderful word.

I cut out a picture that an American news photographer had taken at the Majdanek extermination camp of 800,000 shoes.

Walter James Sass or Walter James' Ass, as some of guys called him, sat next to me in Mr. Benson's physics class. "He's queer," Tilford told me. Walter didn't look particularly queer. He was a big guy. Not muscular, just big boned, and he had an extra large head and wore extra large glasses. "I'm going to marry a girl with a name like Phoebe or Penelope or Paris-dina," he told me.

"A 'P' named girl," I suggested, trying to be amusing.

He apparently missed the humor or was simply ignoring it. "Yes. And at my wedding, I plan on serving lime Jello in a cake tin with pears set into it. They will look like wedding bells. You take pictures; you can be my photographer. The bride…" "The P-girl," I interrupted.

"Yes. She will wear a slightly off-white gown with lime

green wedding bells appliquéd on it and then overlaid with a netting of sparkling white tulle."

I thought of Jack and decided Walter James probably was a homo. For fear of labeling, I didn't much hang around with Walter James' Ass.

We practiced after school. Coach Pete put me at shortstop so I wouldn't have to throw as far. But every day at practice it was catch and throw until I thought my arm would drop off.

"You're late," Sister Mary Leonardo da Vinci said when I arrived for my lesson.

"I had baseball practice," I told her.

"I never would have thought you were the type for baseball. Sometimes the world is just not what it seems," she added rather philosophically and tousled my unruly hair. "But you must also take care of your hands. The piano relies on them, Garnie. Get out your bassoon. That first and then we'll work on your piano." She sat down at the piano and the big black high top shoes touched the pedals as she played a little Bach while I assembled and tuned the bassoon.

The first game was away at Ossian. Auntie Rye, Ernie and Glydece Toddman packed up the Packard with soda and home-smoked ham sandwiches, made by Glydece, and Auntie Rye drove to Ossian. They screamed and yelled and Kenny Kelner pitched a one-hitter and I batted in two home runs, one a bases-loaded, and they just screamed and yelled some more. I rode back on the yellow bus and Arletta Kweever passed a note up to me that I could not only play with her titties, but I could touch her 'thingy with a wet fingar.' That girl could not spell.

The band was learning Wagner's *Rienzi* overture for the spring state concert band competition. Mr. Henvenderson said that, as I read music so naturally, he wanted me to learn to play the piccolo, the string base and the timpani. He particularly needed me to learn the tymps as Margaret Ryan, the regular timpanist, seemed to miss band practice and school a lot. The day after we beat West Union in baseball at home, when Kenny pitched a two-hitter and I hit three home runs, Henvenderson pulled me aside and said "Fuck," and then "Sorry about that. It's a Marine Corps thing. Play the timpani today, Garnie."

"I've never played them before," I reminded him.

"Improvise. It doesn't matter. The baritone will have to cover for the bassoon as well."

I had no trouble hitting the damn kettledrums in perfect timing with the conducting, but Henvenderson stopped the band. "Awful. Awful. The tymps are completely flat."

"I know," I said and bent my ear to the drums trying to tune them.

After band, Arletta Kweever passed me another note written in a scrawl saying that her thingy was waiting for my wet 'fingar' and would I please, please respond to her 'urgancy'.

The Allies liberated Greece. I cut a vertical picture of the long line of German POWs that surrendered at Aachen. I was focused on baseball. I was going to be a Marine. I decided I was definitely, or almost definitely, not going to be a homosexual. I masturbated staring across at the Canadian soldier. Arletta Kweever sent me still another note, this time on yellow paper with lipstick lips smacked on it saying that if I went out with her, she would let me find her 'claitorass' with my 'fingar.'

The French captured Strasbourg. I cut out a picture from

the *New York Times* of Navy Airmen blasting a Japanese battleship near the Philippines. I was beginning to think that blasted, smoke-billowing ships made the most dramatic photographs. The ship was identified on page three as the Yamato and there was another striking photo of the ship worth clipping, as well as a photo of two handsome airmen responsible for the bombing.

Eleanor Greatsinger cornered me in the hall and pushed me against the locker and grabbed me in the crotch. She let go when Miss Smiley came around the corner. After that, whenever I saw Eleanor I ran off in the other direction. She was a junior so I had no classes with her, but she showed up enough to frighten me. I had to talk to someone and I couldn't talk to Tilford about it. He would say 'go screw her. It ain't like you are a homosexual or queer or nothing.' Padric would be the best person to help me. So I managed to escape Eleanor Greatsinger and ward off Arletta Kweever through Friday.

"We need to go to Prairie," I told Auntie on Friday when I came home from school.

"It's not the Saturday we go."

"It doesn't matter," I told her. "I need to talk to Padric."

Auntie asked no questions. She called *LaBelle de Salon Coiffeur Shampoineur Manicure-Nécessaire Pédicure* and made an appointment with Mademoiselle LaBelle.

Rupert asked me after class if he could come over on Saturday. As much as I wouldn't have minded a little cocksucking, I told him I had to go to Prairie.

"I didn't expect to see you today." Padric was waiting on an old lady carrying a yellow umbrella so large that it looked like a tractor umbrella. There had not been the least sign of rain. She tinkled out the door dragging the umbrella.

"I have a problem, Padric. I need some sage — another great word — advice from a wise man."

"Flattery is always good, lad, when seeking help. What's the problem?"

"It's woman problems."

"I may not be your best advisor when it comes to problems with women."

"In this case you are the only one I can turn to. I am not certain whether or not I want to be a homosexual, but I do know at this time that I don't want to screw pussies or play with titties and there are two girls at school that are after me. One of them, if you will excuse my language, wants to be fucked. She has a bad reputation. The guys call her the town pump and she tries to play with my prick right in the school hallway, and the other wants me to go on a date and play with her titties. What can I do, Padric?"

"Fortunately you *have* come to the right person for advice," he assured me.

"I was certain I had. What should I do?"

"You tell them you are going to be a priest."

"But that's a lie. I don't want to be a priest."

"Of course not. That's not the point. But the girls will accept that you are embracing celibacy. Girls are very keen on that. Believe me. It worked for me."

"But you became a priest."

"But it wouldn't have mattered if I had or not. They left me alone simply because I said I was going to be a priest."

"And it worked?"

"Completely."

"Thank you, Padric."

"You are welcome, my young friend. Can I get you a root beer float?"

"I think I will have a chocolate shake."

"A good choice for a would-be-priest, even a fake one. It is what Father O'Tootle usually orders."

I was beginning to think Father O'Tootle probably ordered it a lot. It was not unusual for Father Petroff to be saying Mass at St. Ludmila's and it was rumored that Father O'Tootle often said Mass at St. Gabriel's in Prairie.

We played New Hampton away. I hit no homers but drove in three runs. Kenny pitched a no-hitter.

The Battle of the Bulge raged in the Ardennes. Going into Mass, I had the misfortune of meeting Sister Mary Saint Wulfhilda the Abbess. "Bishop M'Auliffe of Hartford has died. You must pray for the soul of His Grace," she ordered. It was a wonder why he needed praying for and why he wasn't bound directly for heaven, but, then again, I didn't know the bishop. "He had been in an oxygen tent since Monday," she added, as if that perhaps was the reason for which he needed prayers. The Americans and the Philippine guerillas made big advances against the Japs. Older guys were getting drafted. We younger ones, were we to be drafted as well? Was I going to be maimed, blinded or decorated, I wondered. I would have liked to be in the Canadian army, but suspected that was not possible. I thought I was cute enough to be in the Canadian army. I pounded my big dong gazing at the Canadian soldier. The Seventh Army invaded Germany.

I met Eleanor Greatsinger in the hall, and before she could grab my crotch I said, "You mustn't. I am going to be a priest."

"That's disgusting. And it's wasteful and it's papist." That's all she said and walked away, and I don't think she ever talked to me again. She certainly never molested me. She had a beautiful alto voice and she sometimes sang with the tenors and stood not too far from me. And we were both in octet, but I don't think she ever said a word to me there either. She was a soloist at the Lutheran church, but since Catholics weren't allowed to go there, I never got to hear that.

I went up to Arletta Kweever after class. "I can't date you as much as I would like to, or play with your titties or put my wet finger in your pussy. And it is very kind of you to offer, but I am going to become a Catholic priest."

"That's all right then," she said. "I think that is most admirable. You will be a fine priest, Garnie, and not like Father Petroff who, in a sinful manner, diddles his housekeeper."

Later in the day, Tilford cornered me after basketball practice. "What's this shit about you becoming a priest?"

"It's true," I lied. "I have a vocation."

"You aren't just saying that cuz you think you're a queer?"

"No, after graduation I shall go off to seminary. I'll be going first to Loras College in Dubuque." I had worked out a whole lying scenario.

"And you're sure that ain't some big lie?"

"I could never lie to you, Tilford," I lied. I knew full well if I didn't, he would tell everyone that I wasn't really going into the priesthood and then nasty girls would always be wanting to see my big prick.

Rupert wanted to come over after school, but I had a baseball game. We played Fayette on the ballfield at Upper Iowa College and beat them. Kenny pitched a one-hitter and I hit a grand slam homer. Margaret Ryan didn't show up for school

at all. It was whispered that she was pregnant. To my cha-
grin, it was also whispered, that Coach Pete, who was married but didn't have any children, was the father of Margaret
Ryan's yet-to-be-born baby. Margaret Ryan and her mother,
Elestor, who was said to be widowed, though no one had ever
met the late Mr. Ryan, lived in the same building as the Peter-
sons. They called it the town apartment building but, in actuality, it was the old schoolhouse. Henvenderson announced
at band practice, "Margaret Ryan has had the opportunity to
take an ocean cruise and will not be back until fall."

"That's bullshit," Tilford said, putting his flute away. Tilford played the flute but not well. "There are no ocean cruises
in wartime." Of course Tilford was right. No one in their
right mind would take a cruise in possibly mined waters,
even if cruise lines were running. "She's so lucky to be on a
cruise," Arletta Kweever said. Then she smiled and waved to
me as she left the band room. I began to think Arletta was
either being clever or was really stupid.

Rupert wanted to get together and, while Coach Pete had
a firm rule about fucking girls during season, he had made
no rules against cocksucking. But the baseball tournament
play was underway and we were to be gone from school and
the town for the whole week, so I had to tell Rupert no. First,
we were at regionals in Oelwein. Auntie Rye, and Ernie and
Glydece Toddman, packed up the Packard with soda and
sandwiches, made by Glydece, and Auntie Rye drove to Oelwein. The tournament lasted two days and the team and the
Packard drove home for the night and came back the next
day for the championship game. We beat Fayette. But then
it was on to Davenport for the state finals. Auntie Rye, Ernie
and Glydece Toddman packed up the Packard with Nehi

soda and chicken salad sandwiches, made by Glydece, and Auntie Rye drove south all the way to Davenport. They used some Toddman tractor gas for the trip. They, and the team, stayed at the Blackhawk Hotel. I shared a room with Tilford.

"You can suck my dong, Garnie, if you want."

"I don't want to. I ain't queer, Tilford."

"I wouldn't a'let you anyway. I was just testing you."

I really did want to and I think he really would have let me, but I was learning just being around the guys, it was not good to be queer. You could fool around a little bit. A little grab ass was OK. Johnny Moore used to rub my butt in library occasionally and since he sat behind me in physics, sometimes I would reach back and rub the calf of his leg. But nothing much beyond that was acceptable. While most of the guys at least dated, many were also screwing their girlfriends, but it was OK that I did not. It was understood that I was going to be a priest and, as a consequence, was free from having to date or go to parties where there was a lot of petting. There weren't a lot of parties. Not with the war on. Still, the big bands played in Prairie and I went with a bunch across the river to see Tommy Dorsey. There were the team rules. And many of the guys lived on farms and had chores that had to be done and they had to get up at the crack of dawn to help with milking and the feeding of the pigs. That, and war conditions, kept going to parties to a minimum.

Madame Szabolcs, the dowager, came for tea. There had been no word of Ludovic. She looked at me as she nibbled on one of Auntie Rye's deviled eggs made with horseradish and Miracle Whip. "The Nazis exterminate homosexuals as well as Jews. They are made to wear pink triangles in the camps." I wondered how she knew all this.

"They say you're gonna be a priest." Coach Pete caught me alone in the locker room.

I hated to lie to him. "Yeah," I said.

"Should I stop saying 'fuck' around you? I'm Lutheran, so I don't know."

"Fuck, no," I said. "It's only a word."

He laughed and walked away.

We did well at the state tournament — I hit two homers — but in the end we were defeated by Davenport, the largest high school in the state of Iowa. The score was 3 to 2. I hit the homer that brought Ronnie Lestina home, but Kenny couldn't pitch that day because he had pitched back-to-back games already in the tournament and had no arm left. Wilson Holt gave up the three runs.

Fall baseball ended with the tournament. Band practice was getting intense. I was still on the kettledrums that were badly needed for the *Reinzi* overture. I pounded with flare and dramatic tosses. Rupert wanted to come over but always when I seemed to have band practice for the big state competition. The competition was to be in Mason City during spring semester. Roosevelt and Truman trounced Dewey and Bricker. Basketball practice was well underway, and though I didn't make the varsity squad, I played on the freshman team and was doing well. I was getting taller, and as Auntie Rye put it, I would probably be taller than her, but 'that was to be expected, being a man and all and having the genetic makeup.' I sincerely doubted my being a slightly different gender would make a difference in this case. Long before I knew she was my father, I came to a gradual understanding that Auntie Rye was a man in a dress. Drag, I heard it called. A drag queen. I overheard it of her, but never to my face. Only in Davenport at the Blackhawk did I hear some absolute ridicule from players on a Council Bluff's high school team. Coach Pete told them in front of their own coach to "shut the fuck up" and they did.

Tokyo was being bombarded. The Nazis were on the run. The end of 1944 was near; maybe the war was, as well. Milton Bracker wrote in the *Times* about seeing the S-shaped hooks from which prisoners were hung by their wrists before the Zyklon-B gas was pumped in the room. He wrote that it was hard to imagine it was real. But it was real and he had seen the cramped storage room with urns filled with ashes. I scored 21 points in the freshman team basketball game against Fayette. Coach Pete was pleased though he seemed distracted.

Christmas came and only Padric was there and then Father O'Tootle came to dinner after last Mass. And, after a discussion, it was decided not to ask Rupert, being that he was Jewish. It was good to go back to tradition. I didn't miss Field House. We had a smoked ham courtesy of the Toddmans, mashed potatoes, but not home-canned peas as we had eaten every jar of peas that Nancilette Nardo had canned, so we had jarred-by-Nancilette carrots instead, and while the sugarless pie Auntie Rye concocted was with home-canned peaches instead of apple, it was still left on our plates. After dinner I played carols on the piano and we sang and then we sat by the fire. Auntie, Padric and Father O'Tootle drank eggnog and I had some with just a bit of brandy. I was allowed a cigarette but declined. Smoking was forbidden by Coach Pete.

"I'm glad you don't smoke, Garnie," Auntie Rye said.

"Filthy habit," the priest added, puffing cigarette smoke from his lips.

Madame Szabolcs, the dowager, popped by with a Christmas gift — not just a bottle but a case of French Burgundy. "I cannot stay. This is a small thank you. I received a letter from the White House from Mrs. Roosevelt saying that the President was aware. 'Who can imagine the extent of the Nazis' atrocities? How can such mass inhumanity be real?' This is what Mrs. Roosevelt wrote me. And I know the reports of Colonels Kirk and Gully after visiting Natzweiler-Struthof that they find so unbelievable are only the beginning."

"Have you word of Ludovic?"

"Nothing," she said and pulled the foxes tightly and went toward the front door. "*Fröhliche Weihnachten!*" she called back and went out into the cold to her 1929 red Cord Phaeton.

"Do people hate homosexuals so much?" I asked after she had left, but the question was to none of the three in particular.

"Some people do, yes," Padric responded.

"Why?"

"People are sometimes threatened by difference."

"Yes, but fortunately not here in town, so much. Like Milbank the idiot, Carmenite the deaf girl," Auntie responded. "People accept them for what they are."

"Or like weird Elmer who screws his pig," I suggested.

"Excuse me," Padric asked. "You have a man in town who screws his pig?"

"Just a boy," the priest told him. I suspected since he probably heard Elmer Tinkler's confession, he knew best.

"Tilford said people hate queers."

"Tilford may be right," Auntie said.

"Why such concern, Garnie?" the priest asked.

"I am trying to decide whether or not to become a homosexual."

"It is perhaps not a matter of choice," Padric stated and then added, "Come show me the new photos on your wall." It was as if he wanted to discontinue further discussion of the topic.

I awoke on New Year's morning 1945 and stared at *that* wall. The entire wall was filled with photography, mostly torn from newspapers and periodicals and for what purpose? To record a war? Unlikely. Of what use? A few were objects of masturbation intensity. The rest of little value. What of my own photography? A few shots of my penis hidden in a drawer. Another few of my family, which I guess consisted of Auntie Rye, Padric and Father O'Tootle. I had lost my way, my perspective. The Leica sat there on the dresser, potentially able to capture the world, but inert and seeing nothing.

I went down to breakfast. An exciting war breakfast because it was a holiday and Auntie Rye had made a full pot of coffee and had found some eggs somewhere, I suspected from Mrs. Galwaty's 'my hens lay for you and don't cost you no ration points,' and the same went for her butter. Auntie thought it unpatriotic to buy from Mrs. Galwaty, but on occasion she made the exception. So we had buttered toast and strawberry jam that Nancilette had made and some nice bacon from the Toddmans.

Padric had stayed overnight and he came to the breakfast table looking a bit sleepy.

"I've lost my way," I told him.

Auntie Rye poured him a cup of coffee. He cooled it in the saucer and poured it back in the cup. "Padric will help you find it," she said.

"Find what?" Marty O'Tootle said, standing in the doorway looking as sleepy as Padric. I called him Marty now when we were at home, simply because both Padric and Auntie did and he didn't seem to mind.

"My life has lost direction." I dipped my strawberry-jammed toast into the wonderful runny yellow of the egg. "I have ceased to be a real photographer."

"You can become a fine musician," Marty said.

Henvenderson would have me go to Luther College or St. Olaf. I imitated Henvenderson: "You have passion and play dramatically, but you need to learn technique. You have to achieve some fucking technique."

"Garnie, your language." Auntie shook her head.

"I'm only quoting Henvenderson."

"You could try out for the major leagues," Marty suggested.

"I can bat, but I don't have the arm for it and probably never will."

"It doesn't matter," Padric said, "Garnie is a photographer. As Mr. Benson keeps telling him, 'In life you have to be better at one thing than anybody else.' And for Garnie, that's photography. I've taught him everything I can, but I'll find the answer. We'll get you focused, if you excuse the pun, Garnie."

"Eat up, everyone," Auntie Rye said. "We have to get ready for Mass."

"I'll roar over ahead. Padric, you can ride over with Garnie and Rye," the priest said. "Are you serving today, Garnie?"

"No. I'm playing the organ. Sister Mary Leonardo da Vinci had to go to Dubuque. Her father's ill."

"For a high Mass and not a requiem. That's big, Garnie. Do me proud." He got up from the table.

Padric rose as well. "We'll solve it, Garnie. We'll find the answers that get you redirected to becoming the greatest photographer."

And I was redirected. I did find answers. It was in the vision of another man, another photographer. But that was not until July of 1945.

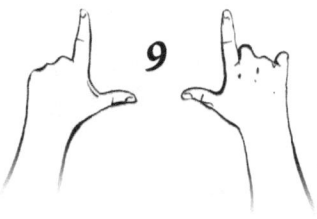

9

Art

It was the year of everything: 1945.

In January I quit moving map pins. The Soviets liberated the largest of the death camps, Auschwitz. In February on page 10 of the Times, next to a Pepsi ad, was a brief article noting that Finnish radio had reported that a German liner, the Wilhelm Gustloff, had been sunk in the Baltic; its passengers, more than 9,000 German refugees, drowned. That was a lot of dead. There had been fewer than 1500 that went down with the Titanic. But I was becoming inured to disasters and they were, after all, Germans. I made no mention of it to Auntie Rye, sitting across from me reading the front page. "Anywhere from thirty thousand to two-hundred-fifty thousand may have been killed in the firestorm bombings in Dresden," she said from behind the paper.

In February, the theatres in New York shut down because of the fuel crisis. The Big-Three: Roosevelt, Churchill, and Stalin met at Yalta in the Crimea. "The Grand Rabbi of Rome has become a Catholic," I told Auntie.

She was looking at a different section of the Times.

"Roosevelt has promised the Zionists there will be a Jewish homeland."

"Where?"

"I can only assume Palestine."

"Sabu, you remember... the Elephant Boy in the movies. He's a tail gunner in a bomber now."

"I consider the Zionist state of greater importance." She sipped her tea. We were out of coffee for the ration-coupon period. Henry Wallace was confirmed as Secretary of Commerce, but I didn't mention it to her. She didn't seem in the best of moods. De Gaulle felt snubbed that he hadn't been invited to meet with the Big Three and declined Roosevelt's invitation for a meeting. I read Auntie a story about an American soldier who found his mother and grandmother living in Manila in the only home the Japanese hadn't burned in the neighborhood. "How heartwarming," Auntie declared. I don't know why she was being so cynical. Perhaps it was because we were out of coffee.

In March, I cut out a picture of fifteen-year-old German troops on bicycles, moving against the Soviets in Hungary. I was nearly fifteen myself and was glad that the war was going well and that I wouldn't be maimed, blinded or butchered riding my Schwinn. A V2 rocket struck Farringdon Market in London killing 110. Tons of napalm and oil bombs were dumped on Tokyo, Kobe, Nagoya, and Osaka. I watched from the front room window as the 1929 red Cord Phaeton pulled up and Madame Szabolcs, the dowager, got out, dressed in bright red, the foxes probably staring at our front door as they wrapped about her shoulders. She sauntered up the walk. Auntie opened the front door.

"Ludovic is in Paris."

"How wonderful," Auntie told her and motioned her in.

The foxes stared directly at me. "Garnie, do you drive an automobile?"

"I do. Auntie taught me, but of course I am too young to have a license."

"Driving licenses are useless pieces of paper required solely as for ze purpose for the state to steal our money." The Dowager gave the foxes a flip with her hand. Their eyes jiggled.

"A fascist plot," Auntie Rye agreed. Auntie Rye didn't believe the government, any government, should have the right to prohibit or regulate driving on public thoroughfares. "South Dakota doesn't require a license."

"But who would want live in South Dakota?" Madame Szabolcs, the dowager, asked.

"There are hardly any trees," Auntie said.

"It's not the lack of trees which disturbs me," the dowager answered. "It is the provinciality of thinking there that disturbs me. Its enforced maternity is a bit like the Nazis, but I digress. Would anyone want to live in that philosophically barren place?"

"Few do," I said.

"My point, exactly. Anyway, I am off to Paris and was wondering if Garnie might drive me to Postville to catch the train for Chicago. For his kindness he may have the Phaeton."

"You mean to drive while you are gone?"

"No, Garnie, to have it. I am not coming back. Ludovic never believed the Germans capable of doing what they did. I knew Linz. It was a great city of great men — Kepler, Bruckner, Wittgenstein. It was also the childhood home of Hitler. I knew the brutal thinking of the Aryan bastards like Hitler who would let the elite SS murder his own barbarian brown shirts and sadists like Ernst Röhm when he no longer had use for them. So with foresight about the Nazi mind, I put aside a great fortune in a Swiss bank just in case, and just in case has arrived. My beloved Ludovic and I will live well in Paris."

"But you must let me pay you for the automobile, such an expensive automobile," Auntie told her.

"No, you have been most kind and the automobile is old and needs new tires."

The next day, sitting quite proudly behind the wheel of the 1929 red Cord Phaeton, I drove Madame Szabolcs, the dowager, and five suitcases and a steamer trunk to the train station in Postville. Like some European countess in a war movie, she and the piles of luggage boarded the Hiawatha. After the whistle blew, I drove off with a powerful sense of ownership. I had my own car and Auntie didn't give a shit whether I had a license or not.

There were reports of kamikaze attacks on carriers in the Pacific. Plans were underway for the invasion of Japan.

I received a letter postmarked 'McGregor.'

Dear Garnie,

When the Red Cross came to Santo Tomas they set up a table where they handed out letters. I expected to get maybe one from my mama, but instead had a pile of wonderful letters. I know this was what you did for me and it made me very happy. A G.I. gave me a chocolate bar and I threw it up. I still am not eating as well as I should but I am getting better. I am really ugly and weigh only fifty-four pounds. The train ride home from San Francisco was long and I was sick. I know you are really pretty (he had crossed out pretty and wrote beautiful instead), but if you

can stand to look at me I would like very much that you
come and see me. Bring your camera, please.
   Your very good friend,
   Robbie.

I drove my new, yet old, 1929 red Cord Phaeton to
McGregor. The trees were beginning to bud and it was a
warm day. Mrs. Bratten was a large woman with breasts like
watermelons and a voice like an operatic basso. She waddled up the steps in her large feed sack dress and I followed
behind. I saw only his head above the quilt. He was wan and
looked exceedingly frail.

"I will leave you," the basso voice said and she waddled out.

"I want you to take my picture." His voice was weak, a
hoarse whisper.

"Are you certain?"

"Yes. I must have it to always remember. Pull down the
cover."

I moved down the quilt and uncovered the naked, emaciated, bone-visible frame of the boy. I took five shots from different angles and then covered him. "Tell me about it," I said.

"People say that, but they don't really want to hear. They
ask and then they tell me how difficult it has been for them
during the war."

"I want to hear."

For an hour, in a weak voice, he told of near-starvation
months behind the barbed wire and how brutal the Japs
were even to the children. He spoke of deaths and the dead
among them. His uncle Raymond, now in St. Mary's hospital
in Rochester, often gave him his own measly maggot-infested
ration. When he finished, he said simply "You are my friend."

"I am. You should sleep now."

"Yes," he said and closed his eyes.

I bent down and kissed him on the lips, not sensually, but with fondness. He opened his eyes and smiled and I left him. The Japs were awful people.

It was the spring of the ugly coffee table. I completed my shop project, a dark stained, solid walnut 28" x 18" coffee table with angled, solid 2"-wide corner legs. It was, in Tilford's words, "fuckin' ugly."

"Isn't that a beauty," Auntie Rye said as I carried the piece of shit in the front door.

"No, it's not," I said.

"Should we put it in the living room in between the sofas?"

"No, we should not! We'll put it in the darkroom to set chemicals on."

"That would be a shame after all your hard work."

"It's where it belongs. Ugliness should be relegated to the depths of darkness."

"I will be honest, since you're so brutal about it. It's not the loveliest coffee table I have ever seen."

"Be more honest, Auntie. It is fucking ugly."

"Garnie, your language."

"Say it. It is fucking ugly."

"That would not be ladylike."

"For once, don't be ladylike. Say it."

She paused for a moment, looked at me and then loudly laughed. "It is really fucking ugly."

We both giggled and I carted the thing off to the darkroom, never to see the light of day again.

I read the *New York Times*, the *Des Moines Register*, the *Cedar Rapid Gazette*, the *Waterloo Courier*, *Time*, *Life*, *Look* and the local newspaper the *Leader*, but I cut no pictures nor added any to the wall in my bedroom. And then there was a picture I *did* cut out. It was the raising of the flag by five Marines and a Navy corpsman on Iwo Jima. The photo was credited to Joe Rosenthal of the Associated Press.

There had been no late band practice *that day*. I shall always think of it as *that day*. So I had come home from school early. I was eating a peanut butter sandwich and drinking a glass of chocolate milk. I never drank white milk. I hated it. I turned on the radio to listen to *Wilderness Road*, a CBS series about Daniel Boone. I sat on the couch half listening and then there was the voice of John Daly. "We interrupt to bring you a special bulletin from CBS world news. A press association has just announced that President Roosevelt is dead."

Auntie came in from the kitchen, wiping flour from her hands onto her apron. "No," she said. And then screamed, "*No!*" She was shaking.

"Mrs. Roosevelt," John Daly said, "has asked that Vice President Truman come to the White House."

"It should have been Henry," Auntie added and then began to sob.

We changed radio stations. Robert Trout said simply, "He died in the war."

"What will happen to us now?" Auntie didn't seem to expect an answer and I gave her none.

There was a loud rap at the door. Before Auntie had a chance to answer the door, Glydece flew in followed by Ernie, followed by Tilly.

"It should have been Henry." Glydece had obviously been crying.

"It should have been Henry," Ernie said.

"It should have been Henry," Tilly added echoing his parents, but it was said more as rote than fact.

"What's wrong with Harry Truman?" I asked.

Glydece, Ernie, and Auntie Rye glared at me. Tilly simply shrugged.

The news went on for hours and we listened. Auntie Rye fried the steaks that Ernie had brought with them and warmed Franco-American spaghetti as her culinary accompaniment, along with the saucepan-heated canned corn. Hours into the broadcast it was announced that Harry S. Truman was sworn in as the thirty-second president by Justice Harlan Stone. "I don't know what will happen to this country now, but I fear the worst," Auntie said and brought a store-bought angel food cake to the table.

"I should have brought cream for whipping," Ernie said.

"Who was to know?" Glydece asked.

"Who was to know?" Auntie repeated.

There were days of mourning. Pages of photos in the papers. The newsreels were about Roosevelt, nothing else. Mournful pictures as the train moved north from Georgia and the people lined the rail lines. It was like the pictures of when Lincoln died. Many of the faces were faces of the Negroes. People were in their Sunday best and the dirtiest of work clothes. It seemed not to matter. Many were crying, but in the newsreels the only sound seemed to be the wail of the steam engine whistle.

I played the timpani at the state concert band festival competition in Mason City. I had a strange experience. Between our preparation practice and our concert, I found a boys' room off on a side corridor and was sitting on the toilet when this guy got up from the next stall and opened the door to my stall and stood there with his hard dick. He was an old guy, maybe thirty or so. He was big, not dressed like a teacher, more like a trucker. He waved his dick at me and said, "Let me see yours." And I shook my head no but showed him anyway and he said, "That is a real big prick for such a young kid." And he told me I should come into the next booth and he would suck me off, and I said no, but I went anyway and he did and I left in a hurry afterward for fear someone would find me there. I had played the timpani with great flourish and we came in first in the competition and Henvenderson said when all the girls were out of hearing that "Fuck, we did great." And we rode the yellow school bus back home. I didn't tell Tilly about my experience. Later I thought about the cocksucker and wondered how he was just able to wander into the school that way.

At home I caught up on the news in the *Times*. One of the five Brooklyn College basketball players expelled for taking bribes to throw games wasn't even a registered student. He just carried books around and got on the basketball team. There were bad floods on the Ohio River, particularly in Cincinnati. As Allied forces moved into Heidelberg, German women and girls attacked the Americans, dropping grenades from second story windows and firing bazookas at them. "Women's rights," Auntie declared. She wasn't a woman. I wondered why she cared, but then she always cared about everyone's rights.

The Brits were building a passenger airliner that had six engines and could seat 168 daytime passengers. "You won't catch me on it," Auntie said. The Allies had taken most of Okinawa. The Russians had taken Slovakia and were moving through Austria. There were problems with Stalin over

Poland. "There will be problems with the Soviets after the war. You just wait," Auntie said.

"I thought you were pro-Soviet," I said.

"That was before; this is now. Stalin is going to cause us problems when this is all over. You'll see."

Japanese kamikazes damaged the battleship *USS New York*. The stars and stripes was raised over the site of the great Nazi rallies, the Nuremberg Stadium. It was an interesting photo in that there was a sense of failed glory in the wetness in which the disorganized Yanks moved. Mussolini and his mistress Clara Petacci were captured by partisans near Lake Como, shot and then hung by their heels in Milan where mobs mutilated the corpses. It was not a pretty picture. The U.S. Army liberated the extermination camp at Dachau. More than 30,000 inmates were freed. The BBC reported that Hamburg radio had announced that Hitler was dead. There was a wedding photo of a relatively unattractive couple, the Reverend Archie Mitchell and his wife, both were killed when a Japanese bomb from a drifting balloon fell near Lakeview, Oregon.

"Hitler is dead," I told Auntie.

"I know. How different it might all have been had it been ten years ago."

It was Monday, May 7. I was reading *A Midsummer Night's Dream* for English and the radio was on, some music, Margaret Whiting singing "There's a Tree in the Meadow" when the news broke. Actually it was more like a whisper. Unconfirmed reports, the newscaster said. German General Alfred Jodl and Admiral Hans-Georg von Friedeburg apparently signed the unconditional surrender of Germany in a railcar. Somewhere in France they surrendered to Ike.

"The war is over in Europe," I called to Auntie who was in the kitchen. "Or at least I think so."

"Well, it's not like we haven't been expecting it these last few days. F.D.R. should have lived to see it." Auntie came and stood in the doorway.

"We should celebrate."

"How? I doubt the town will be having a ticker-tape parade."

"We could drive to Chicago. I bet there will be a big celebration there tomorrow. We could take the Toddmans. Everybody in the Packard. And stay at Field House."

"And who would feed the pigs and milk the cows?"

"I guess you're right." I went back to listening to the unconfirmed reports and Auntie went back to the kitchen. "Harry Truman will be sixty-one tomorrow," I called out. "What a fine birthday present."

She called back, "Henry is younger. Would have been a much better president. Must be only around fifty-six. A much better president."

That was on Monday, and Tuesday at school there was talk about the war ending but not much celebrating. Mr. Benson reminded us the war was only half over and that the Japs had to be defeated and, in the meantime, we should think about our lives and what we wanted to do better than anyone else. Miss Smiley told us as we peered over our Royal typewriters that the war was only half over and we should remember not just our boys in the Pacific, but the women in the service as well. It was said that Miss Smiley had a friend who was a woman Marine, a major stationed in Hawaii. Mr. Henvenderson tapped his baton on his music stand, reminded us the war was only half over and had Arletta Kweever hand out new sheet music. It was the Marine Corps hymn. It was the first time we played it. I was on the tymps, of course, and we played it badly. At baseball practice Coach Peterson reminded us that the war was only half over and then yelled out, "Let's play ball," and we did. We didn't know much about the celebrations, other than what was in the Iowa papers, until we went to the see John Wayne in *Back to Bataan* at the Roxy. The newsreel showed the big celebrations in European capitals, in Miami, in New York, and in Chicago, Carson Pirie Scott had three giant flags that draped the height of the building that must have been twelve stories or more. But the biggest celebrations were in England. Churchill stood on the balcony at Buckingham Palace with the king and millions were crowded along the Mall between the palace and Trafalgar Square. I pronounced the Mall in true British fashion as Pell Mell. I wondered if I should pronounce the cigarettes that way. Perhaps not — the guys might think me affected.

"I could have taken a picture of those flags," I told Auntie as we finished off the popcorn on our walk home.

"I'm glad the Roxy has gone back to real butter. Had we gone and you'd taken the pictures you could have tacked them to your war wall and closed the war with them."

"But the war is only half over," I reminded her.

We didn't win the state baseball championships in the spring, but we did make it to the finals and were beaten by Davenport once again. Fat Field Marshal Göring was taken prisoner. The war raged on in Burma, in the Philippines, and American losses in the battle for Okinawa were staggering. Rupert came over and we talked about the extermination camps. "They're all dead," he said. "There's no way they could've lived through this."

"Your parents?"

"Yeah, and my grandfather, too."

We did a sixty-nine and Rupert said, "We ain't queer."

The war in Europe may have been over, but not all the Nazis got the message and units of the German army still continued fighting in Yugoslavia, Prussia, and Belorussia. We went to Prairie, and I to Small's Drug as usual. Padric was worried. He hadn't had a letter from Johnny Betters in a long time. Johnny was aboard a ship somewhere in the Pacific. "The Japanese will never surrender, not until they are annihilated," Padric said as he stood in his white coat filling a prescription. "The cost in American lives will be staggering."

"Prime Minister De Valera says the Irish are giving twelve million dollars in food and clothing for refugees," I told him, trying to change the subject.

"Johnny will be killed. What a waste this all is."

Heinrich Himmler was captured but committed suicide with a hidden cyanide capsule while being examined by a doctor. The war on Okinawa continued to cost heavy American casualties. Geraldina Lamtouse's father was no longer missing in action. He was liberated from a *stalag* by Yanks. The Germans, for all their atrocities, abided by the Geneva Conventions and he was not tortured, but because of food shortages when Germany began to lose the war, he had lost weight. At least this was what Astania Roms reported. Queen Wilhelmina returned to the Netherlands. B-29s destroyed the port of Yokohama.

The high school band was a concert band and, as we didn't have football, there was no marching except once a year on Memorial Day. Henvenderson said that all that 'marching band blaring destroyed the interwoven acoustical ensemble harmony.' But once a year he allowed it. I played the cymbals, as I could hardly wheel the tymps down the street. Mostly we played "Onward Christian Soldiers" repeatedly, though it was a small town and a short parade so even that wasn't too many times. The guys came over after — many were in the band — and we drank beer and played horseshoes. Tilly's folks were there and had brought a ham, and Auntie Rye had made potato salad with Miracle Whip, and Mrs. Kelner, Kenny K's mother — he didn't have a father — brought an apple pie made with real sugar. Charles, who played football and went to high school over at the county seat and whose picture I used to whack off looking at, was there. Rupert was there and wanted to know if I would like to go up to my room with him. I told him no. None of the parents seemed to object to our beer drinking. Maybe if Dr. Von Hunggor had been there, he would have objected to Don and Dick drinking. Dr. and Mrs. Von Hunggor 'didn't socialize with us' as Auntie put it. She put it down to our being Catholic and their being Lutheran. Yet Doc socialized with Ernie and he was Catholic. After it got dark, most everybody left.

"Could you drive me out to the farm?" Charles asked.

"Yes." I was excited by the idea.

So we went off in the 1929 red Cord Phaeton. He didn't live far out of town, but before we got there, he had me pull off on Garwick Road. "Turn off the engine," he said. I did. He leaned over and kissed me right on the lips with an open mouth and put my hand down on his hard prick.

I pulled away. "I ain't queer."

"Sure you are."

"No. I'm not."

"Have it your way."

We drove to the farm. He got out without speaking a word. I drove home. All I could think about was Charles. Why hadn't I let him?

The battle on Okinawa raged on. Russian soldiers who had been held prisoner by the Germans were freed by the Yanks but were returned to the Soviets, even though they begged not to go. "Why don't they want to go home?" I asked Auntie.

She held the *Times* up in front of her. "Because Stalin will have them killed for surrendering to the Germans."

"That's awful," I said.

"Stalin is an awful man. No better than Hitler."

Germany was to be divided into four occupied zones. Berlin was to be divided into four occupied zones. In the *Courier* it was reported that every Jap — man, woman and child — was being instructed in driving tanks, as paratroopers or as infantry. "It's going to be bloody," I told Auntie. I took down the map pins in Europe. There were reports of mass suicides by the Japs on Okinawa. Rupert came over to tell me he would probably be moving back to Brooklyn. There was no word on his parents or grandfather. We did the sixty-nine. The Brits liberated Rangoon. It seemed to be raining on the victory parade. I didn't cut out the picture. Ike addressed a joint session of Congress.

"Maybe there is hope," Auntie said, displaying a picture from the *Times* of Japs surrendering on Okinawa. She read that 10,755 prisoners are taken. "Maybe the invasion won't be so costly," she said.

"It will be bloody." I poured milk on my Grape Nuts.

On the Fourth of July, we went out to the Toddmans' for a picnic. We had planned on going with the Toddmans to Pike's Peak, not the one in Colorado, of course, but the one overlooking the Mississippi near McGregor, but Ernie had a sick boar. It was his most expensive hog. The pig's corkscrew-like wanger had gotten infected, and since this was the most essential part of this hog, being that its only purpose was to knock up the sows, Ernie needed to stay close to continue the medication sequence. We were having supper at the picnic table in the backyard when the phone rang. Glydece went in and took the call. "It's for you, Rye," she called out. "It's Astania Roms."

I couldn't hear Auntie on the phone, but I didn't have to. Auntie came out steaming and yelling. "That woman. 'Astania,' I asked, 'how did you know I would be at the Toddmans'?' 'Well,' she said, 'I knew that you and Glydece and Ernie and the boys would be going on that picnic to Pike's Peak. I knew after Ernie's prize boar came down with a penis infection that Ernie wouldn't be able to leave, so I knew you would stay to the farm. It was elementary, dear Watson.' Is there anything that goes on in this town that woman doesn't know?"

"Nothing," Glydece assured her.

"What did she want?" I asked.

"Georgia O'Keeffe wants me to call her. Says it's important."

"That's that artist friend of yours," Ernie said. "Use our phone. Call her. I can afford a long distance New York call."

"Well, I don't know if you would call her a friend. I don't think Georgia actually has friends, but she is an artist and she is someone I know rather well. She lives in New Mexico, but believe me, I wouldn't put any long distance call through Astania's switchboard. No, I'll drive to Postville where she can't listen in."

"What does she paint?" Glydece asked.

"Flowers," I told her.

"I like paintings of flowers."

"Not sure you would like these," Auntie told her. "And she paints animal bones, skulls and things she finds in the desert."

"My acquaintance Millet," I told them, "paints vaginas."

"Garnie," Glydece scolded. "No one uses the V word in mixed company."

"And Millet paints penises as well. Can I say penis?"

"Of course."

"It's the pee-word," I said, trying to be funny, but I don't think Glydece got it.

Auntie finished her ham and potato salad at the picnic table and I drank my Grain Belt as Tilly and I wandered off in the direction of the barn.

"You been sucking cock, Garnie?" Tilly asked.

"Hell no," I said. I didn't tell him about Rupert, and I sure as hell didn't tell him about driving Charles home and Charles telling me I was queer.

"That's good," Tilly said.

We stood there leaning against the corn shed drinking our beer. The sun was moving down in the west. There was a sense of peace in the humid warmth of the late afternoon sun. Tilly must have felt it, too. "It's just as if there ain't any war on at all," he said.

"We're going," Auntie called out to me. I wandered back up toward the car. "You're driving," she said and tossed me the keys to the Packard. "I'm too pissed."

"Like English pissed?" I asked in a Brit accent as I opened the driver's door.

"No, like angry pissed at snoopy Astania Roms."

I drove straight through town, passed our Torrington House and headed toward Postville.

"There's talk of dial telephones after the war," Auntie said.

"That won't help much with long distance." I stepped down on the accelerator as we headed out of town.

"Hey. Thirty-five," she reminded me. "Yeah, but she wouldn't have known that we were at the Toddmans."

"What does Georgia O'Keeffe want?" I had never met Georgia, of course. I had only seen her paintings.

"I doubt very much it was Georgia. I suspect she doesn't even have a phone. It's probably Mabel."

"Mabel who?"

"Mabel which, would be more to the question. She's had four husbands. First there was Evans, then Dodge, then Sterne and last, the Indian. Watch that tractor, Garnie. So now she's Mabel Luhan."

"I can see, Auntie. I'm not blind. The Indian?"

"What's a tractor doing out this late? And on a holiday? Her last and present husband, Tony. He's a Taos Pueblo of the Tiwa Tribe."

"They live in Taos?"

"They *are* Taos. Mabel was a rich girl from Buffalo who, after the death of her first husband, Evans, married the even richer Edwin Dodge. She became Queen of Firenze literary society, holding forth in her Medician Villa Curonia." And then Auntie Rye went on and on, all the way to Postville at thirty-five-miles-an-hour, about Gertie and Alice and Leo. And André Gide, Eleanora Duse, Jacques-Emile Blanche, Lord and Lady Acton, and some Indian swami. Until we arrived at the Postville telephone office.

As I sat in the Packard waiting, this guy coming in the direction of the car walked by and smiled at me. He was older, maybe in his twenties, wearing an open blue shirt so you could see his undershirt and the heavy black hair above his collar. In a couple of minutes, the guy came by again, same direction, as if he had gone around the block. I stared. He winked. And when he came by the third time, I knew it was no accident. This time he had taken off the blue shirt and was carrying it slung back over his shoulder, exposing large biceps. He sauntered slowly toward me and then came off the sidewalk and toward the driver's side of the car. At that moment Auntie flew out of the telephone office and opened the passenger side of the Packard. The man sauntered off across the street.

She was out of breath. "Home, James."

I turned the key in the ignition, my thoughts less on what Auntie had to say and more on what the guy with the heavy biceps might have said. But I asked, "Well, Mabel or Georgia?"

"Both," she said. "Georgia was at what I guess is Mabel's… whatever you call it — ranch, cluster of houses, in Taos. I really don't get it. Georgia is not political — well, not political about anything except women's issues. She has always been pissed at Eleanor for not taking a stance on the ERA."

"What's the ERA?"

"It's a constitutional amendment written by Alice Paul… my God, it must be over forty years ago, to give women equal rights with men. Georgia obsesses about it, but anything else to do with politics she won't even hear discussed. She had Charlie and Anne out to Ghost Ranch, for God's sake."

"Charlie and Anne?" I turned off the downtown street onto highways 52 and 18.

"Anne Morrow and her Nazi husband, Charles Lindbergh."

"Charles Lindbergh is not a Nazi. I read in the *Times* that he is flying raids with the Air Corps in the Pacific."

"Who for, the Luftwaffe?"

"Hitler's dead," I reminded her. "So what's politics got to do with the phone call?"

"Sometimes when I get tense like this," she said, "I wish I smoked."

"Calm down." I thought I was the one who ought to have to calm down after that guy in the blue shirt, and I was wondering what might have happened if Auntie hadn't come out of the telephone office when she did. "So?"

"We are going to New Mexico." She said it without explanation.

"Flying? Taking the train? And why do we want to go to New Mexico?"

"I'm not sure *wanting to go* is the way I would put it. It's more an obligation to go and we will be driving."

"Driving all the way to New Mexico? With gas rationing? At thirty-five-miles-an-hour?"

"Yes." She seemed to be thinking aloud. "We can get gas from Ernie, though I can't tell him why we are going. As for thirty-five, well, we might cheat on that a bit driving through Kansas. And we can take turns driving."

"You've driven through Kansas?"

"No, but I can imagine what it must be like. You've seen the photographs of the Dust Bowl. There's that damn tractor again. He isn't making very good time. We'll need the Packard."

"It's a tractor for God's sake." I really didn't want to go to New Mexico and I certainly didn't want to drive across Kansas. It was dry. And not just the air. "You can't even buy a beer in Kansas. Is this some Communist picture-taking thing?"

"You're too young to buy beer anyway. No, it's not a

Communist thing. You know I hate Stalin. But it *is* a picture thing." She paused and looked out the window. Soon it would be dark, but now the late afternoon sky was mostly blue above the rows of the corn not yet knee-high, the green pastures with meandering cows and the still green oat fields. "Have you ever heard of Dr. J. Robert Oppenheimer?"

"Yes, I have been reading about him and his theories. He's made Berkeley what Cambridge was in physics. He went to Cambridge, actually. There he met Bohr, Rutherford, and the others."

"And why are you reading about Oppenheimer and from where did you get the reading material to learn all this?"

"I'm trying to understand quantum physics. When I told Padric, he got the books for me to read from the Campion library. And Marty's been helping me." I no longer thought of him as Father O'Tootle. "He's pretty good at explaining the complexities."

"And what is quantum physics?"

I attempted to explain, but because it was so mathematical it was difficult to comprehend and certainly impossible to explain in non-mathematical terms. "Quantum theory projects the possibility of simultaneity."

"It all sounds like something out of Gurdjieff to me."

"What is Gurdjieff?"

"Not a *what*, but a *who*. A Russian philosopher. More of an occultist."

"No. Not the occult," I said. "This is science. Oppenheimer is also involved in research on stars and the idea of gravitational collapse."

"Sounds even more occultish. His brother Frank needs you to take some pictures for him in New Mexico."

"Dr. Oppenheimer's brother needs me to take some pictures for him?"

"Yes. Well, he's also a Dr. Oppenheimer. Apparently they are both involved in a top-secret weapons project. He and a group of scientists are working on what Georgia and Mabel call a 'gadget.'"

"And they want me to take a picture of the gadget?"

"I would think not. There is a sharp turn up ahead."

"I know there's a turn up ahead." I slowed for the turn. "So what am I to take pictures of?"

She ignored my question. "When Mabel was entertaining the likes of Lord and Lady Acton and the great Duse in Florence, she used to dress like Catherine de Medici and decorated her palace as if she was living in sixteenth-century Italy. When I saw her in New Mexico, she was decked out like an Indian. And her husband squatted at the front door and played a drum and chanted."

"The Renaissance," I said, pronouncing it very British. Though I had mostly given up the affectation because of the guys, there were moments and words which I could not resist. "You were there in Florence?"

"Hardly, no, this was before the Great War. I was far too young."

"The war to end all wars."

"Precisely. It was Mabel's practice, I suppose, for Greenwich Village."

"But you've been to New Mexico?"

"Yes, anybody who was anybody was a guest of Mabel's at Taos. But I really wasn't much of an anybody so I wasn't welcomed very long. And to be honest, I was glad to get out of there."

"Yet you are going back." But she didn't have time to respond as I turned into the driveway of the Torrington House. It was already getting dark. We spent the evening packing. Well, I did. Auntie Rye spent the evening packing, unpacking, repacking, unpacking and re-repacking. "One can't take everything. It's all about decisions," she said.

Or indecision, but I didn't say it.

She called Ernie to ask about the gas, but because of Astania Roms she couldn't ask outright. "Ernie, I really need some jars of canned beef, the canned beef in oil."

I couldn't hear Ernie's response, but he must have caught on right away because then Auntie said, "We are going on a picnic. It's a really long table and needs a lot of food. I thought maybe four jars of beef."

I slept fitfully. I kept wondering if Astania Roms was sleeping fitfully as well, puzzling over the strange conversation between Auntie Rye and Ernie.

We put our suitcases in the backseat to leave room in the trunk for the gas cans and then stopped to fill up at the Sinclair. Marabeline Neisson, the divorced wife of Helmer Neisson, the Chevy dealer, who was 4-F and married to the widow Benevola Eggledorf, who was Lutheran and ran the Jack Sprat, managed the pumps and did oil changes and lube jobs while Sleazy Slim was away in the army.

"Marabeline, I forgot my ration book," Auntie lied. "Will you trust me for the coupons until I get back?"

"You're taking a trip then?" Marabeline's bib overalls were greasy. She wiped the windshield.

"Just a little jaunt." Auntie smiled and Marabeline pumped and the gas rose up a reddish gold into the glass bottle. "Would you check the radiator?"

"Certainly. You can't be too careful in this heat." Marabeline stopped to peer into the backseat as she moved to the front of the Packard. "Lots of suitcases for just a jaunt."

"You know me, Marabeline. Can't go around the corner without needing a change of ensemble." Auntie didn't pronounce the 'ble.' "Always prepared."

Marabeline removed the radiator cap with a rag. "No, you can't be too careful in this heat."

Or Kansas heat. But I kept my mouth shut. I had the Iowa Sinclair map and was the navigator. We drove south out of town on 18, stopping briefly at the Toddmans'. Glydece was there on the porch when we pulled up. Their dog Butt was sleeping near the empty porch rocker. Butt was the only dog I had ever seen masturbate and Ernie took great pride in the achievement as Butt rubbed his pink prick against the porch floor and grunted.

"Don't know what's the matter with Butt this morning. He usually goes out with Ernie." She explained that Ernie and Tilly were out making hay in the west field. I put the cans of gas Ernie had set aside for us in the trunk. "Where?" Glydece asked.

"New Mexico," Auntie told her.

"The artist friend. New Mexico must be the hottest place on earth. Buy a water bag." Glydece gave Auntie a hug and we were out of there back on 18. "What am I going to take pictures of in New Mexico for Dr. Oppenheimer?" Auntie didn't respond and appeared to be concentrating on her driving as she turned off 18 onto route 13 toward Elkader. As we drove through the county seat, I thought of the dead Mr. Emblanci, who had given his life for his country, but I made no mention of him to Auntie. She drove around fifty-miles-an-hour except when we were going through towns, not that it would have mattered much. The state troopers certainly never paid much mind to the state highways and nobody paid much attention to town driving. Strawberry Point was the only town between Elkader and Manchester. "Why do you suppose it's called Strawberry Point?" I asked. The answer was a shrug. Even mostly going fifty miles an hour it took us well over an hour to reach Manchester. We slowed and stopped and Auntie went to the state store and bought a bottle of Scotch and sweet vermouth to make Rob Roys. We went to a local saloon and she picked up a case of Grain Belt.

"I asked if they had any ice," she told me as I loaded the beer case into the trunk with the gasoline. "He told me there was an ice plant in Marion."

I drove. "Why does O'Keeffe live in New Mexico and Stieglitz in New York?"

"You think married people have to live together?"

"No," I said. I thought of my own parents. They certainly didn't live together. "It's just that Stieglitz seemed so sad without her."

"Georgia is Georgia."

"But I wonder why Stieglitz lets her?"

"*Lets* her? Do you think Georgia has to have his permission to live and work where she wants?"

"She is his wife."

"Maybe you're not a misogynist, but sometimes you are terribly provincial."

I did not wish to be thought a misogynist nor provincial. I drove on, not pouting but silent, mulling it over. I was a child of the world. I had been raised to be a child of the world. I knew married people didn't have to live together and that a woman and man could live together, sleep together, without getting married, that men could and did have sex with men, even priests had sex, and that sometimes men pretended to be women. I accepted this because I was, I realized, so cosmopolitan in my approach to life. Yes, my view of life was, well, European. Maybe I had never been to England, but I was still very British and would be going to Oxford. Or was I going in the Marine Corps? I kept on 13 through Ryan; it was a rather pass-through place and I barely slowed down. When we reached Marion and found the ice plant, there was a sign on the gate that said they were out of ice for the season, but that there was electric-made ice in Cedar Rapids and an address was scribbled on the paper. I got out of the driver's seat, grabbed my Leica from the back and took a picture of the sign against the background of chain link and a weathered building.

"Why?" Auntie walked around to the driver's side.

"The ice plant as we know it is a dying enterprise. All ice will be made electrically." I got back in the car and put the lens cap back on. "Henri Cartier-Bresson says that intuitively you must capture the moment. Once you have missed it, it is gone."

"And you know what he said how?"

"Padric told me."

"Cartier-Bresson was a surrealist painter before he was a photographer."

"I suppose you knew him in France as well."

"Actually, I didn't," she admitted. "Direct me to this ice plant."

I took out the Sinclair map that had a little box of Cedar Rapids city streets and directed Auntie Rye to what I thought was going to be an ice plant. It was a Standard Oil gas station with an ice machine and I took a picture of the ice machine. They also sold bright red metal portable ice chests and Auntie bought one in which I put the ice. The chest matched the color of the gas cans in the trunk. Auntie drove through Cedar Rapids, which was awash in smells: Penick Ford, Quaker Oats, and the worst — Wilson's Meat packing plant with its odiferous tannery. We managed to drive close by all three on our way southwest out of town.

It was around noon when we reached Amana. The Amananites had been a communal people and though they no longer took their meals that way, at the Ox Yoke they laid out a noon table for the customers as a communal spread. They seemed not to be bothered about rationing. There was a baked steak and what they called Kessler Rippchen, which was pork chops with applesauce, and also roasted chicken. There were bowls of mashed potatoes, gravy, carrots, beets, peas, spätzle, potato pancakes, hot German potato salad, and turnips. At our table, sitting opposite us, was a newly-wed couple. They didn't tell us. Didn't have to. They were all coochie-cooey. He had the tiniest of noses and she the largest of ears. Further down the table were a middle-aged couple and their three high school-aged kids. The kids were particularly loud and gluttonous and told us they were from New Jersey. They didn't have to; you could tell by the accents. "We are going to visit our son at Fort Leavenworth," the mother said. I hoped it was the military post and not the prison.

As any bowl was emptied, the serving women, all looking well-fed themselves, immediately replaced the bowl with a steaming full one. I offered to try the Millstream beer and was told by Auntie I could have the cream or black cherry soda 'and enjoy it.' The loud family asked if I would take their picture at the table and handed me a brownie. Ugh! The mother was quite beautiful. The husband ugly. I wondered why she had married him. Maybe he had lots of money. They had to have had some to be able to drive their big Caddie all the way from New Jersey.

I took several pictures of the Ox Yoke before Auntie drove us back onto route 151 headed south. I wondered if the marriage would last between the man with the tiniest of noses and the woman with the biggest of ears. I wished I had taken their picture. I got out Auntie's Iowa tour book. It was a little frayed. "Are we going to see the capitol building in Des Moines?"

"I was thinking if we stayed east and then drove south, we could miss the city and the traffic."

"I've never seen a gold dome before," I told her.

"You saw the gold dome at Notre Dame. If you've seen one gold dome you've seen them all."

"I saw it from miles away on the highway drive to New York."

I read aloud to her from the tour book. "'The dome is two-hundred-seventy-five feet above ground level. There are two-hundred-ninety-eight steps from the second level to the dome which is eighty feet in diameter. It is covered with twenty-three-karat gold leaf.' I always thought it was just paint." Now I really wanted to see it. I read on "'The state capital was originally in Iowa City and the old capitol building also has a gold-leaf dome.' We've never gone to see it either."

"No, we haven't. It's now part of the campus of the university." She turned off onto another road, a state highway. Obviously to avoid Des Moines. The road was paved but full of potholes. "You don't want to go to Iowa. You want to go to Oxford."

"If I don't go in the Marine Corps first." All that practice saying 'fuck' would be wasted if I didn't go into the Marines but, if the war ended, there would be no need to go in the Marines, fuck or not. "Maybe we will win the regional basketball championship and we'll go to Iowa City to play in the finals."

"Not likely to happen."

"If we drove through Des Moines, I could take a picture of the gold dome."

"All you have is black and white film." We rode in silence for a bit. "Garnie, what type of photographer do you want to be?"

"One who takes pictures."

"Don't be a smart ass. Do you want to be an artist like Stieglitz, say, or Weston, or be more of a photojournalist like Joe Rosenthal? Or Margaret Bourke-White?"

"Not Bourke-White. I'd have to marry Erskine."

"I shouldn't worry about it. They are divorced and I doubt Caldwell would have had you anyway. But to answer my question?"

"Both, I suppose. Photographic art alone is not enough. A photographer must be an artist first, of course, but making a social statement is important too. Like Berenice Abbott or Dorothea Lange." I realized I sounded a little pompous.

Auntie didn't seem to mind. "What does photographic art mean to you?"

"Vision, I suppose. It is all about seeing, isn't it? Looking at something ordinary and realizing that the most interesting thing about life is its ordinariness. And making the viewer looking at the photo experience how *extra*-ordinary that ordinariness is. Paul Strand's shots of New Mexico are like that. Did your friend Mabel know him?"

"He was part of Mabel's entourage at Taos at the same time as the Lawrences. Stieglitz was his mentor, though I doubt he approved of Strand's fascination for Georgia. Anyone else you would put in the art-social category with Strand?"

"Ansel Adams."

"I normally think of him as the artist."

"He is and yet his photos of the Japanese at Manzanar War Center look like ordinary people going about the most ordinary business until you realize that they are in a concentration camp."

"I am pleased you think highly of Adams. You are about to meet him."

"Ansel Adams?"

"Yes. He will be at Taos."

I sat silently, watching the Iowa countryside, but not really looking at it. I really didn't mind that we would not be going through Des Moines now. We needed to hurry to reach Taos. "You've met him before?"

"Yes," she said, "once in New York. At Stieglitz's gallery. I think Adams learned much from Stieglitz. And he was there in New Mexico when I was at Mabel's."

"'Moonrise, Hernandez, New Mexico.'" The sky, the little round moon. It was an amazing photograph. "And the church at Taos. What's he like?"

"A grizzly big man with a huge beard and he has his nose on crooked. He plays the piano most beautifully and talks a great deal. He and Paul, who was there at the same time, never seemed to tire of talking about photography and spent a great deal of time in a makeshift darkroom that Paul had created in an old shed."

"He has his nose on crooked?"

"Apparently as a child he fell flat on his face during the San Francisco earthquake and broke his nose and it never mended properly."

"If Ansel Adams is in Taos, why does J. Robert Oppenheimer's brother need me to take a picture?"

"I haven't the foggiest notion," Auntie told me.

We rode in silence out of Iowa and into northern Missouri and turned west. We rode many miles in the quiet. I was thinking of Adams and photography. I hadn't the slightest idea what Auntie was thinking about. I broke the silence. "I have to piss."

"Pee," she corrected me. Down the road, she pulled the car off to the side and turned off the engine. "There's a tree over there."

I climbed over the fence, went behind the tree, pulled out my big dick and took a big long piss. When I got back to the car, Auntie had taken out her silver cocktail shaker, along with a martini glass in which she had poured what I assumed was a Rob Roy complete with maraschino cherry. "Would you like a Grain Belt?"

"Yes, ma'am, I would."

She handed me a bottle opener and I dug a bottle of beer out of the red cooler. And there we stood. I wished I had been able to take a picture of us. Auntie sitting there on the trunk in her lemon-yellow frock, very out-of-date 1930s with big brown buttons, and a wide-brimmed yellow hat with yellow veil thrown back. She held her Rob Roy and fingered the toothpick that held the cherry. I stood in my faded jeans, blue dress shirt and penny moccasins, tipping back my beer. I could visualize the frame and was sorry I was not able to step outside myself and snap it. We made, I was certain, a lovely picture. I poured some gas into the tank from one of the cans and we were on our way again. Perhaps it was the heat of the afternoon, perhaps the beer, or maybe the countryside which was becoming tedious, but I dozed, and when I awoke, we were in a city.

"Kansas City," she said. "The Pendergast machine."

"I thought he was dead."

"He is. Harry S. went to his funeral."

I knew better than to say anything further about Truman and gazed out at the city. It was late afternoon, and as we headed out toward Topeka, Auntie stopped at an IGA store and bought potato chips, Velveeta, Wonder bread, and a couple of cold green bottles of Coca Cola. "This will do us until we reach Emporia."

"Emporia?"

"Yes, we will stop at the Harvey House Hotel there and have a great Fred Harvey supper and spend the night."

Auntie drove and I made us each a Velveeta on Wonder. We opened the bag of potato chips and we shared one of the bottles of Coke. It was easier with Auntie driving. Darkness came, but with it lightning, thunder, and a heavy downpour. Driving became difficult and Auntie slowed to less than 35. It was almost impossible to see the road ahead. "Let's hope we don't have one of those Kansas tornadoes." Auntie was squinting as she peered out the windshield.

"We'll need some red shoes, Auntie Em."

"Indeed we will, and a goddamned dog named Toto."

But we didn't have a tornado and finally reached the

Harvey House, a three-story white-stucco-and-red-brick
building on the main street through town. We had lost
a lot of time driving in the rain and the dining room was
closed for the night. We had had the Velveeta on Wonder
and potato chips, so we wouldn't starve, although I was a bit
hungry and looking forward to breakfast.

"You'll have to wear a coat and tie to breakfast," Auntie
told me.

"You've got to be kidding. I thought we were in the Wild
West."

"The civilized Fred Harvey west," Auntie told me. "Good
night." I assumed she was off to her room. She wouldn't find
any lounge bar to languish in, or traveling salesmen to bat
her eyes at, in this establishment. I was left to my very tidy,
very neat, unembellished bedroom. The bed was comfortable and I knew I need not worry about bedbugs, but it was
not the Palmer House.

Auntie Rye was already at a linen-draped table set with
lovely china as I was escorted to my chair by a Harvey Girl.
She was pretty but wore no make-up and her shiny auburn
hair was in a net. Her rather unfashionably long dress was
black and mostly hidden by the starched white apron with
a big bow at her waist front. She smiled and handed me the
menu. Choice of chilled orange juice, muskmelon or California select prunes. "No prunes," I said to Auntie. There
was a choice of oatmeal, corn flakes or Wheaties. Ah, the
breakfast of champions. There was kippered herring on
toast with scrambled eggs, griddle cakes with syrup, French
toast with orange marmalade, and grilled bacon with eggs as
desired. There was toast, muffins, orange marmalade and, to
drink, coffee, tea and milk. I was ravenous and would have

eaten everything on the menu except the kippered herring, despite being British, but I refrained and settled for melon, the breakfast of champions, bacon and fried eggs, toast and coffee. It was delicious. Before we left the dining room, I took a picture of a line of Harvey Girls, standing straight and pretty. Auntie said that with their black stockings and black shoes, they looked like nuns in aprons. I told her I thought they were pretty.

"When did you get so interested in girls?"

"I am practicing to not be a homosexual," I told her.

We stopped at the Phillips 66 station. Auntie bought a Minnequa water bag, had it filled with water and draped on the front of the radiator. "It'll be a hot 'en," the ratty-haired boy in coveralls told us as he finished hanging the bag.

I suspected he was right. The morning country spread flat, but the farms, though further apart than in Iowa, appeared prosperous. I took over the driving and Auntie was reading some novel by Nikolai Ostrovsky. The way she was holding the book I could only see part of the title, *How The Stee*.... It got hotter as I drove and, though all the windows were opened, the air that blew in was hot and flat, like the countryside. The farms were growing further apart and looking less prosperous. "Can you imagine what this country must have been like when the buffalo roamed the plains in great herds?"

Auntie looked up from her book and stared out at the flat land stretching ahead. The road aimed absolutely straight toward infinity. "Perhaps they should again."

As we drove south and west, the country appeared browner, the farms now well apart and their buildings weathered and beaten. We stopped before reaching Wichita.

Auntie decided she would drive. I grabbed a beer from the trunk as we switched places.

"A little early to be drinking beer," Auntie said.

"It's so damn hot."

"You're right on that. Bring me that other Coca Cola from the cooler."

I drank and she drove. Occasionally I handed her the Coke bottle. Just as she had avoided Des Moines, she drove west on 50 before we reached Wichita. She was hitting fifty all the way. There was no rain, but rain clouds gathered in the sky and made things a bit cooler. At least we were escaping the bitter sun. And there were the flashing lights of the state trooper behind her. "Hide your beer," she said. I looked back to see the trooper's car as Auntie slowed and then pulled off the pavement onto the soft shoulder.

"I know I was driving over the speed limit, officer," she said as the Kansas state trooper swaggered up to the driver's side. "But I saw the funnel and panicked. You can see we're from Iowa and not used to tornados."

"You really spotted a funnel?"

"Yes, dropping across a field. It was behind us, and I didn't know what to do but speed up and get away as fast as I could."

"You did right," he said. "You barrel out of here now. When you've gone another twenty miles or so, slow down. OK?"

"Yes, officer. Thank you."

"Git now. Git!"

And Auntie did. She peeled rubber as she pulled back onto the roadway and gunned the Packard.

"Why, Auntie Em, this looks just like the yellow brick road."

"Get out the oil in case we spot the Tin Man." She no sooner said that than the sky opened up and the rain came down in torrents. The wind also began to whip up and she had me close the back windows.

"Maybe you've angered the Wicked Witch."

"No time to be funny." She peered ahead as if trying to find the highway. It was almost impossible to see the road — it was like a river of water. And then the rain stopped just as quickly as it came up. Auntie didn't slow down though until I urged her. The troopers spoke with one another, I suspected. The tornado story wouldn't work a second time. So we continued along the flat 50 toward Dodge City. As we approached the city, an arrow pointed, indicating that it was six miles to the Army Airfield.

Dodge City was a strange town of Boot Hill fame. Many of the buildings were obviously weathered and dilapidated from the recent Dust Bowl years, but there was no sign of the rowdy Dodge City cattle days. "Wyatt Earp, Bat Masterson, and Doc Holliday," I announced as we got out of the parked Packard near what looked like a restaurant.

"You've seen too many movies."

"They were all real. It happened here."

Auntie tottered a bit in her heels after driving for so long. She pointed back down the street with her purse. "I saw some signs in Spanish. Perhaps we can get some Mexican food. You'll like Mexican food, Garnie."

The Café of Home Culinary looked as if it had seen much better days. We opened the torn screen. It was empty except for the waitress with rusty hair and a dirty apron. "Hi," she said. "Sit anywhere."

Auntie made no move to sit. "I would have thought it would be much busier because of the air base," she said.

"It closed. Business has been like this ever since."

"You wouldn't happen to have Mexican food, would you?"
Auntie still didn't sit.

"Naw. The Village is where you get Mexican food. But
mostly only the Mexicans eat it. Estelle Maria. She got the
best."

"Would it be wrong of us to leave and go to this Mexican
place?"

"Why wrong? Estelle needs the business, too."

We were told Estelle Maria's in the Village was just
beyond the Sante Fe Round House. "Of course the Round
House has been torn down." The Village was a shanty town,
like pictures from the Great Depression, and I took photos
of the maze of 'houses' that seemed to be made from railroad
packing, discarded material and debris. There was a hand-
painted sign above the door of a shack that we were assured
was Estelle's: *Copeland jacas a.* "What an odd name, if it is the
name." Auntie stooped to go in the door-less entry ahead of
me. It was dark inside, but cool. And it was good to escape
the heat.

A pretty woman in a clean apron came up to us as we
stood inside. "I am the Estelle Maria. Food you would like?"

"Si, por favor," Auntie responded.

"Today no bull. Today I got pig."

"Carnitas, good. And frijoles, arroz, tortillas, tamales, OK?"
Auntie asked as we were presented with no menu.

A Mexican in an American army uniform sat alone in a
corner. He was staring intently at us. At another table two
men sat drinking beer, smoking and playing dominoes.

"And beer, señorita?" Auntie asked.

"Señora," the woman corrected her. "No beer."

Auntie pointed to the two men in the corner.

"They bring," Señora said.

"May we bring, Señora?"

"Sí."

I was sent to the Packard to pick up a cold six pack of Grain Belt. When I returned, the uniformed Mexican was sitting at the table with Auntie. "This is Umberto Jose Gonzales-Ruiz." I shook his hand. "Will you have beer, Umberto?" Auntie asked.

"I will." His English was perfect. Estelle Maria brought an opener.

"I was asking Umberto if he was here during the Dust Bowl." Auntie popped the caps off the bottles, handed us each one and took one for herself.

"Here's looking at you," Umberto said and tapped his bottle toward us. "I was here, indeed, and on Black Sunday it was so bad you couldn't see your hand if you held it in front of your nose. I was eleven the year of Black Sunday. The dust time was harder for the Anglos than the Mexicans. We had nothing to start with, so we had nothing to lose. And you couldn't grow a garden even if you could find some water for it. The jackrabbits came in the millions and ate everything in sight. And that called for the clubbing. We went out, the whole town, at least the men and boys and even some women, and clubbed all the rabbits to death. It happened everywhere in the bowl. We ate the rabbits, of course; I don't know if the Whites did — probably some; we were all starving and sold the skins."

I took a slug of beer. "Your English is very good."

"I went to Cathedral school."

"Where is that?" I asked.

"Here in town, of course. They call it Sacred Heart, the

Cathedral, the church here in Dodge. We don't have a bishop yet, but there is talk of it becoming the diocese of Dodge City."

Estelle Maria brought our food. The *carnitas* were chunks of shredded pork, served with chopped cilantro. I particularly loved the refried beans and dipped hunks of warm tortillas in them.

"I am so surprised," Auntie said, cutting her tamale with a fork. "I never think of Kansas as being Catholic. It's the Mexican population, I suppose."

"To the contrary," Umberto told her. "There are far more Anglo Catholics in Dodge City."

"Was there really a Long Branch Saloon?"

"Oh, yes, and hotels that weren't much more than whorehouses. There was a boot store and a general store. It was all down on Front Street. Of course, I never saw it, only pictures. It all burned to the ground in the fire of eighty-five. First Dodge was known as the Buffalo Capital, until the bison were all killed off for their bones and hides. Made a lot of bone china, those buffalo did. Then it was the Cowboy Capital, the Queen of the Cowtowns. Those cowboys drove their cattle to Dodge and they were loaded onto the Santa Fe for the Chicago yards. Mostly they drank and whored in Dodge City and then went back out on the range. Dodge City was the wildest of Wild West. Now it makes for good movies. It was funny seeing movies about my hometown with a bunch of guys out there behind the front."

I had seen those Chicago yards and taken pictures of them. And I would take pictures here in Dodge City as well. "Are you home on leave?" I asked, "Do you live here?"

"In the Village, no. We used to, my family. The Village was much larger, but then the railroad needed more land and tore down our shanty and we went to live in a house. It doesn't have plumbing, but it has electric. That was before the war that we moved there. I am the middle of eleven kids. Four of my brothers and one of my sisters are still serving. I've been discharged but haven't got around to buying any civvies yet."

"You were overseas?" I sipped the Grain Belt. He had a lot of ribbons.

"Normandy. But I saw Paris. Ever been to Paris?"

"Yes. Have another beer," Auntie urged him. "This place has a strange name."

Umberto opened another Grain Belt. "It is Estelle Maria's goal. She wants to save enough money to buy a horse and move back to her family's land near Copeland. You know what they say: 'Once you seen Paree, well, it's hard to come back.'"

"You planning on spending your life here?" Auntie asked.

"Until I saw there was another world, I would never have given a thought to living anywhere else. Now I'm not so sure. I survived the Bulge. Life seems to have to be different after that, I suppose. I did my duty for my country. But here I'm not allowed to use the public swimming pool. I'm a spic."

"That's terrible." I was outraged. "Something should be done about it."

"The bishop over in Wichita is trying to get something done about it, and if anybody can get the change, it'll be the bishop."

We finished off our meal with a sugarcoated, lightly-fried dough thing. I decided I liked Mexican food. Auntie paid the meager bill and then left a forty-dollar tip. Umberto walked us back to the car, and after I asked directions to the swimming pool, we shook hands and left.

"I take it you are not planning on a swim."

I was driving. "No. Not a swim." I pulled up near the gate to the pool. Inside was the splash of swimmers. Mostly kids, but all white. I took my camera. The sign read simply: 'No Mexicans. No Blacks allowed.' Not Negroes, but Blacks. I snapped several shots, one with the white kids, though slightly out of focus, in the background.

We gassed up and filled the water bag. I followed Auntie's directions and drove out of Dodge City on 56 headed southwest. "Let's get out of Dodge."

"You had to say it."

"I did."

We drove through Copeland. It was a wide spot on the highway. "If Estelle Maria brings her horse here it's going to double the population." The road was straight and boring. There were no trees, only scrub grasses, and tumbleweeds rolled across the road ahead of me. The compass on the dash said we were headed straight southwest. We passed through Elkhart, Kansas, elevation 3,589, according to the sign, and then into Oklahoma. In places, the soil was red. Though it looked like we were driving on the flat because there was nary a tree and you could see forever, I could tell we were climbing, and the lengthy freight train on tracks that ran parallel to the highway was struggling with two diesel engines. Auntie was reading her Russian novel. "Blacks? I've never heard that term used before. Is it derogatory?"

"I think so. Is or isn't, they still can't swim in the pool," she said.

Then the fog moved in. It kept getting thicker and thicker and Auntie had me pull off. I walked ahead with a flashlight and Auntie drove the speed I was walking. Then the fog lifted and the rains came and I got back in the car. And then the rains came on hard and then harder and then pretty soon Auntie could barely see the road ahead and it began to get darker. "When we come to a town, any town, we are stopping for the night."

We stopped. 'Keyes Pop. 212 Elevation 4160,' the sign said. Gas station 1, closed. Another sign read 'Boise City 16 miles.' There didn't seem to be any light on anywhere in the town. Perhaps all 212 had just got tired of living at 4160 feet in the fog and rain and died. "Can I have a beer?" We were obviously not stopping here for the night.

"When we get to Boise City and settled in at the nice Boise City hotel, you can have two." The freight train and its two engines chugged by. She pulled back on the highway and continued on through the rain, sometimes barely able to see in the torrent, but we made the sixteen miles. There was no Boise City hotel, nice or otherwise. At the edge of town we found the tourist cabins. There was a woman in the office, a large woman with huge braless breasts spreading out from the bib of her bib overalls. She wore a large handwritten name tag that read 'Nettles Quiote.' "What can I get you?"

Auntie, wet and obviously tired, was looking about the sloppy office with its couch and protruding springs. "We were rather hoping to find a hotel here in Boise City — "

"That's *Boise* City, like voice city, not Boise like in Idaho."

"Yes, well, we were rather hoping for a hotel."

"There ain't none. Are you a transvestite?"

Auntie was obviously caught off guard. "Do you not rent to transvestites, Miss Quiote?"

"That's Ki ote, like in Coyote. Yeh, and I rent to anyone. I'm a dyke myself. Although there ain't much dykery around here to have."

I wasn't certain what a dyke was, but I suspected looking at Miss Coyote what it might mean.

"You be needing two cabins or one? Only one bed to a cabin."

"Two, please."

"There's electric, but no plumbing. Outhouse is out back. You can take cabins one and two. They's unlocked." She called after us as we went out into the rain again, "Oh and they each got a radio." She pronounced it 'rad-ee-o.'

I turned on the rad-ee-o but got nothing but static and turned it off and went to sleep. I awoke because I was cold and the single blanket did little to keep me warm. I put on my jeans and opened the cabin door. There sat the yellow Packard covered in white snow. "Jesus, it's July, for Christ's sake." I put on a shirt and wished I had a jacket and ran to the outhouse remembering our own outhouse in the weed garden at the Terrible House. This one was quite different, however. It reeked as much but was a four-holer and, as it seemed gender indifferent, I wondered if others might just come in and sit beside me. However, no one came in, including Auntie Rye, who remarked, as I wiped the snow off the Packard the next morning, "I would shit my pants before I'd use that place."

"Are we having breakfast?" I was dying for a cup of coffee.

"We are getting out of Boise City as fast as we can." She turned on the heater.

"Boise like voice," I reminded her.

"I need a bath." She stepped on the gas.

"I need breakfast." Two hours later we approached Clayton. The heater was off and the windows were open. The elevation, as I read the tour book, hadn't changed, but the temperature certainly had. "Coffee," I suggested weakly.

"Take out," she said and pulled up in front of a restaurant. I came out holding two Dixie cups of hot coffee wrapped with paper napkins so I wouldn't burn my hands. I never bothered with the cream or sugar and we drank our hot black coffee and sped out of Clayton. Had there been a trooper anywhere on the straight flat highway we might have seen the vehicle miles ahead or behind. We seemed to be the only car on the road and Auntie drove along at sixty-miles-per. We passed through Gladstone, which was a building.

"North of here somewhere are dinosaur footprints, still visible," I read.

"We are not leaving the highway in search of dinosaur footprints."

We passed through Abbott, which was an abandoned building and two trees. It was getting hotter. Maybe in the 90s. It was hard to believe we had left snow a few hours earlier. We came to a town. The sign read 'Springer'. "I need a bath," she said.

"I need breakfast."

"We need to find the Brown Hotel," she said.

"How do you know there is such a place?"

"Well, there used to be, anyway. At least Frank Waters claimed there was. Maxwell at Third. I remember that because he wrote a poem about it."

"This is Fourth Street," I told her as we drove into the town.

We crossed a rail track and came to a stop sign. "Maxwell," she said and turned left. And there it was down on the next corner. A striking red building with yellow door and trim. "I need a bath."

"I need breakfast."

She parked the Packard in front of the hotel. "I am going

to get a room, have a bath and change. Two hours we'll spend here and then be on our way. Do you want a room?"

"No, I want breakfast."

Auntie took a bag and checked in. I went into the hotel café and from the menu ordered what was called a green chili burrito and a root beer. It had been a good choice. Full of beans. After that I went out on the street and took a picture of the hotel and some other buildings in the town. The place seemed prosperous. There was a large semi-trailer truck and it had a lot of chrome for a war going on. So I took a picture of it.

A fairly youngish but still older, and big, guy came up to me as I stood focusing on another shot of the big truck. "Would you like to see my big rig," he said.

"Sure." So I got in and he showed me his big rig.

After the two hours were up, I stood out by the Packard waiting for Auntie.

"What've you been up to?" she asked and tossed her bag in the backseat. She was wearing a pale blue dress and large picture hat. I thought it was a bit too elegant for touring but kept my mouth shut.

"This guy showed me his big rig."

"I hope that's not a euphemism."

"No, of course not." She didn't need to know everything. I climbed into the passenger side and rolled down the window. Auntie stuck out her hand, made a U-turn and drove north on Maxwell and out of the town and then turned west. Again we were climbing. We reached Cimarron. The signs indicated it was a historic western town. There were a lot of trees and a lot of Mexicans in Cimarron, but Auntie was not intent on stopping or exploring, and we went through town and began the winding climb up. The road was narrow. The air smelled marvelous.

"Piñon," Auntie said. "The trees."

They weren't really trees — more like shrubs, but it was wonderful to see and smell the vegetation after the empty world we had come from. I took photos from the car windows. Sometimes of the vastness below. We continued to wind up the road, scaling the side of the mountain at times. It was impossible to picture how the world would change forever in the week ahead. And that we would be a small part of it.

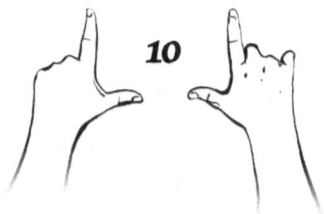

10

The Big Picture

WHAT THE NOSE grasped, the scent of piñon, was powerful as we wound up the mountain road, but what the eye
captured was overwhelming. Light at home — in Iowa, or in
Chicago, or in the East — had been one of contrast. Light
and dark. Here the world was an all-encompassing place
of the sun. It was not opacity, there was still contrast, but
the light was so great that it washed everything. When I
first sensed this was uncertain, but here now with the stark
mountains, the stretching valley below and behind, I was
engulfed in light. Illumination. I grasped what drove Georgia and Paul and, yes, Ansel. It was like journeying to the
moon, a place so different, and I knew I was only beginning
to see it. It made me feel good. Alive.

I thought Auntie seemed almost indifferent to the overwhelming environment. "To hear Mabel tell it, her childhood
was one of deprivation. Not financial, of course, her family
was richer than pig shit on an overflowing manure spreader."

"Like the Palmers, Fields and Gardiners."

"Yes, I suppose." She totally ignored my sarcastic dig. "But despite all the money, according to Mabel, she was totally unloved. Her father, apparently weak and unfeeling, was given to unpredictable temper tantrums and had no use for children, but lavished his affection only on his dogs. Her mother was as strong as her father was weak. She was decisive but cold and self-centered. This, of course, is all from Mabel's perspective. But Mabel isn't the warmest of people. She told me she didn't love her first husband, Karl Evans, and when I asked her why she married him, she said it was 'because he was engaged to someone else.'" We continued winding up the twisting road. "Karl died in a hunting accident and she was left with John, her only child. It's no wonder, with her own upbringing, how she at times seems to ignore and at other times to dote on him. A young widow, she went to Europe for solace and on the liner over met her next husband. Edwin Dodge was an architectural student from Boston. Wealthy, of course. They married and moved to Florence."

"I'm glad we are here." I was still looking out at the amazing world in which we found ourselves. "But why are we here? Why *me* to take a photograph?"

"I can't answer that. I should know and I don't. Perhaps only a whim. When Mabel, sitting like the self-appointed queen atop the world, wants something, she tenaciously pounds away until she gets it. She wanted Lawrence here to write the greatest of novels, based on her philosophic view of life, and he came. He came and was unhappy. And she with him, though she hounded him. And Frieda. And Brett. She wanted Carl Jung to come and take his great collective unconscious and find its ultimate truth here among the Pueblo, and he came and she wasn't even here. In New York the entire time. She wanted Georgia and John Marin and Robin Jeffers and Lillian Gish and Thornton Wilder. And God knows how many others. They all came. Those she couldn't remake, which was practically all of them, she either destroyed or they simply ignored her, as Georgia has done."

"You hate her."

"I don't. No, I don't hate Mabel. I abhor some of her tactics. But I also admire her. She has lifted the veil of Maya and found here amid the Pueblo, from a near Zen perspective, the answer to life. That answer, of course, is that *there is no answer*. But in the insufficiency of discovering that great truth, she is not fully content."

"How do you know all this? You say you haven't heard from her."

"I read her. She is heavily published. Probably the only way to understand her is through her writing. And in it you can also find the venom. You will need to be careful, Garnie. She will mesmerize you. She is driven to envelop herself with the great, the near-great and often the not-so-great, and feed them honey until they are so sated they bare their selves, their fears and intimate secrets." Auntie Rye was clutching the steering wheel with both hands as if she feared it would evaporate.

"She sounds like a gorgon."

"Anything but. Here's what to expect. We will enter a compound of sorts. God knows what it looks like now. She keeps building. They, she and Tony, call it their Big House, but it has some other... some Spanish name. It's really a ramble of a house, maybe even houses; it wanders all over the place as if built randomly. Tony, wrapped in his blanket, will be there somewhere near the entrance, playing his drum. He will recognize our presence but continue playing. Mabel will greet us at the door. She is not a tall woman. Short, actually, but hardly petite. I would not call her stout, but she is solidly built with striking black — no doubt dyed by now — hair with bangs. Her costume — I decline to call it dress — will be Indian. Her eyes will draw you in and immediately she will be your friend for life, of that you will be assured. She will invite us into a room full of people, more famous than not, no doubt." Auntie Rye pulled the Packard off at a widening in the road. "An amazing view." She stepped out of the car and raised her arms out as if embracing the earth. "I hadn't realized that I even missed this."

I got out. New Mexico engulfed me. I had a complete realization of the fullness of it. I felt more aware than I had ever felt. In the spring, when I was taking pictures of a flowering apple and commenting on the scent and shape of the flowers and their beauty, knowing how soon they would disappear and the green apples would form, Rupert had given me a look of disdain. "Nature is inherently boring. You've seen one flowering fruit tree, you've seen them all. Give me the great architecture of Europe, Notre Dame, or the Chrysler building in New York; that's beauty."

"The Japanese find beauty in the fleeting cherry blossom," I told him.

"The Japs have no respect for life. They are miniature slanted-eyed Hitlers."

Auntie broke off a twig and handed it to me. "Smell," she said. "It is cedar." And she pointed to the bluish plant bushing out from near my shoes. "Sage." The scents that mingled with the piñon were pervasive. I became aware of the vastness, the totality of it as I looked out at mountains, clouds, deserted valley below. There was a presence. God was not fourteen images at which one genuflected. It was as if my phonograph record, the last moment of Beethoven's Ninth, was pounding in my ear. I raised my Leica and with extreme care formed the frame and, for the first time, as I pressed the shutter, I understood what Stieglitz meant. What I was seeing — what the Leica had captured, was only a symbol, an abstract equivalent of this experience, this emotion which had so overpowered me. The art was in the emotion that produced the photograph. The universe was vast and I was very small.

"Did you get the picture?" she asked.

"I truly got the picture," I said and walked back to the Packard, not simply elated but enlightened. All this light. It was illumination. Whether or not the equivalency would be realized in the printed photograph, I had no idea, but I had taken the first step. I understood what it was I was trying to achieve. I was only fifteen. Well, almost. And I felt wise. In the moment which had just been, I had achieved a grasp of the nature of life. And it was OK not always to be just a kid. I was a genius, wasn't I?

"Mud," I said as we drove into the cluster of homes.

"Adobe," Auntie said. "This is Taos." And then she added as if more to herself than to me, "To understand Mabel would be to understand Gertie's *Portrait of Mabel.*"

"But who can understand Gertrude Stein?"

"Mabel's personality is like Stein's poetry, fluid and discontinuous." She turned off to the right and up a hill. There was growth — cottonwoods, piñon, yucca and cedar. After a short distance she stopped and we left the Packard there along the roadside and walked through an open unhinged gate in an adobe wall. We went up through overgrowth to an open door. There was no Tony playing the drums. We went in. There was no Mabel, only a large Indian woman standing like a statue in the center of the room facing us. Her face was expressionless. The room was furnished in an odd mix of Indian, Mexican, Italian, Victorian and contemporary furniture and decoration. Despite the eclecticism — I had recently discovered that word — it was elegant. Rather than disconcerting, it seemed as if these objects all belonged lumped together as they were. A large framed portrait, I assumed of Mabel, dominated the room. There was a wonderful perfume about the airy enclosed space: burnt pine or sage, perhaps.

Mabel swept into the room, her overlong dress held up in her right hand. The gown was layered, lacy and of no particular style or era. It was plain yet fabulous. She was short and perhaps stocky if she had stood still long enough to be measured. Her bangs were gray, not black as I been told to expect. She might have been grandmotherly if she appeared less charismatic and was not so much in motion. "Rye. I see you have reached a decision about life." The voice was melodic. A voice, I could tell, one would never tire of hearing.

"I have, Mabel," Auntie Rye responded.

"I always knew you would. Sit. Sit." She reclined in a lounging position on an ornate pillowed sofa. We both found chairs. The Indian woman statue stood in front of me and I had to look around her to see Mabel's face. I sat next to a large black Steinway grand. I wondered if it was in tune.

"I am surprised you say that. When I was last here you said I was an aberration."

"If I contradict myself, well then, I contradict myself. But, admittedly, you were aberrational. You seemed indecisively

unsure of gender. Now you appear settled into noncon-
formity."

"I am. This is Garnie."

"Of course it is. What a beauty you are. Perhaps too pretty.
Are you a homosexual?"

I was taken aback by the question. "I think not." Perhaps
it was the most truthful response I could give under the circumstances. "If the war goes on, I will be joining the Marines."

She ignored that. "Lorenzo once told me that he wondered why nearly every man that approaches greatness tends
to homosexuality, whether he admits it or not. That's about
as close as he ever admitted to being queer." I avoided her
gaze and looked up at the portrait. "Yes, me in a time of
greater beauty. At least Blanche seemed to have found some
beauty in me. He painted Joyce and Proust. He, Lorenzo,
not Blanche, was of course. Queer, that is. Murray and all
that business. Though I think he was afraid of the Blooms-
buggers. I am afraid of no one. Or no thing. Well, war, perhaps. I am — 'was' would be a better way to put it — a pacifist.
Hitler makes that difficult, doesn't he? Politics is all fickle.
Miss Warner's a pacifist. But then she is Quaker, isn't she?"
She gave no indication of whom this 'Miss Warner' was.
"The universe is more contemplative here. The Sangre de
Cristo Mountains are more enduring."

"I stay," the statue said.

"A wise decision, Corisita," Mabel told her. "Why not bring
us some coffee and sopaipillas?"

"Sí." The statue moved and vanished.

"Still," Mabel went on as if not interrupted, "Lorenzo may
have been on to something. Are you intent on greatness?"
She gave me no opportunity to respond. "How many of my

friends. Thornton was queer, though he would never admit it. Bobby, oh, and Carl, but he admitted it. Perhaps Lorenzo was right." She nodded in the direction the statue had gone. "Corisita's husband abuses her. I told her she must stay here. She was deciding. And there is Myron, of course. Have you read *All of Their Lives?*"

"I read *This Man Is My Brother*," Auntie told her.

"Novels don't come much queerer than that, do they? Florence in *All of Their Lives* is me, of course. Myron can be such a queer bitch at times. So mean to me at times. He bifurcated me. One half of me he made most unpleasant. Of course, the other half was lovely. Myron's here. He's got a friend staying with him, if I may be euphemistic." She turned to me. "You are young, my young artist friend."

"I am fifteen. That is, I will be this month."

"And are you a virgin?"

"That would depend on how you define virgin," I told her.

At that moment, as if on cue, a young woman who very much resembled Mabel, including the bangs, although hers were black, whirled into the room. She even wore a dress similar to Mabel's. She was a reflection more than a copy. There was an aura of sensuality about her that I found more disturbing than enticing. I thought of Eleanor Greatsinger and Arletta Kweever. I could hardly announce here, particularly after my Marine declaration, that I had a calling to the priesthood. I also suspected that, to the people living here, it would have made little difference. "I am Bonnie," she announced.

"John's daughter," Auntie Rye said. "You look so much like your grandmother."

"It's more than appearance," Mabel said. "I sometimes see myself as if cloned." She looked up at her granddaughter.

"Have you seen Tony about? I will need him to fetch Georgia or at least let her know that Rye and Garnie have arrived."

"He knew, as he always senses things, that they would be arriving, and he and Frank drove out to *Rancho de los Brujos* to alert Georgia, and over to let Ansel and Virginia know."

"I have a phone now," Mabel told Auntie. "But Georgia in her place at *Rancho de los Brujos* has no phone, no electricity, and no plumbing. She's trying to buy a house. A place in Abiquiú owned by the Catholic Church. She and the bishop seem to go round and round. I don't know if it is over price so much or that he simply does not approve of Georgia. Georgia should call on Willa to have him done in. Perhaps a new bishop might speed up the process. We will make a party of it then. Bonnie, will you tell Brett? She lives here in poverty, but will be moving into a house being built out on Frieda's ranch. Frieda has more money than God now that Lorenzo's dead, and she thinks herself just as omnipotent. Poor Brett gets five bucks a throw for her paintings and I realize I should do more for her. I couldn't possibly buy any of those paintings. I hate them. I do provide a place for her to live."

"Barely. In the winter, the place is like an icebox." Bonnie swung her skirt as she moved about the room. "You should feed her better."

"It's not that I can't afford to, it's just that having her at table is a pain. She is as prickly and cantankerous as a dead cactus and hears just about as well."

We were told food was on the table and went out through a courtyard, past what appeared to be an ornate dining room, on into a large kitchen filled with clay bowls and hanging pots and peppers. We sat around an old wooden table.

Bonnie kept devouring me along with her food in a

lascivious fashion, and I was uncomfortable. "Might I play the Steinway?" I asked Mabel. I would need some self-containment after lunch to escape Bonnie's glances.

"Of course," Mabel told me and handed me a basket of sopaipillas and then a bowl of warm frijoles.

Bonnie finished her coffee, got up from the table, smiled at me — more of an alluring signal — and took her cup to the sink. "I am off to the Pueblo to find Brett. She is painting Indians today."

"Better than the fish," Mabel said as her granddaughter went out. "My God, the ugly fish! Endlessly she paints these ugly fish."

There were photos throughout the living room, but on the piano was a framed photo, more like a snapshot, of three women sitting on porch steps. A younger, black-banged Mabel I recognized as the one to the left. The one in the center was tough looking with a fag hanging from her lips. The third woman was hatted and holding a purse, and would have appeared ladylike but for the strange leg wrappings, the exact nature of which were difficult to discern in the photo. The piano was very much in tune and, after a few scales, I played, as I remembered it, the allegro of Mozart's piano sonata in C. The acoustics in the room were really quite fine and I was pleased with my performance. There was single applause as I finished and I turned to see the clapping came from somewhat small hands on the lanky frame of the bearded Ansel Adams. He was wearing a sloppy black hat. I recognized him at once from his photos. "Nice, yes," he said. "May I?"

I stood up in awe and motioned him to the piano bench. "I'm Garnie Gardiner."

He took off the hat and laid it on the closed piano. "I know." He continued from where I finished, beginning with the second movement. How amateurish my playing seemed in comparison. After the second movement, he continued into the next allegro. I had heard only phonograph records; I truly had never heard a live professional performance, but I knew this must be what it was like. Nuance, variation, and contrast. As the not large hands stretched across the ivory keys, I knew what piano artistry was. He finished. This time I applauded. And as he grabbed his hat, he knocked over the framed photo and uprighted it again.

"Who are the women in the photograph with Mabel?" I asked.

"Frieda Lawrence and Dorothy Brett." He led the way toward the door. "I need to explain why you are here. Let's go for a walk." He turned, it seemed almost wistfully, and looked back at the piano. "Photography is a lot like music." He put on the hat, squashing it around his large ears. "Don't neglect your study of music."

Ansel continued leading as we moved toward the open gate. Tony was now drumming between the gate and the house. I knew immediately who he was. Wrapped in his blanket, he looked somewhat older, but it was the face made famous by the man with whom I now walked. Tony acknowledged me with a look but continued drumming and chanting and did not speak to us directly. Ansel did not interrupt the drummer. "You met Stieglitz." The statement didn't seem to require a response. His voice was hearty. Without introduction to the subject, he spoke to me as if I were the student. "Photography is perception. The analytic interpretation of things as they are. Your camera?"

It was cool beneath the trees. "A Leica Three."

"That will do well for this assignment. Better than my heavy equipment in many ways. At some point in your career, if you intend on this being a career, you will need a view camera for more controlled work. Something akin to a Hasselblad with a multiplicity of lenses. I am a bit of a camera packrat. Probably don't need all that I have."

"I don't know what the assignment, as you call it, is." Walking beside him, as we moved out of the shade into the direct light, I realized how thin he was. Perhaps he didn't eat enough or perhaps it was all the climbing.

"We will come to that." The man had unusual eyes and the crooked nose Auntie Rye had told me about. His overly large ears were made more so by his gauntness. I thought of Lincoln. He walked as I thought Lincoln might have walked, slightly stooped but in great strides. I attempted to keep up with him. "I believe in beauty. A photographer must. I believe in stones and water, air and soil, people and their future and their fate. I follow the tenets of Edward Carpenter. Do you know Carpenter?"

"No."

"He espouses the pursuit of beauty in life as well as art. For me, the purpose of art is to reveal the beauty in life to others and to inspire them. And from Stieglitz, I learned the importance in the artistic theory of subjective equivalence. Let me try to explain —"

"I understand some," I said and related my experience just before we came into Taos.

"Yes, that is it. As an artist, such perception is essential." We continued side by side down the hill along the graveled street. "Stieglitz iterates that a photo must offer the viewer an equivalent vision excited by a previous experience. Perfect objectivity, derived from intuition, linking artist, object and viewer. It becomes that something both distinct and universal, momentary and eternal, the many and the one."

I understood and said, "It is that instant that I, as photographer, have of infinity."

"Precisely, young man. The visual communicated there in the frame reveals the ever-changing, yet permanent harmony, order, and law of nature." He slapped me across the shoulder enthusiastically and we turned off the gravel on to the paved street leading to the center of the village. There was a sidewalk and we stepped up onto it. It was a touristy looking place of adobe and wood structures with post-held roofs, some slightly sagging, extending out over the sidewalk. Ansel opened a screen door and I followed him into a Mexican café. He found a table apart in the front near the window. From the aproned young Mexican woman he ordered food and coffee for us both. I was hardly hungry, having just eaten at Mabel's. "John Marin taught me the need of a oneness with nature. I know that sounds pompous, but like my own powerful Yosemite, it is truer here in the giant sweep of New Mexico than in much of the continent. The Pueblo Indian intuitively knows this. Tony Luhan does not just know the earth; he is part of it. He often knows what is to happen. It is as much part of him as the temporal world in which he lives with us."

I looked about the small room with its chrome tables and torn green plastic seats. There was a scattering of uniformed soldiers of various ranks, smoking and talking raucously among the others, the Mexicans and Indians.

"They are from Los Alamos," Ansel said quite softly,

pointing with a nod of his head at the soldiers. "It is why you are here." He put his finger over a lip buried in the black scraggle of his facial hair, as if to say 'not to be talked about here.'

The food arrived in quantities. I wasn't in the least hungry and picked at it. "Of course it's not all theory. There is the essential of technique. I learned much about tonality and how to achieve it from Paul Strand." Ansel devoured all the food on his plate and several cups of coffee. I realized his thinness was not from lack of consumption. "Aren't you going to eat that?" he asked. I explained I'd just eaten at Mabel's. He reached a fork across. "Do you mind?"

I did not mind. He devoured my food as well and several more cups of coffee. After he finished we went out into the sun and walked away from the village center to the north. "What art, photography, can do then, I would suppose, is to reveal the beauty you, the photographer, find in life, and inspire others with that beauty."

"But I can't do it in the way in which you do and perhaps never will."

"Nor should you. I admire Strand, Stieglitz, Cunningham, Weston. And I have learned from them. What is there is the reality, whatever that is — the flower, the mountain, the sky. They see and I see, but not in the same way, not with the same perception. It's important you accept that. It's about vision, but your vision."

We walked in the sun. I looked up into his deep eyes. What perception he must find with those eyes. "You will need to experiment and should. I was intrigued with the Impressionists and saw for a time my photography through that lens, but then it struck me I should not be evading reality, but embracing it. Here was the power of photography as a tremendously pure art form. The blazing austere poetry of the real. I'm not saying this has to be your way. I am saying it is *a* way and one you might explore in finding your own perception. Even now as you undertake the assignment of the gadget. And I should not call it that. It is more pure terror. It begins at Los Alamos."

"In the café you spoke of Los Alamos."

"Los Alamos was a boys' prep school. It's a bit to the south and west of here. Maybe fifty miles or so, maybe a little more. The Oppenheimer family had a ranch here in the general area. So when Opje was made head of this top-secret program, he chose the prep school location for the site of the laboratories that would develop this hush-hush weapon. The Germans were also working on one. Or so they now tell me." We stopped by the blue water of the river running alongside the street. I had my camera but was intimidated by the presence of the great photographer, and as much as I would have liked, took no pictures. He went on. "I have the mind of the artist, not the scientist, so my explanation is rather basic, but the idea they are after is to create a weapon through releasing vast energy by splitting an atom. It has something to do with uranium —"

"Uranium?"

"The mineral. It contains radium. Glow-in-the-dark paint is made from it. But it is also an element with one of the heaviest atomic weights and a unique nuclear structure. Making fission possible." He picked up a pebble and I thought he might skim it across the river, but he did not. He just examined it as he held it in his hand. "This is just basic science, of course. Fission has been only a theoretical possibility and here at Los Alamos it is being made a reality. Opje brought in mathematicians, physicists, chemists, biologists, engineers, and scientific academicians of all disciplines from the University of Chicago, Berkeley, Cal Tech, M.I.T., and Columbia. Many are European and had fled the Nazis." Ansel examined the flat pebble. And then rubbed it as if it might be magic. "All those minds. It was in some ways appropriate to New Mexico. Ironic in its Utopian scope. A little like the way in which Mabel gathers her artistic geniuses. Most of what goes on beyond the barbed wire we aren't told, but we piece together from the sights and sounds, from the Indians who work out there cleaning the labs and the offices, the houses and the barracks of the new residents. The security people seem to look upon the Indians as if they were furniture, having no comprehension that something important is happening there. There's a hole in the fence on the far side and some Indians go through it and watch movies or buy Cokes at the PX. General Groves runs the Army aspect of it all, Opje the scientific." Ansel slipped the pebble in his pocket and put his arm around my shoulder. "What I am going to tell you now is not gossip gathered by workers there. It is what the other Oppenheimer, Frank, told me in the strictest confidence for a specific purpose. It is a weapon, an atomic bomb. And through the process of fission, the bomb is so powerful that one single bomb can erase a city like New York and its millions of people. It will bring a difference to civilization as we know it. This is what I meant by terror. Terrible."

I stood looking at the moving blue water... the mountains rising beyond and the ancient Pueblo where we seemed headed. I shivered despite the heat. I was no longer a mature photographic student of theory listening to the mentor expound on the nature of beauty. I was now a child. I was suddenly frightened. I wanted to go home to the Torrington House. To the guys. To Padric and Martin. To Tilly. To my wall of photos, where war was pictures, not reality. I wasn't even certain why I was frightened or why I had such a need to go home. I simply wanted to get out of this place. I sensed the terribleness of what I had been told.

Ansel tightened his grip about my shoulder. "It is OK, Garnie."

I looked up into the bearded face and strange kind eyes. "I'm not sure it is." I understood nothing, but I knew it was something horrific. Something awful.

He took a bedraggled small book from his pocket. "My bible, I suppose. It's title is *Civilisation, its Cause and Cure.* Carpenter suggests that civilization is a form of disease that human societies pass through. Civilizations, he says, rarely last more than a thousand years before collapsing. Maybe this bomb will bring about the destruction of this society. But here where it ends it might also begin. For Carpenter, salvation is in a closer association with the land and greater development of our inner nature."

I suppose it was the calmness of Ansel's voice, or maybe the beauty of the running river, the association with nature, but I was suddenly less fearful and moved from his protective arm and stood apart. "How is such a weapon, such a bomb, possible?"

"Nuclear fission. The atom bomb. It's all very top secret. Here in the Pueblo just up the road, sun worshipers came from Mesa Verde, perhaps in the thirteenth or fourteenth century, making it one of the oldest communities in the country. And yet, just a few miles away is the newest of communities. Los Alamos. Both are Utopian, I suppose. One of a living art; the other of living science."

"If it's so secret, why do you know about it?"

"We, that is Georgia, Luis, and I, are being told for a reason. Which I will explain. The bomb, so euphemistically called the gadget, is to be exploded on July sixteenth. Three days from now. What will happen is unknown. Perhaps the atmosphere will catch fire."

"Jesus! You mean the world will come to an end? The apocalyptic fire."

"I doubt that will really occur."

"But you don't know that it won't. In three days the end of the world might be at hand… and you can calmly talk about it?"

"It's a bomb test conducted by the great scientific geniuses of this nation. And I understand it all develops from discoveries made by Einstein."

"If that's supposed to assure me, it doesn't. They are known as Einstein's theories. Theories are not fact. They are unproven."

"Tony has been told nothing and yet he assures me that it will be all right. He saw it all in his head without knowing a thing. He saw a giant mushroom in the sky."

"A mushroom in the sky?"

"Yes, rising like a great cloud. In Tony's vision, we stood about watching unharmed. I trust Tony's insights. He knew you had arrived."

"That pales in comparison to the end of the world." We were nearing the Pueblo. It was quite striking against the afternoon sun. Despite the beauty, I was apprehensive about what Ansel had revealed, particularly my need to be told. "And how am I involved, if I may use a pun, in this picture?"

"You are a minor. Mature for your age, but a minor. What is your relationship with Rye?"

"The truth, though we don't discuss it ever…," I told him, quietly, "Rye is my father."

"I didn't know if you knew. That makes the matter easier. For what I am about to propose will require parental permission. Rye will not be told much of anything, for security reasons, but will have to sign a consent form."

"But I am to be told."

"Yes." And even though there was no one about, he lowered his voice as if the words might float off on the wind. "The point is Opje is worried."

"Oppenheimer?"

"J. Robert, yes. The blast, the explosion of the gadget, all aspects of it are to be photographed in detail by the government — the Army, of course. What concerns Opje is that if something goes wrong, if there is a mass failure, there will be a cover-up. For not just his own protection, but for the nation's interests as well, he wants an outside photographic record of the blast. He is approaching us — by us, I mean Georgia and myself. We are the only two in the know, along with yourself and a soldier, Luis, who will serve as your guide and driver. Frank, Opje's brother, was introduced to me by Georgia, whom he knew from having lived in the area. He asked me if I would be willing to photograph the blast from a safe location. I had no objection, but we immediately realized there was a problem. There is nowhere in New Mexico I can go and not be recognized. The names of all the photographers that came to mind were either too well known or not known to us at all, and whether or not those could be trusted was unclear. It was Georgia who came up with you. At some point, Stieglitz had told her about you. A youth no one would suspect if he went on a mountain camping trip. A youth capable of doing professional work with an unsuspicious 35mm camera, and who also just happened to be the child of someone of our circle. Someone we knew and trusted, Rye Gardiner. Frank thought it perfect. Opje agreed. And here you are."

We entered the Pueblo Village. This was not some touristy thing. Although art and jewelry were displayed and were being sold, the Indians lived here. Wrapped in light colored blankets, the Indian women resembled Bedouins as they tightened their wrappings about them from the heat and light in this oasis. I decided to take a picture of them, despite the great photographer being there, and took the Leica from the case. Ansel motioned me to stop. "You must ask permission first. They will grant it, but you must ask. Otherwise, you insult them."

So I asked and they nodded a friendly affirmative, and there in the Pueblo was my photo that I entitled later when I printed it, 'The Bedouins of Taos.' Ansel led me to the much-photographed church. I did not take a photograph. Ladders leaned against the adobe walls of the rising Pueblo and, as I walked down toward the river where women were drawing water into clay jugs, I had a picture view of the Pueblo against the late afternoon sinking sun. I snapped several shots and then moved back up, where I found Ansel speaking with some blanketed men and drinking coffee.

"Are you going to take my photo?" he asked.

"I'm afraid I could never get it right."

"Probably a little distortion would be helpful. I'm a bit of an ugly s.o.b."

And so I took several shots of the great man from various angles. Then we started our walk back to the Big House. "I came here first in twenty-seven. Paul was here then, or maybe that was when I was here in twenty-nine. That was the year I first met Georgia, through Mabel, of course. I met them all through Mabel. Paul Strand, John Marin, the poet Witter Bynner..." He paused as if he was back in the twenties in his mind. "Marin often used to sit more than paint. He would go out on a morning and just sit silently absorbing the landscape, the Sangre de Cristo. He'd maybe do this for a month, at least three weeks, and then one day suddenly with emphatic moves of his thumb there on the paper would be the mountains. His watercolors were the finest I have ever seen." I walked silently beside the large man, simply listening. "I love John perhaps more than any other man. Yet, we are so different. When we first met, he hated me. I am, as you have learned, loud and gregarious. John seldom speaks, but when he did, particularly about art, I listened and still do. I was playing the piano and John heard me. He loves music, and for that he forgave me for my sin of boisterousness."

"You play with beauty," I said.

"I am an exceptional pianist, but not great. I wanted to be great and was intent on becoming a pianist of world stature. My heart's big enough and my vision, but my hands are too small. So I became a great photographer instead." As we walked along the river, he took the smooth pebble out of his pocket and replaced it back along the water's edge. "They will undoubtedly confiscate whatever photographs you take for them. I am going to give you a second Leica, not as fine as yours, of course, to take with you. If you are able to take photos with that as well, that is the film you can give them. When you return we can develop those from your own camera at Mabel's. Paul turned an old shed into a darkroom. I have chemicals with me, or will have, when Virginia gets here with the car. That way we can make you your own set of prints of whatever you are able to capture on film." He talked more of Paul Strand and his long friendship with Georgia, whom he had met here before meeting Stieglitz in New York. "Stieglitz is not well, you know. Georgia will have to go back to New York soon to be with him. She hates it when she is not here."

As we passed through the town and made our way back up the graveled hill, he spoke of printing techniques, of heavier printing and the employment of selenium toner. "I use techniques in printing to reflect an objective harmony with an inferred theoretical component."

"A theoretical component?" I asked.

"Yes. Say I am trying to recapture the individuality of human existence as it relates to the universe in the frame. I can heighten the perception of the idea through techniques in printing. There is choice of paper. I opt for a simple high gloss paper over any textured paper. It's about choice of lenses and filters, seeking tonal range."

"Do you teach these techniques?"

"I do, but also I am going to be originating a program, a degree in photography at the California School of Fine Arts in San Francisco. Beginning in the fall we will have a department of photography. I can teach techniques, but I can't teach the intuitive grasp of the moment, an essential of photographic art. That each artist has to find on his own. In the end, it all comes down to vision. Your music will help you, though. Visualization in musical terms is extremely useful. Thinking in the abstractions of tone, volume, rhythm, phrasing and their relationship will free you from the bonds of representation and let your unconscious mind loose. So Kandinsky would have it. It's musical composition and mood." He stopped beside a large rather beaten-up Pontiac station wagon with wooden panels and a large rack mounted on the roof. "Virginia is here."

The rear of the wagon was filled with cameras, tripods, and boxes that I assumed were packed with other equipment. He opened the unlocked rear door and searched around for a box, found it and took out a Weston exposure meter. "You will need it," he said, handing to me.

"You mounted the tripod on the rack?"

"Yes. It gives me elevation and mobility."

As we stood there talking a man rode up on a horse and dismounted. "Ansel," he said. He was a big man, hatless, and with a full head of hair. Rather hunky for an old guy, probably in his forties. He gave me a look, rubbed me across the rear in passing and said, "Nice little butt, kid." Then he led the horse around the wall and disappeared.

"That's Myron," Ansel said. "Ignore him. He's harmless. A novelist. Writers, painters, poets. Sooner or later they all come to *Los Gallos*. The place does have a name, although Mabel just calls it the Big House."

Later at dinner I had not only Bonnie ogling me but Myron Brinig as well. I guess it was good to be popular, but there were times when I'd rather not be. Dorothy Brett brought her big ear trumpet to the table and people still shouted at her. Georgia sat quite upright. She was a presence.

There was a charisma about this woman in black who sat mostly silent but fully attentive to the conversation. It was an elegant spread at the elegant table in the elegant dining room. A man addressed as Spud sat next to Myron. Tony tended to speak monosyllabically and consumed vast amounts of whiskey. He offered me a glass. Auntie Rye said emphatically 'no,' that thin air made one drunk on very little alcohol. I looked up as someone I knew entered the room.

"I'm sorry I'm late." Prince Jablonowski took the empty chair next to Myron. He winked at me and then he leaned over and kissed Myron on the lips. It was not something I had ever seen before. I was uncertain how I felt about it. I was embarrassed and yet I approved. I thought of Charles. Sometimes sex was so conflicting. "Millet has a new show in the Village," the Prince said after the kiss.

"More swelling vaginas?" Brett asked.

"No. She is portraying the female breast in the singular," Jablonowski screamed at her.

"A one-titty show," Myron offered. "I don't find it appealing."

"You wouldn't, Myron," Virginia Adams suggested without rancor.

Mabel, however, was more venomous. "I would have thought a titty or two might have been appropriate to the splendor of your pulp fiction."

"Ouch," Myron said. "I'm sorry I'm not addressing the great cosmological inquiries of our universe."

Frank Waters, the other novelist at the table, looking quite frumpy and drinking whiskey, stated that Pueblo cosmology portrayed a universe in which man, woman, and nature, body and spirit were in a correlatively balanced interdependence. All their rituals and ceremonies were undertaken to assure harmony with nature and to assure that cyclical changes in nature would continue to occur. Spud was in accord, suggesting they were produced on a level apart from the temporal aspects of life. "Neither time nor space. Even their fertility rituals are void of any sexual symbolism. Would you not agree, Tony?" He raised his glass of whiskey in Tony's direction.

"Mabel say it Apollonian," Tony responded.

"Yes. I came to this place a total Dionysian, devouring life with a frenzy for fear I would emotionally starve, I suppose. Now I live far more in the vision of the mind," Mabel told them.

"Are you saying you are no longer interested in sex, Mabel?" Brett asked her.

She yelled back in the direction of the trumpet. "I'm always interested in sex, Brett. I perhaps don't practice as much as I would like." She glared at Tony as if it might be his fault.

"It is true," Georgia said. "The Pueblo are Apollonian. They avoid any sense of personal authority or possession."

"Except for Tony and his car," Frank said.

"Tony's hardly the ideal Pueblo. He lives here," Myron suggested.

"Not always," Tony said.

"Not always," Mabel echoed.

"Tony lives in his car," Ansel said.

Bonnie got up and walked around to the head of the table and gave the braided-haired Indian a hug. "Quit picking on my Grandpa Tony."

"It is true," Virginia said. "There is a total integration and organic connection between the individual and the community."

"Yes, no distinction between work and living space, play and art," Georgia agreed.

"And all are grounded in religion that has love at its source." Mabel motioned for Bonnie to pour her another beer.

"And the greatest of these is charity," Virginia quoted the Bible. "The Pueblo are a people of charity. They are courteous, generous of nature, and pacific. The Pueblo, unlike so many tribes, are not given to marauding and war."

"If the latter is so true, Virginia, why have so many gone in the Army?" Myron winked at me.

"For the honor of country," Ansel answered for her.

"It is not their country," Myron said.

"It's been their country for thousands upon thousands of years," Tony said.

"And hopefully will be more fully again," Mabel said. "When we are crushed by the mechanization of our civilization."

I thought of the bomb. I thought of the burning atmosphere. What would be left of not just our society but of the Pueblo society as well?

The conversation turned from the Pueblo to the nature of life itself and evolved into a discussion of the imagination of the mind. "What Pound does with words is create the picture," Brett said. There was no mention by Auntie Rye of his pro-Nazi politics, which she usually went off on. He, nor William Butler and Maud had apparently ever been here, though their friend Ella Young, some Irish revolutionary, had come as guest of Ansel and Virginia. At least that's what I gathered from the talk. Sometimes it was hard to piece things together.

"Edward's credo," Ansel added to the continuing conversation about the poets. "'To see the thing itself is essential. The quintessence revealed itself without the fog of impressionism.'" Everyone seemed to know who the Edward was he was quoting. I was too shy to ask.

Manuel brought in the dogs and Mabel fed them some bits of meat from the table and then went out to the kitchen and returned with a chocolate cake. Bonnie brought in the coffee.

"This is good cake," Frank said.

"And I know," Mabel added, as if it was a ritual with them, "'but not like Miss Warner's.'"

"Nobody makes cake like Edith Warner," Virginia added. "How's she doing?"

"Up there in years," Frank responded, "but surviving. We can't eat there anymore."

"Why ever not?" Auntie Rye asked.

"Los Alamos," Frank told her. "Security, we are told. Her only allowed customers are military, scientists and family from that barbed-wire monstrosity on the mesa."

Ansel turned to me. "Miss Warner ran the Otowi Switch. There was a narrow-gauge branch line that used to run down from Colorado to Santa Fe and she ran the station. Had a tearoom there and it was a wonderful place to eat. Grew everything herself. The station used to service Los Alamos Ranch School. Then in forty-one they shut down the line and tore up the tracks to use for the war effort. She continued the tearoom, however, and we used to go up there often to eat."

"Never served alcohol, though, and you couldn't bring your own." Frank washed down his cake with whiskey. "She didn't allow it."

"She was a Pennsylvania Quaker. Opposed to war," Georgia said. "Strange, now her only customers are men of war."

"And women," Brett chimed in. "There's a passel of WACS

up there. You see 'em in Santa Fe. What do you call a passel of WACS?"

"A wiggle," Frank suggested.

"A wampum, maybe," Myron added. "I hear they charge for services rendered."

"Enough," Georgia told them. "That is sexist." She turned to Auntie Rye. "And we should leave soon."

"Are you well, Garnie?" Prince Jablonowski asked.

"He is fine, Jabby," Auntie Rye told him.

He looked at me as if the answer was insufficient.

"I am fine, Prince." But I wasn't sure I was. I was anxious about the assignment.

The plan was that we were to follow Georgia in her Model A over to *Rancho de los Brujos* in the Packard. Accommodations had been made for us at the dude ranch. The next day I was apparently to meet Frank Oppenheimer.

No one said anything for a moment. As if to break the awkwardness, Auntie Rye asked, "How did she happen to come out here from Pennsylvania?"

"Miss Warner? For her health," Virginia told her.

"Santa Fe is nothing but people who came out here for their health," Brett added.

At that moment we all looked down the table toward Tony, to see an Indian in an Army uniform, a sergeant, who had come in and was standing directly behind the older Indian. "I'm sorry," he apologized. "There was no one about and the gate was open."

"It always open," Tony leaned back and told him. "You welcome here."

"I am Luis. I have come to see Mr. Adams," the soldier said, looking about as if to determine who might be Mr. Adams.

Ansel stood up. "I thought it was to be tomorrow at *Rancho de los Brujos.*"

"There has been a change," the soldier said.

Ansel followed him out of the dining room into the open court.

"What's that all about?" Myron asked.

"Nothing that should concern you," Georgia told him.

"Has Ansel been nosing about Los Alamos with his camera?"

"OK," Tony said. "All OK."

Ansel came back into the room. "Garnie, Rye, could you come out please?"

We stood up and followed him out into the courtyard and then down to the gate. We could hear Myron ask to be told what was going on and Georgia replying a simple emphatic "no."

The sun had not set and it was still light out as we walked down near the cars. Ansel stood taller than the other three of us. "Rye, the timetable had to be moved up. I talked to Garnie about the assignment this afternoon. He knows the nature of it." He looked directly at me. "You are willing to accept this photographic challenge?"

I hesitated and then responded, "Yes."

"May I be told what it is?" Auntie Rye asked.

"I'm afraid not," Ansel told her. "But Garnie is a minor. I need your signature."

"I don't know if I should if I can't be told."

"It's OK, Auntie."

Auntie signed. Luis stood there as if on guard duty.

Ansel led me over to his station wagon. From the back he first took out a soft case that looked a little like a gun case. "This is a super telescopic lens. I call it my astrolens. I was going to give you instructions on using it. Now you will simply have to read the manual, which is in the case with the lens. I think you'll figure it out. You're a smart kid. Yes, I suspect you will." He handed me another gun case. "This is a telescope with its tripod. Here are two other tripods." He held those himself. "And this bag has film, assorted lenses, filters and another light meter. Another camera, thirty-five millimeter. A Zeiss. The telephoto lens will fit it. Oh, and here's some binoculars." We put the equipment in the trunk of the Army-insignia-marked drab brown sedan. There was already what appeared to be camping gear in the trunk.

"Clothes," Auntie Rye said and went to the Packard. She came back with jeans, a shirt and some socks.

"Put them in here," the sergeant said, and held out a saddle bag. "I've got a jacket and cap for him. And some boots, some more socks and gloves."

"It's July, for God's sake," said Auntie Rye.

"This is New Mexico and it gets cold in the mountains." His head gear was a piss-cutter which he wore tilted appropriately. It gave him a cocky air.

"What mountains?" Auntie asked.

But the sergeant didn't respond. And they stood there together as Ansel led me off toward his station wagon. "I thought we would have time to go over the possibilities, not that I know much of anything about the gadget. My simple advice is to spend a lot of time, if you have it, to set up all three cameras. On tripods, of course. The telephoto will require the most attention, and will have the greatest difficulty in focusing. Focus in on the object totally. You are going to lose background as well as foreground. I wish I was going to be there with you. It could singularly be one of the most important photographs of the century."

"I wish you could be there, too. Is there any way?"

"None." We started back to where Auntie and the sergeant stood silently. "And be careful with the telephoto lens," he whispered. "My house didn't cost as much."

Auntie gave me a kiss and I started to get into the passenger seat. "No," the sergeant said. "Backseat."

I got in and, with a wave goodbye, we drove off. What in hell was going to happen now? "Why do I have to sit in the back?"

"Because I am the chauffeur and you are the bratty general's son off on a camping trip. That's the story, if anyone asks."

We drove in the direction of the setting sun. "It's Friday the thirteenth."

"That's good luck. Want a cigarette?" He handed me a pack of Chesterfields. "Whatever the White man thinks of as bad luck, the Indian thinks of as good luck."

"I'm not an Indian."

"So you are not." He handed back the cigarette lighter and turned off onto the main highway. "What should I call you?"

"Call me the bratty general's son." I decided it was not his fault I was here. "No, sorry... I'm Garnie. What am I to call you?"

"Sergeant when anyone else is around. Luis when it is just the two of us, which will be most of the time. Your Auntie, she's..."

"She's what?" I puffed on the cigarette and handed the lighter back.

"You know?"

"No, I don't know. Say what you mean."

"OK. Your Auntie is a man, right?"

"My father."

"I'm sorry. I didn't mean anything. It isn't really any of my business, is it?"

"That's right. It's none of your business." The road was a marked US highway and paved, but it had lots of ruts and holes and we bounced about a bit. "Were you overseas?"

"Yeah, I was in England and France."

"D-Day?"

"Yeah. Lucky to get out of that one alive."

"So why are you here? Doing this?"

"So why are you?"

"I asked first." I took a long drag on my cigarette. Sitting back there facing his neck below the shorn black hair I felt a bit like the bratty general's son being chauffeured. He had taken off the piss-cutter.

"Because the Oppenheimers asked me. Reason number one. Before the war I worked for them up on the ranch above the Pecos Valley. A place called Grass Mountain, but they called it *Perro Caliente*."

"Does that mean hot dog?"

"Yeah. I guess they took one look at the place and said 'hot dog' and the name stuck. Opje's… the other scientists call him Oppie, but on the ranch he was always Opje. Anyway, his wife, Kate… her folks had a ranch up there, too. Her family has lots of money. The old man, Julius Oppenheimer, he had lots of money, too, but I think he lost a lot of it during the Depression. Anyway, when I came back from Europe my orders were to report to Santa Fe. Hell, it meant coming home, so I had no complaints. I got to Santa Fe, reported to one-oh-nine East Palace, as we call it, and Dorothy, she runs the place, told me to hang around for a truck to take me to Los Alamos. 'Ain't that a rich kids' boarding school?' I asked her. 'No more,' she said. 'Now it's a top-secret, hush-hush place.' So I went up there and there was Opje, blue-eyed Opje. Since he was wearing civvies, I kinda wondered what he was doing on an Army base. So I asked. He just smiled like he always did and told me he was 'working for the government on something big.' And when I asked him what I was doing there, he said, 'Driving for baby brother Frank.' And Frank walks in and throws me the keys and I have been driving for him since. Kate, she had me over for dinner. She doesn't entertain enlisted men much and the guys talk about her like she's this uppity, better-than-all bitch, but she treated me like family come home."

"And that was reason one, you said. What's reason two?"

"Well, I guess I can talk to you about it because it sure won't be a secret from you after what you see. The bomb. I ain't supposed to know as much as I do, but you can't drive Frank around, him and the other scientists and even Opje sometimes to Santa Fe and even Albuquerque, without hearing things. It ain't just a gadget. It's a bomb and it's a big one, an A-Bomb, as they call it, and you will be taking pictures of the test, and if it goes well, they will be dropping it on the Japs."

"On a city?" We had driven through a place called Pilar and were approaching, according to the sign, Embudo. Any bomb, a dinky bomb, would obliterate those places.

"Yeah."

"A lot of civilians will be killed."

"Yeah, and I realize they are only Japs, but they're still people. But the thing is, it will bring an end to the war. There could be a million Americans killed if we have to invade Japan."

"And you'd be one of them?"

"Yes. I've done my time. I don't need to go to Japan now and get killed." He offered me another cigarette. I shook my head no. "And you — what is your reason for doing this?"

"I want to become a famous photographer like Ansel."

"Mr. Adams is famous?"

"Yes, one of the most famous photographers in the world."

"I didn't know that," he said. "Fancy that, I met somebody famous." He suddenly pulled off the road. "Have to piss. Get out and take a look below."

While he peed, I went over to the edge of what appeared to be a canyon and, despite darkness coming on, peered down from a great height to a raging rapid river twisting through the rocks below. "Jesus."

"That's something, ain't it?" He was zipping up his fly. "That's the Rio Grande. We'll be seeing more of it, but not like this. The other way up out of Taos. It's even deeper. You can't get across there. The highway just ends, but they're talking about building a great bridge over the canyon. After the war, of course."

"It's something," I said. Had it been lighter I might have gotten out the camera and taken a picture. Instead I climbed into the backseat again. Luis asked a lot of questions about my life and what Iowa was like, and I asked him a lot about Europe and the war. "I am thinking about becoming a Marine," I told him.

"You may not have to if the bomb's a big success and the Japs surrender."

"Do Marines say 'fuck' a lot?"

"More so than the Army, I think. Yeah, I'd say that about the Marines I met. A lot of 'em are dying in the Pacific. Guys fire and kill and then there are guys that shoot photos of it. You could be one of those."

"But they get killed, too, the photographers?"

"Yeah, saw more than one at Omaha. That's for sure."

"Did you like the English?"

"I liked the girls. They didn't care that I was an Indian, like American girls. They didn't even care if a guy was Negro. There is a scientist, Klaus Fuchs, well, he's a German that escaped from Nazis and all that, but he lived in England for a time and sometimes he would talk to me about life over there."

We talked about England and scientists and stuff and drove through two towns which were kind of combined, Española and Santa Cruz. "Santa Cruz was once the capital of this territory. Ain't much left now but the old mission." Going south from there were signs for Santa Fe. But we didn't go there, at least not at once, but, instead, at Pojoaque Luis turned right and we drove along a real rough road. There was a road block. An Army jeep was parked diagonally across the rough pavement. Two soldiers with armbands clearly marked as MPs walked up to the sedan. Luis reached over and from the glove compartment withdrew some paperwork which he handed to one of the MPs. No words were exchanged until the MP returned the papers. "And the kid?"

Luis spoke softly, acting as if I wasn't supposed to hear. "A General Mitchell Tyler's brat."

"Never heard of no such General."

"Neither had I until now. British. He's here for the you know what."

"Gotcha." He went back to the jeep. Both men got back in and unblocked the road.

"A bit of OK, that," I told Luis in my best English accent.

Luis drove on. We were climbing. The light was disappearing in the western sky. We came to a one-lane bridge. Here he stopped the sedan and honked before crossing. On the other side, he pulled off onto gravel, a parking pull-off of sorts "This is Otowi Siding. Miss Warner's tearoom is right there. Pretty famous."

"I've been told about her chocolate cake."

"That's pretty famous, too. Of course, I've never had any. Never been inside the place, though I've sat in this parking place often enough waiting for the boss."

And so we sat. Luis told me about the Denver and Rio Grande narrow gauge railroad that ran from Antonito, Colorado in the mountains to Santa Fe, and how Miss Warner used to operate the station and started her tearoom to serve the passengers. "It ain't a Fred Harvey's, I suppose, but it was considered pretty grand in these parts."

And then I heard the sound of a baby crying. It was a sort of wailing and continued for a bit. "Did you hear that?" I asked Luis.

"Hear what?"

"The baby crying."

"Not a baby. That was a coyote."

"Do they sound like that?"

"Sometimes. Sometimes they just howl."

A car pulled up, a Buick, not an Army car. "The boss," Luis said. He got out and opened the door for me. A tall lanky man wearing a hat and rumpled suit climbed out of the driver's side. He was smoking a cigarette which he threw to the gravel and smashed with his boot toe.

"Young Mr. Gardiner." He shook my hand but did not

introduce himself. "You look like a proper lad. It's been explained to you by Adams, right?"

"Yes, sir."

"That's swell then, isn't it? Do you have any questions?"

"Where am I going?"

"Luis will see that you get there. That's what matters, really. Do you ride?"

"Ride, sir?"

"Horses. I thought maybe being from Iowa you might ride. Well, it's no matter. Luis will teach you. He knows horses. He'll make a regular cowboy out of you in a day's time." He turned to Luis. "Is he well-equipped?"

"I have a warm jacket and cap for him and a pup tent. Plenty of water and rations. A rifle in case of a mountain lion or anything."

"Ever shot a rifle?"

"Yes," I said. I had gone squirrel hunting once with Tilly, though I wasn't looking forward to any encounters with mountain lions or coyotes. "Are coyotes dangerous?"

"Naw," Luis said. "Not unless you're a baby or a kitten. They're just dogs."

"Ugly dogs," the man in the rumpled suit said. "But you don't have anything to be worried about."

"Luis will be with me."

"Not all the time. Luis will get you to the top of the mountain, but he has to be with me at the time."

"At the time I'm photographing the bomb — "

"The gadget," he corrected me. "This picture-taking is not exactly on the up and up and we can't have anyone asking questions about my driver. The only reason you are doing this is to ensure we have an unofficial record of what occurs."

He took out another cigarette and lit it. "I met Rye some time back in New York." He did not elaborate where. I hoped, for the sake of what I was embarking upon, it was not at Madam Rodowckinski's and that he was not a Communist and this was not some sort of Communist plot.

"There is one other real important element." He handed me dark glasses that were like goggles with dark side panes that would fit snug. "These are polarized. It is essential to protect you from blindness. Have them on, and when you see the first flash of light fall to the ground, cover your face."

"How am I to take a picture that way?"

"In about a moment you will be able to get up. You take the picture. The blast will be a cloud. You take the picture of that, but after, hold on to your camera. Sound travels slower than light and when it reaches you it might just knock you over."

"My camera will be on a tripod."

"Well, hang on to it. Good luck." He went back toward the Buick. "Think of it as doing your bit for the war effort." He got in the Buick and drove off. I got in the backseat and Luis got behind the wheel. He honked the horn, drove over the narrow bridge and we went back in the direction from which we had come.

The MPs waved us down again. "That was quick," the same MP as before was the one who stood at Luis' window.

"This is getting a bit tedious." I spoke in my best English accent with a touch of brattiness.

"Change of plans," Luis told him. "Now we are to go to Sandia."

"I don't envy you." The MP waved us on.

It was dark as we drove through Santa Fe on into Albuquerque and Luis got us a room at the swanky El Vado Motel on Route 66. Motels were a new thing for me. Even the word. And it was a lot nicer than tourist courts. There was a carport adjacent to the room. The neon sign had an Indian in flashing headdress. The exterior of white-painted adobe with blue window and door trim proclaimed the newness of the place. Inside, the beamed ceiling and brick floors reflected the southwest. The room was big, with twin beds. Luis left me alone to go out and pick up some beer. He came back with Mexican beer, something called Dos Equis that had two XXs on the label. We drank beer and played cribbage and, after that, I fell asleep easily despite Luis's snoring.

In the morning, we had lots of coffee, burritos, and *huevos* and then headed south from Albuquerque. It was Saturday, July 14. It was not an ordinary day, of course. I was sitting in the backseat of an Army sedan, moving along a highway that bordered the Rio Grande to a destination I was not certain of and to a future over which I had little control. All I knew was that we were going to the Owl Café in a place called San Antonio for the 'best chili cheeseburgers ever.'

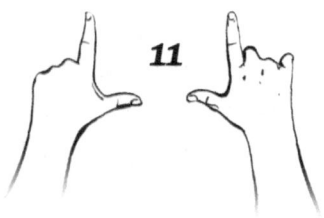

11

The Photo

We traveled south. "When we get to San Antonio we will have the greatest chili cheeseburger ever," Luis repeated. For what I heard about Indians, who according to popular perception were monosyllabic, Luis sure talked a lot. Maybe it was his time away, his time in Europe. That was mainly what he talked about, how much better he was treated in England and France than in the U.S.

"Would you rather be there?"

"No, course not. And right now it's so bombed out it looks like a New Mexico reservation junk-car yard. The trouble with cars in New Mexico is the weather. They don't rust away. They just get older and junkier." Near a place called Polvadera we pulled off to the side of the road to let a convoy of Army trucks, lights on, drive past. "Headed for *Jornada del Muerto*," Luis said.

"Does that mean Journey of the Dead?"

"Yes, a single-day's journey of the dead man. It's where the bomb will be detonated."

"Doesn't sound like a place I want to go."

"You'll be above it… looking down."

The convoy passed. There were large flatbeds with their cargo hidden under canvas. There were trucks with troops in dungarees visible from open flats. There were staff cars and there were trucks laden with crates. No one pulled over to ask us any questions. "Let's get to San Antonio and the greatest chili cheeseburger ever." Luis pronounced chili, 'chill-lay.'

A passenger train, not a streamliner, but a simpler train, moved parallel to the road. It reminded me of the train that had brought Miss Lilith to Barrington. It was strange seeing Prince Jablonowski at Mabel's. He brought no love from Millet with him, but, then again, she would not have known I would be in Taos. According to billboards, we were approaching Socorro. "Won't be long now until we reach San Antonio."

"And the greatest chili cheeseburger ever." I pronounced it 'chill-lay.'

Luis laughed. He had a funny little laugh that included quick short breaths. At the junction of 380 we arrived in downtown San Antonio, which consisted of a saloon, the Owl Café, a grocery store, a dry goods store, a movie theatre, and a boot shop. Luis parked near the Owl Café and I followed him in. He immediately turned around and pushed me back out.

"What's wrong?"

"It's full of scientists. I know most of them. At least on sight. Shit!" He led me off to the boot shop and bought cowboy boots for me. They fit but took a little getting used to walking in. The heels were higher than the penny loafers I had been wearing. From a rack of cowboy hats in the boot store he took off one hat and plopped it on my head.

He made me keep the boots on as well, leaving the store. He carried the big shoebox with my loafers jiggling inside. We went to the saloon where he got a six pack of Dos Equis and a couple of packs of Chesterfields.

"Now what?"

"We might as well head on out."

We went back to the sedan, me in my new boots. I tossed my cowboy hat in the backseat and was ready to climb in.

"You can sit up front now if you want."

And I did. He drove east out of town on 380 and I could see the lights ahead. It looked like a major roadblock, but Luis turned off before it on a graveled side road. There was a little sign that read 'San Pedro.' After San Pedro, which was really not a town, just a few houses, the road turned into two dirt tracks. The Rio Grande was out the window on my side of the car. There was sage, but now there was other foliage — mesquite, Luis called it — and cottonwoods, and I even saw some willows. There were other channels of the now flat and less rapid Rio Grande and, as we drove down alongside the water, there were ponds and spreads of marshes. I saw a flock of cranes. And then ducks and geese. "What was that?" I yelled out.

"A roadrunner."

He seemed pleased that I was so excited. And I yelled out again when I spotted a deer. "This place is called a *bosque*," he said. Which in Spanish would mean literally forest or woodland. It was maybe a woodland, hardly a forest. "Just think... the ancestors of these geese and cranes have been coming back to this place, migrating here, as long as my people have lived upon this land. Thousands of years." We continued on the winding dirt track that edged the *bosque*. "I went to the

Black Forest in Germany. I bought a cuckoo clock." To the east a single mountain rose up from the flat land on which we were driving. It looked so lonely. "Little San Pasqual Mountain," Luis said. How many miles we drove through the wet countryside I was uncertain, but in the mid-afternoon Luis turned off onto another dirt road that led in the direction of the *bosque*. There were some weather-worn buildings, crude adobe, and a corral. A tall, amazingly handsome Indian in cowboy dress came out of the adobe. He approached the car as Luis stepped out. The cowboy nodded but didn't speak. "My cousin, Jorge," Luis told me. "This is Garnie," he told his cousin.

"Howdy." The amazingly handsome Indian cowboy took my hand. He had amazing big hands to match his amazing sculptured face and his amazing dark eyes. He was an Indian, without a doubt, but I had not seen any as handsome in my time thus far in New Mexico.

"Garnie's never ridden before," Luis said.

"There's nothing to it," Jorge said. "It's like taking a piss. It's all in getting and keeping your hands in the right place."

Jorge heated up some chili on a wood-burning range and warmed some tortillas for us. Afterward, I changed into other Levis and a plaid shirt, and learned to ride. I took to it naturally and the brown mare seemed content with me. I smelled a bit like a horse. We washed up at the pump. The water was cold as hell. Jorge fried some thick bacon and warmed frijoles and tortillas. We drank beer and played poker. Poker was new to me and I lost miserably. Jorge talked more than he had at first. He told us that just south of where we were was one of the big battles of the Civil War, the Battle of Valverde.

"Out here in the middle of nowhere?"

"Out here," he said. "It was one bloody battle. Lots of casualties. The South eventually won the battle, although it raged for days. I think the Indians fought on the side of the Confederacy in that battle, although I don't think they really gave a shit at that point who beat what White man."

I had tanked down enough beer to sleep soundly in the rope-spring bunk. I awoke to the caw of birds and the honking of geese. I looked up to see the handsome Jorge towering over me. "Time to rise," he said. I felt like saying let it rise and I'll suck it off for you, but I didn't. Though I did take a little time getting out of the bunk until I got rid of my raging hard on. I dressed and put on my cowboy boots. Jorge fed us more beans and more tortillas, this time with side pork, as he called it. I drank lots of coffee and finished off with a trip to the shit house and beat off while I was there. We packed the camping gear and the photo equipment on a mule. I was most careful of the handling of the telephoto lens, aware of what it cost. Luis and I waved goodbye to Jorge and began the Sunday morning trek across the flatland, and then began the sharp climb up the San Pasqual. Luis led the mule and I struggled to stay on the mare as the climb became steeper. We left the trees behind and the mountain was sage, tumbleweed, and mostly rock. The sun beat down. It was Sunday, July 15, and at home I would have been walking to Mass.

"That ravine over there is called Pussy. It looks like a woman's pussy. The way the rock forms around the split."

"My mother paints vaginas. I mean pictures of vaginas."

"What on earth does one say to that?" Luis forced his horse up the incline.

"There's not much one can say," I told him and followed the mule up amid the sharp rocks.

It was mid-afternoon before we reached the peak. There was not a lot of flat surface, certainly not a mesa, but enough that I would be able to make camp and set up the tripods. I looked down into the barren valley to the east. There were lava beds below to the south but, between San Pasqual and the mountains across, there was a spread of glistening white.

"It's called White Sands, but it's not sand at all. It's gypsum, and through it is *Jornada del Muerto*. Can I see your binoculars?"

I dug in the mule pack and got out the binoculars. Luis searched the valley below. "There, I found it. There is Trinity. Here, look."

I took the binoculars. There was a tiny structure, like an oil derrick I'd seen in magazine photos. "Trinity?"

"The bomb site. That tower. The bomb is mounted on that tower. I drove the boss down there a couple of days ago. The bomb wasn't there then. It probably is now."

I could barely make out the tower; I certainly couldn't determine from this distance if there was any bomb on the tower.

"The buildings nearby are what was the MacDonald ranch. Now they are government property. All the wiring and record-monitoring equipment is in those buildings. There's a bunker down there for the observers, if they aren't all killed in the blast."

"Thanks for that," I said. It began to drizzle and we set up the pup tent. "You won't be able to have a fire. It would be visible for miles. You may see some smoke signals. I wouldn't put it past some of the Indians in the area. Keep your rifle handy. I don't think you'll need it, but better safe than sorry. Anytime you have to use the flashlight, keep the light facing down and to the west as much as possible. Better not use it when you don't have to."

We unpacked all the camera equipment. I took several pictures of Luis. He smiled as he unpacked food, water, and other supplies. We covered them with a small tarp, and threw down another tarp for me to sit on. I wished I had taken a picture of Jorge. I doubted I would have the opportunity later.

"The elevation here is about five thousand feet. Down there, Trinity is at about four thousand. The blast is set for four-thirty a.m. tomorrow. It is now fourteen-twelve." He took off his watch and handed it to me. "Use this. It's set on Mountain War Time. It will be more accurate for you. In case it rains, the blast might be postponed, so if it doesn't go off right at four-thirty, don't be alarmed." Luis made a finger-count inventory of the supplies. Then he put his arm around my shoulder. "Here's the battle plan. Near the time, put on your goggles. Else you'll go blind. And drop to the ground, face into the ground. I'm told there will be a flash of light ten times brighter than the sun. In a few moments you can open your eyes, get up and take your pictures of whatever there is to take pictures of. In a short time the sound blast is supposed to hit you and it will be powerful. I will be there at an observation point to the north and a little closer to ground zero. God willing, I will see you mañana." With that, he let go of me, climbed up on his horse and led the mare and the mule away. The last I saw of him was the cowboy hat as he made his way down the mountain. I snapped a shot of that hat on the horse from above.

The drizzle stopped. I set up the telescope on its tripod and got a much closer look at the tower. I could now see the egg-shaped bomb atop it. I could see the figures of the men below, moving in and out of the MacDonald ranch buildings. I set up the cameras, all three, and, with the Zeiss and the telescopic lens attached, took photos of the tower that looked like an oil rig and its egg bomb. In the distance, I could see the rising dust of a vehicle approaching the site. That, too, I photographed. I played with the aperture settings and used the Weston light meter. I tested the settings on both the Leicas as well. I drank some water from the canteen. It tasted metallic. I opened the ammo box and took out a bullet and loaded the rifle. If I was going to be a Marine I would need to really know how to fire the weapon. But I hoped I would not be using it on this night. I looked through the rifle scope and saw nothing but sky. Maybe I could shoot the bomb now, from its tower. I knew that I didn't possibly have the range, but the powerful thought pleased me. It began to drizzle. I took off the telephoto lens and covered all three tripoded cameras with the tarp on which I had been sitting and moved under the pup tent.

Darkness came. And there I sat. Lightning tore the sky and thunder followed. Up there I seemed so close to it. And despite being under the pup tent, the rain blew at me, but it failed to disturb the coyotes — they cried and barked and yelled. I touched the rifle that lay next to where I squatted. I had no intention of sleeping. That would be far too dangerous. I used the flashlight inside the tent to check Luis's watch. It was a long evening. I ate a can of Spam, two chocolate bars, and canned beef stew. I drank more metallic water from the canteen. The rain let up a bit and I peered through the telescope. There were lights visible at the Trinity center. Then there was more rain and I covered the telescope and crawled back under the pup tent. The waiting was now driving me a little mad, but I thought it must be much worse for those down at the site, although they at least had each other's company. I thought I heard something and grabbed the rifle, but nothing appeared and I set it back down. I drank some more water. It stopped raining.

I thought of the blast and how powerful it might be. I unwound the cameras from their tripods. With a military knife that was with the equipment I dug holes for the feet of each of the tripods. I rammed the feet down into the holes and then anchored them with rocks. I remounted the cameras and refocused each. I sat down again at the opening in the pup tent. I got up again and draped the canvas over the camera. I sat back down again. I got up and peed behind the tent. I sat down again. I drank more metallic water. It finally was four o'clock. The sky had cleared. I uncovered the cameras. I affixed the telephoto lens to the Zeiss. I checked the focus once more on each of the Leicas. At this point it was difficult to determine the light factors. I went through the routine in my head. I had the goggles ready. I looked through the telescope. There was activity at the site. I put on the goggles. Four-thirty came. I waited. I checked the watch constantly. Finally five o'clock came. There was no blast. I checked my goggles. There was no blast at five after, nor ten after, nor fifteen after. I suspected there was to be no blast. Yet I had been warned to be patient. I checked the security of my goggles. Five twenty-five and then five thirty.

And then, at five thirty-one, as the blast of light came, I fell to the ground and buried my face in the tarp. And I knew the light was brighter than any daylight I had ever seen. I arose and, still with the glasses on, saw the shape beginning.

I threw off the goggles and manned the cameras and began clicking, refocusing, adjusting the aperture and settings on all three and I clicked away and reset and clicked some more and checked the frame. There was no time for the theory I had heard so eloquently from Ansel. There was nothing but haste. And yet... Jesus Christ! What a sight!

And then the power of the moment overtook me. Life could never be the same on earth. Not after this. A force had been released which could not be put back. I needed to focus. Not the cameras, but myself. I had to embrace the emotion, recognize the power and take the greatest photograph ever taken. I needed to frame the moment. After that initial intense light, a giant ball of fire formed. It was all immediate and quick, but I became part of that ball of fire and I shot it on all three cameras. I was snapping and advancing the film, but always aware of what was happening and that I was at the core, at the center of this changing universe.

An orange and red column arose. I could feel the heat. It was like standing at an open fireplace. I let the heat engulf me as I photographed the rising column that kept moving higher and then spilled out like a fountain. That, too, I captured through the lenses. It was all fast, but so was I, but not uncoordinated, not willy-nilly. I was in pain, but I used that pain to capture what I must contain within the frame. Spilling out away from the column a giant cloud shaped like a mushroom formed. There was a blue aura surrounding the cloud. It formed and reformed like musical variations. Tony and his vision. Would we be OK? And then it came. The blast! And an enormous roar! It must be what being inside a tornado was like.

I was nearly forced off my feet, but I hung on. I clung to

the Zeiss with the telescopic lens. The blast kept coming. It must have been five minutes long, though it seemed longer, and, when it passed, I could see the cloud breaking apart and drifting to the east. It was like a death shroud disintegrating. I had escaped. I was alive and the tripods stood. I sank to the earth and sobbed. I didn't know if I was crying for myself, for humanity, or for the Japs... for I understood now what was to come. I got up and took the last pictures of the dying cloud. I was glad Luis was not here. I was glad Auntie Rye was not here. I was glad Ansel was not here. I had taken what would always be the most important photograph I would ever take. Probably not the best, but always the greatest. And for that to be, I had to be — not just myself but *by* myself — alone. It had to be solitary. And I was.

I knew what had been unleashed here could not be put back. What I had seen, few had witnessed, but I had captured it in the frame, an emotional frame tied to who I was, not as Garnie but as a person of the earth, linked somehow to the *bosque*, the cyclical nature of life.

Later, in the daylight, I looked through the telescope to the site where the tower had stood. It had been obliterated. There was nothing left but a hole, a crater, and it looked like a green mirror. Something out of *Snow White* or some other Disney movie. It was so unreal. This was a place that road-runners called home. After a while, sitting there shivering in the morning light, the world appeared the same, yet I knew it could not be. I got to my feet and unscrewed the cameras from the tripods and dug out the tripod legs. I repacked the camera equipment. I unloaded the rifle and put the bullet back into the ammo box. I put away the knife and drank some metallic water. I knew I should open some rations, but the thought of food made me ill. Eventually, I took down the pup tent and rolled it up. I sat there atop the mountain that had appeared to rise so solitary from the barren land. I, too, felt solitary.

It was midday when Luis arrived with horses and the mule. He barely greeted me when he took from his saddlebag a black box that had some sort of meter on its face. A cord dangled from it with a device on the end and, holding the box in his left hand, he ran the device over my body. "What the hell?" I asked.

"It's OK. Just minimal. You're clean."

I simply stared at him.

"I am so damn sorry." He looked almost like he was ready to cry. "This is a Geiger counter. It detects radiation. There has always been an element of danger from radiation from the fallout. That cloud you witnessed was radioactive."

"And you're telling me now? But you knew of the danger before? Bastard!"

"I know, Garnie. I wanted to tell you. To warn you. You should have been told before you agreed to come here. They wouldn't let me. I should have told you." He kept repeating, "I should have told you. I was wrong."

"Yes. It was wrong." I was careful not to say he was wrong.

"There were problems with radiation to the east of here. Because of the drift of the wind. There was no problem here to the west, but there could have been. You could have been in great danger and you should have been told."

"I understand. But it is over now." I became the directing adult. "Let's pack up and get out of here." As I hung the cased rifle on the mule pack I said to Luis, "Perhaps I should use it on you."

"You should." He spoke seriously.

"Luis, I am kidding."

We spoke little as we made our way down from Little San Pasqual Mountain in the heat of the day. Occasionally we stopped to drink water. He had brought fresh water with him.

"You won't have to die now in Japan."

"Perhaps it would be better if we did."

"No. As much as I may realize now more about the universality of life, we did not start this war. Millions of American men have died because of what Hitler and the Japanese began. There is a distinction between American life and Japanese life."

"You think?"

"I know." And I did believe that.

We wound our way down the mountain trail and arrived at the little ranch beside the *bosque*.

"Where's Jorge?" We unpacked the mule and put the stuff into the sedan's trunk.

"He was going into town. Have you slept?"

"I haven't."

He took an army blanket out of the trunk and tossed it into the backseat.

After he got the horses into the corral and the gate closed we headed out, not north on the dirt road but to the west through the *bosque* on an embankment. When we reached the main channel of the Rio Grande, there was a kind of floating raft, a ferry of sorts that was rope-and-pulley operated. Luis pulled it up to the bank and drove the sedan on to it. I was glad to see we didn't sink. Then, using the rope, he pulled us across to the other side. After we hit the highway, I slept, fitfully, but I slept. In Socorro, Luis pulled off and parked in front of a Mexican restaurant. I followed him in, still half asleep. We sat at a wooden, oilcloth-covered table with wooden chairs and were handed menus all in Spanish. "What would you like?" he asked.

"I don't know the food. Order for me."

While we waited, I picked up a newspaper. It was all in Spanish and I showed it to him. He turned to the next table. Two elderly Indian men sat there. "Por favor," he said and pointed to the paper.

"Si," one of them said and handed him the paper, which he handed to me. I read aloud to Luis. "'An explosive magazine at the Alamogordo air base blew up Monday morning and the flash, sound and shock were seen, heard and felt in areas more than one hundred miles away. The flash was intensely white and seemed to fill the entire world. It was followed by a large crimson glow. The flash lasted only a second or so. It was so bright that Miss Georgia Green, a blind student at the University of New Mexico, who was being driven to Albuquerque by her brother-in-law, Lieutenant Joe Wills, asked, "What's that?"'"

"I seen it," one of the older Indians said.

"Me too," said the white-aproned old Mexican man who brought our food to the table. "That must have been one shit pile full of explosives." We drank Dos Equis with our lunch and then headed north.

I slept. North of Albuquerque, at a town called Bernalito, we stopped for an evening meal and had steak rather than Mexican food. We drank more Dos Equis and had cigarettes. I had some apple pie and we got back in the sedan. "Do you want me to drive for a while, Luis?" I asked.

"I would say yes, but we're going to be leaving the main road and taking a shortcut."

"To Taos?"

"No, toward Abiquiú. To *Rancho de los Brujas,* sometimes the Whites around here call it Ghost Ranch. It translates as Ranch of the Witches. I don't much believe in a lot of the Indian shit I was raised on. They even talk of little dinosaur bones being found 'round here. Who ever heard of little dinosaurs?"

"Not me." I slept again. I awoke once and asked where we were.

"Cuba," he said.

"I am glad you speak Spanish."

"We could have more fun in Havana than this place," he said. He drove on and I slept. There were traces of dawn as we reached *Rancho de los Brujos.* He found the parked yellow Packard and we loaded my pack and the photographic equipment into the Packard's trunk. I found Auntie sleeping in the adobe and came back out without awakening her.

"I was told the artist arises early," Luis said. "We can drive there."

"Do mean Georgia O'Keeffe?"

"Yes."

"I thought you didn't know any famous people."

"Didn't know she was famous. Frank, Opje and Kate would sometimes come here on weekends to get away from Los Alamos. I guess they knew her from the old days."

The Model A was parked and Georgia sat in a wooden chair outside the little courtyard of the rundown adobe. "I was expecting you." She didn't get up.

"Are you like Tony?" I asked.

"No. I saw the light. Literally, yesterday morning. I rather guessed how long it would take for you to get back here."

"Do you need me any longer?" Luis asked Georgia.

"No. I'll take over," she told him.

Luis came over to me. I expected an awkward hug but didn't get one. Instead he shook my hand. "It was an experience. I am not certain a good one."

"You will not have to die now," I reminded him.

"But is the cost worth it? I'll be off." He started to move away.

"The film," I said and handed him the canister, the one with the film from Ansel's Leica.

"Ah, yes, the film."

He drove away in the sedan and I stood there looking at the middle-aged woman, who sat there hatless in the cold morning air. "Are you traumatized?" she asked.

"To the contrary. I am exhilarated."

"You got *the* picture then?"

"I got *the* picture." I sat down on the ground facing her. The earth was cool, hard, and grassless.

"That's all it need be about it, right?"

"Yes. Of course, until it's developed and printed, I won't really know."

"But you felt it?"

"I knew at that one moment, that one particular click of the shutter, that I understood for just that one time what life was and yet it was fully beyond my understanding."

"That is art," she said.

We sat there, still and silent, and listened to the sound of morning.

"Is it the end of civilization?" I broke the silence.

"Does it matter? The blue will remain."

"The blue?"

"The hole in the bone. The blue. If white bone, as I picture it, were to rot, to disintegrate, as all physical matter must in time, the sky, the blue, remains, for that is eternal, infinite. The universe will continue without us. It did after the dinosaurs that roamed this country before us perished. And it will remain after our greed and cruelty have destroyed humankind. Hitler may be dead, but war hasn't ended, and after we drop this bomb on the Japanese, there will still be more war. It doesn't matter. Because if we don't exterminate the race through war, we will find other ways. We live on this planet which has finite resources. The Dust Bowl showed us life without water. Life without water means no life for this race. And, sooner or later, we shall consume all of the water."

"I hate to see it so bleakly."

"Your truth is not necessarily my truth. To be art, it only need be your truth."

Auntie came running down the dirt road toward us. She wore cowboy boots and an oversized cowboy hat. She looked just damned silly. But I didn't laugh. I got up off the ground and Auntie ran up to me and hugged me so hard it hurt.

"Auntie!"

She let me loose. "I was so worried. Are you all right?"

"I'm swell."

"You're not a child any longer, are you?"

"No. I've lost my English accent."

"It was like a weird daylight here on the mountain and I just knew. I just knew. And Georgia wouldn't tell me a thing." She turned to Georgia. "How can you be so damned stoic?"

"A life of practice. I have great patience."

A woman seemed to come out of nowhere. "You do, don't you, Georgie?"

"Don't call me that," Georgia told her.

"Of course, Georgie." She poured us coffee from an enameled blue pot into enameled blue cups. She had a folding stool on her arm and she unfolded it and sat on it. She was not introduced. The four of us sat there, drinking coffee, awaiting the dawn.

I steered the Packard through the New Mexico morning mountains and Auntie Rye navigated. It was an unalarming day, as if nothing was wrong in the world. The sun brought the usual illumination to the sky and the mountains and early day shadows. "Who was the woman who brought the coffee?"

"That's Maria Chobot. She lives there. Tends to Georgia's every need."

"Are they, you know?"

"Lovers? No. Maria would have it, but Georgia would have none of it."

The sun was high in the sky by the time we reached *Los Gallos*. Ansel was already there and we went out to the hut that served as a darkroom.

"I sealed out the light," he said. "The place was like a sieve."

We developed the film. There were strips from both the Zeiss, close-in views, and from my own Leica. It was from the Leica strip that I saw it. "This one," I told him. "This is the one."

"*The* photograph?"

"Yes, *the* photograph."

"Yes. I can see it. I can feel it."

Then began the long process of dodging and burning. We spent a good part of the day dodging and burning until I felt it was right. It was the layers that Stieglitz spoke of. The white clouds high, luminous, seeming to float apart from

the darkness below. And within that darkness was the glow-
ing mass of dust, not yet formed into the mushroom that
appeared in some of my other shots. It was intense, and just
below it was a strip of brilliant off-white. I knew in reality
that it had been a luminous green.

"It's better in black and white," he said as if reading my
mind.

"Do you want a copy?" I asked.

"No. I must not. If someone found it among my photographs, they would think it mine."

"I'm sure no one would mistake it for yours."

"Yes, they would, Garnie. It is that good. You must give
up your thoughts of Oxford and come out to San Francisco."

"I have decided to do that already."

I kept his words with me: "It is that good."

THE DRIVE BACK to Iowa was long and we were both impatient. But I had shown Auntie the photo and talked now
about the experience.

"It is evil. There at Los Alamos — they have brought a
great evil into the world. It must never be used," she said.

"It will be used against the Japanese." I did not say Japs. I
knew they were people and I knew they would die.

"No," she said. "It must never be."

"It will be. To save the lives of all those American soldiers.
To save Luis's life."

"You can't make it personal."

"But it is personal," I told her.

We got home to the Torrington House and waited. I told
no one what I had seen, nor what I had photographed.

"He won't do it," Auntie said.

"He will," I said.

We waited.

"He won't do it," Auntie said.

"He must," I said.

On August 6, Truman spoke on the radio. "Sixteen hours ago an American airplane dropped one bomb on Hiroshima. It is a harnessing of the basic power of the universe. The force from which the sun draws its power has been loosed against those who brought war to the Far East."

The Japanese didn't surrender.

On August 9, the bomb was dropped on Nagasaki.

The Japanese didn't surrender.

ON AUGUST 14, Hirohito announced the surrender of Japan. I took out my photograph and looked at it. Millions upon millions had died in Europe, in the Pacific, and in Japan. And, in the end, it came down to this. It looked so beautiful, black and white on glossy stock.

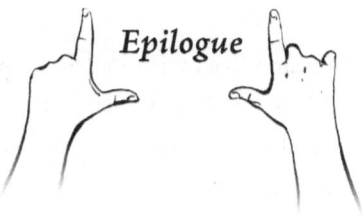

Epilogue

WE WON THE fall state Baseball Championship beating Davenport High, but Kenny K pitched four straight days and destroyed his arm. Without him we didn't make the spring regionals and his hope for a career in the majors was finished. We did win the state concert band championship, but Margaret, without any mention of a baby, returned to play the tymps and I went back to the bassoon.

In the summer of '47, we had a parade on the Fourth of July and, as Mr. Henvenderson was going to teach at Luther College, he didn't seem to care anymore that we were marching. We played the *Liberty March* and I tinkled away at the glockenspiel.

In '48 I graduated. Valedictorian, of course. Since I was not going into the Marine Corps I curtailed my use of the word fuck. I decided definitely not to go to Oxford, but to go to the California School of Fine Arts in San Francisco and study photography in the program established by Ansel. Minor White had become the director. Father Martin O'Tootle left the priesthood and moved to Prairie du Chien, where he taught high school and lived with Padric. I saw them often. Johnny Betters did not return to Prairie but was living in San Francisco with another ex-sailor. Perhaps I would see him when I got out there. Millet embraced Op Art and her optical vaginas were displayed at MoMA.

Tilly got an athletic scholarship to the University of Iowa and became a Hawkeye. Sister Mary Leonardo da Vinci left the Presentation Order and joined a women's band in Chicago. I put off going to CSFA for a year, so that I might go around the world. Auntie had given me the trip as a graduation gift. I didn't exactly take the Grand Tour of old but backpacked through a lot of devastated Europe and went to Egypt, the Greek Isles, and India. I didn't come home as soon as I had planned but went on to Australia. I was doing a lot of interesting photography and visited Borneo and the Philippines. In Manila, I took pictures of the University where Robbie had been a prisoner. I sent him a photo and he wrote back saying that he wished I would come home so he could kiss me. Fall passed and I missed getting to San Francisco in time for classes, so I decided to stay abroad for another year and went back to Europe. Auntie wrote often. Sometimes it was difficult for her letters to catch up with me. She had been to Chicago and to Field House and wondered if I wished to keep it. And I wrote her that I did. And she went to New York and said she saw Madam Rodowckinski, who was not well. And I wrote back telling her to be careful, that there was a lot of anti-Communist talk in the government. And she wrote back that she was able now to buy a new girdle. I spent New Year's in Paris with a Swede who was pretty hunky, and I tried to find Sylvia Beach's bookstore but learned the Nazis had closed Shakespeare and Company back in '41. In

February I went back to England. I met up with Rupert, who was now living there with his grandfather. We did the sixty-nine and Rupert declared, "That didn't make us queers." I went to Oxford and explored, and though I was sorry in a way that I wouldn't be going to the University; I was looking forward to CSFA. I corresponded with Ansel and promised him I would be home in the summer and off to San Francisco in the fall. Tilly scrawled a note, now and then, admonishing me not to do any queer stuff and to tell me that Geraldina Lamtouse was p.g. but wouldn't tell anyone who the father was. I rented a brand-new MG-TC and sped north on the left-hand side of the road and, in Lincolnshire, made a point of driving across the 'umber. I didn't speak Brit, but I was a bit 'ammered at the time from a few too many pints.

In May 1950 I returned home. The Toddmans had a picnic out on the farm in June and the guys, mostly home from college, were there and we played ball. Charles wasn't there, but I was told he had married a girl from Elkader.

And then on June 25 North Korea invaded the Republic of Korea in the south without warning.

Tilly drove into town. "We gotta join up. The Marines," he said.

"Yeah," I said. "Fuck."

Acknowledgments

I would like to thank the two amazing women whose work, editorial genius, and support made this novel possible, my long-time agent Liz and my publisher Lynn.

About the author

GENE FARRINGTON is a Professor of English at Notre Dame of Maryland University of Baltimore. He is the author of *Breath of Kings*, an historical novel of 10th-Century England, Normandy, and the Daneland, and *The Blue Heron*.

A P E R T U R E

Book club questions

- Garnie, the narrator of *Aperture*, is a precocious 10-year-old boy when the novel begins. He is also fixated on penises and comes to the conclusion that he is homosexual. Do you think sexuality is on the minds of children? How old were you when you began to think about yourself as a sexual being?
- On the first page of this novel, Garnie tells the reader that his parents are "gone" and he doesn't know for sure what that means or where they might be. He is under the care of Auntie Rye, who is a very unusual individual. Discuss Auntie Rye as a guardian for Garnie. When did you come to realize who Auntie Rye is?
- Discuss what you came to understand about Garnie's parents and heritage. Garnie accuses Auntie Rye of killing his parents. In what way do you see Auntie Rye doing just that.
- Farrington provides a clear picture of a small town in Iowa during the time of World War II and shows how each individual fits into the overall running of the town and how each individual knows his/her place. Do you think small towns have changed in any significant way in the last seventy years?
- Auntie Rye has access to a considerable amount of money and knows some of the most famous people of that era. Did you learn anything new about any of the famous persons depicted in the novel? Discuss the impact of these famous people on Garnie.

- Early on, Garnie decides that he will become a famous photographer. How does that decision play out and shape his life?
- Farrington moves the story to several intriguing locations and has Garnie interact with a whole cast of characters in each one — from Chicago to New York, including the Village and Harlem; and then to the Southwest. Which was your favorite location and adventure?
- Before reading this book, how much did you know about the Manhattan Project and Los Alamos? How did you feel about Garnie's assignment?
- Farrington does not shy away from portraying the good and the bad in people and institutions. Did this bother you? If so, what offended you? If not, what poke-in-the-eye did you enjoy the most?
- If you can imagine Garnie beyond the last page of this novel, what is he doing and where does he live?

The Blue Heron
A novel by Gene Farrington

You'll visit Jamestown, Virginia; the Chesapeake Bay; Washington, D.C.; London, England; Munich, Germany; Avignon, France and various other spots in between—in the here and now. You will also observe Jacobin London and the founding of the Jamestown colony in the 17th Century. You will get insights about what was happening from a David and a Molly from both the past and the present—as well as from Native American Opechancanough, who was taken to Spain as a young man and educated in the ways of the white man who inserts himself in the here and now, via email chats. It's magic and spell-binding. Just hang on and go with it.

Gene Farrington mashes the past and the present as only a post-modern novelist can, always conscious of the impact of words, even as he fractures time and melds characters in such intricate ways that you will be amazed at how time means nothing... how the traits and qualities of ancestors get passed along—through time, through blood. By breathing life into historical figures as well as the fictional ones, Farrington forces us to reconsider: what is history... what is fate?

Water street press

The Hot Monkey Love Trial
Lawrence G. Townsend

Bert Gropes is a reclusive twenty-six-year-old who lives with his mother in Woodland, California, and he's about to get fired, again, from a job he loves: teaching social studies. Unknown to Bert is that before he was even born, someone genetically altered him in vitro. A single gene from a Libidoan monkey—an oversexed great ape—was inserted into Bert when but a wee bit of biomaterial.

As destiny plays out, Bert finds trouble of biblical proportions. He's accused of terrible crimes in Tennessee for his role in the death of a thrill seeker who downloads an app developed for sexless farm roosters but that's been repurposed for human use as the ultimate electronic tonic: Hot Monkey Love. Senator Ray Hoffenworth comes home to Tennessee to be the prosecuting attorney. The defense, offered by Bert's celebrity animal rights lawyer, captures the world's attention: Can a defendant with a single nonhuman gene be tried for murder as a person?

It's the Scopes Monkey Trial all over again—except the story's DNA has been mutated, recombined with strands harvested from today's news, and twisted into a tale that only the coming age of biotech could dish up.

Water Street Press

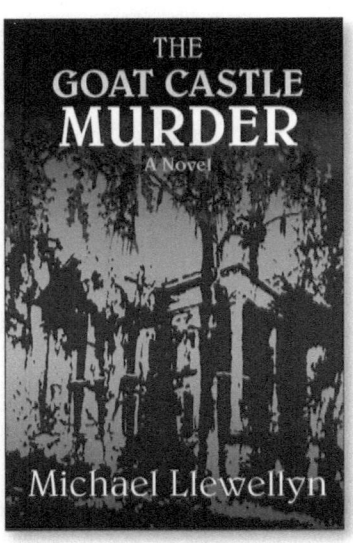

The Goat Castle Murder
A novel by Michael Llewellyn

Before the television age, when "crime of the century" meant something, the public was unduly captivated by murder. This was especially true during the Great Depression, when Americans were desperate for escapist fare. The more bizarre or glamorous the crime, the greater their fascination, and few intrigued more than the events of August 4, 1932 in Natchez, Mississippi. The brutal shooting of spinster recluse Jennie Surget Merrill grabbed instant headlines with tales of fabulous wealth, beautiful women, European royalty, Southern aristocracy, a U.S. President and the Confederate President, army generals and ambassadors, not to mention madness, incest, racism, bitter internecine feuds, vertiginous falls from grace and eccentricity in spades. The case became known as the Goat Castle Murder.

Michael Llewellyn has combined the facts of the case with new revelations to breathe life into these eccentric Southerners. The result is a compelling novel, *The Goat Castle Murder*.